EVA F

THE
HIGHLANDERESS

VOLUME 1 OUT OF 5
ENJA'S VOYAGE

For additional Bonus Material
please visit

www.highlanderess.com/clan

and follow the process outlined there.

Caught in the chaos of warring lands,
Where love ignites 'midst bloodied sands,
Enja stands with fate in hand—
Duty calls; she must command.

Shall she yield to passion's flame,
Or lead her kin to endless fame?
In battles fierce, with blade she fights,
And carves her name in legend's might.

A warrior queen, defying all,
Who dared to rise, to heed her call.
She shattered norms, claimed what was hers,
And stood where only fate concurs.

Yet love doth whisper soft and near,
Shall peace in passion soon appear?
Or will she forge a path of power,
And stand alone in victory's hour?

Bear witness to her epic quest,
Of rebellion, strength, and fearless breast.
For in her heart, unyielding reigned,
The spirit of a queen unchained.

For my boys. I am so proud of you!

My dearest reader:

From the desk of Eva Fellner

Welcome to this Voyage! In everything I've written across the five volumes of The Highlanderess, I believe in the extraordinary power of liberty and leadership inspired by higher values.

You are holding in your hands the first of five volumes of a heroine's story of bold emancipation set against the harsh backdrop of 14th-century Scotland—one of the most challenging times for women, ever.

Driven by the motivation to forge new and difficult paths, our heroine embodies the spirit of adventure, boldly stepping into the unknown with courage and determination. Enja is a cool, James Bond-like character, wielding her katana and proudly bearing her tattoo, originally branded on her as a slave, which has since pivoted to become a powerful testament to her strength and resilience.

As her journey unfolds, the voyage itself becomes a powerful reflection of the modern high-performance warrior—a fierce and unyielding fighter, both in her world and ours.

These values often transcend what we encounter in today's business world and cultural contexts. The purpose and mission of the five Highlanderess volumes are to emphasise and celebrate these qualities, showcasing how Enja—and women in general—can develop into outstanding individuals with strength, wisdom, and a deep sense of purpose.

In this first volume, through the journey of Enja and the other characters, I aim to portray a narrative where leadership is deeply rooted in family values. You will discover that some families don't need to share the same blood to stand together with decisiveness, freedom, vision, persistence, and even natural healing. By weaving these elements into this historical novel, I hope to inspire you to recognise the potential within yourself and the people around you. From the very first moment, you should understand that this historical series isn't just about telling a powerful story set in mediaeval Scotland; it's about encouraging a shift in today's perspective towards more meaningful, compassionate, and empowering leadership for both women and men alike.

The Highlanderess is a literary series of five volumes that follows Enja and her clan. The five books—Enja's Voyage, The Quest, The Clan, Enja's Fight, and The Legacy—bring to life a world where an exceptionally strong woman leads with both strength and grace.

All the stories are filled with powerful themes of connection, bravery, and outstanding healing knowledge that would be great for many to have today. By engaging with this historical narration, you are invited to explore new ways of thinking about pioneering and community building.

At the end of this volume, there's a special note for you that might just spark a change in your life and in the lives of others. You'll reach it at the perfect moment for you. For now, we will prepare you for that with Enja's Voyage, which I hope inspires you to embrace the values she represents.

Now: Enjoy this book!

Eva Fellner

Chapter 1

Scotland in May 1307

W hat the devil has gotten into me lately to stumble upon such a mess? I couldn't shake that thought all day long—it kept echoing in my mind. The heavy dress stuck to my body, wet with sweat. The chest and waist were laced up tightly, with only enough room for shallow breaths. The tailor had done a good job. The tight collar threatened to suffocate me, and the brocade bodice rubbed uncomfortably against my ribs. It's your own fault, I thought, you probably want to prove yourself to everyone again, Enja.

The bridesmaids had placed the bridal wreath on the white silk fabric as a sign of my chastity. Under the veil that covered my face protectively, I grimaced at the thought of my own folly. I scanned the ranks of the bystanders as I walked slowly down the aisle. Nobody suspected anything under the veil other than the face of a typical Scottish bride. More precisely, they expected the face of Elisabeth Armstrong, the beautiful daughter of the powerful clan laird, Alexander Malcolm Armstrong. In size and hair colour, Elisabeth and I hardly differed, but otherwise, we were probably as different as day and night.

Durham Cathedral was overcrowded. The English families looked at me with a mixture of boredom and disgust. If only they knew. With painfully slow steps, I moved to the altar on the arm of the old laird. "Slowly," the aged lady's maid of the Scottish princess had drummed into me. "Slowly." So, wearing my boots, I put one foot in front of the other, always careful not to stumble over the hem of the dress that they had forced me into, which was much too long. I felt ridiculous in that outfit and feared that no one would be convinced by this deception!

The maid had tried to assure me that in this dress, I could even fool the old laird himself. Laird Armstrong had resolutely put the plaid with the colours of the Armstrong clan around me and fastened it with his wife's silver brooch. None of the English guests in the church had seen his daughter before, and all of the Armstrongs were fully aware of what was about to transpire.

The tailor had made sure that my arms, hands, and neck were carefully covered with fabric up to my chin, as appropriate for a chaste bride. Thereby, he also cleverly covered my fair skin and my strong muscles. Underneath I wore black trousers so that I could get rid of the bridal dress if necessary. The tightness and the heat of the outfit made me feel like a tethered beast.

The laird next to me held my hand, and with a serious expression, nodded affirmatively. It had been his idea to escort me to the altar instead of his daughter so as not to have to marry her off to the English baron Henry de Keighley. For this he risked the enmity of the English king, not to mention his life. And I was offered as the best suited person for such a daring deception since, for me, it was a matter of personal vengeance against King Edward as well as a sign of resistance. In the battle against the despised English, all means were right and proper. I realised that the plan to assassinate the baron at his own wedding was brazen, but it was possible.

In these days, Edward I, King of England, weakened by illness, shrewdly wed the women of the Scottish nobility with the English barons and lords in order to ensure the consanguinity of the difficult-to-control clans. The other way around, Scottish aristocrats were required to marry English ladies. If the aristocratic families refused, they were threatened with death for high treason.

Some of the old Scottish clans were unpleasantly surprised by the English king's marital politics. One day, the battle-hardened Scottish clan of the Armstrongs, led by the proud chief Alexander Armstrong, whose seat lay between Cumberland and the Scottish border, were outraged to hear the news that Chief Alexander was now to give his only daughter in marriage to Baron Henry de Keighley of Lancashire to support Edward's peace plans. The chief's protests fell on deaf ears.

Alexander's beautiful daughter Elisabeth was to be a pawn in the gruesome game that Edward played with his feudal lords. The English king, deeply in debt by his failure in Flanders and the Scottish War, tried brutally to subjugate Scotland, whose rebellion he regarded as a revolution in his own country. Cruel executions of high traitors were intended to deter and nip the resistance in the bud. But they only continued to kindle the wrath of the Scottish noble houses.

Confidently, I squeezed the calloused hand of the old knight next to me. He must also be very nervous; I could clearly hear his gasping breath. We had now completed the march on the stone floor up the aisle in Durham Cathedral, all the way to the altar. Henry de Keighley was already there, looking at us expectantly. Not really a bad looking man, I noticed briefly, but unfortunately, he was English.

Politics required sacrifices; that had been the motto of my Grandmaster, the assassin leader Hassan I-Shabbah. I couldn't suppress a smile. With my free hand, I felt for the dagger, which was carefully hidden in a fold of the dress. How good it was to feel the cold steel of the weapon under my fingers. Immediately, my heart stopped beating quite so fast and my breathing calmed down a bit. What a mockery of fate that no one would examine the bride for weapons. All the men here had to lay down their weapons in front of the holy church.

It would be an easy game for me. The groom had no idea. Before he even recognised me, he would be dead. A strange premonition came over me, as always, when my senses were focused on an impending assassination.

The young Baron de Keighley was a little taller than I and slim and athletic. In courtly fashion, he bowed his head as I approached him. He took my hand from the laird's arm and kissed it. He carefully helped me straighten my dress so that I could kneel on the bench that had been provided. I had practised this a hundred times over the last few days to make it look as graceful as possible.

I didn't hear anything about the actual ceremony. Again and again, my glances slid to the wooden choir stalls, then to the altar with the stone pillars on each side. Bishop Antony Brek's monotonous phrases interested me as little as the sentences dutifully repeated by my groom. His voice did not match his appearance; it was far too high. Without really thinking about it, I also repeated the previously spoken sentences. The seconds passed by, and impatiently, I waited for the moment when Henry was to raise my veil to kiss me.

That was the moment in which he would be distracted and vulnerable. That's when I would strike. I took a deep breath. Again, the voice of the bishop rang out. Then the voices of the many people behind me, who answered his prayer. Now was the time.

"You may kiss the bride!" The bishop's words were the cue. I turned toward the man next to me. He raised both of his hands to lift the veil. Carefully, he pulled it up over my face.

Bafflement. That was the first thing I saw in his eyes as they wandered from my mouth to my forehead, to the small tattoo of the cross above. His expression was one of surprise.

Only when it turned into a grimace did I know that my dagger had not missed its aim. It was the ugly mask of death that now covered his visage. I stabbed him above the fifth rib, near his breastplate, directly in the heart. He died instantly.

Suddenly, all hell broke loose in Durham Cathedral.

The self-appointed Scottish King Robert de Bruce seemed weaker than ever in the following days. For months, he had been hiding in the Hebrides in the far north of Scotland to avoid his pursuers, the English troops. Edward the First. once again assembled his troops to deliver a final blow to the Scottish resistance, which repeatedly flared up like an inflammatory hotspot in the contested land.

The people in the borderlands between the two rival kingdoms had little peace. Their region became the destination for Scottish as well as English robber-knights, who took advantage of their insecure position in no-man's land like wolves in a herd of sheep. The unity of the Scottish clans came heavily into play since the families banded together to protect themselves against the despotic advances of the outlaws of both countries.

In any case, the noble families of Scotland were, in the main, powerless, and heavily under the influence and authority of a ruthless Edward, whose forced intermarriage between the people of both nations caused a great deal of suffering.

In a desperate attempt to save his daughter from such a marriage, the clan chief, Alexander Malcolm Armstrong, turned to Enja, an assassin from the Orient, who firmly resisted all English aggression and who would murder the English bridegroom. With her daring and unusual fighting techniques and abilities, she had almost become a living legend in the Scottish Highlands. The bards of the country now mentioned her in the same breath as the exploits of William Wallace or James Douglas.

Lady Enja von Caerlaverock could never have imagined how that fateful wedding in Durham Cathedral would alter the course of her life. On that unforgettable day, May 7, 1307, she unwittingly penned a new chapter in the vibrant saga of the Scottish bards' exploits.

Berwick, a few days later.

The inn in the tranquil town of Berwick was bustling with activity that evening. As one of the few establishments offering guest rooms, it was a favoured gathering spot for traders and travellers alike. That night, the taproom was filled with guests from every corner of the kingdom.

Berwick-upon-Tweed, situated in the contested borderlands, had long been a flashpoint for the bitter struggles between the Scots and the English. Just a few years earlier, in August 1305, the town's mayor displayed the severed arm of William Wallace, who had been brutally quartered, in the market square—a grim act that fuelled resentment among the locals. Politically, the town swayed back and forth between English and Scottish control, like seaweed caught in a shifting tide.

The Scottish bard Alistair MacMhuirich, famous in the Highlands, was sitting comfortably in a corner of the spacious dining room. Surrounded by noisy gossip, he had eaten the dish of the day, a stew with vegetables, barley meal and wild boar bacon. With relish he brushed the leftover food out of his greying beard and let out excess air with a belch. Basking in the warmth, he had taken off his felt cap with the plaid, placed it next to him on the bare wooden bench, and ordered a second beaker of Uisge beatha, the Scottish whiskey, from the stout maid. Despite her bulk, she moved nimbly to the bar to get the jug.

Indeed, the bard had managed to attract the attention of visitors by announcing outrageous reports from neighbouring Durham. In no time at all, the landlord and guests of all types had invited the educated storyteller to a plate of stew and the Scottish liquor to catch up on the latest news. The cold of the night barely managed to counter the heat of the crowd and the fire that shot up in the fireplace. Even the fighting dogs finally shut their snouts to hear the bard's words.

Alistair looked around at the traders and travellers that now hung on every word that crossed his lips. He wiped his mouth with the back of his hand. But it took another sip of the high-proof brew to loosen the tongue of the bard.

"Worthy ladies and highly esteemed gentlemen," he said, beginning the ritual that had emerged as an established evening's entertainment in the Highlands for centuries. Even the great leaders of all the Highland clans listened to this man when he had something to say.

A murmur and hiss went through the crowd, and now the last guests in the room finally fell silent. Curious, they leaned toward the person at the table for one, who was besieged by the English as well as the Scots, the maids, and the cooks.

"A few days ago, the sixth Sunday after Easter, the young Lady Elisabeth Armstrong, the only daughter of Alexander and Catherine Armstrong, and the Baron Henry de Keighley, Knight of Shire in Lancashire, were to marry"

This news had been proclaimed a few weeks ago, so Alistair was only repeating what many already knew. He cleared his throat, and in a hoarse voice, let his words sink in.

"I was invited to the celebration as a bard for the Armstrong family and am expected to report on the wedding."

"Was the bride as pretty as she is said to be?" A young maid interrupted shyly and was immediately rebuked by a grunt from the stout cook. You don't interrupt a bard.

But the cosmopolitan man with his silver-grey beard, who was well past forty summers, smiled indulgently and said, "She is as radiantly beautiful as the light of the sun when it is reflected in the sea in the evening."

A deep sigh escaped the women who had gathered around him in large numbers.

"She just didn't show up, unfortunately," Alistair continued dryly, delighting in the perplexed faces of the audience. A laugh like a billy goat pealed from his mouth. His beard trembled with the rhythm and his shoulders shook. Again, he allowed himself a draught from the pitcher, and stirred up an expectant tension.

"As it happened," he finally explained, "the real Lady Elisabeth had been replaced by another person who stepped through the church to her bridegroom to marry him before God and the Church!"

"In her place?" came the horrified shouts. "Then it wasn't Lady Elisabeth who stabbed the baron?"

This time even the cook didn't seem to have anything against the maid's question, who now put her hand over her mouth in shock. Of course, the news of the bridegroom's death had long preceded the bard and still horrified the people of the city. Now they had a witness who knew all the details of this incredible story.

"But no!" confirmed the bard. "On the way to the wedding, the carriage was stopped and the rebel Enja von Caerlaverock exchanged places with the bride, who was brought back unharmed. Lady Enja, who has taught the English what fear is in many battles, had agreed to walk to the altar instead of Elisabeth, and then to stab the bridegroom on the spot and rebuff the king."

This sparked a discussion in the back rows, including some voices that the bard recognised as English. Alistair spoke in Scottish Gaelic, which all residents of the border country spoke or at least could understand.

"How do you know for sure that it was Lady Enja?" interjected a clearly English voice provocatively.

"How could this woman get so close to the groom? Surely, he must have realised that it was not his bride?" asked another with a heavy Welsh accent.

Alistair raised the goblet with the brown liquid to his lips again and took a sip with relish. As he lowered the drink, he belched loudly, showing his appreciation for the host. At the innkeeper's suggestion, a maid quickly brought him a small wooden board with pieces of cheese, which the cook had made himself from the milk of his goats. Gratefully, Alistair picked up a piece with nimble fingers.

"Well," said the bard with his mouth full, "it is said that not even the bride's father knew that it was not his daughter who was under the bridal veil. Then how should it be for the groom who had never seen her before?" Not a muscle twitched in his face as he sent forth this lie into the stale air of the taproom.

"As is customary in noble houses," he explained succinctly, "the king determines the marriages on paper. Normally, the spouses see each other only on the day of the wedding. In fact, the bride wore a veil that hid her face. Otherwise, the black cross in the middle of her forehead, which Lady Enja has borne since childhood, would have been noticed."

"A cross? In the middle of her forehead? How cruelly disfigured must this woman be?" The sympathetic comment came from one of the women.

"I can assure you, dear people, this beautiful woman wears this mark with such pride that it simply forbids this assumption .... In any case, the bridegroom had no chance because the moment he lifted the veil in front of the altar to kiss her, her dagger struck him right in the heart."

"Oohh," gasped the women in the room. "That's unheard of!" said one of the women. "No lady is that sly!" said another.

With a narrator's calculation, the bard let the outbreak of female indignation have its effect without comment. In the meantime, he took another sip of the Uisge beatha, which the host had made himself.

"Did he look handsome, that knight Henry?" crowed the young maid, who had previously asked about the woman's appearance, and earned a rebuff from the cook's elbow.

The question elicited a raised eyebrow from the narrator. He nodded gently, raised his eyes thoughtfully to the ceiling, and with a mischievous smile under his beard, explained, "Baron de Keighley was tall and slim. His finely cut face was very pale, and a black beard graced his chin. He would certainly not have been a bad husband for Elisabeth Armstrong," he mused, "if he hadn't been English."

This provoked a lot of laughter from the audience, to which the English only responded with derogatory outbursts. The atmosphere in the room was filled with the tension that prevails in places where men of different origins meet.

"I hope they killed the murderer on the spot!" someone shouted in English and was cursed wildly by the Scots.

Alistair knew how to keep the audience under his spell by holding up his hands soothingly and asking for silence. A young servant hastily put some wood in the large fireplace. He didn't want to miss any of the story, either. He sat back down just in time to hear the bard's next words.

"The brave warrior who had wedged herself into the wedding dress with the green and blue colours of the Armstrongs was now exposed to the English guards without protection. As you can imagine, Durham Cathedral was crowded. The bride's Scottish family and her clan had been relegated to the back of the church, while the English nobility stood in the front rows. Women, children, knights and nobles watched helplessly as the young Henry de Keighley was stabbed to death by a murderess before their eyes!"

Actually, Alistair not only repeated the shocking scene, but managed to arouse the horror of the audience anew. He leaned forward and struck his fist with force on the table, which made everyone in the audience hold their breath in shock. "But apart from the murderer," he hissed menacingly, "there was not a single person in the church who had a weapon at that moment!"

With big eyes and open mouths, the amazed audience stared at Alistair.

"Not a single one ...", the bard repeated. He theatrically raised his right hand and clenched it into a fist.

"Lady Enja was the only one with a dagger in her hand and thus held Bishop Anthony Brek in check; he was so afraid that he almost wet his vestments!"

This time, the laughter came from all sides; after all, it was not every day that a bishop was so clearly a dupe.

Alistair MacMhuirich sat back and studied his audience. In addition to the servants and maids, there were also some merchants and Scottish knights among his listeners. Surely, they would put a little silver in his cap later that evening. He patiently let the laughter die down before telling the rest of the story.

"I was standing in the back with the family of the Scottish bride. Suddenly, a burning bale of hay fell through the open side window—and then another! But the bales were damp and smouldered more than they burned. They covered the church in thick smoke. You can imagine the panic this created with all the women and children!"

A look around at his audience confirmed that they knew of the dangers of such fires. Insufficiently dried hay had often caught fire in the haystacks and the fire surprised people in their sleep. The wood crackled in the fireplace, seemingly in agreement, and a few glowing logs slid along noisily. The people looked reverently into the bard's face, who now leaned forward conspiratorially and lowered his voice.

"The screams of the people alerted the guards, and they attempted to enter the cathedral against the current of those who wanted to escape from there. In the midst of this melee, the murderess managed to drag the bishop with her. Despite thick billows of smoke, I could clearly see the woman in front of the high altar respectfully saying goodbye to the priest with a slight bow. Now I knew it was her. Enja von Caerlaverock!"

Challenging anyone to disagree, he looked around.

"I could look directly into her beautiful face with the painted cross between her eyes. She looked proudly in my direction and raised her hand, perhaps to ask forgiveness for the Armstrong family. I was frozen by the gesture. How gracefully she stood there ..."

His gaze wandered into the distance, as if he saw her before him. Without haste, she then slipped out of the dress under which she was wearing men's clothing, and carefully placed it on the altar. Then she put the dagger in her boot and swiftly climbed the ornate high altar.

He pointed with his hand to the ceiling, which was barely two yards above him in the inn. All eyes followed his hand movement upwards.

The bard bridged the meaningful pause with a strong sip from his goblet, which the maid immediately refilled. The countless spellbound eyes were now fixed on the face of the man who had been an eyewitness to these extraordinary events.

"I've never seen a person, let alone a woman, soar nearly nine yards so quickly. It was as if she had wings that lifted her up and made her disappear from view forever ..."

Now some of the audience members turned pale. A winged murderess? But the bard hurried to erase this image by quickly following with the explanation.

"She had worked her way up the ornate stone pillars on the left and right of the altar, up to the window, opened it, and swung through it like a cat, under the angry roar of the English people present. The people ran in panic in all directions." With that, he spread both his arms to a brilliant climax.

"She escaped?" squeaked a horrified voice that actually belonged to the fat cook. A film of sweat had clearly settled on his balding head.

"Why was she able to escape from there?"

Other heads nodded in agreement. Everyone imagined how the church must have been surrounded by the English, Scots, and a large crowd of onlookers. Such an important event drew people from everywhere, not the least of which were merchants selling their wares.

"Well," the bard crossed his arms over his chest and raised his thick eyebrows, "apparently, she had accomplices outside the church who had positioned themselves with a hay cart in front of the altar window. She jumped on the hay cart and hid in it. The cart then left the church grounds unobtrusively and the perplexed guests were at a loss. Neither the Scots nor the English found their tracks. She seemed to have vanished into thin air, and with her, the hay wagon pulled by a black stallion—a horse as black as the night, with eyes that could see into the souls of every sinner." At this last sentence, his voice deepened, and a shudder seized the audience throughout the room. Only the crackling of the logs and the sighing of the women could be heard as Alistair MacMhuirich sat back contentedly and turned his cap upside-down on the table to receive his tips.

This was his story. At least, it was the one meant to reach the ears of the English king. The old laird had paid him handsomely for it. Alistair MacMhuirich had been part of the daring plan orchestrated by the young woman. "Edward will have you quartered as a traitor!" he had warned that madwoman from Caerlaverock back then at Hermitage Castle in Cumberland, the seat of the Armstrong clan.

"He's already tried, Alistair," she had replied with a laugh, "and he won't succeed this time either. Those who challenge the devil will reap death." Her eyes had sparkled like ice crystals as she spoke.

How could he ever forget her...

Chapter 2

Iceland in 1289

Tam-tam, tara-tam, echoed through the mountains, where the small huts of the inhabitants blended inconspicuously into the forested valleys like mushrooms merging with the background. Tam-tam, tara-tam, the drumbeats vibrated in my ears, signalling the start of a ritual: the handing over of a young girl. The closer we got to the spot where the ship waited, the louder the drumming and the singing grew, as the people prepared for the most important event in their community. Tam-tam, tara-tam…

It was early in the morning, the moon had not yet fully retreated from the night sky and wrestled with the sun over the transition from darkness to day. Various shades of grey defined the silhouettes of people and the landscape.

The whole village had accompanied me and my mother, and now the crowd was singing and dancing, moving en masse towards the sea. There, torches lit up the grey of the waning night, revealing their glowing, excited faces. The excitement seemed to capture everyone who walked with me down the steep path from the village to the jetty to witness this moment. I would have felt almost as sublime as them if I hadn't known that a turning point in my life awaited me down there by the sea. It would be an agonising separation that I couldn't avert. This was my destiny.

As if the excitement surrounding him left him completely cold, my wolfhound, Rocca, cheerfully panted beside me, his tongue hanging out of his chaps like a wet rag. From time to time, his clever eyes looked at me curiously; for him, it was just another outing together with the family.

With mixed feelings, I now waved to the people who had all come to say goodbye to my mother and me. I should be proud like these people and especially my family here. But the thought of losing loved ones, family, friends, animals, still gnawed at me. My heart was heavy when I walked down from the village for the last time, to the jetty where the ship was waiting for me. Every single stone and stalk on this path was so familiar, and holding my mother's hand, I absorbed every little detail like a sponge to keep it in my memory forever. My little feet could hardly keep up with her firm, unhesitating steps.

There was a chill in the air on this spring morning. Although the days were already getting warmer, the nights were still bitterly cold. The north wind blew so hard in my face that it brought tears to my eyes. Or were they caused by the pain of farewell?

My mother squeezed my hand. She seemed to sense that I was struggling with myself. She smiled at me cheerfully as we walked the last few metres to the jetty on the weathered wood of the pier. My legs were tired because of the long walk, so she slowed the pace a little. Or was it just to see the faces of those who had loved her and me? Friends, relatives, the whole village actually, had come to celebrate this big day with us.

The view back was impressive: a dense cluster of people stood there, wrapped in thick fur skins against the icy winds, at the edge of the sea. They screamed and shouted, and many also sang to the gods who were to protect my mother and me on our journey. Numerous torches surrounded the whole scene, which had become a wild and powerful spectacle. Even the fog that hung majestically over the water and mixed with the smoke of the torches seemed to pay homage to our journey.

My father, who had been following us silently, came up to me, took me into his arms, and pressed me firmly to his chest. The thick fur, which he had thrown around his shoulders like a blanket, tickled my nose. I will never forget its familiar smell of leather, smoke, and fish oil, while enjoying his caress with an intensity that arose from the certainty that it would be the last time—the last time before I grew up. Then he held me at a little distance from himself and looked at me with a serious expression. His bright blue eyes with their sharply drawn black brows looked lovingly at me. Long, light hair surrounded his face tanned by the icy air. Bright beard stubble glistened on his face, framing his smile like stars around the moon.

"I'm very proud of you, Enja. The whole village is proud of you, and we are sure that you will not shame us. No matter what happens, the gods, your family, and all our people are with you. Don't ever forget that!"

My heart made a sentence, and I had to swallow before I could answer. "I'm going to make you proud, Papa," I said, "just like all the other girls made their fathers proud before me!"

This seemed to make an impression on him, because he kissed me again on the forehead before abruptly letting me go. Maybe he didn't want me to see his tears. I noticed them, but I would never have said a word.

My sister, Jalla, in her leather dress with the embroidered fur collar very similar to mine, was now pressing herself close to me. She had remained mute all the way to the pier and did not react quite so warmly, which was understandable under the circumstances. In tears, she handed me a bouquet of flowers, sniffled, and quickly turned around and disappeared behind the countless legs of the surrounding crowd, whose feet were wrapped in sheepskins held together by leather cords. Jalla was the only one who didn't understand all of this and wasn't proud of me. She was only infinitely sad, but in her quiet way, could not say so. It gave me a stab in the heart, and I wanted to run after her just when my father decided to push me towards the jetty.

Now it was time: our ship laid majestically in the water; at the bow, a mighty dragon made of carved wood bared its teeth and threatened anyone who dared to approach. I was always afraid of this demon, which looked like a petrified beast riding on the water that could come to life at any moment. Anxiously, I stole a glance at the wooden head as we passed the bow, and followed my mother, her long fur coat flapping in the wind, along the narrow path over the footbridge. Mama hoisted me over the railing of the ship onto the rough wooden planks without effort and followed me with a big step onto the boat. Then she turned me away from her so that I could look back to the shore, with both her hands placed proudly on my shoulders.

"See how they rejoice! A chosen one from our village. That's you, my daughter!" she said to me proudly.

A shiver went through me. In fact, I was indeed the chosen one. What an honour! For one moment, like a cold shower that almost took my breath away, a wild resolve supplanted my sad thoughts. This pride and the firm hands of my mother saved me from jumping back over the railing of the ship, which was now moving away from the shore as the villagers roared. As if guided by a ghostly hand, the dragon's head seemed to move towards the open sea. My gaze caught the faces of the people in the front row, illuminated by the early morning light, for the last time. I desperately tried to internalise forever the image of the large figure in the middle, which was unmistakably my father. His hair danced in the wind, and his face shone from the tears that he shed.

"I will never forget you, Papa!"

It was only when the black mass of the island had swallowed people's silhouettes and all that could be seen was their faint outline protruding out of the sea that I realised my face was hot from the tears running over it. Gently, Mama wiped the wet drops from my face with her sleeve and took me in her arms.

"Everything will be fine," she murmured. "If you see us again one day in the hereafter, you will be like the gods. You alone have the power to do so with your destiny."

Despite all the great expectations and intentions, I just didn't feel up to great deeds at that moment. Sobbing, I burrowed into the lap of my mother, who gently cradled me and stroked my hair.

"Enja!" An elbow jabbed painfully into my rib. "Wake up, you stupid girl! You're dreaming with your eyes open..."

I blinked, turned my head towards the hissing voice, and looked into large, dark eyes set in a freckled face framed by brown curls. A worried look scrutinised me.

"Is everything alright?" the voice whispered again.

"Yes, of course," I stammered, a little dazed, and also whispered, "I was just somewhere else in my thoughts."

"I noticed that," Jasemin remarked mockingly. "You had a very glassy look ... pssst, Master Abdallah has already seen you; he will surely…"

Jasemin stopped in the middle of the sentence. The said master had just cast his falcon-like gaze at me as she leaned in my direction. Master Abdallah was a haggard-looking man; his unevenly striped kaftan hung on him like a bedsheet on a clothesline, and his nose resembled a beak, sharp-edged like that of a falcon. His eyes matched the imposing centre of his face. They lay deep in the eye sockets and now flashed at me furiously. His head was covered by a blue turban, the end of which he had draped loosely over his shoulder. He crossed his arms, looked at me sternly and bowed his head gracefully.

"Do you sully my lessons again with your unworthy chatter, Enja? Where do you get this self-confidence? As if your words were more important than mine? Come here to me, immediately!"

His words came as a threat—quiet, demanding, arrogant. How I hated being judged by him! But what else could I do?

I did not want to be punished for disobedience, so I untangled myself from my cross-legged position, stood up, and stepped in front of him. I wasn't very tall yet and just reached to his stomach, but I answered his furious gaze with respect.

He clearly enjoyed showing his power in front of the other children. As a strict and also somewhat arrogant teacher, he was not used to contradiction, and now he made me suffer for it. Slowly, he looked over the children squatting on the floor and back to me, making me feel my indignity. The small room was pleasantly cool; it lay in the shade of a large palm tree, and the open air-slits in the walls allowed a pleasant breeze to cool the hot air.

Still, the sweat formed on my forehead. I knew, of course, what was to come, and I was preparing inwardly for his attack. I hadn't followed his lessons, and he had noticed. What would he come up with to punish me? His hand lay heavy on my right shoulder and pressed it down firmly; he deliberately wanted to make me small.

"Tell me, Enja," his anger echoing through his soft voice, "how do you translate 'don't talk when the teacher speaks' into Farsi?"

I thought for a moment and confidently spoke the Persian words. After a little pause, I put another phrase behind it— the translation of his title and his name. His face did not indicate whether he thought this was right or wrong; he only looked at me with his dark eyes, sighed, and then started again.

"You don't pay attention, but you still understand me." This was not a question; it was a statement.

"Uh, how do you mean that ...?"

"Translate!" he hissed impatiently.

I swallowed in disbelief but followed his order.

His face twitched; did he disguise a grin?

This time, he addressed me in the language of Persia.

"How do I do this? I don't know, Master. It... it's in here," I said hesitantly, and I pointed at my forehead, embarrassed. "And it's suddenly there..."

Even I realised how stupid this sounded, and I looked at the floor, ashamed. My bare toes dug into the hard ground. The other children began to giggle, and Jasemin was among these traitors.

"Come to my study today after the evening meal. I need to talk to you."

An outstretched arm directed me to my place. I settled down again gladly next to Jasemin, who held her hand in front of her mouth so as not to make any noises. Her cheeks were red, but her gaze was trained stubbornly downwards.

Master Abdallah looked at me thoughtfully and snapped his fingers. "Quiet!"

Not a minute later, he spoke about the subjunctive, probably inspired by our little battle of words—his girls now all attentive listeners. Master Abdallah was indeed a strict Farsi and Arabic teacher. If he was in a bad mood, a blow with his stick could also be expected. If he was in a good mood, his lessons were even fun, and his mood improved when his students made no mistakes. So, I wasn't punished this time because I had done everything right. It's strange, however, that he wanted to speak to me alone later. Was something wrong?

So while sixteen girls followed his lessons attentively and diligently practiced Arabic numbers in Farsi, my thoughts drifted back to the ship on the open sea once again. And to my mother.

We had been on the water for hours now, with no end in sight. There was no land to be seen anywhere, just the endless sea with its unfathomable depths.

I clearly remember my mother standing proudly, high up at the bow of the ship, right next to the dragon's head. Her hair was braided, smooth and white, woven like silk threads into a work of art. A few strands were plucked out by the wind, which played a lively game with them. The early spring sun warmed our faces a little, but the breeze was even more refreshing. She faced the sun. High cheekbones framed an even, classic face with a long, straight nose. Her closed lids hid the deep blue eyes that were so similar to mine. She was a beauty, a goddess. Anyway, my father called her that, and he certainly knew what a goddess looked like.

Her beautiful face turned to me, and her lips twisted into an uncertain smile that barely disguised her discomfort. "Seems like we're going to have a rough night; the weather is changing in a few hours. Try to go to sleep right now. Who knows if we're going to get much tonight."

Since I had never experienced 'a rough night' and had no idea about what was coming, I left it at that. She willingly stretched out her arms, and I clung to her. Smiling, she wrapped me in her coat, made from the warm fur of a polar bear that my father had killed with his own hands. I was able to cuddle close to her body. Her nearness and warmth allowed me to be the little girl that I still was, and with a pleasant feeling, I asked, "May I sleep next to you, Mama?"

"Of course, my love; come, we'll lie down next to this crate, where we'll be protected from the wind."

There happened to be a large wooden box on the deck, which probably contained ropes and rudders. It provided us a sheltered place from the wind, but still let us enjoy the warmth of the sun's rays. I curled up tightly in Mama's lap under the coat and watched from under its hem how the men on the ship were doing their work. Quietly and without talking loudly, they did their jobs, tying ropes, nets and chains, and tying loose boxes and barrels, as if they were preparing for a strong storm.

My limited view reached just as far as the horizon, with whitecaps bouncing all around in the endless water. Papa said we would be travelling for a few days and there would be a lot more water to cross; weeks would pass before we reached my destination. What will become of my sister Jalla now that I am no longer there? I thought. Will she miss me or forget me?

Papa had told me about the other girls who had taken the same journey each year. They were to assist the gods in the battle against the volcano Hekla, who, from time to time, opened his big mouth to devour everything that stood in his way. People, animals, houses and even entire villages! I was just not sure what to do on the way to be well received by the gods, but my father had looked at me proudly and assured me that I would be accepted by the gods at Olympus without pain—a great honour, which was bestowed on very few girls in our tribe!

The thought that my sister would now have Papa and Rocca all to herself annoyed me a little. But I had my mother to myself now, which wasn't bad, either. My little hand crept into her wool vest, my head lay leaning on her chest, and the world around me became unimportant. She had wrapped her warm fur coat protectively around me to keep the cold winds away from me, at least a little.

With the even rhythm of the waves accompanied by the creaky lullaby of the ship's planks, I fell sound asleep.

Mama suddenly lurched so violently that she cried out. Immediately, I was awake. A lightning bolt had struck one of the masts with a crack so loud that it resounded in my ears. The mast splintered and hit the ship's planks with a huge noise. Ropes, sails, and wooden parts flew through the air. The men were able to save themselves by jumping to the side, but everything happened fast and furiously.

With great presence of mind, my mother tore me away from our sleeping place before it also fell victim to the faltering mast. Pure chaos prevailed all around us. Again and again, the lightning flashed brightly over us. Frightened, I clawed onto her leg, which was wrapped in soft leather. In disbelief, I stared at the ghostly scenery: glistening light that illuminated the surface of the deck in snapshots gave a glimpse of the devastation. Like bones, the charred shards of the main mast reached up from the bottom of the ship. Around us, the sea was foaming and hissing, the wind whipping the rain almost horizontally over the deck. It was a shocking sight! At that moment, the ship suffered a heavy blow and left us both tumbling toward the railing where we sought to hold on. The torrential rain made the seafarers' hair stick like wet algae on their faces as they tried with all their might to drag the mast into the water. In rushing around, they severed the rigging, which still connected the mast and the sails to the ship. Unfortunately, the greater part still hung on deck, and the mast barely moved from the spot. For the first time, I felt something like fear among the experienced men; the casualness and calm had given way to desperate hectic effort.

Mama held me in front of her tightly with both hands. We had moved further and further back along the railing to the stern, and I felt the ship rolling and roaring under us. Desperately, we clung to anything that could not be washed away. The bent mast put the hull in a dangerous position, and we propped ourselves up at the rear end of the ship's edge so as not to fall over the railing. Water hit hard over the bow of the ship every time it plunged toward a wave. The demon's head, flashing its teeth, fought against a wall of water, which, in our helplessness, mocked us, and gurgled, and demanded sacrifices. Would we be the next?

Eventually, I felt Mama bind her shawl around my chest; cleverly, she attached me to her own body with the cloth to make sure I wasn't going to be swept overboard.

"I'm not leaving you alone, my little one," she whispered in a firm voice into my ear, as if she had guessed my thoughts. But I saw her fingers trembling. "The gods will protect you; you are..."

A loud noise drowned out her voice, and a huge arsenal of lightning illuminated the horizon. Behind me, I felt my mother's body recoil. She had seen it, too! I was still small, and everything around me seemed big, but I thought that what I saw in the flash of white light was incredibly huge. Mama, too. A black wall had risen up threateningly right in front of us, the height of several ships moving in our direction, like a mountain that had been set in motion to crush us.

Behind me, a terrified cry emanated from my mother. "By all the gods, what is that!" And all of a sudden, time stood still.

We stared at the giant black wave without realising what was going to happen. Even the sailors gave up their efforts to clear the ship again. They just stared motionless at this billowing wall that had appeared in front of our bow, because they knew there was no chance of escape. Fate had caught up to us with a wave of death.

As if in slow motion, I saw that water monster pushing the ship up in front and lifting it along the wall of water into a vertical position. The wooden hull rattled and groaned under the load. The mast, now destroyed, rumbled past us into the depths and, with it, a few lost sailors. The screaming of the men was drowned out in the noise; I could hear my mother's screaming only because my ear was so close to her mouth. I saw the dragon's head still steadfastly breaking the crest of the waves, then the ship turned over on its back, and the black water embraced me, and all those who shared my fate, with its icy arms.

All was suddenly quiet. Very quiet. The sounds of shattering, the bursting and cracking of metal and wood were smothered under water. I could hear a dull bubbling and felt my mother smashing about and paddling vigorously. Maybe, only maybe, I heard the screams of the sailors. But could one hear screams underwater?

I remained surprisingly calm. The panic of the previous day gave way to a sense of certainty. I accepted my fate and let myself float. And in the blackness of the deep, I felt strangely safe, somewhere between heaven and earth, as if the sea had welcomed me like a guest. Was it the water or the peace? The cold was not unpleasant; I always felt comfortable where others froze bitterly. I almost felt it was beautiful underwater, had it not been for the shortness of breath and the burning in the lungs. With a whoosh, we penetrated the water's surface, paddling wildly, wheezing and panting; Mama had managed to bring us both back to the top. She had sacrificed her polar bear fur, which now floated through the depths of the sea. Gratefully, I soaked up the precious air.

"Are you alright, Enja?" Panting, Mama choked out the question as she frantically doggie-paddled on the water's surface.

"Yes ... I'm fine! Please let me swim on my own!"

I was still tied to her, but now she pulled the shawl away from me, trembling, and held me fast with her hands. She knew I could swim well. She was probably just afraid that the raging water might pull me away from her. It was now easier for her to stay on the surface because she no longer had to carry my weight.

The sea around us was still raging, although the waves were a little flatter. In a lightning flash, we tried to recognise parts of the ship, but only a few broken pieces could be identified. The giant wave must have crushed the ship and buried the men under it. How and why we were able to survive was a mystery to me. In the meantime, I felt the coldness of the water slowly moving into my bones. As comfortable as I felt in the water, the cold would kill us in no time.

"We won't survive long if we don't get out of here. Look out for something floating, maybe a piece of wood from the ship..." Her voice sounded weary, she shivered from the cold, and small clouds of steam came from her mouth. The lightning slid further behind the horizon, and the thunderbolt followed at greater distance. The dark, grumbling clouds withdrew with the thunderstorm and sought new victims. The waves no longer roared and did not rock us back and forth quite so angrily on the agitated surface. But the moon came out behind the clouds, shining bright and round. It hung loftily above our fate, illuminating our misery in full light. Far and wide there was no human soul, no land, and no ship in sight.

"Will we die now?"

My voice was just a whisper, but she could hear it over the rattling of her teeth.

She wheezed as if the cold had frozen her lungs. "No, it must not be, it simply must not be ...!" came from her trembling lips. Her growing desperation was palpable in every fibre and made me cry. My proud, confident mother no longer knew what to do. Her helplessness became a reflection of my dwindling hope.

Was this the end? Could it be that the gods had sent us on this journey to kill us? Wasn't I the chosen one, or were they angry about something?

I saw similar thoughts in Mama's face illuminated by the moonlight, even if she tried not to show her fear. Her lips were moving. Perhaps she was praying for a little miracle. How small humans were when the gods waved their fists!

I paddled wildly with my arms to keep myself afloat. Again and again, water splashed into my face and my eyes, which were already burning unpleasantly from the salt. But at least a little bit of warmth was generated in my body from the effort.

Suddenly, I saw something that caught my attention: "Mama, look, there!" I pointed to a shady shape not far in front of us, something that was floating in the water. "It floats! Maybe it can carry us!"

With a final mustering of our dwindling forces, we managed to swim to the object, which was quite stable in the water. It was the wooden crate next to which we had slept. It must have come loose from the ship, and now it was drifting upside down in the sea. Mama helped me pull myself over to its surface, and I lay stretched out on the crate like a dead fish, struggling for balance.

"There iss sp ... space fff...for two!" I cried, trembling, clinging to the wooden handle of the box. Mama tried to pull herself up, and the wood bobbed dangerously under the surface of the waves. She stopped immediately and let herself slide back into the water. The base wavered menacingly from left to right. Her head protruded just a few hand-widths from mine out of the water, pale and in deep shadow. Her wet hair shimmered silver. She was breathing calmly and flat now, almost as if she were gaining strength for a new attempt. But she didn't move, holding the box only at the edge. What was going on with her?

"Mama, you have to get out of the w... water, n... now!" My voice was very thin, like her voice before; fragile. I knew what was to come and fought against fate with all my might. I closed my eyes and clenched my teeth until they crunched.

"You can do it, I'll hold you..." I managed to say.

The water seemed spiteful, cold, and deadly. When she spoke, her voice was soft and sounded infinitely tired. She had stopped shivering. "The wood is not strong enough to carry us both, only you. It will save you. You will live, Enja. You are the chosen one, and the gods will help you."

Now I could see through my weakened senses how her strength was failing. Her voice was just a whisper. "I love you, little one. I will always be with you. Here, take this and wear it. It will protect you. It is the bond that unites us!"

Using the last of her remaining strength, she pulled the cord with the amulet off her neck and stretched out her trembling hand. I grabbed it just before it could fall into the water. It was the oval stone with which I was always allowed to play when I sat on her lap; it was smooth and black in a silver setting on a leather strap. Determinedly, I put it around my neck, and it seemed to me that something from my mother had just passed to me: warmth or strength? I couldn't tell which. The stone just seemed warmer than my own body, perhaps still from ... from her? Suddenly I realised what she was up to ...

"Mama, stay with me!" I barely got the sentence out of my mouth as a wave of horror rolled over me and took my voice away. The next moment she let go of the box, slowly drifting away from me, her head only a dark, wet, and ever smaller shape in the infinite expanse of the sea.

Her last words reached me only as whispers over the water, as if she had already become one with her wet grave.

"Don't give up, Enja, you now carry my force within you." Her head was nothing more than a dark, ever-shrinking outline in the vast expanse of the sea.

My vision suddenly blurred with tears, and everything seemed to melt away. Silence enveloped me as the sea stopped bashing my wooden crate, as if it wanted to rock me to sleep. Gratefully, I surrendered to a leaden fatigue that, for the moment, eased my pain and pulled me into an exhausted sleep...

Chapter 3

Two days later...

I wasn't sure what was waking me up, whether it was the light of the first rays of the sun or the rocking of the waves. My hands and feet were numb with cold, and my head throbbed. My tongue was swollen, and my lips felt cracked. I had drifted helplessly on the surface of the water for a second night, with no fresh water and no food. Perhaps it would have been better to meet my end in the depths of the sea with my mother, rather than dying in agony on a wooden crate. But I was afraid of death, and even more so of breaking the promise I had made to my mother.

"No," I croaked with difficulty, "no, I will not die, I will live…"

My eyes had run out of tears; they were dry and swollen. I blinked with great effort. As I carefully licked my lips, the salty taste of the sea intensified the cruel thirst that gripped me.

Day and night seemed to have become one, and I lost all sense of time. Around me I saw only water—endless, deep, black water—as if the rest of the earth had been swallowed up by this never-ending mass. The thought of my mother's death constricted my throat.

I could still see her face, and her sad eyes were still before me, burned into my memory. The last picture of her remained, floating lonely in the waves, even when I closed my eyes. She had fought valiantly for me, saved me, but gave her life for it. Where is she now?

According to the faith of our fathers, she would enter a new world after death and assume the rank she had earned during her life. I hoped she was happy where she was now. Maybe she was looking down on me from there? That gave me new strength. She shouldn't see me struggling with my fate, possibly losing the fight. If she could see me, could she also hear me?

"Mama, I miss you!"

Desperately, I was looking for a sign of life, for her face, the face of a goddess. But I hardly recognised anything near me, my vision was blurred, my eyes were now burning like fire, and I squeezed them tightly against the pain. "Mama ..." I sobbed again and again, and my voice died in a dry croak.

"Hoohoo!" The sound penetrated to my ears. "Hooohooo!"

Mother? I doubted she would call to me like that, but what does such a call represent? Had she changed into a different life form? Into a bird or a dragon that was turned into wood like the demon on our ship's bow? Such stories were told by the adults at the fires in the evening ...

"Hoohoo," it resounded, and a shadow fell on me. A big shadow. It was a ship. I heard the creaking of the wood and the beating of the waves against the hull sooner than I could recognise it as such. Now there were also several voices shouting excitedly in my direction. I couldn't understand them; they spoke a different language or a dialect. Our people did not have much contact with other tribes, but sometimes travellers came through our village and sold all sorts of things. We children were always excited and curious, so I knew one or the other sounds of foreign languages.

But this language, which now reverberated in my ear, sounded strangely melodic, throaty with high and deeper tones that I had never heard before. The strangers pulled my floating home of the last few days nearer with a boat hook, and one of the men climbed overboard, skilfully grabbed me around the waist, and let the others pull him up. He laid me down on my face like a wet sack on a barrel that smelled rancid. My arms and legs hung down without sensation. My tongue lay thick in my mouth. Thirst! screamed my innermost, I need something to drink! But I couldn't get a sound out of my throat, as if it had completely dried up.

My saviour smiled and spoke a few words of this throaty, melodic language, and I shook my head weakly. I didn't understand it. That was all I could manage; my arms and legs were dead weight. He propped me up like a doll and started massaging my hands and feet. All the while, he talked to the other sailors, all of whom had striking dark skin and dark hair. Their eyes were also dark, almost black. But the individual faces were so varied, as if someone had tried to bring as many different types together as possible in this small place. My lifesaver was tall and slender, and he had a youthful face that would have been friendly had it not been for a scar that left an ugly bulge from his temple almost to his ear. Apparently, as a consequence of his injury, his ear had been cropped. This wound had undoubtedly been very painful once.

He could sense that I was watching him, and he smiled again, somewhat too lopsided. Slowly life returned to my limbs and the pain proved to me that I was still in one piece, but tears welled in my eyes, and I held my breath. No, I wouldn't scream!

Next to him, a small, fat man with a ring of light hair tried to bring life back into my limbs, which he managed to do quite well by moving his sausage-like, warm fingers rhythmically over my hands and feet. Just when my limbs started to feel like my own again, he ran off to get a blanket. It stank of urine and was torn, but I gratefully accepted it. The fat man flashed a nasty grin and showed a bite that consisted only of a few black teeth. He spoke to my saviour in this throaty language, and based on their facial expressions, they were probably discussing what they intended to do with me since, again and again, their dark gaze was trained in my direction.

The younger man hesitated for a moment and examined my necklace. He took the stone hanging from the leather strap in his hand and turned it carefully. There was something like disappointment in his appraisal, and he dropped the stone, shaking his head.

The little fat one barked something that sounded aggressive to me, and he contemptuously adjusted his expression. His eyes lay in the deep shadow of his eye sockets and sparkled dangerously. Immediately in response, the already dark face of the younger man darkened by another nuance, whereupon he barked back. I instinctively pulled my legs closer to my body and wailed, "I'm thirsty!"

It was a desperate attempt to draw attention back to me because my throat hurt so much. They fell silent at the same time and looked at me again, as if they had forgotten that I was still there, but they didn't understand me.

"Drinking," I repeated, underlining my words with a clear gesture of my hand.

Their nodding made me feel relieved, and immediately the fat man handed me his leather bag with water. It was stale and slightly salty, but it was a tonic; the best I had ever drunk! The two men watched me with interest in their dark eyes as I greedily emptied the leather bag. Then I poured some of it into the hollow of my hand and washed my face. Gratefully, I returned the bag and wiped my sleeve over my forehead and cheeks.

Only now did I realise that they were poorly dressed, with dirty cloths held together with a belt wrapped around their bodies. There was a dagger—a large dagger with a curved blade—at their side, also secured by the belt. The men wore wide trousers that ended in leather shoes, greasy and worn.

Armed men are always dangerous, my father had said, so I was on guard, as if it would have made any difference at all in my situation. I was completely at their mercy. What if they threw me overboard again because I was worthless to them?

The other men seemed to be resuming their tasks; it was a big ship. I leaned my head back. Yes, a large ship with two masts and many sails. I wondered where they were taking me. They didn't know me, and I couldn't tell them anything. What did they intend to do with me?

None of the men on the ship made any attempt to do anything to me. On the contrary, they gave me a piece of bread as hard and dry as the nuts that Mama always opened by hitting them with a stone. But I was grateful at least to soothe my growling stomach, even if it took a lot of spit to soften it in my mouth. A little later, one of the boat boys brought me some soup in which I could soak the bread. It was like a feast for me ...

My leather dress, richly embroidered by my mother over many hours of work, was still wet, and in the fresh wind, I started to cool down again despite the blanket, and trembled. The boat boy, just one head taller than I, saw this and brought me below deck into a dark chamber. There lay some straw and a few scraps of fabric, but it was at least warm and dry. It smelled uncomfortably sharp and mouldy and reminded me of rotten fish in brackish water, so I made sure that I didn't accidentally sit on a dead fish or its remains.

The young man hung an oil lamp by a hook on the ceiling. That was very nice because I was often afraid in the dark. He observed me unobtrusively as he did this. We were alone in the chamber, and he spoke to me quietly in this throaty language. I shook my head, so he knew I didn't understand him. Without letting me out of his sight, he came and knelt in front of me, his face serious and almost expressionless. Hesitantly, he took a strand of my sticky hair into his hand and looked at it curiously. It was white, like my mother's hair, and in contrast to his pitch-black hair, it was striking. The two men on deck had also curiously inspected my hair. I shyly took the strands back from him, and a small smile appeared in the corner of his mouth. He was haggard, but his face had somewhat of an innocent expression, and his eyes were now blinking curiously like that of a child. Surely, he hadn't been on board this ship with its eerie figures for very long.

The lanky boy asked me something that sounded like "amrad baida," and pointed to my hair. I shrugged. He rubbed his fingers against each other, a sign of wealth with us. With him, too?

I shook my head to tell him I had nothing with me. He looked at me compassionately, stood up hastily, and retreated to the back wall of the chamber when he heard the two men who had taken care of me were returning. They had brought a small jug, perhaps with water?

In addition, they brought a cloth, which they rolled out next to me, and a small, artfully painted container closed with a wooden stopper. I turned it in my hands. I had never seen anything like this. It wasn't clay or wood, and the painting was so fine and delicate ...

Perhaps they will bring me back to my people, it suddenly occurred to me. If only I could make myself understood!

I tried it with a few words and even more gestures. But the two men just looked at each other and shrugged their shoulders. It appeared they did not intend to bring me back to be ransomed by my people, so what did they want from me? My gaze fell back on the small vessel in my hand. Did what it contained have something to do with it?

I was still crouching on the straw as the fat one stepped behind me, took the vessel away from me, carefully placed it at my side on the floor, and then bent both my arms backwards. I resisted only briefly because he was far too strong, and it hurt me as soon as I resisted his intentions. He skilfully tied a rope around my wrists and laid me flat on the floor. He pressed the back of my head on the straw with one hand, and with the other he held my mouth.

In desperation, I started to wriggle and struggle, but he held me tight. The long-haired man with the scar on his face grinned crookedly. It looked as if he was taking pleasure in my helplessness. These two men would hurt me, I was suddenly sure of it, and I used all my strength to tear myself away from him. But the tall younger man knelt on the floor, put his long leg across my thigh and clutched me. Faint anger shot through my stomach: what were they up to, why were they treating me like this?

They didn't say a word; it was as if they had done this a few times. Each of them knew exactly what to do. Yes, it was routine, and with this realisation I became cold with fear. My heart was pounding because of struggle or fright, I couldn't tell which. I could hardly get enough air through my nose, and my frantic breathing made my nostrils vibrate.

The hand holding my mouth smelled of rotten grass, sharp and disgusting. I bit it and the fat one grunted angrily, took one of the scraps of fabric that lay next to me, and stuffed a piece into my mouth. I choked and screamed against the disgusting counteraction, but it was just a miserable whimper which, even to my ears, sounded ridiculous. They tied my legs and then waited leisurely until I had calmed down to some extent. Angry, I snorted through my nose and grumbled into the fabric as my tears flowed. Shortly, however, I calmed down a bit, and my breath resumed its regular rhythm.

The scar face crouching on one knee next to me asked me something with his choppy words. Judging by his tone, it sounded like "Onward now?" and I stared at him like the hare at the axe. I had no idea what was coming, let alone an answer. But he didn't expect an answer either because he grinned and unwrapped the piece of bright fabric that lay next to the water carafe. It was a piece of thin metal, pointed at the front. He opened the delicate vessel, briefly put the metal pin in it, and pulled it out immediately. A dark liquid dripped from the pointed underside. The hands of the fat one now again covered the sides of my face. His foul breath was right above me, and I could see the dark metal tip moving between my eyes. Then I vigorously pressed my eyelids closed and held my breath ...

The pain was horrible. The metal tip pierced my skin between my eyes, over and over again. It was almost as if he was constantly pricking the same spot, but in fact he was making a deliberate line. Yes, he drew a line with his stitches! And in between, I heard the vessel ringing quietly as he repeatedly dipped the pen into the liquid and carefully brushed off the metal tip at the edge.

Apparently, he was satisfied with the line, because he wiped the place he had painted with a wet cloth and looked closely at his work. I opened my eyes and looked at him, irritated. I realised with horror that he dipped the pen again and, oh, by all the gods ... I tried to scream despite the gag in my mouth, but only produced a dull howl.

Scarface did not let my panic irritate him at all. The grip on my head only became stronger, and I quickly stopped fighting back. My head was already throbbing from the pressure and my futile efforts. He stabbed again to the left of the already razor-sharp line and, agonisingly slowly, drew another line vertically to the existing one.

Stitch, stitch, stitch, then dip into the vessel. Stitch, stitch, stitch, immersion. When he wiped the wet cloth over my forehead again, he also wiped off the sweat that had formed there. The merciless grip detached from my head, and I allowed myself the hope that it would be over. What had they done to me? Why did they hurt me so much? If mother had been here, she would have driven the two to take flight with her curses alone.

I missed her so much …

Apparently satisfied with their work, they packed up their torture tools and got to their feet. With his dirty fingers, the fat man patted my cheek, and I would have liked to slap his hand away, but my hands were still bound behind my back. They removed the rag from my mouth and only unfastened the shackles from my feet. Clearly, they didn't want me reaching for my face. Then they left me alone with my confusion and pain. My head continued to throb and pound, the two lines between my eyes burned and pulsed. It took a long time before I could finally fall asleep, utterly exhausted.

Muza in the year 1293

The class ended earlier than usual that afternoon. The heat had seeped into our dimmed study room, making us grow weary quickly. Master Abdallah sent us back to our rooms with a few tasks, as he was yawning, too. A thick film of sweat glistened on his dark, wrinkled skin.

"Don't forget to come to me after supper, Enja." His voice was subdued, and his gaze gave nothing away. He turned and walked down the shaded corridor with his scrolls under one arm and his flowing kaftan billowing behind him. Jasemin nudged me from behind and laughed softly.

"Maybe he'll give you a few extra hours of Farsi?"

"I don't think I did anything wrong," I replied defiantly, though I wasn't entirely sure.

We crossed the sunlit square more quickly, as the stones beneath our bare feet were hot from the afternoon sun.

"Should we go down to the thermal baths? Now that it's so hot, most people are asleep, so we can lounge undisturbed."

Jasemin looked at me with anticipation. She furrowed her brow and frowned, and the pierced black lines between her eyes assumed a whimsical life of her own. I nodded, smiled at her, and we headed towards the thermal baths in a good mood. This area of the palace was laid out deep in the catacombs and sparkled with a basin of hot water carved into the rocks. There, the inhabitants, women and men, were able to separate, wash and relax. Oil lamps illuminated this area and reflected in the basins, and the light sources divided into a multiplicity of small, dancing points of light. Jasemin had the same cross on her forehead as I: a long vertical line was drawn with a short crossline that traversed the long line further down, right between the eyes. It looked like the inverted sign of Christ, as the muealam alquran, the Qur'anan, told us.

It was the sign of the fallen cross of Christians, pierced in the forehead, and for every inhabitant, the visible sign of my submission. I was a serf, belonging to another person in both body and soul, and was worth as much or as little as a piece of cattle.

At that time, on the long journey aboard the ship, I learned the language of the Arabs so well that the sailors could explain the meaning of this sign to me, my fate, and what to expect. The two men who had fished me out of the sea were traffickers and made me a slave with this sign. With such a rare and lucrative catch as I, they rubbed their hands, because light hair was particularly in demand among the slave traders.

I would certainly be sold to a man, they said, who paid a high price and certainly treated me well, they were sure. Maybe they said that just to reassure me. In any case, the two were firmly convinced that I was a prized prey, and gave me plenty to eat and drink, while they generously helped themselves to a liquid from a clay jug, which in a few hours led to greater merriment than even the prospect of a good trade.

On this journey, they also explained the name of the country from which they came and to which I would return with them. They called themselves Earabiin. The country was far to the south, where the sun went down; in their language, it was called 'Ardu Alearab. My father once told me that there were countries that were very hot, that the people there worshipped another god and therefore were not happy. For this one god does not give them water, and therefore, they must suffer greatly. We, on the other hand, had our own god for water and for fire and for ...

"Look, Zahra had the same idea," Jasemin suddenly cried, and I spotted our friend walking down the stairs to get to the underground bathrooms. Her bare, petite feet slapped rhythmically on the floor.

"Zahra!" We both shouted at the same time, and the noise stopped immediately. A pale girl with pitch-black hair on the stairs looked back expectantly and smiled shyly at us. She was very petite but definitely older than Jasemin. I had no idea how old she really was, but she was much more womanly than I.

At least her silk jilbab bulged in places that were still completely flat on me. And also, her pubic hair had already grown in. I could always observe that well in this bath without it being noticed. Jasemin and I, on the other hand, were still quite bald between our legs.

We walked in our fluttering silk dresses, the jilbabs, down the last steps to the women's chambers. On the way there, I impatiently removed the delicate veil that covered my hair as I passed the endless oil lamps that illuminated the vault carved into the natural stone. It was agreeably temperate down here, as the heat could not penetrate to this depth. In fact, at this time of day, there were no bathers here, and we were able to undress undisturbed and dive into the water, which was pleasantly warm by the underground springs. What a difference from the cold water in my homeland! My memory of it was still very vivid and always connected with frozen blue lips. Here, on the other hand, everything was very warm, even the water. The only refreshment we girls felt was when we lay naked on the smooth stones of the thermal spa stairs to rest, because the water on the skin provided cooling. It was a real luxury, intended for the ladies of the house and for the girls who had the privilege of receiving lessons here.

Perhaps I was lucky to come here at that time. When I arrived at the port of this huge city, which the sailors called Muza, it didn't look good to me. It was so hot and stuffy that day that the air flickered. The snarly Abadin, the younger of my two tormentors, swapped my leather dress for a straight-cut hooded dress made of plain linen upon arrival. They left my feet without shoes, which was not necessarily pleasant in the hot, sandy dirt of the harbour pier. The men had taken my sturdy boots from me a long time before and had probably sold them expensively for provisions, but in the wafting heat, they would certainly not have been pleasant for me, either.

After weeks without solid land under my feet, even sand and dirt were a welcome change, and besides, I really enjoyed the new feeling of hot sand between my toes.

Abadin and the fat Burak, who had told me their names at some point in the weeks of our sea voyage, took me to a place in the port city of Muza that looked like a marketplace. In the middle of the flattened clay court, surrounded by mud houses, there was a kind of pedestal made of coarse wood, on which some children sat, stood or lay. They stared at me bluntly when I arrived with the two men, their faces emaciated and apathetic. They were exposed to the heat and the blazing sun. The smell of sweat and urine affronted me unpleasantly with the wafting air. My own sweat ran down my back and legs in rivulets. Did I also look so miserable? I hoped not. At least I didn't feel that way since I had enough to eat and drink from my offenders, who were grinning expectantly.

A slave trader, sitting in the shade with a straw fan, stood up and greeted the two with a submissive bow. His kaftan was dirty and stuck to his sweaty body. His face twitched strangely, which irritated me quite a bit, and reluctance was clearly written on my face. It was only after a long and noisy negotiation with the typical expansive gesturing among these three despicable persons that I changed hands for a bag full of coins or gemstones. To catch a glimpse of the bag, I stretched my neck as far as I could, but as loud as the negotiations were that had just taken place, the handover took place quite inconspicuously.

It was only when the greasy and contentedly smiling trader led me away from the two to the pedestal and tied my hands on a leash like all the other children, that I realised I would now be sold like a piece of cattle. I was very young at the time, but the feeling of having become an object moving from one hand to the next, just like all these people on this leash, made me feel deeply ashamed.

Abadin and Burak nudged each other and patted each other on the shoulder, satisfied and with full pockets, ready to convert the acquired hard cash into liquid at the next stop. Based on their satisfied grins, they had apparently received more than they had hoped, and in this vibrant port city, they would certainly find plenty of ways to spend their fortune.

As if to mock us hopeless children around this time, the city seemed to linger in crippling silence. The midday heat made the sand in the streets glow and the air flicker. Few people were in transit in the withering heat, and only moved about when it was absolutely necessary. I had let my gaze wander around at least to distract me from the sight of the sad figures around me.

After the many weeks below deck, I was certainly no longer dew-fresh, but still strong enough to eat on my own. A few of the skinny and ragged children here were no longer able to do so. They stood limply lined up on the rope like rag dolls, and the few people whose prying eyes landed on us in the marketplace only rudely wrinkled their noses.

To protect against the strong sun, I pulled my hood over my head and crouched as unobtrusively as possible. Maybe no one wanted me? Nonsense, I told myself, then the trader probably wouldn't have paid so much for me. The conspicuous twitching of his face had worsened every time he looked me in the face. Had he perhaps cheated my two henchmen?

In the late afternoon, I had even dozed a little. The mud houses blocked the unbearable heat with cooling shadows, which also reached as far as the marketplace. Clearly noticeable, the shops and the market came back to life like a bear from its hibernation. Voices, music, and laughter penetrated my ears and attracted my attention. The city had filled with life again—travellers from all corners of the Orient, sailors, and the merchants who offered their goods. Even a few of the children who were tied together shed their apathy to see what was happening around them.

Inconspicuously, I could watch the people rushing past us. Some stopped and looked interested, others pointed to this or that. They were not afraid to touch the poor little figures, to undress them or to examine their teeth, like my mother if she wanted to buy a piece of cattle. At that moment, I felt just like such a piece of cattle, exhibited in a marketplace for sale to the highest bidder.

It's good that my mother couldn't see me like this. She probably would have cried. The thought of her made me close my eyes. No one should see that I was sad. I missed her sorely, my father and Jalla, even the stupid wolfhound puppy that she spoiled so much. The tears welled up hot under my eyelids and ran down my cheeks. I had to swallow hard before anyone became aware.

Until now, I hadn't really been noticed among the children who had been offered for sale because I had buried myself deep under my hood. But an elderly gentleman in an impeccable white kaftan woven with gold threads and a turban richly embroidered with glittering gemstones studied with sharp eyes the long line of ragged figures He pointed very firmly at me and the slave trader grinned in my direction, nodded affirmatively, and then quickly scurried over to me. With a quick hand movement, he pulled the hood off my head and let me get up.

The turban wearer's face brightened visibly as he spotted my hair colour. He climbed the stairs to our funeral stage and stopped in front of me, slightly disgusted. Presumably, the stench was annoying to him, suggested by his wrinkling his nose. He had a stern face with a small, dark, pointed beard, and his mouth was pinched. It wasn't until he looked at me directly that the corner of his mouth moved up a little—to a smile? If it was a smile, his eyes remained strangely immobile and cold, which frightened me.

With his right hand, he turned my face from left to right. Slender brown hands bared my teeth, and he wrapped my hair around his fingers. I had been allowed to wash and comb it after our arrival in the harbour, and it was now shiny, like silk, in his clean palm. He was a very well-groomed and expensively dressed man, which I concluded from his richly embroidered kaftan and the gold and gem-studded dagger on his belt. As he approached me, I noticed a pleasant, somewhat sweet smell of spices. Apparently, there were also rich people in this country because his hands were clean and well-groomed, and they did not smell when he pulled my lips back. Surely, he had never had to work with them. With shudders, I remember that he must have recognised the numerous gaps in my dentition, but I couldn't tell if he was estimating my age or just my health.

His appreciative nod finally lit up the slave trader's face and his black eyes sparkled like the gems on the stranger's turban.

The well-dressed stranger had my shackles loosened and, to my shame, took off my kaftan. He looked at me with penetrating glances, as if he were checking a gemstone for its authenticity. Again and again, his gaze travelled to my hair, which shone like silver in the sun, and took a few steps around me, nodding his head every now and then. Eventually, he let me put my kaftan on again, but my hands remained free.

Now was the time for the negotiation of my price, which was very much reminiscent of the theatrical performances of the street artists who entertained the visitors here. The two threw numbers back and forth at each other's heads, which were once violently negated by one side, then by the other side, and in between, the one sulked first, then, again, the other.

Eventually, they came to an agreement, and the stranger wordlessly handed the trader a few gold coins, which he accepted with many bows. Then the rich man with the fine-grained hands grabbed me by the wrist and led me down the stairs. On the same day, I had changed my owner twice, and at first, I didn't really know if I should find it good or bad. It was good that I was able to escape this hopeless place, but now I had no idea where I was going to go from here. Only so much was clear: the stranger was more preferable to me by far than the slave trader!

With dispatch, my new owner pushed me through the dense crowd to a group of men in long robes and colourful headscarves waiting for him on a side street.

There I came across the ugliest horse I had ever seen for the first time. It was huge, had two humps on its back and shaggy fur. Its head hung from a strangely curved neck with hanging lips. I stopped in shock, but immediately strong arms lifted me up and sat me on the creature.

It felt as if I were back on the wrecked ship in heavy seas. The men in their white kaftans just laughed at me, but at that moment, it didn't matter at all. Anxiously, I clawed my way into the blankets that were fixed between the two humps and focused on not falling from this hellish animal. I felt certain that some folks had no doubt already broken their necks in a similar situation.

One of the men tied my animal to other equally ugly horses. They were heavily loaded with a wide variety of goods. Together, we left the city. In addition to the many blankets, boxes, and clay jugs, I was also in the middle of it all as the latest acquisition of this troupe, whose intentions I did not know. Should I become a work slave like so many other children? Or would they try to track down my family to extort ransom? But how?

I didn't even know my full name at the time and didn't know where I came from. The realisation stabbed me in that moment like a knife in my chest. All I had was my memory, the face of my mother, my family, and the oval stone I wore around my neck, so worthless to my henchmen that I was allowed to continue wearing it. At that time, I rode with strange people towards an uncertain future, farther and farther away from home.

On our way, they gave me plenty to drink from their water skin, which was probably made of the leather of goats, since the scent reminded me of the animals at home. It was a familiar smell in a completely alien world, and I had to suppress the desire just to giggle. Nervousness, tension, fear, all these feelings dissolved with the familiar smell of goat leather. Had I gone mad with homesickness?

Carefully, I looked around on my swaying mount. The men who accompanied the rich nobleman had faces darker than I had ever seen before. Again and again, they smiled at me with their bright white teeth, took the water skin from me, and gave me a dark fruit, which tasted wonderfully sweet. They called it datiln, and I decided that I could certainly live where such fruits would grow. It was my desperate attempt to come to terms with my fate. Still, enough to eat and drink made it easier.

The water basin here in the small swimming grotto was equipped with a marble bench at the edge. All three of us had retreated here. Their lower bodies in the warm water, Zahra and Jasemin washed off the soap with a soft sponge that grew here in the sea. At least that's what they told me when I asked about the strange object. It was a yellow thing with holes, soft as feathers. It absorbed the water and let it go again when you pressed it. It was wonderful on the skin, and in combination with the soaps and oils, which were bottled in small carafes standing around in large numbers, a boon for my senses. We washed each other's hair, massaged it with flowery-smelling oil until it was tender as silk, and then combed it with an ivory comb. Even Jasemin's unruly curls gave way under this loving treatment. Zahra had patiently struggled with the comb on my hair and was about to weave it into a knot on the top of my head when she burst out curiously:

"Where do you actually come from, Enja?"

And as if she were embarrassed to ask, she apologetically and hastily added, "I've never seen a colour like your hair before. Blonde hair, I already know from the Roman slaves, but your hair is white like the mane of a golden horse, only much softer and delicate like silk."

I took great pride in my hair because it was the same as my mother's, the hair of a goddess. But I kept this circumstance to myself. I didn't have to think long to answer that question because I couldn't say much about it.

"I don't know where I came from. I was too small to ever ask. I just know it was very cold where I lived. The ground barely thawed in the summer before winter came back," I said, somewhat quietly. It's good that Zahra couldn't see my face because she was behind me.

"Brrr, that's certainly awful. Always freezing, isn't it?" said Jasemin, who was sitting in the water in front of me and was now looking at my expression, rubbing her nose again so that the slave cross on her forehead was crumbling in waves.

"We never really froze. We were used to the cold and had warm clothes on."

My hands pressed the sponge and air bubbles formed underneath where the holes were. I felt a stab in my chest when I thought of my family. Had Papa and Jalla ever received a message about what had happened? Or did they still believe us to be at the destination of our journey? Surely the ship had already been missed since its people should have returned at some point.

"Honestly, it's too hot for me here in this country. I sweat all the time, and the sun blinds my eyes during the day. I always have to stay in the shade and cover myself from head to toe; otherwise, I will turn red like a lobster in hot water!"

I laughed cheerfully to hide my sad thoughts. It sounded kind of strange even to my ears. Was I really so different from the other girls? Not only in appearance, but also in my thoughts?

Zahra had now braided my hair and looked at me, leaning over my shoulder. "The women here are all wrapped from head to toe anyway," she said in amusement. "Why should it be different for you?"

Annoyed, I looked at her grinning face. "With my people, the women also walk around covered from head to toe, but because of the cold!"

Then they laughed out loud, and I wondered if I had said something funny, but I couldn't recall. Jasemin cackled like a monkey who had devoured stolen datiln and was holding his belly. "Why are you complaining that you have to cover up here?"

"Because I melt in this heat like snow in the sun and would like to swim naked in the sea, just like the boys in the water basin in the city!" My voice was loud, angry. But that wasn't what silenced the two chuckling girls.

"You want to bathe naked in the horses' bath? With the boys and the horses?"

The horror was now written in capital letters on Zahra's face.

I grinned when I realised that I now had her full attention. "Yes, and then gallop with the horses in a chase over the dunes!"

My hands made a big arc. I was in my element. They wouldn't laugh at me anymore.

"May Allah forgive you for your arrogant chatter!" exclaimed Jasemin, her hand in front of her mouth. Oh, she sounded like Master Abdallah!

"You don't mean that seriously!" was Zahra's response.

Her horror just egged me on: "And I will take the biggest and fastest stallion and ride with the boys ..."

I threw the sponge, which I had kneaded ecstatically the entire time, far from me, and it landed with a smack on the wall of the grotto.

The two girls fell silent and looked at me with big, incredulous eyes, as if I were from a strange world, and maybe I was. At that moment, I felt that I was actually different. I didn't want to live a life like these two. I didn't want to accept my fate as we were told. I wanted to get away from here. And that was also what I wanted to make clear to them.

We were trapped here. We were being trained like soldiers, as slaves, for a role that we had to play. Yes, we had to learn languages, study the Koran, play musical instruments, and we learned to care for our bodies, but the goal was to serve a man and entertain him perfectly, in every way. I had been here for four years now and learned very quickly, no matter what it was.

I picked up everything like the sponge I had just thrown against the wall. I was docile and willing, and even in chess, in a very short time, I could do better than Master Abdallah, who became more and more suspicious of me the more often I checkmated him. But I never considered letting him win. Maybe that's what made him so distrustful?

I quickly learned that only the most beautiful girls came to Fahrudin Abd al Qadir, our noble gentleman and owner. Like me at the slave-market in Muza, he always chose each individual personally. I still remember with shudders the strict gaze of the well-dressed Arab in the noble kaftan, who bought me from the merchant in the boiling hot port city.

His girls were considered the most coveted slaves among tribal princes and rulers, and he was paid for his services. Sadly, when Fahrudin found an honourable buyer, the girls left us again, with many tears. Friendships were therefore always finite. Zahra, too, would soon leave; at the last inspection, she was chosen, and her future master would soon come to pick her up.

I could actually count myself lucky if one day I could live in luxury and splendour as the mistress of a rich Arab, like Zahra and all the girls before her. And yet I didn't want to submit to this life. I wanted to be free like the boys and the beggars at the horse pond. But I was a slave, and I was also a girl, like my two friends. This meant that my fate was predetermined. My days as a child were numbered; soon

I would be a woman, expected to serve a man and endure whatever he wanted from me.

Zahra and Jasemin looked at me with a fear that I could hardly comprehend. They were certainly not afraid of me, even if I sometimes allow my feelings to be a little too obvious. But they were afraid of what I was planning, of what I was. I was amazed that the two of them had not fled the baths in fear after my outburst of emotion. They felt my determination at such moments, but there was no alternative for them. Rebellion against this fate was accompanied by severe punishments. My thoughts alone were a threat to every other girl. I had known for a long time that I had to leave here and go a different way. Not a day went by when I didn't think about fleeing, but I didn't have a plan as yet. But I definitely had a goal. I pondered how I could defy my fate. Perhaps the two girls were right; in my anger, I was sometimes unpredictable.

In fact, both were anxiously silent and pursued their ablutions all the more intensively. They scrubbed their backs and all parts of their delicate skin with a small brush, so as not to create rough calluses somewhere. The knees and elbows especially always received an extra treatment. Silently and with a defiantly pursed mouth, I helped them with their feet, just as they did with me. Jasemin put my foot on her knees and scrubbed my nails with the brush with practised movements, and even used her own nails to help remove particularly stubborn dirt.

Suddenly, an astonished sound came out of her mouth, and she paused. All eyes were on my foot, which she held there on her knee.

"Enja!" She looked at me with big, wide, dark eyes, her mouth half open. "What kind of strange toes do you have?"

Strange? What was so strange about my toes? I had ten like everyone else ...

"What about my toes?" I asked insecurely. Now Zahra had also bent over and examined them from close range.

Jasemin held my foot a little higher and began to bend my toes apart one by one, as if she were cleaning the gaps. I still hadn't noticed anything strange.

"Oh," Zahra said breathlessly, "but that looks really weird; is that skin?"

And as if all this weren't embarrassing enough, Jasemin took the piece of skin between her fingers and pulled on it. I hastily removed my foot from her lap, and I didn't know whether it was in shame or terror. Both looked at me with great astonishment, and Zahra pointed her hand at my foot again.

"I've seen this with a frog, he also had such skin between his toes, but he only had three ..." She fell silent.

I looked down at my foot and pulled it closer to me. In fact, just below the toenail, a thin skin stretched between my big toe and the second in the row, which connected the two. I saw the same with the other toes. Quickly, my glance went to the toes of the other two girls, and they even lifted their feet to show me that they didn't have this skin between their toes.

"How do you know that it may not be missing from your toes? Maybe you don't have normal feet," I remarked defiantly to downplay my insecurity. I hadn't really noticed the difference. To top it all off, the two had pulled one foot out of the water and inspected each other.

"I've washed a lot of feet," Zahra remarked confidently, "but I've never seen anything like it!"

That was it, the proof of my otherness, the first indication that I was different, and not just in mind. There lay my self-confidence, a tingling in my back testified to my fear and the realisation that I was indeed different from the two of them here; a fear that now overwhelmed me like a wave in the sea and took me with it.

I jumped into the water and escaped into the deeper part of the pool. I submerged myself and let the warm water carry my feelings. This wonderful wet element that I felt so connected to. That had already given me so much comfort on the one hand and on the other had taken away the dearest of all, my mother.

Chapter 4

Master Abdallah received me after supper in his study, a room cluttered with papyrus scrolls, curios from his many travels, and an abundance of dust. He had me stand on a soft, knotted rug in front of his desk, acting as though I were invisible. Leaning over a papyrus scroll, he murmured words I couldn't understand, his finger tracing the narrow script here and there. My bare toes dug into the soft, cool fibres of the silk carpet.

His deliberate disregard made it clear how insignificant I was to him. Bored, I began counting the papyrus scrolls stored on the shelves behind him, reaching three hundred and twenty before he finally looked up, sighed, and leaned back in his chair, arms crossed, his face more lined than usual. I noticed a further cabinet of papyrus scrolls standing by the door.

He studied me for a while, cleared his throat, and placed his hands on the table in front of him.

"Enja," he began carefully, before I could count the other rolls, "although physically present during my teaching in class, your mind is elsewhere. Your only contribution this week was asking what day it is and whether it will be as hot tomorrow as it is today."

His black eyes looked at me disapprovingly.

"You don't respect me!" he stated harshly. He raised his beak nose up a little higher, reminding me again of the falcon that has located his prey.

"I would like to reprimand or punish you for it." He grimaced in annoyance as he searched for words. Fuelled by his own displeasure, he got up and began to cross the room with his arms folded behind his back. "But you seem to have learned more than the other girls in the few weeks that you have been taught. You can answer any question and translate any sentence correctly. How is it that you are so far ahead of the others, even though you don't seem to be listening?"

He had walked completely around the table once and was now standing in front of me, his eyes sparkling like black gold. His brow furrowed; a thought seemed to be forming behind it. Suddenly, his hands grabbed my shoulder painfully.

"Tell me, have you spoken our language before?"

I opened my eyes in disbelief. "No, I have never spoken Farsi before, but I am grateful that I can learn it from you, Master Abdallah." I lowered my eyes. Students shouldn't look directly into their teacher's eyes.

His gaze studied me intensely, as if examining my every word. His lips were pressed together in a line and my knees went weak. He shook me impatiently.

"Look at me, Enja! You have been here with us for four years now, since our generous Mr. Fahrudin Abd al Qadir bought you at the market in Muza."

Like a carpet. The thought shot through my head bitterly.

"You had the honour of educating yourself, even studying the Qur'anan and learning musical instruments for four years. You are a girl with extraordinary abilities. You learned the language of the Persians with ease."

After a pause, he added, "And also my mother tongue ... "

He let go of me, folded his arms behind his back again, and paced back and forth.

"How old can you be now, Enja? Do you know?"

He paused for a moment and looked at me carefully; his gaze rested on my chest. I shook my head in shame. I really didn't know. Confused by his words, I bowed my head and looked at my toes, which were so strangely shaped, and which would always remind me that I was different from others. Did he also suspect it?

"I surmise that you're probably about ten years old, younger than Zahra in any case. In a year's time, you will be ready to be sold to a man. Your prospective master will consider himself fortunate to have such an articulate harem maid, so readily taught. Perhaps you can even be useful as a teacher of your master's daughters. Your price will be very high."

At these words, his voice assumed a conspiratorial tone, as if only he knew what I was worth. "You are something truly unusual . . ."

I smiled. My mother always said that, too. I wasn't sure if the conversation went well or bad for me. A sense of satisfaction filled me, for I was a good student, and he thought I was grown enough to be resold.

But suddenly the admiration in his voice gave way to a cold, professional undertone. He was again the teacher reprimanding his student.

"Unfortunately, you do not yet have the necessary devotion to serve a man. Despite my best efforts, you are completely lacking in humility and modesty. I see your pride in every fibre of your body: in the way you hold your head, in the way you stand in front of me, and in the way you look at me."

I raised my head, and my eyes nervously searched his gaze. His eyes had lost all warmth now. I had to swallow; the conversation had taken a completely new turn.

"Again, you look me in the eye instead of lowering yours. You have to learn to withdraw yourself. You are still a girl, but soon you will be a harem maid, and as such, you have to submit to the will of the man, to submit to him completely. You do what he tells you and you do it without hesitation. Do you think you can do that?"

His black eyes bored into mine. His words struck my pride like lashes.

"Will you be able to serve a man without will?"

My mind was racing, whirling like snowflakes in a storm. A man like Abdallah? I thought to myself. No, hardly. But what about other men? I pressed my lips together. I had obediently fixed my gaze on the floor. I knew that, otherwise, I would give my thoughts away.

"Did you hear me, Enja?" His voice became urgent; he was very close to me now, only half a step away. I could hear his heavy breathing right in front of me.

"I ... I will do everything I can to be a good servant, Master. I am an avid student, and I have learned a lot from you. I'll be honoured."

Even I could tell it didn't sound honest.

As if he had guessed my thoughts, he slipped a finger under my chin and lifted it. Blue eyes stared into black ones. He didn't believe me; I knew that. I didn't believe myself. But he said nothing, and his face remained immobile.

"Your words speak a different language than your eyes. In your eyes, I recognise the pride and temperament of a young horse. They are clear and beautiful, just like you. It was my wish to train you because I felt that you were special. But I have to break your will, Enja. You are too strong. You will soon be old enough to leave here, and then you have to be a different person; otherwise, you are worthless to our master. I'll have to break your pride even if it hurts, because I like you. But in this country your pride is an obstacle. See what follows now as punishment. This will continue until you become a devoted slave. Please forgive me ..."

He let go of my chin and walked out the door, his caftan billowing. One of the eunuchs who guarded the girls' rooms had been standing in front of it the whole time and now entered. He belonged to my Lord Abd al Qadir's as his personal bodyguard. He was massive, his skin almost black and shiny, probably a Nubian like most of the eunuchs here. He could not speak; not only had his testicles been cut off but his tongue as well. He was a mute instrument of his master, who carried out orders without a will. A dull premonition seized me. I glimpsed the frightened faces of Zahra and Jasemin in front of me.

I am special! The thought surged defiantly in me. At some point you will see it, I swear!

The fat eunuch grabbed me with his huge hands and pulled me through the door to one of the many water basins that provided some cooling. It was filled to the brim. I screamed in panic when I realised what he was up to. He pushed me effortlessly against the edge of the basin, arched my arms behind my back with one hand and pushed my head under the water with the other hand. My scream became a useless gurgle. I quickly stopped struggling and cursed myself internally for not taking another deep breath instead of screaming.

I fought valiantly against the devastating reflex to breathe. I felt dizzy, my lungs cramped, and without wanting to, at some point, I sucked water into my windpipe. It was a terrible feeling because the onset of the coughing spasm led to even more water getting into my lungs. My chest seemed ready to burst at any moment. I roared again in despair, but no sound came out; there was no more air in my lungs. My fists clenched the stone edge of the basin in agony, but the iron hand held my head in the water. It flashed through my mind, a few more seconds and it would all be over. Let yourself go, it's over ...

My body no longer had any strength, and I went limp. As if he had seen my end coming, the Nubian suddenly yanked my head out of the basin. Water shot out of my mouth and a violent gagging and coughing seized my whole body. Twitching helplessly and crying, I knelt on the dusty palace floor. The eunuch left me, mute, and without even looking at me.

Chapter 5

Muza in 1293

The day of Zahra's departure was marked by a fierce northeasterly wind, whipping desert sand through the air and forcing those outside to cover their noses and mouths with cloths. The entourage of the wealthy merchant, who had acquired Zahra in exchange for gold coins, camels, and a great deal of silk, stood in the palace courtyard. The fringes of camel harnesses and blankets fluttered up and down, spinning in pirouettes with the waiting group's scarves and shawls like dancing dervishes.

Zahra stood with me at the entrance of the palace, her eyes red from tears. I held her hand, trying to comfort her as best as I could. The veil over her face concealed her inner turmoil. We other girls were also shielded from prying eyes by the silky fabric, allowing us to discreetly follow the ceremony.

Our great and kind Mr. Fahrudin Abd al Qadir insisted on personally handing Zahra over to the merchant. She was wrapped in a beautiful silk dress, which richly embroidered with pearls and trimmed with gold threads. As a sign of her high standing as a harem maid, she wore a lot of gold jewellery on her wrists, in her ears, and even on her nose.

To accommodate the jewellery, we had to poke additional holes where necessary. With her fair skin and silky black hair, Zahra was as beautiful as a Persian princess that day.

We washed, depilated, made up, and dressed her for hours before she faced Fahrudin's critical gaze. Still without a veil, he examined her from all sides, his arms crossed behind his back, and we saw him nodding appreciatively again and again, relieved. He then gave Zahra the pear-bellied barbat, a little lute that she was the only one of us to play in a perfect manner. It was his parting present, and she immediately fell on her knees in front of him and kissed his fingers. That was really very generous and showed his immense appreciation.

I secretly suspected that Zahra was Fahrudin's best-paid girl so far because I had never seen one of his students receive a present. The clothes, jewellery, and all accessories were provided by the buyers, and the richer they were, the finer and more elaborate the additions were. Zahra had deserved everything. She was a beauty with many feminine qualities that men held in high esteem. Her price was extraordinary.

Zahra's new master was a little older, as I saw under my veil. He treated her politely, took her by his hand and led her down the dusty steps of the palace, where we had been allowed to live and study for several years now. Melancholy and a little pride ran through my chest. I would never see her again, but—and I was sure of it—she would be treated well, better than many other slaves could expect. Perhaps one day he would even recognise her as a favourite woman. Her life was now in this man's hands.

Since we were never allowed to go outside the walls of the palace, I seized the opportunity and took a curious look at my surroundings. I moved to the edge of the group that had gathered around the couple. Zahra was lifted onto one of the ugly animals that I had learned were called camels. The veil swirled around her, making it impossible to see the expression on her face. The gemstone glued to the centre of her slave cross sparkled briefly in the sun before the bright veil covered her whole face again. No, she wasn't smiling. None of the girls smiled, and the sadness of parting was oppressive in the air. She turned her head in my direction one last time. A little nod and we both knew: it was a goodbye forever.

The group with about six camels and an equal number of men started moving; this was the opportunity I had long waited for. Under the protection of the palace guards who lined the path out of the inner courtyard, I ran alongside the camels, waving as if I wanted to accompany Zahra to the gate. As the group crossed it, I slipped past the startled guards and ran off down the busy street in the other direction. I heard some shouts go up behind me, but I hoped I'd find a hiding place sooner than the palace guards could organise a search party. That's how I imagined it. Distracted by the many guests, no one paid any attention to a little girl who simply disappeared into the crowd.

This turned out to be a mistake because a couple of mounted guards had indeed noticed me. Before I could find a hiding place in the windy alleys, one of the guards caught up with me and easily pulled me onto the saddle in front of him.

It had been the first attempt to escape since I had encountered the water basin, and I knew I would face the same ordeal as the last time I disobeyed. In fact, Fahrudin's henchmen immediately took me to a basin. I stared dully into it; it was filled to the brim with water. I remembered with horror the excruciating procedure of my last disobedience, only this time I was not afraid.

The Nubian came up to me with soft steps. My gaze fell on his indifferent, mask-like face, whose eyes looked as lifeless as if they were made of glass. With an iron will, I prepared for what was about to happen to me. After the last time, I realised that it was only the beginning of a process designed to break my will. For me, it was the beginning of my fight against a force majeure that forged me into a certain role I definitely did not want to fill. The pain and shame of the torture had brought me to the realisation that I would rather suffer and perhaps die in the process than continue to serve as a slave to Fahrudin Abd al Qadir.

Since I knew that we girls could only be inflicted with pain that did not leave any visible traces on the bodies, lashes or fists were out of the question. With a lot of practice, I had developed a technique that allowed me to hold my breath longer than usual. My father showed it to me once so that I could dive deep into the sea. With short breaths, I pumped more air into the lungs than necessary and then let it out again in a controlled manner. Underwater, this not only had the advantage that I could go deeper than with normal breathing, but also that the pressure on the chest lessened with the outflowing air. Here, in Fahrudin's house, I practised every evening, as I had then with my father, holding my breath so deliberately that I could survive in the water basin for as long as possible without cramps.

This time, too, the Nubian held me under the water until my mock convulsions convinced him that I was about to drown. I had learned firsthand how the human body behaved in such a situation, and now I also knew when to cramp, cough, and relax. Since they always left me alone, nobody noticed that I regularly recovered from the attacks far too quickly. To keep up appearances, I always waited a little longer before venturing back into my room, dripping.

After the first incident, I lay in Jasemin's arms for hours and cried bitterly. When I had calmed down a bit, I sniffed, wiped my puffy eyes and nose with the back of my hand, and told my surprised friend, "I will stop crying from today on. I am not weak, my will is strong, and the gods will help me get out of here."

Startled by my words and my sudden change of heart, Jasemin opened her eyes wide, looked around vigilantly and hissed, "Enja, you are not allowed to name your gods! Have you already forgotten everything? Haven't they hurt you enough?"

Defiantly, I straightened up in the pillows we were both sitting on and clenched my fists. "They won't force their will on me." I sniffed defiantly. "They won't break me."

Jasemin's brown eyes studied me in the torchlight from the small oil lamp. "You're serious, aren't you?"

She turned away from me a little and looked at our legs, which we had stretched out next to each other on the sleeping carpet. As if what she wanted to say was a big secret, she whispered in my ear, "I'm pretty sure by now that you don't belong here. Your gaze is far too direct. Your shoulders and whole posture are too proud to submit."

She paused for a second.

"On the outside, you are a beautiful girl. You have flawlessly white skin. Your hair is as fine and smooth as silk; it shimmers like silver when the sun catches itself in it. And your eyes are blue as the sea where the light illuminates the depths. But your eyebrows and eyelashes are as black as the night and yet as fine as if a master had painted them. Your high cheekbones give your face something noble. I haven't met anyone like you before. Your appearance is as unique as your character."

Jasemin took my hand and pressed it to my heart. Her voice was conspiratorial: "Can you hear it? There the heart of a lioness beats, there the blood of a warrior flows, proud and strong! You don't belong here; you have to flee as soon as an opportunity arises."

Her words echoed in my chest as I kneeled soaking wet and trembling on the hard stone floor in Abdallah's water basin after another torture, trying to control my heartbeat. They had tortured me once more and punished my disobedience. But that was enough. They wouldn't hurt me again; at that moment, I seemed to have overcome my fear.

Back then, Jasemin had said what I was feeling and confirmed to me what I had always suspected. I had quietly hugged my friend, who was brave enough to utter those words that night, then I made a plan. For the first time in my life, I took my fate into my own hands. Jasemin visibly shuddered when she realised what she had just said. She was literally afraid of her own courage.

Shivering, she spoke the words that I will never forget: "I will help you, Enja. Even if it means I will be punished, I will help you escape." Her whisper was very close to my ear.

I leaned my head back a little and whispered to her, "I'll find a way out of here. Nobody will be able to break me ... and one day I will take you with me, and we will be free— free as the wind!"

We held on to one another for a long time that night. Two girls so different and yet ready to risk anything to help each other. I sincerely hoped that I could keep my promise. The gods would surely help me ...

Chapter 6

I once discovered a beautiful butterfly and asked my father why its eyes were on his wings. He laughed a lot, put me on his shoulders, and walked a few steps to the edge of the little mountain in front of our house. The jagged cliffs were still covered with snow at the top, but the plants had already fought their way to the surface, and the flowers shimmered with bees and butterflies. Father pointed to the snow which, as it melted, accosted the valley as a raging brook, and patiently explained that certain animals would adapt to the colour of their surroundings. The polar bear is as white as the snow around it, and the squid in the far seabed assumes its stains as soon as it hides in the sand. Thus, they're not noticed by their prey and could strike when they least expect it. Animals that were potential prey also protected themselves by adopting the colour of their surroundings, or even pretending to be an animal they were not. The butterfly, which was now dancing in front of us again, protected itself by wearing large eyes on its wings, thereby deceiving birds.

In my room, it was completely silent except for Jasemin's even breaths. From outside, at most, came the screeching of a monkey fighting over food with one of his own kind; otherwise, hardly a sound penetrated through the small window, which was covered with a narrow net of flax. A few stars could be seen through the mesh there in the clear night that was already advancing toward morning.

I lay on my pillow that I shared with Jasemin, and my mind raced. Her narrow body turned restlessly from side to side. Perhaps she sensed the inner restlessness that seizes us humans before a special event. She was afraid of my escape—I knew that—but she would do anything to help me.

I was very proud of her and had found a real friend in her. While I put my hand on her arm soothingly and stroked her gently, I tried not to think about tomorrow. After class, Master Abdallah had reverently told all the girls today about an important visitor who was coming from the big city of Baghdad because of us—a Grand Vizier who was looking for harem maids for the son of his sultan.

"The good reputation of the Fahrudin house and the fact that particularly beautiful young women with light hair are for sale here," Abdallah proudly announced, letting his falcon nose rest on me for a few seconds with a meaningful look, "prompted the Grand Vizier, now in his prime, to rush directly to us in the palace. He will have these and other women brought to Baghdad for his master and his young son Chalil's approval."

My heart jumped. Was that my chance?

Master Abdallah's eyes had sparkled with joy in his deep eye sockets. Understandably, this news had excited everyone in Fahrudin's palace, because a man as important as the Grand

Vizier would buy not just one girl, but several. We learned that a whole delegation was already on the way to Muza. Even Fahrudin was in a good mood and was seen rushing through the palace with a billowing caftan. Presumably, he had to quickly create space in his treasury for the expected gold coins.

A large delegation also meant a large number of soldiers, camels, and horses, and where there were many people, it was easy to lose track of things. I saw my chance in the small classroom. My gaze, which crossed with Jasemin's, said a lot because she smiled at me and nodded almost imperceptibly, knowing about this special opportunity.

In the sultan's harem, Abdallah had explained to us, there were chief wives and concubines of exclusively Muslim origin. The sultan's descendants were only allowed to come from the direct bloodline of noble families who met these criteria. The harem servants, on the other hand, were allowed to be slaves of Nordic origin. Jasemin and the other girls would find their calling here and call the most influential house in the Arab world their new home.

It was said that the Sultan Qualawun had up to eight hundred women in his harem. His son Chalil was probably just about to build his own harem. Apparently, he had discovered his preference for light hair, which increased my chances of being chosen. Fahrudin would send five of his most beautiful girls to Baghdad. The lighter the hair, the more generous the Grand Vizier is when it comes to payment.

Master Abdallah unconsciously rubbed his hands at this news. His pride emanated from each of his words, and he also purposefully named the five girls who would travel with the Grand Vizier the next day. He didn't look me in the eye when he pointed to me and Jasemin, but I knew he was giving me a chance here to escape my fate of being sold by Fahrudin to an inglorious man. It was his last favour that he did me, but also the final farewell.

I didn't like Master Abdallah very much, but I was grateful to him for letting me go, so I included him in my evening prayers along with my family and Jasemin.

So, we would embark on a journey, Jasemin and I, which would hopefully give us an opportunity to escape this palace and the oppression of Fahrudin. We would spend a few days on horses or camels, and I hoped this would be the opportunity to find freedom forever.

Jasemin had calmed down a bit with my hand on her arm. She seemed to have fallen into a calm, deep, and dreamless sleep. When my excited heart finally fell into a slower rhythm, I fell asleep too.

It was just as I had imagined: the delegation of Sultan Qualawun al-Mansur Saif ad-Din Qualawun al-Alfi consisted of sixty-three camels, two hundred and twenty horses, and a corresponding number of soldiers, armed to the teeth. Of course, we were in a troubled country.

Master Abdallah told us in class that the Arabs, with the help of the Mamelukes, would drive the Crusaders back from the Holy Land and gradually recapture the cities in Lebanon on the Levant coast. For him, Sultan Qualawun was a great hero because he had captured Tripoli, an important strategic fortress in Lebanon, albeit with high human losses. He never got tired of praising this hero. The death of the many people was reprehensible to my taste, but the Sultan was of divine descent after all. It was said that he was feared for his irritability and that he slew his own people just to take his anger out on someone. But who knew if that was true?

The sultan's success was less important to me. In any case, his entourage was large enough for me to carry out my plans, and my excitement grew steadily as we were prepared for the trip.

At the moment when the long convoy left for Baghdad, one might have thought the desert itself was in motion. Rider for rider, camel for camel lined the entrance to the palace and headed north amid much shouting from market traders, curious bystanders, and Fahrudin's people. The brightly coloured robes of the Grand Vizier's bodyguard, as well as saddlery and harnesses of the horses and camels, were like the splashes of gemstones in a pompous mosaic.

Jasemin and I had been brought to one of the sedan chairs strapped to the backs of the camels with great jubilation. We could sit next to each other and were protected from the sun, wind, and prying eyes that were trained at us from all sides. We were clad in silk, gold, and precious stones and strolled out of the palace as if we were already the sultan's brides.

"Look, the people leave everything behind and watch the caravans!" Jasemin's enthusiasm knew no bounds. Again and again, she pushed aside the small curtain that covered our litter left and right. Her cheeks flushed with excitement. She pointed this way and that and was as happy as a little child. It was a great day.

Our camel was accompanied by a tall eunuch who occasionally gave us a smile. He was one of the sultan's men who were supposed to bring us safely to Baghdad. I had never seen him before. Unlike my previous torturer, he seemed to have a gentler disposition. A shy smile came over my lips as our eyes met.

It was a three-day ride to Baghdad along infinite dunes, oases and rocks—past landscapes that were as dangerous as they were beautiful—and I learned to appreciate the simple needs of camels. Hardly any other animal would survive the long journey with so few breaks and little water. The horses were always slower, needed more rest, and made more laborious progress in the sand with their hooves. In fact, in the heat we lost two horses that were actually intended as gifts for the Sultan. We women were protected from the eyes of the men, but I learned a lot about our trip through our eunuch, whom we were allowed to call Babo.

"Tomorrow morning, we will ride another two hours, then we will see the gates of the big city. The sultan's palace is on the hill overlooking the city. They will see us from afar, but the slow pace of our horses will detain us a while longer on our way through the city streets." His voice was low and filled with a respect that testified to many years of submission.

"Will you accompany us to the palace, Babo?" I was curious if he would stay with us.

"I'll hand you over to the harem servant; he will then accompany you."

With that, he turned and set up our camp. It was going to be the last night together for Jasemin and me, and I could see on her face that she had the same thought. Tomorrow, I would leave her; my plan was set. Over and over again, we had mentally acted out what we had to do.

We held on to each other that night. One last time we whispered to each other that we would meet again, and one last time we prayed together for our two fates.

We had heard that Baghdad was a grand city, but this place surpassed everything I had ever seen. The caravan came to a halt at the crest of one of the larger dunes, allowing us to glimpse the city's walls and formidable fortifications over the shimmering sand. Master Abdallah would always wax lyrical about this fascinating city whenever he spoke of it, and we girls had hung on his every word with awe. Now, seeing it with my own eyes for the first time, my heart leapt with excitement.

Battleground of fierce conflicts, Baghdad was the lifeblood of the eastern Arab empire and, under its ambitious Sultan, a thriving metropolis. Rarely had so many religions coexisted in one city: Jews, Muslims, and Christians, alongside a certain degree of prosperity. This was my first impression of the vibrant city that would become my home—though not quite as the Sultan might have envisioned.

Behind the curtains of our litter, I began to prepare for my escape. I put on simple bloomers, the so-called sirwal, which we could beg from servants of the palace, and the typical waistcoat, which was buttoned at the front. Both were made of the light-coloured cotton fabric from which most of the garments of the common people were made. Not new, but at least clean. I slipped into my pants and vest and freed myself from all the gold and precious stones I was wearing. Jasemin stuffed everything together with my silk dresses under the pillows on my side. A wide belt completed my disguise.

Now came the part that was hardest for me: with a sharp dagger that Jasemin pulled from her hair, which had been freed from the veil, she cut my long hair into short, fringed layers. With a sigh, she tucked the strands under the pillow. Then she held out the pot with the soil that we had gathered together. I smeared it on my face and hair until I looked like one of the street kids who always loitered in front of our palace. We even soiled my otherwise well cared for feet with dirt. My hair was now dull, the delicate skin of my face was covered with reddish soil, and where the tattooed cross had been visible, there was now a lump of dirt. Jasemin nodded approvingly.

"They'll think you're a street boy, no question about it." There was pride in her voice and a little concern for me.

"Will you really take me away from here one day?"

She looked at me with her beautiful brown eyes that were filled with tears. Still, there was hope in her voice.

I gently stroked her loose, curly hair, which, in the diffuse light of the litter, looked much darker than it normally was.

"Of course! I keep my promises," I affirmed, feeling like the big sister Jasemin never had. But the knot in my throat would not loosen. There was a little fear, plus pride and a strange excitement that spread across my back, making my heart pound and my stomach flutter.

The noise in the street announced our imminent arrival. Even the animals moved a little faster as they made their way through the streets of Baghdad up to the palace. I gave

Jasemin a tight hug, with a silent promise, and then carefully pushed the curtain aside. Before us lay the magnificent gates of the palace, which were still closed. All the animals came to a standstill to wait to be led through the right wing one at a time. Only now did the large right gate open. I saw it from a distance. It would be some time before we passed through this eye of the needle. In addition, many people were there to await the arrival of the caravan. Babo stood on Jasemin's side of the camel and held it tight.

My senses were fully focused on my upcoming adventure when I suddenly felt Jasemin's hand on my shoulder. I turned to her and looked into her troubled face. She handed me the dagger she'd used to cut my hair.

"Keep it. It will always remind you of me, and maybe also serve you well one day. I will hardly need it anymore ... "

I looked at the dagger in my hand and only now saw how nicely it was made. It was the typical dagger that women liked to wear hidden in a skirt or belt. It was small and narrow, extremely pointed, and so sharp that it could also be used by a man to shave. This special dagger was in a small silver shaft with beautiful engravings, set with tiny precious stones that shimmered in colour.

"I can't accept that, Jasemin!" I replied, deeply touched, and held out the dagger to her again. "It's worth more than anything I've ever owned in my life."

Jasemin smiled sadly. "It's my mother's legacy. I always kept it well hidden with me, mostly in my hair because it looks like a hairpin. They will take it away from me because I am not allowed to own anything where I am going." Her voice was urgent. "Please take it with you and keep it for me, because you are the only one who knows how to appreciate its true worth."

Moved, I took the tiny dagger and put it in my belt.

"It will always remind me of you, Jasemin. It stands for the bond of our friendship, and if I see you again one day, I will give it back to you," I promised in a firm voice and looked outside again to avoid her sad eyes. I found it hard to concentrate on my escape as a tear ran down my cheek.

It had to be quick now. All eyes were still directed ahead. I forced myself out of the litter on the other side as quickly as possible and now hung with my arms on the wooden frame that held the litter in the middle of the wobbling back of the camel. I carefully measured the distance to the ground with my eyes. We had been assigned a big camel and I didn't really dare to jump, so I climbed down a short distance on the saddle cloth with the knotted coloured ribbons and let myself fall lightly from the cord into the dust of the sandy road. Immediately, I crouched on the ground so as not to attract any attention. I slowly slid sideways towards two barrels that were stored on the side of the path. At the same time, our camel was led a few steps forward by Babo, and I would almost have been kicked by the following camel if the eunuch who was running by had not pushed me out of the way with his foot.

"Get out of the way, boy," he called out. "Otherwise, you will be trampled!"

I didn't need to be told twice. Relieved by my successful camouflage, I sat up and ran as fast as my legs could carry me. With a pounding heart and trembling knees, I ran away from the palace and along the dusty path into the city that welcomed me so promisingly. My father was right: the squid had successfully adapted to its environment. Dirty like all street children in this city, I plunged into the hot and dusty crowd of the busy street.

Excited, I stopped and looked back at the caravan. My chest rose and fell under my heavy breaths. Nobody had noticed my escape. I could hardly believe my luck!

From now on, I was a little boy who had just got his freedom back—a freedom that I would never give up again.

Chapter 7

Scotland in 1304

When the sun shone in Scotland, the heather bushes bloomed, and the air buzzed with bees diligently gathering honey, a serene atmosphere would settle over the land, masking its true state. Those were turbulent times that shook the country. England's invasion of Scotland had faltered; King Edward was severely impacted by the Scottish wars of independence, losing soldiers, horses, and crucial territories to the rebels. Under the leadership of William Wallace, a peasant army rallied to the charismatic knight, boldly supporting his fight for Scotland's freedom. The borderlands between the two countries became frequent scenes of dramatic attacks. It was no wonder that the English troops felt uneasy in this harsh land, rife with opportunities for cruel ambushes. Nevertheless, they had to ensure a steady supply of provisions, horses, weapons, and food. The English forces ruthlessly compelled the beleaguered Scottish peasants to distribute their belongings to the soldiers. The Scottish people's hatred grew with the audacity of their occupiers.

But there was no sign of these troubled times this morning. The quiet of the early day was only broken by the occasional neighing of the horses which, with astonishing dexterity, grazed the finest tufts of grass that the heathland had to offer. Here in this fertile area between Galloway and Dumfries, on the border between the two divided countries, the grass grew lush and thick.

The two girls who looked after the herd lay in the shade of a large oak tree, under its wide branches. While one of them dozed sleepily in the shade, the other girl kept her gaze wandering attentively to the forest edges and then back to the grazing horses. The twelve mares with their foals barely moved away from the two girls, as if there were an invisible bond between them. Two falcons circled above them in search of food for their offspring, accompanied by the numerous songbirds and wild chickens that found plenty to eat in the heather-covered landscape.

The stream that flowed not far from the oak provided enough water for the people and the animals. Fresh and clean, crystal-clear rivulets pearled through the stones and moss-covered boulders, which stood out black against the lush green of the grasslands. Emma, who kept watching the horses and then observed the surroundings carefully, picked up a blade of grass and chewed on it. Movement on the opposite hill caught her attention. She put her hand over her eyes so as not to be blinded by the sun.

She had clearly seen a small group of riders as they trotted down the path that both girls had taken with the herd that morning. She knew immediately what this meant because the English banner was visibly blowing in the wind. Excitedly, she nudged her sleeping companion in the side with her foot to wake her up.

"Lily! Wake up!" Her tone was low but urgent. "Wake up and take the horses away from here! The English are coming. I'll try to detain them to buy you time."

Lily startled, with eyes still heavy from sleep, but recognised the urgency of the situation immediately and quickly went to the lead animal, which was grazing peacefully with its foal not far from her. The young women both wore coarse linen trousers and loose tunics that allowed them to ride like men. It was easy for her to pull herself, as supple as a cat, onto the mare's back. Without a bridle or saddle, just by thigh pressure and shifting her weight, she steered the animal, an older but still pretty mare, past the herd, repeatedly but quietly calling out the names of the horses that followed her immediately.

The movement of the animals had not escaped the notice of the men on the hill, who were moving faster now. Emma swallowed hard when she found her suspicion confirmed: the group was indeed after the horses. She had been warned several times by her foreman that this was a common practice of the local occupiers, and so she was prepared accordingly. In spite of this, her heart was pounding as she took the delicate crossbow in her hand and, trembling, equipped the double barrel with two arrows. Two of the five men separated from the group and cut their way in the direction of the fleeing horses.

"Stop!" shouted Emma in a firm voice and aimed at the first of the two riders who galloped after the fleeing horses.

"Stand still or I'll shoot!" She repeated the order.

Emma dropped to one knee and aimed, with the crossbow on her shoulder, a position she had practised often enough. Both riders recognised the danger and tore at the reins to bring their horses to a standstill. Behind them, she saw Lily disappear into the forest with the herd. Well, Emma thought with relief, now I just have to give her a little head start.

"Who are you, and what do you want here?"

Her voice sounded firmer than she felt. The riders to her right were so close now that she could see their faces. One of them was easily recognisable as a knight in all of his combat equipment, from steel boots to helmet. On his tunic he wore the colours of his knightly family, white and blue stripes punctuated by red falcons. Emma didn't know what his name was, but he was an English knight, and his standard identified him as such.

The other two, who didn't leave his side, were dressed more simply. Their helmets only covered their heads and not their faces. Instead of the metal shirt, they were dressed in leather and with the obligatory breastplate, but on their chests were the telltale colours and the emblem of the English king, yellow on red. They were soldiers of King Edward, also known as the "hammer of the Scots" because of his unyielding attitude towards the Scottish people—their people.

The hand that continued to aim the crossbow at the two riders in front of her trembled slightly. The English knight had stopped to her right and angrily raised the visor of his helmet with one hand. His arrogant look fell on Emma. He obviously thought she was a boy because of the way she was dressed. He sported a red beard and his face registered annoyance that he was required to deal with such a pathetic incident.

"My name is William de Valence, a knight in the service of King Edward of England," he said with as much authority as he could put into his words. "We are assigned to collect horses for the army in order to put them in the service of the crown. These horses are thereby confiscated!"

His voice grew even louder at the end, as if it annoyed him to have to explain the situation to a stupid horse herder. He hadn't really expected any serious resistance, so it bothered him that the boy with the bright voice was still holding on to his crossbow and not even lowering it a little. The knight's eyes were fixed on the two riders who stood between him and the tree line, waiting for his orders and looking somewhat uncertainly at both the knight and the archer.

"The horses belong to my feudal lord, and you must first ask him if you may have them, my lord; under no circumstances can I hand them over to you."

The cheeky reply made de Valence turn his head in surprise to examine the steadfast boy a little more closely. Surely, he could not seriously dare to oppose the Crown?

"You alone against all of us and against the Crown of England? What a stupid brat you are! If you dare to shoot, I'll kill you myself."

He turned a little in the saddle and gestured for the two men to overtake the horses. They immediately released the reins and stormed off. They ignored the call of the crossbowman behind them. It was only when one of the two fell off the saddle with an arrow in his neck that de Valence realised that the boy was serious and that he was a damn accurate marksman. Before he could warn the second rider, the second arrow hit him in the back, and he fell from his horse with a groan. Before the doomed man touched the ground, de Valence spurred his horse and shot forward on his heavy battle-ready steed, towards the archer. With a frightening roar, he pulled a morning star from the loop of his saddle and brandished the dreadful weapon with a force that bore witness to years of practice and merciless effort.

Emma lowered the crossbow. With the death of the two soldiers, she had given Lily a few valuable seconds to break away with the herd.

From the right, the knight now came rushing towards her with his terrible battle cry. She had dreaded this moment because it took too long to load the weapon with the two arrows. Although she reached for the quiver with one hand in a practised movement while drawing the bow and laying the arrow with the other, it was no longer possible for her to fire it. The knight had quickly shortened the distance to her.

She had already turned to face him, still on one knee, so as not to lose her balance. Her fingers were jittery and nervous, her stomach fluttered with excitement, and she couldn't load the weapon in time. She saw the mighty knight racing towards her. His roar mingled with the thundering of the hooves and the puffing of the huge battle horse. Emma knew she was doomed and her efforts were in vain; she froze.

The metal spikes of the morning star struck her chest with a terrible thud. The force of the impact made her slim body spin through the air like a ball until she landed on her back. She stared up at the knight vaguely and as though through a thick fog. With a repulsive cold-bloodedness towards his enemies, he had stopped with his horse beside her, calmly inspecting her injuries.

In her shock, she felt no pain but could hardly breathe and felt a lot of blood running out of her body, and with it, the hope of survival. Emma did not dare to look down; instead, she looked fearfully into the immobile face of her adversary, who was now enthroned on his horse above her, eyeing her with a cold look.

William de Valence spat once and reattached the morning star to his saddle. His two companions had come to a stop beside him. Their questioning looks turned from the gaping wound in the girl's chest to de Valence. Indignant, he gave the order to catch the dead soldiers' two horses.

He was about to turn away when a long black arrow with unbelievable force first killed one rider of his retinue, and seconds later another arrow killed the second. Both men sank lifeless from their horses.

William de Valence turned with his steed, ready to fight the unknown archer. His anger over the futile attempt to capture what was believed to be safe prey surged fiercely. He would show this peasant pack what it meant to stand against a Valence and thus against the will of the king! But what he saw then made him hesitate. Something was very wrong here. The sight that made him pause gave him goosebumps. He had never been afraid of anything in his life, but now he felt as if he were looking straight into the abyss of hell. Even his horse snorted and shied, as if it felt the same way.

In front of him, directly on the hill that he had previously descended with his soldiers, loomed a rider dressed entirely in black on an equally imposing black stallion. The stranger slowly lowered his arms with the arrow and longbow, as if to give him an opportunity to react. The third arrow was probably meant for him, but no arrow pierced armour. The face that studied him was carved from wood. Not a muscle moved in it. Cold blue eyes eyed him with devastation. The rider's skin was pale like that of a dead man, and framed by white hair that was strictly tied back. A few loose strands fluttered against the horse's mane in the light breeze. And when Valence squinted in order to see more clearly, he saw a black cross at the bridge of the nose.

All the tales about the black rider came rushing back to him, sending a chill through his veins. He felt as though Death himself had arrived to claim him. Instinctively, he crossed himself. His horse, equally unnerved by the apparition, began to rear back, and before he knew it, it broke into a gallop as though the devil were chasing them. He made no attempt to rein in the horse.

Instinct is one of the best weapons a trained warrior can use. It helps to assess difficult situations correctly or not to get into one in the first place. Or else it dictates an action. And it was pure instinct that set me in motion when I saw Lily chasing the horses out of the forest. She would never expose the foals and pregnant mares to such a pace were they not in danger. And there was no trace of Emma, a young but very skilled archer who was supposed to protect the herd with Lily.

I pressed my heels against Taycan's flanks and gave his nervousness a target. He too seemed to feel something and danced excitedly. We raced in the direction from which the herd had come and got as far as the hill. Emma lay on the ground. Her chest was badly injured, or she may even have been dead. Two soldiers were in the process of catching the horses of their dead colleagues, who were lying a little farther away with arrows in their necks. In a split second, I made a decision and pulled my longbow out of the saddle. I hit the first rider in the neck with the first arrow, and immediately afterwards the second also fell dead from his horse. I wanted to take some time for the knight, because he obviously had Emma on his conscience. Only a morning star tore such a terrible wound as the one in Emma's chest. And this well-dressed nobleman on his warhorse had such a weapon tied in a loop on his saddle. I lowered my longbow and waited to see how he would react. I had to get my anger, which seized me at the sight of the injured girl, under control again. You couldn't tell what was going on inside me, but I had just passed his death sentence. The only question was how to do it.

The knight in the valley eyed me from the back of his horse, which was prancing restlessly, and crossed himself. Good thing, so he took me seriously. Then something unexpected happened: the knight took up his reins and his horse reluctantly threw his head up. But he didn't come up to me; he turned away and let the nervous horse run free. In a thin cloud of dust that only slowly settled down on the narrow dirt road, he disappeared as if the devil were after him. So, he didn't even want to face a fight, the damn coward!

I clenched my fist furiously and shouted something like that after him, but he couldn't hear me anymore. On the one hand, I would have liked to chase after him; on the other hand, my Emma was down there in agony. I decided to take care of her first and postponed his death until a later date. He wouldn't get far with me on his heels, even if he should ride straight to hell.

My stallion stopped next to the girl after a short sprint down the hill. I jumped off before the horse had stopped and knelt down beside Emma, shaken. She was lying on her back, her eyes wide open. Her breath came out of her as a rattling, gurgling sound. It took no medical training to know that the gaping wound in her chest meant her death. The fear showed in her large hazel eyes, and my heart contracted in pain. My brave Emma paid for the fight for my horses with death.

Deeply moved, I took her hand, which was freezing cold from the blood loss and shock, and gently straightened her upper body to make it easier to breathe. Her lips trembled; my arm, which was supporting her upper body, was instantly soaked with her blood. With my free hand, I held her head as tenderly as a child's and plucked the sticky blonde strands of hair from her face. She had cut it off because long hair always got tangled in her crossbow. Now it was dull and wet with sweat.

She would die in the next few minutes. Again and again, a tremor seized her that made her slim body shudder. There was nothing more I could do for her, only ease her death. And so, I held her tight and spoke to her, calmly and gently.

"I will avenge your death, Emma. None of my warriors die in vain. Not even you. I will find this knight and make him atone a thousand times over."

Despite my low tone, my voice was firm and determined. It gave no indication of my anger and conflict—a useful trait

I'd acquired over the years. Emma's eyes, which fixed on me gratefully, lost some of their fearful expression and ultimately prevented me from jumping up and riding off immediately. Those last few minutes were all I could give this brave girl, and I gave them to her from the bottom of my heart. How often have I now accompanied loyal comrades into death, held their hand, and tried to take their fear away. And yet it always affected me deeply. As always, my soul took on the guilt of her death and let the dark flow of my conscience swell deep inside me.

A gurgling cough shook Emma's slim body. Her eyes grew dull, the lids trembled. Once again, she tried to get up with the last of her strength and formed a few words with her lips: "... death ... warrior?"

I understood immediately, squeezed the limp hand and confirmed her last question: "Yes, you will receive the burial of a warrior, with all honours. You were a brave girl and gave your life for all of us. Let go now, my little Emma; go to your God and go in peace."

Emma closed her eyes and suddenly looked almost content. As she took her last breath, her face relaxed before the life escaped from her body.

I took a deep breath and looked up from Emma's dead body into the faces of the warriors standing around us, where grief and pain were combined. They had hurried over from Caerlaverock Castle, our home, and were now standing side by side with me next to the slain girl. I had no words. So loud was the pain in my head over the loss that I couldn't comfort myself or the others. My back tingled. The rage that I knew so well came back to me and drove away the grief. Good thing. I needed it to tear myself away from the corpse and take up the pursuit.

Someone gave me a rag to wipe my hands. I placed Emma's head gently on the ground and got up. I stared dully into the sad eyes of the bystanders, who either bowed their heads or looked at me expectantly. The fighting spirit glittered in their eyes and an anger that mirrored my own. I turned to my horse, who whinnied at the scent of blood, and reluctantly lifted its head.

Resolutely, I climbed into the saddle, nodded briefly to those present, and gave final instructions to bring the body back to the castle and prepare everything for the funeral. Taycan, who snorted in irritation, seemed to sense my determination and threw himself forward to start running. Indeed, his power had a calming effect on my mind, and I let his will flow. I was sure we would be back in time for the funeral service—with a lock of hair from Emma's murderer as a grave object. The wind blowing on my face dried her blood on my skin and clothes, as well as the tears on my face.

The tracks left by the knight and his powerful horse were as easy to read as the letters on Master Abdallah's papyrus scrolls. He had about an hour's head start, and I allowed my stallion to take the lead. I was puzzled that the knight had not sought a return route to England but had ridden deeper into Scottish—thus enemy—territory. Even on the run, a wide arc back would have been possible, but he had stayed the course almost stubbornly north.

Soon the well-developed roads, which were used by the English troops for the heavy iron-shod wagons, became overgrown, denser and narrower, and seemed more like beaten paths. His tracks were still clearly legible, the iron horseshoes dug deep into the soft ground. He had apparently slowed down his pace so as not to harm his horse. I did the same with Taycan, who had sweat dripping from his throat. He was tough and strong, but I had all the time in the world. In addition, the path became more and more rocky and the risk of stumbling increased.

I realised why he had ridden deeper and deeper into enemy territory when the tracks suddenly changed in a clearing. In addition to that of the battle horse, there were now more hoof prints. Almost all of them were the typical size of the shod English horses, not the smaller bare hooves of the Scots horses, so he had met his own people and had known that they would be waiting for him here.

Taycan moved forward briskly, seeming to sense the enemy nearby, and I had to hold him back so as not to rush straight into the troops. Based on the tracks, I estimated the number of riders to be about ten. That changed my plans a little because I had to catch his helpers in a suitable place to get to him.

It wasn't long before I found their abandoned resting place by a small river. I had never been to this part of the lower highlands. I guessed that we were way past Dumfries, which was part of Clan Douglas land. I had been travelling at a brisk pace for four hours, now completely off the beaten track, as if the English were looking for a hidden destination.

Even so, they made no effort to cover their tracks. The knight was probably very sure that he would not be pursued or attacked. Everything was still rumpled where they had rested; the grass hadn't straightened up yet, so they were pretty close.

I turned Taycan slightly to the east and rode a parallel path to that of my enemy. Sometimes, when the wind was favourable, I came so close to them, I could even hear them laughing out loud. The wind came from the west and was already warm because of the mild climate of the sea, so they could neither hear me nor could the horses smell Taycan's scent.

At a fast pace, I overtook the group at a reasonable distance. The valley that we had now left behind had no junctions or crossroads. At some point, therefore, they would pass along the narrow path that led alongside a stream at the end of the valley. Taycan fell into a slow trot, and I surveyed the surroundings for how they could be useful, given my numerical inferiority. To the left and right of the path, the rocky walls of the mountain formation into which the brook had been eating for centuries, rose up steeply. At one stretch, the already narrow path narrowed further because a boulder had fallen from the sheer mountain wall. In addition, the rocky path had a slight incline where the horses would find little traction. The riders would have to walk around the boulder itself, in single file.

I positioned myself behind the rock and drew my sword from my back holster in one smooth motion. I was safe here because the bend in the path and the rock protected me from being discovered too early. The ivory handle now rested familiarly in my hand. The rare weapon was as sharp as no other sword. I looked lovingly at the reflection on the slightly curved blade, the perfectly forged metal, and the beautiful engraving on the handle. They were Chinese characters; the name of the master who had once owned this sword, Kang Shi Fu. It had taken me some time to find out that it was his name that was engraved there. I sent a little prayer to Shi Fu, my Grandmaster and teacher, who made me the warrior I was today. The old Chinese warrior had been like the father I had missed so much all my life. He held a special place in my heart, right next to that of my family.

The beautiful summer day would end in a bloodbath, as it should have. The sun set slowly on the horizon, as if it wanted to cleverly evade the coming events. The light of dusk turned the sky orange and made leaves and trees shimmer golden.

I traced the line of the blade with my fingertips, careful not to hurt myself. The hardness of the metal made me feel safe. Despite the coolness of the early evening, I felt warmth creep from my back into my stomach, and my senses began to focus.

I could clearly feel the vibration of the ground as the riders came down the path I had passed earlier; they were a stone's throw away. My stomach was very warm, my breathing was calm and even, my body adjusted to combat mode. I closed my eyes. I didn't have to see them, I felt them. My senses told me clearly what I needed to know: they rode in pairs, with the knight I was looking for in their midst. Ten soldiers accompanied him. I heard the clatter of horseshoes, the clink of metal weapons and harnesses, the groaning of the leather saddles, the snorting of the horses, the laughing of the men.

Now they stopped for a moment, the boulder forcing them to split up. A loud command rang out and the soldiers began to move. The first trotted around the boulder and into my field of vision. I opened my eyes.

William de Valence had recovered. After an egregious and unprecedented fear made him turn back, he galloped his horse north. It took a long time before he could think clearly again and the eerie figure on the black horse faded from his mind's eye. He scolded himself for avoiding a fight for fear. But there was something so different about this figure, something that, deep down, had made him fearful.

His nickname was William the Brave, but at that moment he had forgotten that. He told the escort that he had met on the way to the Highlands that a large group of savage Scots had ambushed him and his people. Only he managed to escape. In a few days, they should reach the castle in Stirling, which was in English hands. Perhaps they would meet one of the numerous marauding gangs of this traitor William Wallace who were up to mischief here. He would be glad to put an end to this scoundrel, this traitor to the English crown.

His party came to an abrupt stop in front of a huge boulder. His foreman instructed the soldiers to go around the stone one at a time, as only one horse could fit through the narrow gap. Impatiently, he held his horse in check to let the soldiers pass. The first four had just slipped through when a scream rang out on the other side that went through his bone to the marrow. It wasn't the battle cry of a wild Scotsman, it was the roar of a man in fear of death. Damn it, of course! It was the perfect spot for a trap!

"Everybody back! Come back at once!" shouted Valence with all his might. He pushed his horse forward past his soldiers and pulled the sword out of the hip holster. The cries of battle reached him vaguely from the other side. The last soldier who had passed the rock now came back with his horse. He screamed in pain, his arm completely severed just below the breastplate. Valence jerked his horse back, startled. The injured man and his panicked horse pushed into the assembled soldiers in front of the rock. Valence was foaming.

"Nobody goes to the other side! Take care of Kerrington and stay together!"

Most soldiers first had to calm their animals down before they could help their comrades. One dismounted and helped the injured man off his disturbed animal, whose eyes rolled until they shimmered white.

"How many are there?" shouted de Valence as he nervously pranced his horse in front of his people and the narrow entrance to the path. The injured man couldn't utter a word, just a wild stammer that was drowned out in the stamping and neighing of the other horses.

"Talk!" he yelled at him gruffly, but Kerrington's eyes rolled back into his head as he passed out. William de Valence tried to organise his thoughts. Three soldiers did not return and a fourth was seriously injured. How many enemies were there behind the boulder? Why didn't he hear anything from the other soldiers? Were they dead?

With clenched teeth, he gave the order, "We'll ride back and take another route before we lose any more people!"

He pulled his horse around and galloped away in the direction they had come from.

"What do we do with Kerrington?" asked the soldier holding the unconscious, injured man in his arms.

"Leave him here. He'll only slow us down."

Worried faces showed how harsh this order was, yet the soldier let the one-armed man slide to the ground. He was about to get back on his horse when a black rider shot out from behind the rock with a sword and cut off the head of the first soldier in line. The second soldier, whose horse's hind legs slipped off the sloping path in shock, fell over backwards and the heavy horse's body fell on top of him. A stab in the neck of the stumbling animal made it hard for the trapped rider.

The third soldier died by the murderous weapon before he could scream. The fourth even crossed a blade with the black rider before he too was robbed of his head with a round blow. Now there were Valence and two soldiers left. The knight roared like a wounded stag when he realised in frustration who his adversary was. One who decimated his troops as if they were just lambs at the slaughter. The pale face of the black rider was frozen in a determined mask, and the thirst for revenge flashed in the blue eyes.

No, this time he would fight back! If death wanted to get him, he would face him. William de Valence hadn't lost a fight, and he wasn't going to lose it to death.

I had him trapped. Fighting the few remaining soldiers hadn't been a great effort. They were poorly trained swordsmen and worse riders. I was not surprised that the Scots taught the English to fear.

The remaining two soldiers, one on the ground and one on horseback, defended themselves with little skill but loud roars. The one on the ground didn't even get to draw his sword, and the soldier on the horse was simply thrown from the saddle by Taycan when my mighty stallion rode his mare. He was an easy target for my sword.

The knight I was targeting was more difficult to fight. He was protected by his armour, his sword was longer and heavier than mine, and he fended off my blows with an ugly crack of metal on metal. Again and again, the blades clashed against each other. I had to admit to myself that he was an experienced fighter who was familiar with all the tricks.

However, the weight of his heavy armour hindered his mobility and quickly tired him. The heavy metal made every movement a test of strength. He groaned and snorted. The mighty blows grew more impatient and angrier. My agility and, above all, my speed, made it difficult for him and visibly frustrated him. My right foot tapped the front shoulder of my stallion. It was his sign to harass the heavy gelding of the knight, and in fact, in the end, he stumbled him. The horse sank in on its forelegs and let the heavily armoured figure tumble forward over its neck and on to his back. I looked around hastily, recognised this one fighter as the only danger, and therefore stepped down calmly from Taycan so as not to expose him to the danger of the angry knight's desperate slashing.

In a rage, the knight pushed himself up from the ground, tore the helmet with the red plume off his head and yelled at me, "Who the hell are you? How dare you attack the royal escort and with her, a knight of the crown! My name is William de Valence, and I will teach you what it means to mess with me!"

He threw his helmet on the ground, and it clattered over the rock. His voice almost cracked. He stood in front of me, snorting and puffing, his fists clenched. His short red hair stuck out sweaty from his head. His face was flushed and hot from the exertion, and his eyes glared at me with murderous lust. His teeth were bared like a wolf snarling menacingly. He was definitely dangerous and aggressive to the core; it would have been a mistake to underestimate him.

I didn't answer him; I just pointed to the sword in front of him on the ground that he had lost in the fall. He stalked awkwardly on his iron-clad legs, took it up with an angry snort, and attacked me in almost the same motion. I parried each of his blows with powerful counterblows, and the exhausting movements soon made him pause, panting heavily.

The sweat rolled off his forehead, his red beard glittered, his open mouth twisted into an incredulous, mocking grin. He shook his head in frustration. I looked him straight in the eye; they were brown like young chestnuts. But suddenly a shadow fell over his pupils, a bluish tinge. I was spellbound. What was that? Had blue flames reflected in his gaze? But I saw no fire anywhere.

"Who are you? What kind of weapon is that?" he croaked now in turn, his chest heaving up and down heavily under the breastplate. He sounded puzzled.

"My name is Enja, and I will kill you with this weapon as you killed my Emma. Nobody harms my girls. And your king means nothing to me."

Resolutely, I tightened my grip on my sword, trying to translate my words into deeds, but his brown eyes flashed at me. My next hand movement was supposed to separate the head from the torso, a clean cut with little effort. But the strange blue flicker in his eyes seemed to slow me down, and I felt a terrible pain in my stomach. Instead of fighting back, I was still looking into those goddamn eyes. His gaze caught me like an evil spell. Now he was staring at me triumphantly, the blue sheen gone. His mouth twisted into a sneering grin. I saw the movement of his lips, and his voice came to my ear, muffled as if through a thick cloth.

"But today, you cursed woman, death will take you." And he pulled his sword out of my body with one jerk.

Overwhelmed by the pain, I gasped and dropped to my knees. I pressed one hand against my stomach. Hot liquid ran over my fingers. The pain was terrible, but even more terrible was the anger that gripped me. Hot rage over his grin, his triumph, and my own inability to finally hunt down this knight and avenge Emma.

How could that have happened? There had been no one faster with the sword than me! Nobody had hurt me so badly before. What was wrong with me?

I closed my eyes in irritation and saw Emma lying in front of me. Her lifeless young body. The pain paralysed my body and mind. The ivory grip on my weapon became heavy and slipped out of my right hand. Still on my knees, I narrowed my eyes and looked at the knight as he raised his arm with the weapon to strike again. My defencelessness shook me to the core. Without lifting a finger, I awaited the fatal blow.

But apparently my opponent changed his mind, turned around, shaking his head, and stumbled back to his horse. He seemed certain that I was going to die and didn't even bother to finish his work.

Forgive me, Emma. I couldn't avenge you.

Chapter 8

Scotland in the year 1304

I'm really sorry, James!"

The guilt in Hugh Douglas's voice was all too evident. He allowed his black horse to trot alongside his older brother James's brother's chestnut bay one more time, trying to ignore James's icy glare.

"I had fallen asleep. My God, I was awake all night, and after those endless hours, I just got tired! I should have…"

"Enough," his brother growled. "I'm not discussing it any further. It was a long and unfortunate night. Let's leave it at that." Impatiently, he dug his heels into his horse's sides, and it broke into a gallop.

James had to rein in his anger to prevent his younger brother from feeling the full force of his wrath. At just sixteen summers, Hugh was old enough to join the attacks on the English, but still lacked the experience of the men around him.

They had lain in wait for most of the night until, at last, the English troops rode towards the clearing in the forest where they had been waiting in the trees. The spot was perfect for an ambush. If the English had only half crossed the clearing, they would have offered the troops an excellent attack surface from the front and behind at the same time. But that idiot of a brother had to fall from the tree just when the enemies had not yet reached the clearing. Hugh fell asleep and tumbled off the tree like a little child out of his crib.

James couldn't believe it. He ground his teeth. His brother and companions struggled to follow him. The wind tore at his hair, which hung wildly in his face.

"How do I explain that to Father?" he muttered to himself, shaking his head. His brother should have just stood in front of him and confessed. He already knew how Father would react. William Douglas's rage was legendary, and his tantrums often ended with teeth knocked out and broken noses. Most ran away when the dark clouds of resentment crept over his face. Perhaps he could somehow cushion the inevitable blow by telling him about the two they had killed, but too many of the English had escaped. No, it wasn't a success. And on top of that, he had to save his little brother from death. God forbid, Hugh had fallen at their feet like a sacrificial lamb ...

His little brother had always been a handsome boy, loved and pampered by everyone. He would never forget the sight of him, with the dishevelled dark hair and the perplexed expression on his face as he sat on his behind, seeking orientation—the English not a hundred yards away. James rolled his eyes once more as he thought of the scene that, to his horror, had played out right before his eyes.

James reacted immediately. He also jumped from the tree, and with him, his surprised followers. At the same time, he let out a battle cry that made even the birds fall silent with fright, and he and his men threw themselves at the English.

Unfortunately, they only caught two of the soldiers. Everyone else escaped in time.

"He still has a lot to learn, and his mistakes are the quickest way to learn," he heard a voice behind him say. Unimpressed by his anger, Lachlan McKay, his foreman and best friend, approached from behind. His mare, quite a bit shorter than James's tall gelding, struggled to keep up. Frustrated, James reined in a little to let him catch up.

"Tell that to our father," he replied angrily. "I hope he's already had breakfast when we get back; otherwise, Hugh will be his first appetiser this morning."

He looked grimly at Lachlan. His eyes were directed forward to the path. Suddenly, he looked tense and reined in his horse. James instinctively did the same. Lachlan gestured silently to a point ahead where the path was narrowed by a fallen boulder. Dark figures lay spread out on the ground in front of it, horses and people.

"English soldiers?" James asked, saying what Lachlan was thinking.

"If I see the colours correctly, yes. But who besides us was supposed to kill the English, and here, on our land?" he remarked.

"Did someone get ahead of us?" Hugh's bright voice came from behind. He had come to a stop behind them with the rest of his people.

"Who makes such a mess and doesn't clean up afterwards?"

His brother's wild grin reminded James of his own carefree days before he, as a contender for his paternal inheritance, had been drawn to duties that matured him more quickly than he would have liked. He nodded over his shoulder to Hugh.

"We'll find out!"

An uneasy feeling crept over him. These soldiers had strayed too far from the main line to be accidentally ambushed. Someone had checked out the group. And who should do that if not a Douglas?

Slowly and with his eyes always on their surroundings, James's group started moving. They left the horses and approached cautiously. None of the English soldiers survived. One leaned a little to one side with his back against a tree in the shade. Lachlan went around the rock with a couple of men and took a closer look around.

The dead were all soldiers of the king. Apparently, they had all been killed with clean, well-aimed sword blows. Too clean for simple robbers. It was clear to James that this group was a delegation that Edward had sent to Scotland to supply the individual garrisons with horses and provisions from the surrounding villages. He didn't like it at all that they were travelling on his land.

"What happened here?" he asked, more to himself.

But Hugh heard him. "They came from the south," he speculated, pointing to the boulder. "The rock is an ideal place to attack a large group. There must have been several who attacked, but none of them appear to have been wounded. The limbs were completely severed. They were probably killed by well-trained men, and the weapons must have been very sharp."

"Well recognised, Hugh." James marvelled at the boy's powers of observation. His anger was gone for now.

"But why didn't they cover their tracks, collect the weapons, or at least take the horses with them?" he mused, pointing to the English horses that were grazing peacefully nearby.

Hugh rubbed his chin, which showed the first fluff of beard he was so proud of. "Maybe they were disturbed?"

The seriousness on his face showed James that one day he would become a considerate man, once he had overcome his youthful hastiness.

"There are three soldiers on the other side, all just as dead as the ones on this side, "McKay shouted as he turned around the boulder again. "No one to be seen anywhere anymore."

"Ten dead," said the older Douglas and turned to the corpse at the tree, which was only visible as an outline in the shade. "Who could have done that? A neighbouring clan?"

His gaze fell on the face of the motionless person. If he had taken her for a younger soldier at first, he now recognised his mistake. His chin dropped.

"Damn what ...!" and he started walking.

"That's a woman," he uttered when he was standing in front of her seconds later. Lachlan, who came to a stop next to him, uttered one of his curses, which slipped loosely from his lips and made many blush in shame. James poked his elbow in his ribs and hissed, "Shut up, you idiot! Maybe she's still alive!"

"It doesn't look like it," Lachlan said carefully and looked at the woman. "Pale as a corpse. Besides, she's wounded; look, the hand on her stomach is bloody."

He pointed to the middle of her body. In fact, the hand seemed to cover a wound, and the clothes were soaked in blood. Meanwhile, Hugh had joined them, too. He leaned down carefully and cautiously touched the woman's shoulder. "Hey, beauty, are you still alive?"

He grinned boyishly again. James snorted.

"She's unlikely to say no, you idiot." He didn't like it all. He was uncomfortable and couldn't figure out what had happened here. The woman looked strange: white hair tied back, elegant features, black eyebrows and eyelashes. The lips were pale but full and sensual. Her clothes were particularly unusual. Black trousers with a tunic, and over them, a leather vest. She wasn't dressed like a Highland woman, but neither was she dressed like an English woman.

Just as his gaze stopped on her nose, over the base of which a cross had been painted, she opened her eyes. James got a strange pang that made his scalp tingle. Her eyes were blue, as brilliant a blue as the flowers in his mother's garden. They were surrounded by black eyelashes, like the frame of a picture. She fixed him with large pupils, as if she had been in the dark for a long time and blinked to get used to the light.

James cleared his throat and considered saying something useful. He didn't mean to scare her. Who knew what she had been through.

"My name is James Douglas, son of Lord William Douglas," he introduced himself formally, "and you are on our land.". Inwardly, he rolled his eyes at himself.

The woman closed her eyes again. There was nothing to suggest that she understood him. Hugh nudged her again. "Hey, talk to us, or don't you understand us?"

Slowly, very slowly, her upper body leaned to one side and threatened to tip over if Hugh had not held her. Her head fell forward on her chest.

James looked at Hugh and almost laughed at the awkward way he tried to support the woman but didn't know how or where to touch her. He had no idea how badly she was hurt. That she was still alive was indeed a good sign. He intuitively made up his mind.

"Lachlan, have the bodies buried and collect the weapons and horses. We'll take the woman to Douglas Castle, where the healer can take care of her injuries. As long as we don't know who she is, we can't leave her here."

"What if it's an English woman?" interjected Lachlan.

"Then my father will be happy about a hostage," James replied grimly.

Shaking his head, Lachlan set about gathering the men. He didn't look enthusiastic, but James didn't care. He took the woman in his arms, careful not to touch the wound.

Hugh eyed his older brother suspiciously. He didn't like the suggestion to take the unconscious woman home, but he had no better solution. He followed his brother on his horse to help him mount his load. Perhaps the appearance of this mysterious woman would save his father from his obligatory fit of anger. It wasn't far to Douglas Castle. He hoped that she would survive the ride until then ...

Lord William Douglas stared at the large, calloused hands that had frightened many an enemy. He would have loved to put them around the neck of his second son, Hugh, who was sitting across from him with his head drooping. Only the presence of his young wife, Eleonore, and her hand on his thigh prevented him from teaching the rascal a lesson once and for all.

Around him, the clan members had gathered for dinner in the great hall, which could hold almost three hundred people, and which even served as the warriors' sleeping quarters in winter. The noise level was kept within limits because everyone wanted to hear something of the expected punishment of the young Hugh. Only the kitchen staff and the maids, unimpressed by the tension in the air, scurried eagerly through the room to serve the food and cider.

While the simple clan people sat on the roughly hewn benches at the wooden tables, the Douglas family and their closest confidants had taken their seats on the raised platform where everyone could see them. So, the view of Hugh, who sat across from his father and stubbornly stared at his hands, and especially his red ears, escaped no one.

Damn it, if James hadn't reacted so quickly ...

William Douglas felt a sudden surge of worry and anger. His fist closed on the clay jug in front of him and he imagined it was Hugh's throat. With a crunch the vessel gave way and let the rest of the sour drink splash in all directions. The servants tripped over each other's feet to clean up the liquid and the broken pieces.

He was feeling a little better now, but his anger just wouldn't fizzle out. He felt his wife's warm hand rest on his thigh like an anchor. His sinister gaze slid back to his son, who had only briefly looked up, and had to swallow when the clay jar burst. Now he dutifully looked again at his hands, which he had folded in his lap. His father actually managed to moderate his tone and struggled to maintain his composure. Even so, his voice sounded menacing as he said, "Get out of here, Hugh, before I forget you're my son. You will sleep in the stable for the next few months, muck the horses, and think about whether you really want to become a warrior or end up as a priest like your cousin."

Hugh turned pale so his father thought he was unfit to fight for him. It was harder than any corporal punishment because it hurt his pride. He had expected everything—screaming, beating—but not this accusation. It hurt. He swallowed his shame hard, got up slowly, and looked into his father's eyes.

"Please forgive me, Father. I made a big mistake. I put myself and our people in danger. But I will not go to the monastery. My place is here. I want to fight for you, for our family and our people. But I accept your punishment."

His voice trembled a little and he had to swallow again and again, but he held up well. Resolutely, he turned around and marched out of the great hall into the rain that drove people into the houses that day. He barely felt the cold drops lashing his face as the relief of having gotten away from his Father's fury drove him voluntarily into the stable to take up his work.

His brother James, who was sitting next to his father, breathed a sigh of relief. The old warrior had apparently calmed down a bit as he got older, or was it the positive influence of his gentle wife, Eleonore, who now looked at William with a smile?

Eleonore was his father's second wife. His father had married her after the death of James's mother, and it seemed that she could soothe his quick temper. James was William's eldest son, and his mother, Elisabeth, died giving birth to Hugh when James was just three years old. He took his own goblet and drank the diluted cider, which came from the apple trees his mother had planted herself.

That morning, with the injured stranger in his arms, he had arrived at the gate of the castle his family had lived in for generations and had placed her in the care of Lady Douglas who, along with the healer, had immediately looked after her. The strangely dressed woman hadn't woken up since the brief look they'd exchanged under the tree. He sincerely hoped she would survive. Her eyes had fascinated him too much. It had only been a brief moment, but he felt as if he had looked into her soul. It was enough to overwhelm his thoughts.

Who was this woman? Where did she come from? James had counted ten horses, dead and alive. But counting her, there were eleven people who were found. Had she come with the soldiers or met them? How he would have loved to hear her voice, even once. Her clothing was unusual for a woman because it was little different from that of a male warrior. But it was made of good material; her boots, too, were of the finest craftsmanship. The weapons in her leather vest were unusual and also made of the best ore.

"Are you thinking about that woman you brought with you, son?"

Torn from his thoughts, he turned his head in shame to his father, who was staring at him with shrewd eyes, and nodded.

"You don't seem to mind that I brought her to your castle," he replied, evading his question.

His father leaned back in the chair a little and crossed his arms over his broad chest, smiling coldly.

"I see it the way you do, James. As long as I don't know who she is, I treat her like a guest. She may even be of use to us. She must be one of the escorts you saw there, so she holds a high position, and rich families pay good money for their relatives if someone wants her back."

Everything was always so easy for his father. What if she were a prisoner of the English? Again, James saw her before him in his mind—those eyes ...

"Maybe she's neither Scottish nor English. She was wearing unusual clothes. Is it possible that she comes from France?" interjected Eleonore.

James and William looked at her with irritation. James didn't know how she could judge, but the possibility wasn't a bad guess. Eleonore looked at him expectantly from across the table.

"A French woman who makes common cause with the English?" His father frowned, and he too began to ponder.

"Since Edward's daughter-in-law Isabelle is French, this should be obvious," said Eleonore.

"Mmmh ..." mused Lord William from the other side of the table. "Since Edward is looking for an alliance with the French against the Scots, I wouldn't be surprised." With that, he secretly agreed with his wife, which surprised James.

"Damn the English! Now that the Scots are pissing on their feet, they are looking for the help of the French. But they won't succeed. King Philip has very different problems than us Scots. Ha! Let Edward choke on it!"

Lord William had risen from his chair with a jerk, left his seat at the high table, and was now pacing up and down with his arms folded behind his back. His face darkened as always when he thought of the hated English.

"Have you seen, James, what a single Scot with the necessary courage can do to the cowardly English?"

James nodded, knowing immediately who he was talking about. William Wallace had been the hero of his childhood and spoke to his father from the heart. What he could not do himself, he trusted this imposing man to do; namely, to unite Scotland and lead it to war against the English. Lord William was an active supporter of the freedom fighter and thus one of the first from the nobility.

Now his blood was pumping, and his voice rose to make it resound with all his might in the great hall.

"The Scots will no longer allow themselves to be exploited! We have the God-given right to be masters in our own land. And just because Edward doesn't like that and he needs our money, he tries to incorporate Scotland. But he won't succeed. I would rather die than submit to England!"

He raised his fist as if he wanted to strike the English king dead. The men in the hall also raised their fists, and battle cries rang out. The name Wallace was also mentioned here and there. High spirits prevailed and people began to tell each other stories of the successful battles that had been told dozens of times, but repeatedly extolled the Scots' bravery. Everyone liked to listen to those more often.

James smiled to himself. How his father always managed to rouse his people was a mystery to him. He himself grew up in Paris during the struggle for freedom. He had only recently come back to his parents' house and enthusiastically joined his father's fight against the occupiers. Douglas Castle was located on the borderland between England and Scotland and was often the scene of battles, raids, or hostage-taking. James's father was an unpredictable, nefarious fighter and hoped his son would show the same enthusiasm for his politics. But between James's passion and William's hatred, a few years of life experience were missing.

A movement on the great stone staircase that led to the upper chambers caught his attention. The old healer, Mairi, was just coming down the stairs with her basket. The stone stairs led in a straight line from the sleeping chambers to the great hall that his forefathers had built. In the gigantic castle hall, the walls of roughly hewn stone stretched high, only to be closed off by a soot-blackened wooden ceiling. The thick beams were richly decorated with carvings and, in addition to the roofing, also held the heavy iron chandeliers that lit the hall with hundreds of candles. The walls were adorned with woven tapestries and weapons from generations past. Above the raised end of the hall was the shield with the coat of arms of the Douglas clan—three white stars on a blue background.

The foreman, Lachlan McKay, who was sitting at the other tables with his men, let out a whistle that silenced the hall. All eyes turned to the old woman, who slowly made her way through the hall, past the large fire and the rough tables of the curiously staring clan people. She wiped the sweat from her face with a sleeve before stepping to the heavy wooden table on the raised pedestal.

With a small bow, Mairi greeted the master of the house, who had meanwhile taken his seat again. With an impatient wave of his hand, he asked her to speak.

"How is our guest? Will she survive?"

"My laird," she began in an uncertain voice, "I washed this woman and tended the wound. I sewed the cut as best I could. The wound was deep and in a part of the body that does not heal well. For the time being, I can't do anything for her but pray."

It was as quiet as a mouse in the hall. Everyone tried mightily to make out what was said, and sat attentively, listening alertly. Only the patter of rain on the roof and the crackling of logs in the fire could be heard, however. Those in front passed the news in a whisper to those in the back.

"Did she wake up again?" James asked the healer.

"No, sir. She remained unconscious the whole time."

"Thank you, Mairi; you stay with her until she wakes up or dies."

She answered William's clear command with an eager nod. She half turned, then seemed to change her mind and turned to her master again, who raised an eyebrow impatiently.

"One more thing, my laird," she began hesitantly. "I noticed something." Her gaze went hesitantly from one to the other at the high table. The old woman had William's full attention.

"Are there any indications of her origin?"

"Hm, not that, but ... she is very tall for a woman."

"Nothing unusual; the northern women are sometimes tall," objected the old laird.

"But she also has very strong muscles," the old woman began again.

"Maybe she works hard?" William was getting impatient. "What is so strange about her, woman? Speak up!"

The healer looked into the expectant faces of the people and then back to that of her laird and said hesitantly, "She has a mark on her skin."

Lord William brushed her note aside with an impatient wave of his hand. "Above the nose. I know. A tribal affiliation, perhaps?"

"Not just over the nose, but also on the back."

This made him sit up and take notice. "Also a cross?"

"No, a dragon."

William exchanged a look with James. Eleonore's mouth was open in astonishment. Women who had pictures tattooed on their skin?

"Are there any other pictures on her body?"

"No, just one thing." The old woman coughed and looked at the floor, embarrassed.

Lord William cleared his throat. "And?"

"Well," she hemmed and hawed, "the dragon fills the whole back, from the neck to the base of her spine." Her voice became lower and lower during the sentence; the silence in the room made her uncomfortable.

Lord William had to bend over to understand her better. He thought he had misheard. A dragon? Pierced the skin all over her body? A terrible thought suddenly crossed his mind.

"God help us!" he shouted suddenly, got up so quickly that his chair flew backwards, and his fist hit the table with a crash that made the healer step back in horror and fall over the step. His face was flushed with anger and his eyes bulged from their sockets.

"The English have sent us a druid to bring us to our knees!" An angry scream rumbled from the men's throats through the entire hall.

Voices. I heard voices. They were far away, but I heard them, so I haven't been to hell yet. I clearly felt my muscles ache; the wound burned and throbbed. My tongue was dry and heavy in my mouth. But I was alive!

I opened my eyes carefully. The first thing I saw was an intricately carved wooden ceiling. I let my gaze wander around the room. Two windows, a dark wood table, a chair, and a chest with an iron lock. I was lying on a bed with furs, soft and warm. There was a clay jug on a box next to the bed. My clothes and boots were carefully folded up next to them. I was wrapped in a cloth under the warm fur.

The voices swelled, became quieter, then louder again, and they came from outside this room. They could be clearly heard above the pattering of the rain against the leather hides on the window.

As I tried to sit up, the pain in my stomach taught me a lesson, and I almost passed out again. I carefully lowered my torso back onto the bed. Then, memory captured my thoughts like bolts from the blue: the pursuit! The knight who pierced me with his sword; Taycan; the face that studied me.

The face? In my head, small pieces came together to form a picture: It was the face of a tall, handsome man with dark hair and friendly brown eyes. The nose had a little kink, as if it had been broken once. Why was this picture so clear in my memory? Was I dreaming?

The voices grew louder. I had to go out and see where I was. I gritted my teeth hard and rolled onto my side. With one hand, I freed myself from the cloth that covered me only to find that I was naked underneath. My gaze fell on a large wound that slanted about four inches to the left of the belly button.

"By all the gods …" I exclaimed, staring in disbelief at the small stitches in my skin. I only vaguely remembered what had happened. In my last breath, the knight had given me a devastating stroke of the sword that left me defenceless. How was that possible? Up to now, no one had ever been able to beat me in a sword fight. Why suddenly this knight who was not even among the best of his trade? So many men hadn't stood a chance against her, and Emma's killer, of all people, got away with his life?

With a shaky hand, I grabbed the jug on my left and took a long swig of the clear water. With every sip, I felt the life come back into my body. I carefully put the jug down and picked up the cotton shirt that was folded up on the bed. Nothing of my clothes could be seen in this room. I gasped briefly, pulled the garment over myself and stood up with shaky feet. When the room began to spin, I immediately sat down again.

One more try. The third time, I stood up. The bedpost served me well. I propped myself up and slowly moved further into the room. It was about six feet from the bedpost to the door. Three steps, door, done.

It wasn't locked. I pulled it open and the babble of voices grew louder. My pulse was racing. Where am I? Am I among friends or foes?

From the door, a dark corridor led to the stairs; apparently, I was in a castle, which would make sense given the rich furnishings of the chamber. The strong smell of fire and smoke reached to the upper floors. It mingled with the smell of cider, food, and unwashed men. I propped myself up against the wall and made it to the stairs. The walls spun around me for a moment and I closed my eyes, waiting a few seconds for it to subside. When I opened them, it was dead quiet in the hall. Countless pairs of eyes stared up at me from the diffuse mixture of smoke and human vapours. They had discovered me.

There he saw her, at the top of the stairs, proud, upright as a cliff in the waves, as if she weren't about to die, but were actually challenging him. James couldn't believe his eyes.

She was one of those beauties from the Scottish sagas and legends that the ancients passed down to one another around the campfires across the wild country. James knew that a lot of it was invented, and some was fictitious, but it was said that there was always a kernel of truth in every story. And one of these beauties from the legends was now truly standing in front of him in a shirt that bared her shoulders and legs to her knees. But her inappropriateness didn't seem to bother her in the least. She looked with her blue eyes at the high table of Lord William, his son, then at the warriors and servants in the hall.

Everyone present was completely surprised. Nobody moved. Even the dogs lolling around the big fire didn't make any noise; they just pricked up their ears. Only Callie, an alert girl with heart and mind, ran up the stairs with a plaid shawl and threw it over her guest's shoulders. Despite her attentive gesture, the proud stranger did not look at the maid.

Instead, the woman's glance had stopped at James Douglas. She must have recognised him. She began to move cautiously, step by step, step by step. Everyone clearly saw that the lady was in great pain. The girl who had put the Douglas scarf around her was holding her elbow anxiously for support, but she ignored it. Her long white hair fell far over her shoulders and shimmered like liquid silver on the dark fabric. The woman kept eye contact with him as if he were the rope she was using to balance as she moved along. The dark circles under her eyes betrayed her exhaustion.

James looked sideways at his father; even William's mouth hung open. Seldom had he seen his father lack words, but this was clearly such a moment. James's mind was probably the first to start up again. He got up, walked briskly around the table, and pushed a chair towards her, on which she sat down, exhausted. She closed her eyes and moved her lips as if she were counting. She was probably fighting nausea.

Damn it, what was wrong with this woman? Half dead a moment ago, she was now dragging herself down the stairs and sitting—how unbelievable!—sitting on a chair in front of him at that moment. How could she have made it this far with such a wound? He studied her face curiously as she sat so close to him.

The woman's skin was very pale, and her forehead was sweaty. He saw a shimmering bluish vein pulsing on her temple. The black cross was clearly visible on the bridge of her nose—the short side down—strange. Was she really a druid? In any case, her exotic appearance matched his father's guess.

There was restrained restlessness in the hall; some began to whisper; others nodded or shook their heads.

Suddenly she opened her eyes and found James studying her. His eyes fixed on her face. She raised an eyebrow questioningly.

"Forgive me," James—remembering his manners—managed, embarrassed, "can I do something for you, my lady?"

"Can you speak?" William Douglas burst out, who had straightened up in his chair and was now leaning forward curiously.

The strange Lady closed her eyes again for a moment. He had asked her in English. This was the most common language on the border, including on the Scottish side.

"Father, you see, she's still too weak ..." James wanted to object, but he got no further.

"She came down here on her own two feet, so she'll probably be able to talk!" William roared impatiently and hit the table once more with his fist, making the jugs rattle. His face had turned that dangerous red colour again. Apparently, he had regained his temper.

Callie backed toward the kitchen to get out of harm's way. Lady Douglas put her hand on her husband's elbow, and he took a deep breath. She didn't take her eyes off the mystic woman at her table when she whispered to him, "Maybe she doesn't understand you at all if she is French?"

Lord William sniffed and grumbled that she might be right. As a scion of the Scottish aristocracy, he was also able to speak French, but he did not like to use the language.

"So ...?" he tried again in inexperienced French. "Comment vous appelez-vous—what's your name?"

The beauty smiled, the corners of her mouth curling slightly, revealing even, white teeth. James was still standing next to her, afraid she might slip off the chair in her condition. The other reason was that he could hardly avert his gaze from her face; she had literally captured it. Her eyes were now fixed on his father. They shimmered like crystals, bluish, the pupils large and black like her eyelashes. The look she gave his father was as icy as Loch Ness in winter.

She moistened her dry lips with her tongue, inhaled briefly, the eyelids fluttering in pain, then opened her mouth and spoke. "Enja." And after another painful breath, "My name is Enja."

Her eyes closed as she passed out and slipped off the chair into James's arms. He raised his head worriedly and looked at his father. Lord William straightened up and crossed his mighty arms over his chest. His mouth twitched, but he nodded to James. With the silent consent of his father, he carefully carried her up the stone stairs to her room. Again, he held this strange woman in his arms. She was heavy and firm, very different from how women usually feel.

James bit his lip. His thoughts were getting out of hand again. Sure, he liked women. But unlike his father, he didn't let anyone wrap him around his finger. It annoyed him immensely that Eleonore had such a grip on his father. She was so different from his mother, who would never have contradicted his father.

No, that would never happen to him. A woman shouldn't impose her will on a man. Annoyed, he shook his head, pushed the door to the bedroom so hard with his foot that it thundered against the wall, and carefully laid Enja on the bed. His nose came close to her hair. He frowned and pressed his nose once more into the silky white-blonde hair. He really couldn't smell anything because she had no body odour.

Callie, keenly aware of her duties, had eagerly accompanied him to the chamber and now put a jug of fresh water on the table. She hadn't noticed anything that he had observed. She pulled the woollen scarf off Enja's shoulders and rolled her back into the cloth she was previously in.

Meanwhile, James withdrew from the room. After closing the door behind him, he paused for a moment. Should he tell his father? But it would only cause more confusion; better if he kept it to himself for now. Did the woman realise that she had only narrowly escaped her own misfortune? Then he remembered how consciously she had chosen her words when she answered his father. She hadn't answered him in French or English. She used Gaelic, which is common in the Scottish Highlands, without an accent. She made his family understand that she was an ally, even if she was not Scottish. So his nose had not deceived him in the truest sense of the word. This woman was no danger to his clan, but she was to blame for the death of the English. That much was clear to him.

The girl with the chubby cheeks and the clever eyes had brought me soup. My stomach cramped at the smell of bread and meat, but I patiently allowed spoon by spoon to be pushed into my mouth. Like an old woman, I sat hunched over in bed with this funny camisole that was much too small for me. I estimated the time to be early noon, although I couldn't see the sun from this side of the window.

"How long did I sleep, lassie?" I said, with cracked lips. Because I didn't know her name, I used the Scottish word for girl. Since there was Gaelic shouting in the hall, I assumed that she could understand me. Indeed, she looked up briefly, blushed, and dipped the spoon back into the bowl.

"Two days and two nights, Mistress. You were weakened by your ...", she cleared her throat, embarrassed, "by your visit in the great hall."

She had a beautiful voice, even if the guttural language was slightly harsh.

"But you were very lucky—the stab in your stomach did not destroy any important organs. And Mairi was able to contain the fever very quickly. You have a strong mind and a healthy body, Mistress!" she continued admiringly.

She offered me another spoon, which I gratefully accepted. It wasn't the first time that the strength of my body surprised me. As if I were made for the dangers of this time, I thought fleetingly—or I was just luckier than other people. Thoughtfully, I looked into the face of the well-fed girl who was trying so hard to look after me.

"Since I'm still alive, I suspect that Lord William decided to hear my story before he kills me," I guessed, between two spoons of the strong broth.

I had to assume that the elderly gentleman at the high table was the Douglas clan chief, the father of my lifesaver. The fact that he hadn't even introduced himself to me at the table strengthened my suspicions. Only a man of high rank could allow himself such rude behaviour.

The strawberry-blonde girl blushed again, this time down to the roots of her hair, which I found very sympathetic.

"Lord William would certainly never kill a woman!" She shook her head vehemently. "Not without reason, of course," she quickly corrected.

She dabbed my mouth with a cloth and pushed the empty bowl back onto the tray. Before she had a chance to ask any more questions, she got up quickly and turned to the door. I clearly felt her insecurity, but also her curiosity.

"Say," she began again, "what does the cross on your forehead mean? Has it to do with religion?"

Most of the Scots in this area were Catholic. They automatically connected the cross with the suffering of Christ; it was the sign of their faith. I smiled kindly at the shy girl; I had heard this question all too often.

"In the Orient, the cross is the symbol for people who have forfeited their rights. With the cross one becomes the property of another person until one's own death."

"And whom do you belong to?"

Of course, that was the next question.

"Nobody. I have regained my freedom, and I will never belong to anyone again. The cross on my forehead reminds me every day how quickly one can lose one's freedom."

"But you are a woman. How can you ever be free?"

Her curiosity amused me and made me smile happily because I understood her question all too well.

"By teaching men to fear."

She smiled shyly again because she understood, and without blushing.

"By the way, my name is Callie. If you need something, I'll be outside." She curtsied politely, turned around, and opened the door. Suddenly, she bowed low and gave way to someone standing in the massive wooden frame.

It was James Douglas, the man I couldn't get out of my head. I owed it to him that I recovered so quickly and that I could already eat something again. Tall, he towered over his father by almost a head. He hadn't inherited his beefy stature, however; instead, he was rather slim and wiry. But he had the same brown eyes that seemed so warm on him and so cold on his father. His wavy, dark brown hair was tied at the nape of his neck with a leather cord. A shadow of a beard emphasised his angular chin. He had inherited a number of masculine features from his father: the strong nose, which was slightly bent, and the area around the eyes. But the eyebrows weren't nearly as bushy and thick; they were rather narrow and curved, and he moved them skilfully to make his facial expressions more pronounced. Perhaps his mother had immortalised herself here. With his full lips and noble pallor, there was almost something grand about him.

I almost thought that he was a witty person, but the thought dissipated as he stood in front of me with his arms crossed, imitating his father's posture, a pose full of arrogance.

I leaned back on the pillows, pushed my chest out a little, and tried to maintain a little dignity despite my deplorable condition. While the Douglas heir was simply but properly dressed, I cut a significantly worse figure in my shirt.

"I already introduced myself," he began hesitantly, "but I suppose you didn't really notice me out there, where we found you."

He paused his thoughts and raised that beautiful eyebrow.

"I am James Douglas, son of Lord William Douglas, whom you met earlier in the hall."

With my head tilted slightly, I nodded slowly.

"Very pleased," I replied. "You already know my name."

That brief statement made him smile, and he nodded knowingly, turning a little and looking out the window as if to avert his gaze from me. The windows were open at this time of day and the sun dared to throw a little light into this chamber. Of course, he did some research. A female warrior is to be known in the highlands.

"You are my father's guest as long as you're recovering from your wound. But it would be nice if you could tell me a little bit about yourself. The situation in which we found you." He cleared his throat uncertainly. "It was more than strange."

He looked everywhere now, just not at me.

"Why isn't Lord William coming to question me?"

I wanted to know. His neck turned a little red.

"Well," he hesitated, and examined the toe of his boot carefully, "you are my guest. I have brought you here, so I have to take care of you, too."

"Then help me out of bed, my lord! I could take a few steps and walk with you. Here in this bed, I'm rusting like a nail in a bucket."

Startled, his gaze travelled down my flimsy nightgown. "I'll get Callie. She can help you in getting dressed ..."

"Pah! There will be nothing of that sort, young man. I don't need help getting dressed," I angrily spat at him.

His prudishness enraged me, and even more so my helplessness.

He tentatively took the dressing gown that hung over the chair and handed it to me with his face averted, but a smile played around his mouth.

"Young man?" he repeated mischievously as I pulled on my red coat. "You are probably not older than I?"

I held out my hand to him, which he took without hesitation to help me out of bed. I smiled.

"But much wiser!"

I stalked around the bed to the door on unsteady legs.

He laughed. It sounded carefree, and his eyes danced along with it. I had the feeling that the soup in my stomach didn't agree with me. I put my hand on my stomach to calm it down. Certainly, it came from the pain of the wound, which now and then felt like a malicious stinging.

He led me carefully to the door, bowed, and kissed my hand. The touch raised goosebumps on my arm. His gaze was serious, but one eyebrow was raised mockingly, and he imitated my snippy tone: "You have yet to prove that."

I gladly accepted the challenge. We took a few steps across the courtyard and had the opportunity to get to know each other better. It was then that I realised that James

Douglas was a witty narrator. Of course, he was educated by his upbringing in France, but cleverly avoided my questions about the politics there and the relationship between France and Scotland. When he tried to engage me in a conversation about the incident in which I was so badly injured, I went monosyllabic and asked him to go back the way we had come. He understood that I didn't want to talk to him about it.

As an attentive listener, he changed the subject. Something seemed to be burning in his heart. "How is it that you have a dragon on your back that the healer—with all due respect—described to us in detail?"

I had to laugh for a moment, which I immediately regretted, because the pain in my stomach punished this outburst of feelings. James was still holding my elbow for support, and I felt his grip tighten. He wasn't going to let go of my arm, or this subject.

"Well," I began thoughtfully, "the dragon is the symbol of strength, power, and death. Hardly any other symbol combines these three components better. I chose it because it symbolises my career like no other. It's my talisman ..."

"Talisman?" He perked up. "Then you are something like a druid or a shaman?"

There was a sense of awe in his voice.

"No, I wouldn't say that. I chose this picture myself and had it painted on my back without a religious meaning."

"Did you do that voluntarily? What woman lets herself be ravished like that?"

"Ravish?" My horror was not feigned. "But this is the adornment and pride of every warrior. I have nothing to be ashamed of!"

The young man shook his head without understanding.

"I'm afraid I don't understand you. You are a very beautiful woman. Why would you ... "

"... Why would I rather be seen as a warrior?"

At the same moment, he stopped and stood in front of me. With great self-confidence, I looked directly into his warm-hearted eyes and added with a smile, "Because I am a warrior, and whoever knows me will not doubt it."

I noticed unmistakably in his look the disbelief that I had seen in many men. In the meantime, I was no longer surprised that in this country my views embodied a worse evil than that of the Antichrist. Apparently disappointed, he now turned away from me, absently took my elbow again, and slowly walked back to the door of the side entrance through which we had come outside. Beyond it was the staircase, which reminded me with every step that the knight's sword had badly damaged my stomach muscles.

After some time of deliberation, he said in a muffled tone and without looking at me, "I see something special in you. You are proud and brave, but never forget you are still a woman. If your dragon wants to develop his power, then this can only be done with a man by your side."

With a gallant movement, he bent over my hand, kissed it, and politely said goodbye. On the way back to the room, he left me with Callie, who hurried over as soon as he had said goodbye. His words cut deeply into my soul because he didn't tell me anything I didn't already know. In this land, men had power and law on their side. One look at the company at this castle and I could see it for myself. It was time for the dragon to show what it could do.

I was doing amazingly well, the wound was barely pulsating, and my appetite had returned. The healer informed me that she had personally cleaned and sewn the wound. The skin was already firmly back together, and she could take out the stitches. A wound of this size could have caused a lot of problems, so I saw it as a stroke of luck to recover so quickly. After just a few days in bed, I was able to walk to some extent and even carefully do a few exercises that were supposed to restore my muscular strength. The only thing that annoyed me now was my severed abdominal muscles, which would take longer than the rest of the tissue to regain their original strength. Today's walk on Sir James Douglas's arm from the room over the stone stairs to the great hall was therefore no pleasure for me. Without wanting to, I uttered a low, painful sound every third step.

Apparently unimpressed by this, his Lordship William Douglas and his wife Lady Eleonore were already waiting for me in a room next to the great hall, which probably served as a writing room. There was a smell of leather and wood here, and a large fireplace kindled the pleasant warmth in the small room, which was lit by a small window. The dawn light made Lord Williams' hard features look a little softer, and when he smiled at his wife now, I could see something of the young James in him, whose face hadn't been furrowed so deeply by life.

Both looked at me expectantly as I carefully stepped into the room. I nodded briefly because a bow was still not possible. An old, gilded chair by the large, solid wooden table was vacant, and James showed me there. Only now did I become aware of another person who hadn't caught my eye because he was in a kind of box with two pairs of wheels attached to it. The box was next to Eleonore, and her hand kept going back to the bundle of humanity that lay inside. It was a child, but a bit bigger than a toddler, that shouldn't really have to lie prone. There was something strange about his face. James caught my eyes and shook his head warningly. Why shouldn't I ask?

Eleonore ignored James' warning looks. She, too, had seen my questioning look. As she began to speak, I heard a mother's love for her child in every word she said.

"This is our son Matthew. He was born with difficulties and is not like other children, but I love him very much because he sees the world as it is, and I learn every day to see it with his eyes."

That made a deep impression on me. Eleonore might be young, but she looked more mature than most women her age. My respect for the petite lady of the castle grew with every passing moment. She had fought for an influential position at the side of her husband and brought love and reason to this male-dominated castle life. Her positive influence also reached as far as my host, who now cleared his throat and said, "We tried everything, but no healer could help him. He will probably remain a cripple forever. But as long as I live, he will be respected. Because he is also a Douglas, like all of us."

I stepped closer, curious. Oftentimes, a disabled child was seen as a disgrace and a punishment from God by the church. My guess was more of a blood disease or an injury to the brain. Head injuries in war victims produced symptoms similar to those of this child. Perhaps when it was born, it had been treated roughly and its soft head was crushed. But of course, I didn't say that. Nobody here had to know more about me than necessary.

But this child here was lucky in misery. It was loved and treated properly. Hardly any of his companions in fate survived the first few months; they were often abandoned out of fear or starved to death. Matthew seemed to be a little over five years old by my estimate.

He smiled at me, hit the edge of the box with his clenched fist, and squealed happily. In contrast to his father, he seemed to be in a good mood, while William looked at me with a dark expression from the other side of the room. Infected by his cheerfulness, I held out my hand to Matthew, which he finally grasped after three attempts, and nodded to the child with a smile.

"Pleased to meet you, Matthew Douglas. My name is Enja, Enja von Caerlaverock, and your resemblance to your father is simply amazing!"

In fact, I couldn't find anything that would confirm his paternity, but that lie slipped easily from my lips with a smile. A loud squeak and hoot from the box confirmed to me that he understood more than most believed, and his father smiled despite my daring words.

"He seems to like your humour, Lady Enja."

"Which cannot be said of everyone in the room," I countered and sat down on the vacant chair, accompanied by Matthews' happy laugh.

"Proud words from a woman! If a man were to say it, I would answer him accordingly. But my upbringing—and my dear wife—don't allow it."

He took her hand and kissed her lovingly. James twisted his mouth in disgust. He didn't seem to like his father's submission.

"Your wife is a very clever woman who possesses virtue that is not remotely close to mine. Please don't be considerate. I don't expect any forbearance," I demanded and looked at him with my head held high.

Thoughtfully, he dropped her hand again and stood up. His imposing figure obscured the flickering fireplace and cast a shadow over me. His son had withdrawn in silence to the right wall, where he could follow the conversation and perhaps intervene.

"Well, then tell your story, because believe me, consideration is definitely not one of my virtues. If I see you as a danger to my clan, then you will not survive the day alive."

In order to make a strong impression, at least physically, I leaned back slightly in the chair, crossed my arms, and nodded appreciatively.

"That is the language that I like better."

How good that the pulling pain in my stomach kept my mind wide awake.

I thought feverishly about what to tell the chief of the Douglas clan. The Scottish Highlands are patriarchal through and through. A woman had nothing to say; she was the property of her father or, later, of her husband. With a few exceptions, women were uneducated, and in addition to the task of giving birth to an heir, perhaps also had responsibility for domestic matters. I cautiously gave Lord Douglas only small bites that were easier to digest instead of turning his worldview upside down with the whole truth.

"So, you rode after the horse herdsman's murderer with the foreman of your clan and met the English knight and his soldiers. The foreman killed everyone except the knight, who wounded you with his sword. Then he took care of you and left you behind to get help?"

Suspiciously, the lord summed up my statements.

"Yes," I confirmed, nodding without blushing, "and before he came back, your son found me and brought me here."

Disbelief was written in large letters on his furrowed brow. James' face was blank. I tried not to look at him, but instead looked steadfastly into the face of the clan chief. He ground his jaw, and the tendons on his cheeks tensed. Repeatedly, he looked dubiously at Eleonore, and she spoke in his place, very unusual for a wife.

"You are very brave for a lady, and your wound heals faster than our healer predicted. You are unusually tall and strong, you have a large picture of a dragon on your skin… "

She paused for a moment and with one look, got her husband's consent to continue.

"What are you? Are you a druid?"

Her gaze was so expectant that I was inclined to confirm her suspicion regardless of the consequences. It was the same question James had asked me in my room. Apparently, a druid was an extraordinary but accepted person.

The room was quiet for a short time; only the crackling of the logs in the fireplace and the boy's gurgling could be heard. I had to say the right thing. Otherwise, I wouldn't be able to leave here. I leaned forward carefully, forgetting about my stomach muscles, and winced a little.

I closed my eyes in pain, exhaled slowly, opened my eyes again, and replied, "I come from the country where the holy war is raging. I ended up there as a slave when our ship went down with my mother. I fought for my freedom and self-determination for many years. In search of my father, I finally found a home for myself and my people in Caerlaverock Castle with the Maxwells' clan. I look different and I am different from the Scots here, but I see the country as my home. And there's one thing I'm on par with everyone here: If a damned Englishman kills one of my people just because he wants my horses, I'll kill him, even if I declare war on England—so I'm just the same as a damned Scottish lassie."

William leaned forward during my speech. He stared at me, and I met his gaze. Slowly, very slowly, a smile crept onto his face, which turned into a chuckle and finally led to roaring laughter. All eyes were on him, and Matthew squealed with fervour.

Eventually, we all came back to reality, my stomach muscles ached, and William wiped the tears of laughter from his face. Finally, he got up, took a few steps towards my chair, smacked me on the shoulder with his big paw, still laughing, and held out his calloused hand. A sharp pain travelled through my body; however, my expression did not change.

"No matter who or what you are, Enja von Caerlaverock," he said with a grin that showed all the teeth that had not yet been knocked out, and made his features seem less intimidating in one fell swoop.

"But you are on the right side, and whether woman or not, Scot or not, I like you!"

So, Lord William had a soft heart, was a generous host, and was well ahead of his compatriots. I had had a completely different experience with the local Scots, and especially with the neighbours of my lands.

He had insisted on having dinner in my honour that day. It had been an offer of peace, which I gratefully accepted, but only on the condition that I could participate in it in my own clothes. I gratefully stripped off the shirt, which smelled so disgustingly of illness, and washed myself as best I could in a bowl provided. Callie kindly helped me.

I pulled the wide-cut trouser legs over my legs and wrapped and tied them at the hips. I left the belt around the tunic a little loose so as not to tear the wound open. Then I tied my hair in a bun at the back of my head. To do this, I put the small dagger, which was stuck in a shaft with fine, glittering gemstones, into the twisted bun with practised fingers. Callie had carefully placed it in a chest next to my bed, along with my weapons and clothes. Unfortunately, the leather vest was destroyed—first by the sword stroke and then by the healer who had to cut it up when she had tended my wound. Callie had sewn my tunic and washed out the blood. The girl now examined my appearance with a scrutinising look.

"You are an admirable woman, my lady. And even in trousers, you are more beautiful than many a lady in the most splendid dress."

The charming blush again crept across her face, and I gratefully squeezed her hand.

"If you ever need help, Callie, you can always come to me. You have been a loyal friend to me, and I never forget a good deed."

A shy smile was the answer, and I made my way cautiously into the hall to attend the clan's feast. The roaring could already be heard in my room. Plenty of ale and uisge beatha—a hard liquor with a colour like honey—had fuelled the mood.

As a guest of honour, I was allowed to sit next to Lord William at the family table. Next to Eleonore sat Hugh, freshly washed, who this evening was permitted to come out of the horse stable. James insisted on sitting next to me. It was a relaxed evening; the tension of the last few days had given way to a friendly atmosphere. The conversations served to quench curiosity rather than to distinguish between friend and foe.

To avoid further questioning, I studied Matthew, who had captured my heart. He always seemed in a good mood, and my words made him even more cheerful. I was forced to talk to James, but I couldn't help but feel that he expected more from me than the answers I'd given his father. He repeatedly attempted to engage me in conversation to find out more about me. As he did so, his brown eyes studied me with an intensity that, oddly enough, was not uncomfortable. Before he realised my peculiar weakness towards him, it crossed my mind that I should say goodbye early so as not to have to sit next to him for too long, but the rare pleasure of juggling well-chosen words with a skilled conversationalist finally made me stay in my place.

I suspected that he wouldn't believe my story. Too much went unanswered, and James, like his father, did not let my heroic answer blind him. He was a sharp-witted man; that he let me know. He kept coming back to the incident with the English. His questions revolved around which weapon had killed the men and who had helped me. At this point, I persisted and let him grope in the dark. For me, it was like a game of chess; every move had to be carefully considered, and I was hard to beat. James turned out to have a brilliant mind and was sure to become a clever laird of the Douglas clan one day, especially since he was nowhere near as irritable as Lord William.

The evening was not really over yet; the sun was just casting the last rays of the sun on Douglas Castle and bathing the thick walls in orange light. The drunken clan people who sat in the great hall began to sing or shout, whatever escaped their throats, when the horn suddenly rang out at the main gate. It announced visitors. Most of the Douglas men stayed where they were, some well past the point where they could even walk. Some didn't react at all and just stared glassily into their jugs.

The doors to the hall were pushed open hard, and one of the lookouts shouted across the hall, "A rider is approaching our castle, my laird! Shall we let him through the gate?"

Lord Douglas stood up, swaying, braced himself with difficulty on the table, and roared with all his might: "At this time of night? Let him in! What the hell! All men who can still walk, f-follow me!"

And he was the first to stalk uncertainly through the door into the courtyard. This led to confusion. Drunk men stumbled aimlessly, falling over chairs and legs. In between, the servants rushed like frightened deer to save plates, goblets, food and drinks from the staggering figures.

I sat calmly where I was and tried not to show any reaction. James had got up and stood next to me instead of following his father out into the yard. He crossed his arms and looked at me carefully. Cunning fox!

"Can it be that you know exactly who is coming to visit us here?"

I rose carefully until I was face to face with him. He was a whole head taller than I. His dark brown eyes bored into mine. His expression didn't tell whether he thought me friend or foe.

"Yes, I've been waiting for him."

"Him?" he asked, tilting his head slightly. The furrow between his eyes deepened.

"Hal, my foreman," I explained and paused. When I saw his eyebrow raise questioningly, I added: "The one who killed the English."

I imagined I saw something like slight disappointment behind his unfathomable expression. But he had himself well under control, because he nodded towards the door and said only briefly. "Then we should go to greet him."

He offered me his forearm and I gratefully accepted his help. Slowly, we followed the others through the chaos in the hall to the outside. Everyone who had gathered there in the meantime looked spellbound at the main gate, which was now pushed open by the few guards who had remained sober. In addition to numerous burps and curses, Chief Douglas stood upright with his legs apart like a rock, despite the binge drinking, ready to sweep away any unwanted guest with his eyes.

The sun had long since set. The courtyard was now illuminated by the midnight sun, which lengthened the evening by a few hours and made torches superfluous. It was a strange mood, a brightness without sun, and it coloured the surroundings in an idiosyncratic light almost as if the gods had lit torches, but they were nowhere to be seen. There was no shadow, either; everything around me was illuminated by the same diffused light—a strange phenomenon the likes of which I had only seen here in Scotland in the summers; a phenomenon as strange as the rider who was coming up the hill, and with him a feeling of familiarity. Once again, I was happy to see Hal. He trotted calmly towards the castle on his huge white horse.

Enja, at James's side, tightened her grip on his upper arm. She straightened a little more as if to underscore her authority, and watched intently as the rider rode leisurely through the archway as if he were visiting the church and not the court of the mighty Lord William Douglas.

James Douglas admitted that his men had seen better times than they had tonight. The sheer number alone should have been enough to intimidate the stranger. Instead, the man rode into the courtyard on the sturdy white horse as if he were the boss of this half-drunk bunch, albeit a pretty grim boss by the look on his face. James unconsciously swallowed when he saw the arsenal with which the stranger was armed: two axes crisscrossed in his belt, a mighty broadsword peeked over his shoulder, and a bow with arrows and a heavy shield dangled from the saddle. At the same time, the giant looked intimidating on his own.

Under his too tight tunic, impressive muscles stood out, dancing with every movement. His leather vest was scaled like fish skin with overlapping layers of leather. The loose trousers only hinted at the mighty thighs; the huge feet were in leather boots. The stranger was enthroned like a colossus on the white horse, which proudly stretched its large skull and neighed. The imposing destrier warhorse was noticeably large, his chest broad and strong like that of his rider; even the hooves were the size of a plate. His dark mane came down to his shoulders. The eyes and nose were also tinted dark, while the rest was piebald. Somehow, horse and rider fit together and formed an impressive unit.

Enja let go of James's elbow and took a few steps forward, smiling, with her arms crossed. The mighty warrior on horseback nodded to her.

His head surpassed anything James had ever seen before. Up close, he could see that the massive skull was completely shaved and went straight into a thick, short neck. One earlobe was torn off, and an object he couldn't make out was hanging from the other. His forehead was painted black, and the paint ended in wild shapes and lines that stretched over his head like snakes. They wrapped around his green eyes, which were so intense that they seemed to shine even across the distance of the courtyard. Those eyes stared at him now as if James were the plague of Egypt. He nervously switched his weight from his right foot to the left and at that moment, was downright grateful to Enja that she had withdrawn from his arm in time because he didn't want to attract the holy anger of this man under any circumstances.

His green eyes wandered to Enja, who now stood upright like a statue only a few metres away from him. He looked her up and down sharply. His eyebrows drew together;

something seemed to be bothering him. His voice sounded hoarse, and the tone matched the menace of the man. "Are you hurt?"

Enja shook her head. "Not worth mentioning," she replied and made a dismissive gesture before crossing her arms over her chest again.

"Mmmh ..." the rider muttered. The white horse shook its mighty head impatiently and lengthened the reins with its bridle.

"I've been waiting for you." That sounded reproachful.

"I've been busy, Hal," Enja replied sharply, as if she wanted desperately to prevent him from blurting out any truth that would blow her story apart.

James raised an eyebrow and Lord William cleared his throat. His men were strangely uneasy, as if they would rather be in the hall than out here with this strange rider, and he raised his hand firmly.

"This lady is my guest, and if you are a friend, you are welcome to join our celebration. If not, move your behind to where you came from!"

Only a slight shuffle in his voice betrayed that Lord William had looked too deeply into his goblet.

The monosyllabic rider unwillingly looked over at the clan chief, grunted something incomprehensible, and turned back to Enja. His huge arm shot forward, and he opened his hand.

"Come on now!" he ordered her impatiently.

Enja sighed and just shook her head at such impolite behaviour but made no move to contradict. It was fine with her; she wanted to get out of here as quickly as possible, so she politely turned to the head of the clan, and Eleonore first, made a small bow that cost her a little groan, and said, "It seems to me that I have to leave you tonight. I hope for your understanding. there are important tasks waiting for me."

The female warrior blinked in amusement.

"Please accept my best thanks for your hospitality and the extraordinary services that you rendered. My special thanks go to your son James for the rescue and care."

She tilted her head in his direction. She winked at him and her mouth played a mysterious smile.

"Our ways separate here. But be sure, if you need an ally, ask about Enja in Caerlaverock. I am linked forever as a friend with the Douglas clan."

She nodded briefly to James and Hugh and moved to Hal. The rider tensed noticeably. He seemed to be in a rather bad mood and radiated something that made the hair stand up on the back of James's neck. It was better not to have this man as an enemy, but he feared he was already. Enja's hand on James's arm had not escaped the green eyes.

Enja put her hand in that of the mighty warrior, and in one swing, he pulled her onto the horse behind him as if she were just a flyweight. Without a word, the colossus turned the white horse and trotted away as leisurely as he had come.

Just as James was wondering if he would ever see her again, Enja turned around again and looked at him with her blue crystal eyes. Involuntarily, he straightened up a little and hesitantly raised his hand. Enja did the same, and there it was again—the mysterious smile. Something strange happened at that moment that he didn't understand: was he just imagining it, or was part of him actually walking with her, leaving a void that hurt?

Lord William grunted something incomprehensible, turned around unsteadily, and waved his restless entourage back into the hall with a gruff gesture.

Chapter 9

Baghdad in the year 1295

I had been wandering the town for days. My newfound freedom was limited to the questions of where to find something to eat and a place to sleep. Under Fahrudin's care, I had never needed to think about such matters. Now, I found that I spent a significant portion of my time searching for food. Each morning, I watched the merchants and craftsmen set up their stalls. Occasionally, I could lend a hand and, in return, receive a bit of fruit or a few of my beloved datiln. Sometimes someone would slip me a piece of bread out of pity.

I was just lying in the shade of a palm tree, sleepily watching the hustle and bustle in the midday heat, wondering where I was actually going and how I should survive in the near future, when out of the corner of my eye, I saw a loaf of bread falling from one of the baker's boxes. He had lost it in passing. Every lunchtime, the baker delivered his goods to the harbour bars. I immediately noticed two competitors who might also have observed the bread dropping on the street. But the happy circumstance went unnoticed by the boys, who had made themselves comfortable between the sacks opposite.

I got up as inconspicuously as possible, strolled down the alley to the place in the street where the bread had fallen, and paused for a moment. My eyes searched both directions of the almost empty street for people who might get in my way. But nobody seemed to notice me, so I ran swiftly, grabbed the piece, and darted nimbly into the next alley. I stood breathlessly behind an open door and listened for shouts or quick steps. Nothing.

I looked proudly at my prey, and my stomach growled. I bit into the bread so quickly that I almost choked on it. Oh, what a delight! It tasted like fresh cardamom and was so crisp it must have come fresh out of the oven. Satisfied, I strolled down the small alley with my bounty when I suddenly heard footsteps behind me. A chill ran down my back and I stopped involuntarily. My heart was pounding.

"Don't you want to share the bread with us, little one?" I heard right behind me. It was a boy's voice. I turned around slowly, still chewing on the big chunk. In front of me stood the two street children who had been lying in the shade opposite on the market square. The taller one had crossed his arms over his chest and looked at me with a challenging expression. The second ducked down and peeked nervously from behind the other's back.

"Not really," I declared firmly. "I'm hungry, and this fell in front of me," I held up the bread, "quite by chance at my feet."

I quickly took another bite and chewed on calmly since I didn't want to show my nervousness.

"You're hunting here in my area, and if someone gets something here, he'll share it with me, too!"

The bigger one pointed his forefinger threateningly in my direction.

"Who are you anyway? I've never seen you here," I replied with my mouth full. "How can you say this is your territory if you aren't here?"

I was surely not going to be intimidated that quickly, and I still had the bread in my hand.

"My name is Khalil and the boy behind me is Laith. I am the leader in this area, and if you want to continue begging here, you will please subordinate yourself and give us some of this!"

He pointed to my piece of bread, and I swallowed the bite with difficulty, which had just become very dry in my mouth.

"What is your area? If I know, I'll go somewhere else."

After all, I didn't want to step on anyone's toes. The big boy grinned mischievously, spread his arms and proudly said, "Everything here. All of Baghdad is my area, and now bring me the loot!"

I looked with regret at the remaining piece and then looked at Khalil. It was enough for the three of us. With a sweeping gesture, I tossed him the larger part. He caught it deftly, tore off a small piece and gave it to Laith, who devoured it greedily. He was quite a bit smaller, thinner, and dressed in only a frayed sirwal, oriental harem pants. His right arm ended in a stump that was just as filthy as the rest of the boy. He hastily stuffed the bread into his mouth with his left hand.

Khalil stared at me and followed my gaze, then gave a mean grin.

"Never seen anyone who got caught, huh?"

"Got caught?" I croaked, startled. By now, my mouth was as dry as the desert. "Doing what?"

The two laughed scornfully. "Well, while stealing—just like what you just did," Khalil explained to me with a grin.

"I didn't steal anything. I just picked up the piece of bread that was lying in the dirt," I replied angrily and threateningly raised the remaining breadcrust.

"Tell that to the executioner when you stand before him." Khalil grew serious. "You're new in town …"

It wasn't a question. He frowned, wrinkling his forehead, which was as dirty as mine but without a tattoo. Then he crossed his arms over his chest and spoke with astonishing authority. "You look nimble and agile. Why don't you come with us? We'll hunt together and you can count on our protection. We stick together, whatever happens. Often other gangs come and try to drive us away, but we hold our territory."

Khalil had spread his legs and looked confident.

"Of course, you have to beg and steal, but by doing your share, you can stay with us."

It occurred to me that the protection of a group would really be of help to me. I nodded and shook hands with him. Khalil laughed with white teeth that stood out strangely against his dark skin, took my hand, and asked me my name. For a moment, I felt a little dizzy, I hadn't really thought about it yet. What was my name now? Enja wouldn't work ...

"E ... Ewan," I stuttered my new name. It was still a little strange to me, and difficult to say.

"Ewan," said Khalil loudly, and once again squeezed my hand firmly, "welcome to the Usamas, the lions of Baghdad!"

Laith hurried to shake my hand as well, even if it was only with his left. The shy boy was a handsome guy, but much too skinny. His skin was dark like that of so many locals, his eyes were a beautiful grey-blue, like those of the pigeons that were hunted by the hawks and therefore were only seen in the cities. I suspected he was the bastard of a western slave because his hair was golden under the dirt.

Khalil, on the other hand, was well-fed and strong, his jet-black hair sticking out in all directions, and his dark eyes sparkling cheekily from under his head of hair. His trousers were still whole, and he had procured a vest that stretched over the front of his handsome stomach. The colours were faded from the sun.

"Come on, Ewan," he said, tilting his head in another direction, "I'll introduce you to the others."

He ran through the alleys swiftly and finally climbed a ladder, with his little shadow, Laith, right behind him. We reached the upper storeys via the ladders, and from there down again into the side streets. There were fewer people there than near the market square, and we made far more rapid progress.

At that pace, I had trouble following the two of them as they quickly climbed up the ladders, then down again, ran by narrow houses, and finally into a market hall with meat waste. It stank horribly. Thousands of flies covered the food that had been carelessly tossed away, and I held the piece of bread in front of my nose. Khalil led me to a secluded room that was empty except for a few benches and tables. The dim light obscured the filthy floor that I could feel between my toes. A little astonished at this dead end, I looked around, and an oppressive feeling crept into me. Had he lured me here on purpose?

Khalil whistled softly with two fingers in his mouth, whereupon a ladder was lowered through a small hatch in the ceiling. Khalil heaved his plump body up first, then I followed him, and finally Laith. Narrow faces stared at me wide-eyed as I stepped through the hatch. It was dark; the room had no windows. Only the hatch in the floor let a little of the scant daylight into the former attic. A few belongings were scattered on the floor.

They were all children, maybe between six and twelve years old. Even the leader, Khalil, I guessed to be no more than twelve. The exception was a small boy who had to be much younger than the others, maybe four years old. He was

184

holding the hand of a larger child with similar features. His brother?

I waited for Khalil to introduce me to everyone, and I greeted each child with a handshake. I discovered that two other hands were missing, confirming that the punishment for theft was chopping off the hand. All the children had one thing in common: they were hungry, and they looked greedily at the piece of bread. I held out my hand carefully to the leader. Khalil took it from my hand and handed it to one of the boys, who took a bite and passed it on.

There seemed to be an order of precedence because the sequence was not random. The last was the little boy, but there was nothing left for him. Already slightly apathetic from hunger, he hung his head, whereupon his brother gave him a small piece of his already small bite.

The situation shook me. The children were free, but they were slaves to their hunger. Their miserable existence pained me.

"Where do you find your food?" I asked everyone.

The beggar kids looked at their spokesman, Khalil, as if he were the only one who knew.

"We split up into different groups that patrol at special times of the day. In the morning at the fish harbour down on the Tigris, at lunchtime at the bakers who deliver to the inns, and in the evening, we try it with the market tenders who don't want to take their products back with them and who give us generous gifts of food. We only steal sometimes."

That brought him a well-deserved grin from all of the little faces.

"But woe if the Rabahs or the Junays come. They'll beat you up, and the booty is gone!" Laith crowed from behind Khalil in his bright voice. And a few more names were thrown in that meant nothing to me. They were probably the names of other gangs of beggars, and my stomach felt a little queasy. My hands sweated, but I didn't show my insecurity and asked, "Can I go to the market with you tonight? I already know a few people there. Maybe something will fall off for us."

The children laughed and whispered, but Khalil looked at me carefully before nodding. Apparently, nobody wanted to go to the marketplace. How would I know what this street life meant? For me, it was the most exciting adventure of my life.

In just a few weeks, I learned how one carefully but inconspicuously observed people, distracted them, and then relieved them of their bounty. Most of the time, it was about food; only rarely did we steal items because people were so angry when it came to personal things. Not infrequently, we could barely escape our captors, but we were all the more pleased about the successful outcome of the raid when we did.

I learned that the mercenaries, or Asakirs as they were called here, rarely hunted us children. They were not interested in capturing us because we were not lucrative prisoners who were ransomed by their relatives. So, they only upheld the law for as long as people observed them and they had to show that they were doing their job properly.

The Asakirs came from entire family clans who were trained and specialised in observing the laws in Baghdad. Their position was a lucrative source of income, and unfortunately, they were thoroughly corrupt. I learned that very quickly because not only were we looking for prey, but our observations sometimes turned into involuntary spying. More than once I saw innkeepers, traders, or noblemen handing gold coins to the Asakirs. Perhaps they are buying liberties that they would otherwise not have? Or even protection, as Khalil gave me?

Since we couldn't pay the mercenaries to look the other way, I learned to look out before we struck. If an Asakir witnessed a theft, he had to do something to protect his reputation. They were actually quite easy to recognise since they wore white Sunni turbans, most had a full beard, and they were dressed in light tunics with a red waistcoat that was embroidered with a gold border. In addition to the curved dagger in their belts, they also had a sword strapped to their backs, the scimitar, a curved sword that was also used for beheading because of its sharpness. In all honesty, I had never seen any of the Asakirs pull it out of his belt, let alone use it. Presumably, they were mainly used for masculine ornamentation.

It would have been pure paradise if the other gangs of children hadn't kept ambushing us, robbing us of our hard-earned booty, or even beating us up. To have such a tough fighter as Khalil in our midst, who deterred most opponents by his appearance, had advantages. On the other hand, I had to compensate for my lack of strength with speed. My tactics consisted of distraction and lightning-fast slamming with anything I could get my hands on. Oh, I was fast, very fast!

I had really learned a lot from Master Abdallah, reading, writing, arithmetic, and I was able to quote the Koran, but nothing could have prepared me for life among the street children of Baghdad. My little friends gave me lessons in sneaking up, running away, and lying, which they belittled and called "ingratiation." And they taught me a discipline that soon made me the best among the Usamas because I benefited from my tremendous jumping ability and my speed: the house run.

If there was one thing I loved, it was jumping from and to houses and ladders at a speed so fast that no one could catch up with me. In addition, I preferred to go hunting in the evening or at night. For one thing, I was far too easy to spot during the day. My light skin, white hair, and last but not least, the cross on my forehead immediately brought me under suspicion.

Too often, I heard someone shout "It was the boy with the light hair!" in the market square, and then had to run like a weasel. Another reason was that my eyes could see at least as well during the night as they did during the day. As sensitive as they were in the sun, they saw keenly at night, like a cat. How often had I seen cats develop large, black pupils at night?

Laith noticed that, too. With a thoughtful gulp, he spoke to me about it once. He had noticed that I didn't even need the moonlight at night to stalk Baghdad safely. I didn't make a sound or take a wrong step.

"Night Star" became my battle name, and I was mighty proud of it. For me, it meant what I always wanted to be: free and independent. For the first time, I had friends whom I could protect and who were there for me, too. Baghdad's lions were like a small family. We stuck together, protected one another, and warned one another. Sometimes a new child came along, while others disappeared—like little Benjamin, who always held his brother's hand. He got weaker every day, and one day he just didn't wake up. We threw his body into the Tigris. His brother didn't seem sad, so I spoke to him about it while we were standing on the bank. I thought of my mother, how she had drifted away from me in the water, how her face had become smaller and smaller on the horizon, and the memory almost took my breath away.

The boy just stood there and put his hand over his eyes to gain some shade; the sun was shining low and made the water glitter like crystals. In the distance loomed the endless sand-brown silhouette of the city of Baghdad. As with a paintbrush, the houses were smeared with the dust of the desert. The rows of houses disappeared into this sea of sand.

"Are you sad?"

"No" he said calmly. "We all have to go to paradise someday. Benjamin just goes a different way than me; a shortcut. Ultimately, we all get there—some sooner, some later."

His words were so clear and he seemed to possess such wisdom that I would not have believed him capable of it had I not heard what he said. I couldn't reply and swallowed the emotion that welled up in me.

"Benjamin might not have been my brother at all. I don't know. He was with my family when they abandoned us both."

I looked down at the floor.

"Why did they do that?" I asked carefully. My voice sounded uncertain. I struggled with my own memories. The farewell to my father, the crossing, my destination. Had my family abandoned me, too? What was my destiny anyway? And why did the suspicion solidify that something was wrong with my memory? What had happened to the many girls who had set out on the same path every year, as I did? Not one had ever come back. To get rid of these disturbing thoughts, I shook myself. Little Benjamin's death seemed to go deeper than I wanted to admit.

"My family were market people; every mouth was one too many, and I was too small to earn anything. When I woke up one day, everyone was gone, and Benjamin was in my arms."

Strangely touched, I hugged this lonely boy and began to suspect that none of this left him as cold as it appeared. He was trembling and I hugged him with both arms. At some point, we both started crying because of Benjamin and everything we'd lost.

In the following months, I found that I was increasingly struggling with the heat and the harsh glare of the sun. During the day, I spent almost all my time at the horse trough, located not far from the town at one of the flooded river valleys of the Tigris. The proximity to water had become a vital necessity for me, a physical requirement. The filth and the heat were overwhelming. The water there was my only means of washing, and I took advantage of it daily. I would race anyone who challenged me, swimming alongside them. Laith, who had become a loyal friend and companion, even placed bets on my behalf.

At first, I rejected Laith's idea of shaving my hair off and protecting my scalp with a turban. But in spite of my cleanliness, I couldn't get rid of the lice that cavorted on every child's head. It didn't help that we plucked them out of our hair every evening; the next morning, it itched and we scratched again. At some point, the decision was made: the hair had to be taken off.

Laith asked for a bar of soap from the soap monger's stall that smelled peculiarly of rancid olive oil. But it lathered up well in warm water. He soaped his hair first and then I shaved it with the little dagger Jasemin had given me, carefully sliding it over his narrow skull.

Satisfied with my work, I ran my hand over his bald head. He grinned from ear to ear.

"Now the lice have to look for a new home!"

That made me laugh, but he also looked so strange without hair. Everything about him was now thin and smooth like the end of his arm stump. Would I look so weird too without my hair?

Much more skilfully than I thought, Laith shaved my head, too, and we both laughed for a long time. We imagined what a face the lice would make when they found out that we had robbed them of their house and home.

From that day on, I was only seen with a turban that covered my head and thus the treacherously marked forehead. Tarik—the translation of my battle name, Night Star—soon became known as one of the fastest and most cunning thieves in Baghdad. The town's beggar children said of him that at night he stole his prey as silently as a cat and was able to hide away as if his shadow had merged with that of the city.

But what use was the best reputation as a thief if there were others who envied it? In retrospect, I was sure that everything was planned. They wanted to hand us over on purpose, because otherwise I just couldn't explain why the Asakirs were there so quickly that night.

That fateful evening, Laith and I had followed a drunk who had stumbled out of one of the numerous taverns. We followed him like a shadow and soon found that he was alone and suitable as a victim. We stayed close on the heels of the slender man, who was remarkably well dressed and wore the khanjar, a crooked dagger typical of Arab noblemen, on his belt.

The nobleman staggered to the corner of a house in the shadow of an inn that was closed and relieved himself there. He looked around uncertainly, then swayed further and eventually sat down heavily on one of the crates scattered around. We could clearly hear him grunting and burping.

Laith and I waited a little longer, then crept up on tiptoe. He just responded with a sullen grunt when I nudged him with my foot. Finally, confidently, I put my hand in his belt and pulled out a pouch while Laith furtively kept an eye on the deserted street.

I carefully took out two silver coins and put the pouch back into his belt. I nodded to Laith, and we ran briskly back to our camp. My heart was pounding. Two silver coins! With them we could finally buy new fabrics for clothes that we needed so badly. Laith's sirwal barely covered his bum.

We looked forward to seeing the excitement on the faces of our gang and scurried up the ladder that led into the attic of the meat hall. Usually, we were greeted with curiosity, but this time, it was strangely quiet. Had everyone already gone to sleep? How long had we been on the road?

It was only when I let go of the ladder and stood in the room that I could see why it was so deadly quiet. The members of the Rabahs held the children of our gang around me. They threatened them with knives, sticks, and all kinds of weapons. Khalil was held by the leader, who towered over him by more than a head, and spoke first.

"I couldn't do anything, Tarik. They ambushed us." His voice sounded angry.

"It's okay, Khalil. I'll give you my booty and let them go."

It never occurred to me to endanger all the children because of two coins. The enemy leader's eyes fixed on me.

"Very sensible, Tarik. We don't want trouble. Put them down in front of you so that I can see them."

I dropped the two coins on the floor in front of me, clearly visible. Without hurrying, I took a few steps back and watched the Rabahs leader closely. For a second, he let go of Khalil and leaned curiously towards the coins. Carefully, he took them in his hand and examined them in the weak light that came up from below. He turned a little towards the hatch to get a better view. His long black hair curled like wool around his fair face.

What was going on in Khalil when he thrust the great leader of the Rabahs to his death, I couldn't explain ... It happened terribly quickly. A movement out of the corner of my eye. Khalil's face dashing forward resolutely. The moment burned hard in my memory.

"No!" I shouted with all my might and rushed to the hatch through which the Rabahs leader had fallen. Khalil was carried away, too. Both fell with a terrible roar, until a dreadful sound abruptly ended their screams. For a moment, it was deathly quiet.

We stood rigid with shock. The blood had drained from my face, too. I felt it tingle up to my lips.

"I'll climb down and check on them. Pull the ladder back up behind me and close the hatch. No matter what, don't open it. Do you understand me?"

My voice was trembling. The children nodded conscientiously. Whether Usamas or Rhabas, all looked equally horrified. I climbed the ladder carefully, rung by rung, and a completely dishevelled Laith followed me.

"You don't have to come with me, Laith; who knows what it looks like down there?" I tried to hold him back.

"I'll follow you everywhere, Tarik. I am your shadow," he whispered, trembling, but his voice sounded strangely convincing.

With so much obstinacy, I just rolled my eyes and continued to climb down. When Laith standing with both feet on the ground, I had the ladder pulled up again and the hatch closed. Maybe someone had heard the screaming and would come and see?

A little more light fell from the windows onto the floor of the hall, and I could quickly make out the two bodies lying there in the dirt. One of them was on top of the other, and together with Laith, I pulled the boy on top off the one below. He opened his eyes and moaned. Below him, Khalil became visible, his back on the floor; he stopped moving. I shook him desperately.

"Khalil! Khalil!"

My voice sounded hollow. I knew he was dead. Blood oozed from his ears and nose. His eyes were open. Black and lifeless, they stared at me as if asking for forgiveness.

Laith bent down to the other boy, who was moaning softly now.

"Hey, what did you do?" he exclaimed in horror. "Why did you come here?"

The great Rhabas leader only moaned.

"Why didn't you look for another victim?"

Suddenly, a rough male voice echoed through the room. Laith and I winced and turned around in shock in the direction the voice came from. The dark outlines of a black figure stood out against the gate that had previously been the entrance to the hall, but now both wings were missing.

Then another figure arrived, with a torch that cast a ray of light on the cruel scene, and in the dancing light, I was able to recognise who the two men were. They wore the

Asakir red vests. Now the nobleman, whom we had last seen as a drunkard behind the tavern, and whose silver coins I had stolen, joined us. He was suddenly as sober as the two henchmen who grinned triumphantly at him.

"We've finally caught a big fish in our net here. Two of the leaders are lying there, and that's the one they call Tarik. Their punishment will keep this city calm for some time."

They loomed threateningly and moved forward to arrest us. They held their curved long swords in front of them to keep us from escaping. Laith had a look of agony on his face. Did he know what would happen to us now? I took a hasty step towards the approaching men and stood in front of the trembling Laith.

"I was the one who stole your money, Mister! Nobody else was involved. I can give it back to you."

I clenched my fists and tried to keep my voice firm. It made me feel braver. The nobleman stood squarely in front of me and laughed.

"You little busybody! You want to divert suspicion from the others, but I know that nobody here is innocent. We've been trying to track you down for many months. And you … ", he growled and stabbed me in the chest with his finger, "you are one of the worst plagues in this city next to the rats."

He turned to the Asakir and barked: "Take them all directly to the governor, and throw the dead one into the river."

197

He laughed disparagingly, then took the two coins that had fallen next to Khalil's body and gleamed in the firelight. It was a trap. A damn trap! And we were fooled by these corrupt scoundrels. This nobleman had just pretended to be drunk and let us rob him. His henchmen then only had to follow us to our hiding place. Why hadn't I noticed that?

The other children! My gaze shot up unobtrusively; the hatch was still closed. By all gods, at least they were safe. But Laith and I were lost. That evening the cards were being reshuffled.

The governor hadn't even opened the door for us at first, but sent word via his sleepy, yawning servant that he would not interrupt his night's sleep because of three street children. With that, he left the nobleman to decide on the sentence. It was as if luck had finally left us. Our fate was sealed. The two Asakirs kept us between them, so we had no chance of escape. We even had to support the Rhabas leader, whose leg protruded at a grotesque angle. His face under the black curls was pale and twisted in pain.

"Chopping off a hand above the wrist is the standing penalty for theft," announced the nobleman, proclaiming our verdict so triumphantly, as if it were the best news of the day. He transferred us over to the rough hands of the two henchmen. With brutal force, they dragged us to the market square where the sentences were to be carried out the next morning. We were supposed to spend the night before our punishment under the watchful eye of one of his underlings. With a smug smile, he let us know that he would provide for a competent executioner with a sharp hatchet and, of course, for a Medicus to take care of us.

A terrible shiver ran through my body. Laith was in shock and trembling incessantly. I hugged him and wanted to be brave for him. His crying and the occasional moaning of the other boy, whose leg they had barely splinted with a piece of wood, was the only thing I heard that night.

The night had settled over us like a silky blanket. It was quiet and still warm in the city that had lain all day in the heat of the sun. Between the stalls of the market people, we sat in the sand, which at lunchtime glowed like an oven, but which now offered us a soft and warm place to sleep at night. I was far from sleep, my heart rumbled in my chest like a startled chicken, and my nose was running from suppressed tears.

How could it have come to this? Khalil was dead. Had he been a pawn? Would Laith and I share the same fate tomorrow? Would we be branded for our lives because someone feared for his good reputation?

This much was certain: tomorrow, the Rabahs boy and I would lose our right hand in front of the onlookers, while Laith would lose his last remaining hand. What was to become of him then? Another stab went through my chest. He would never be able to work again, only beg, if he survived. Many people had already bled to death during this ordeal or died from shock. I had to listen to a number of horror stories when we children waited for sleep in the dark, small attic room. Laith survived it before. Would he get through it again? Would I get through it?

The market was very busy that morning. The order of the day was severing the hands of children. The executioner had already arrived, only the promised Medicus was not yet present. Laith had cried all night and was now lying apathetically in my arms.

I hadn't slept for a moment. My head ached from my thoughts and anger over what had happened. The executioner set up his block of wood calmly in front of our eyes. He was wearing the black clothes and the red vest of the Asakirs. Instead of a turban, he wore a mask that only exposed his eyes, mouth, and nose. No matter who was under this mask, he should not be recognised, because his job did not make him very popular among the townspeople. Now he put a log on the block, took aim, and rammed his huge, curved axe into it. He repeated this a few more times, and every time the cutting blade hit the wood and it cracked, I winced. It was an ordeal that the executioner obviously enjoyed, and that took all our courage away. The edge of my turban was now soaked with the sweat that ran down my forehead in rivulets.

The Medicus, who finally arrived, first took care of the boy's broken leg. After all, he owed that to himself and his guild. He was a small, older man who didn't look at us. His hair was covered by a brightly coloured cloth that he had tied around his head with a ribbon and that fell to his shoulders to protect him from the sun.

So that I wouldn't have to watch him straighten the bone, I looked the other way. I nervously kneaded my hands, probably for the last time. My unsteady gaze went over the market square, where quite a few onlookers had come together.

There! In the shade of the palm trees, I caught a glimpse of the other street children. They had all come! Rhabas, Usamas, children of all ages crowded anxiously against the walls of the houses as if they feared they would be brought before the executioner together with the three poor delinquents.

The executioner had now stacked the freshly chopped logs into a pile and lit his own fire with the guard's torch. After inserting large black pliers and a hook, he stood upright with his arms crossed next to his block of wood. The muscles of his upper arms and broad shoulders indicated that he had been practising the art of sword cutting for many years. His expectant look under the black mask first fell on us three trembling children, then he looked over to the Medicus.

201

He came to me resolutely, took Laith out of my arms, and placed him in front of the Medicus. Laith let it happen and kept his head down. The Medicus had a wrinkled but not unfriendly face with little button eyes that seemed to capture everything that was going on around him. They fixed on Laith, and he spoke to the terrified boy in a calm, aged voice.

"Can you hear me, child?" he asked, lifting his chin with one hand. He shook his shoulder lightly with his other hand. "What's your name?"

Laith didn't answer. The Medicus took his small left hand, felt the pulse, and frowned. After a while, he looked at the executioner carefully; the latter just shrugged his shoulders, arms crossed over his chest. The nobleman, who had just hurriedly arrived, went to the two waiting henchmen and asked, a little short of breath, as if the end of his patience had been reached, "What is the matter with the boy?" His voice had a coldness that did not allow mercy to be expected.

"He's apathetic and his pulse is very low. I would like to give him a little more time," replied the Medicus thoughtfully.

"Nothing doing," replied the man with the khanjar in his belt, shining golden in the sun. "He's just pretending to be deaf so he can escape his punishment!"

The Medicus sighed in dissatisfaction but finally nodded to the executioner, and one of the Asakirs roughly grabbed Laith, dragged him to the wooden box and put his left arm on it. The executioner raised the massive ax. But suddenly Laith came to life again: he began to fidget, his white face twisted with terror into a grimace, gasping for air, and when the axe darted downward in one swift blow, I screamed with him.

Laith's left hand fell from the block of wood. He slid lifelessly to the other side, where the Asakir left him carelessly.

"What about him? What about Laith?" I shouted. I wanted to run towards the battered body. A rough hand held me back.

"Let the Medicus take a look." My guard stopped me angrily as I tried desperately to tear myself away. A hard slap in the face sent a sharp pain through my skull and took my breath away. From my eyes, blurred with tears, I saw the Medicus lean over Laith, take his pulse, and finally shake his head.

I felt sick. I could hardly believe it. They killed him. Laith had not only lost his second hand, but his life, too! Panic gripped me like an iron fist. Something happened to me that made me scream like crazy. Completely beside myself, I used all my strength not to have to go to this block of wood that stood threateningly in front of me. Strong arms grabbed me, carried my wriggling and screaming body there, and brutally pushed me down. I screamed and hissed with all my might, and my tormentors struggled just to hold me. The executioner struck out again. I suddenly fell silent in fear of death as the huge sheath of the axe hung over me like a threatening shadow. Then it zoomed down.

I expected a crash, a splinter like before with Laith, but it was only a dull, hideous thud. My head was turned away by one hand and held in place as if with screw clamps, so I only saw the faces of the audience, who suddenly put their hands over their mouths in shock. Then the pain hit me like a wave. It took my breath away and exploded in my head. My eyes finally went black.

It was the Medicus who reacted first. Despite his age, he swiftly ran to the boy with the unusual eyes and pulled him away from the wooden block. He hung unconscious in his arms like a wet sack, and the blood soaked his bright robe, turning it a deep red. The executioner cursed, "Put him back down, you quack, and with the next blow, he'll be finished!"

"Stop!" called the Medicus, his fragile voice loud enough even for the noble, who hurried over. "It is not allowed to hit the same delinquent twice! The executioner has to let him go! The punishment of the delinquent is carried out with the first blow. That's the law!"

With one arm, he clutched the boy, holding his wrinkled, knotty hand protectively in front of him. The nobleman looked impatiently at the executioner, who shook his head and shrugged.

"I can't understand why the hand is not off. That has never happened to me. I aimed precisely," the hangman moaned.

Ignoring the two, the Medicus laid the boy on a blanket and pressed a cloth and one of his leather straps on the wound to stop the bleeding. The unconscious child's skin was cold, showing the seemingly unreal blue veins under the skin. The little turban that hung crookedly over his face was sweaty, sticky, and stained with drops of blood.

It was immediately clear to the Medicus that something was wrong here. But he also had no explanation for what he had just seen. His hands trembled as he tended the wound. Usually, he had his emotions under control; he had attended executions too often for that. Taking care of injuries to torture victims or determining death after an execution was routine for him, and as a Medicus, did not normally affect him like the fate of this boy here.

What had just happened, and why did this boy's strange face so captivate him? Was it his eyes or the way he proudly held his head? He had to find out …

"The next one!" the noble shouted out between pressed lips. It was the Rhabas leader who was now being dragged in with his wooden splint tied to his leg. He howled loudly in fear or pain. The executioner aimed precisely this time; after all, he wanted to prove to everyone that he knew his trade. The audience held their breath, and with one blow, he severed his hand precisely from his forearm.

The boy's piercing scream was drowned out by the applause of the audience. The Medicus, who had hitherto leaned protectively over Tarik, taking care of the arm, now reluctantly left the still unconscious child on the floor and hurried to the next bleeding stump. Unbelieving and angry looks were directed at the hunched over child in the turban. There were screams of retribution, but also pleas for mercy.

The Medicus glanced briefly at the nobleman, who was discussing loudly and furiously with his henchmen what to do, then at the child on the floor. He realised that he had to react quickly. It was a miracle that this delicate little hand was still hanging on the child's arm! And as a healer, he knew how to read such signs. Why Allah chose him for the decision remained a mystery to him. He was old and couldn't protect the child, but at least he had to try. Inshallah—God willing ...

The old healer had closed the stump of the third boy's arm with a red-hot iron and then bandaged it. Now he gave the body and the surviving boy into the care of the executioner, and with great effort, picked up the still unconscious Tarik from the floor. The crowd finally broke up, grumbling that there were no more punishments. The market had come back to life, customers were waiting, and making money was more important.

"Stop!" shouted the nobleman and stood in the way of the old man, his face marked with anger and disappointment.

His eyes flashed angrily at the Medicus, sweat stood on his forehead, and he had saliva on his lips from screaming.

"Where are you taking him? I'm not done with him yet..."

The old man looked at the child in his arms, then at the face disfigured by rage. In a voice that sounded old but firm, he said, "I'll take the boy with me. After all, I could use help now. Eyes that see better and hands that are calmer than mine. Since the boy here is a slave and no one has made a claim on him yet, I am doing so here."

"A slave?"

The nobleman's jaw dropped. Indeed, the boy's soiled turban had slipped slightly from his face and the mark on his forehead was clearly visible—the slave's cross. As if to underline his demand, the Medicus ran his thumb over the mark. It literally seemed to glow on the white skin. The nobleman turned angrily with his fists clenched. He glared fiercely at the executioner and his two henchmen, who looked down in alarm. Without saying a word, he trudged to his governor with the two perplexed Asakirs in tow. He didn't have good news.

Chapter 10

Isaac ad Din Abu l'Abbas washed his hands with soap at the only spring in the oasis. Again and again, he scrubbed away the scent of death, blood, and fire. He then dried his hands on a clean cloth and rubbed his tired eyes. Exhausted, he squinted into the dim light of the small fire he had kindled near his wagon. Beside the fire lay the slim figure of the child he now felt responsible for. Their encounter had changed his life in an instant.

The child was a sign that there were people who were different—people destined by Allah for a higher purpose, much like Jesus, Moses, and Mohammed have been once. Isaac didn't know why Allah had chosen him to help this child, but he was determined to fulfil his task. As a devout Muslim and scholar, he regarded it as a rare honour. What his task entailed, however, was still unclear to him. For now, he had saved this child from a cruel fate.

Isaac sat down next to the little bundle wrapped in a blanket. He stared worriedly into the pale face of the child who lay sleeping before him. He grumbled and growled, unable to put into words what made it so special. He only saw one child, something he was denied in his life. He had long since buried the dream of a family.

While he was washing the child, he was surprised and irritated when he noticed that he had saved a girl. Why should God send a girl to speak to believers?

But the sign was not deceptive. A miracle had indeed happened, and he had witnessed the greatness of Allah. He had taken another look at the girl's hand in awe. It was cut halfway to the bone, but the rest of the arm was uninjured. He had seen it with his own eyes: the executioner had aimed exactly at the spot above the wrist, the axe had slipped off the bone and had bored into the block of wood instead of the arm.

Isaac shook his head, reviewing the images over and over again in his mind. Allah must have truly great plans for her!

He had sewn up the wound and dripped some of the clear liquid from one of his vials onto it. Then he had wrapped neat bandages around it, with a wooden splint, and pinned them in place.

After endless brooding, Isaac bent down to the sleeping girl and checked the little patient's hand, feeling her pulse again. The skin was cold, but the pulse was steady. With a satisfied grunt, the old man pulled the covers back over the child and got up with a groan. A short, hard cough shook his lanky body and made him pause. With shaky hands, he carefully wrapped his utensils in a leather roll and put them in the worn bag in his wagon.

From this pocket, he took a water pipe and a bag of small balls. With a wooden spoon, he pressed the small white balls from the bag into the bowl above the glowing grate and went back to the fire next to the sleeping girl. There he put hot coals in the grate with a stick and put the hose in his mouth. With a few quick breaths, the contents of the bowl glowed red and he greedily drew the smoke deep into his lungs. He coughed, but not quite as persistently as before.

Isaac sat down next to the wooden wheel of his wagon and stretched out his legs. Slowly he relaxed, his thoughts became lazy, and the cough never returned. The night fell over him like a blanket. Now and then he could still hear the snorting of the draft horse, which was recovering after the hot day, and the night call of the owls waiting for their prey. He comfortably embraced the long-awaited tranquillity that took hold of him. Allah was now in control of his life. From now on, a lot would change, yes, maybe for the better. He released his thoughts into a deep sleep full of beautiful images; his old body floated weightless and pain-free in a gentle dream. There was the slightly bitter smell of poppy seeds in the air.

I woke with a dull throbbing in my head, a sensation only surpassed by the sharp pain in my arm, which felt strangely heavy. The memory of what had happened jolted me upright, and the light blanket covering me slipped down into my lap.

My hand! I thought only with difficulty of the last moment before the devastating blow. Everything was clear to me again: the blow that had struck my arm, the doctor's surprised face, the cry of the crowd, my own ...

I looked at the stump of my arm, which was as heavy as a piece of lead, in confusion. The bandage was bloody, but there was no sign that my arm was shorter than the other. I carefully compared the lengths, moving my fingers carefully. Everything was still there!

How could that be? I heard the speed of the axe as it went down. I would never forget that terrible crack of the axe blade on the bone. The executioner had hit me above the wrist, where the bandage was now bloody. I looked at the carefully knotted bundle of cloth in disbelief.

Then I let my gaze wander over my surroundings. The pounding in my head had subsided a bit since I sat up straight. I blinked to clear my head and vision, and a smell settled in my nose that irritated me; slightly bitter, but not unpleasant.

Finally, I saw the old man with the mouthpiece of a water pipe in his outstretched right hand, leaning limply against the wheel of the big carriage. His body was comfortably relaxed, as that of a person in deep sleep. His headscarf prevented a better look at his face. But I also recognised him without a closer look: it was the old Medicus. Apparently, he had taken me out of town and now I was here with him in the desert, in the middle of nowhere.

My eyes fell again on the wagon with the large wooden wheels, which had a strange structure. Behind the driver's seat was a large, closed box with a door that was now open. From its roof hung loads of dried herbs, vegetables, and even snakes and chicken feet—the usual paraphernalia of a quack roaming around towns and villages. A little further away, an older grey horse with a drooping back was chewing on a bag of dry grass. Despite his age, he was well fed, his eyes glancing at me as if I were a competitor for his food.

My eyes wandered back to the blissfully sleeping old man by the wagon wheel. I got up cautiously and found that I was naked. My God, he knows! I felt boiling hot. He knew I was a girl! My hand went to my mouth before I could make a suspicious sound. Panicked, I looked around for my clothes, which I found neatly folded next to my blanket. I dressed quietly and with awkward movements. I held up my bandaged hand so as not to aggravate the painful throbbing.

Then I crept on tiptoe to my rescuer and kneeled down curiously. The water pipe had lost its ashes, and I took it in my hand for careful consideration. The belly with the water was carved entirely of wood with strange signs and runes. The mouthpiece on the hose was somewhat flattened and dark with saliva and smoke. I smelled it with fascination, and the slightly bitter smell in the air could clearly be attributed to this device.

"That's opium, my child," a rusty voice suddenly croaked in my ear. Startled, I looked into the face of the old man, who was studying me with his little weasel eyes—but not angrily, because he smiled gently.

"Opium is balm for my coughs, and the direct way to sleep!" he explained to me mischievously. His smile curled happily in the corners of his mouth and let some of the gaps between his teeth show.

I dropped my shoulders in relief. He wouldn't hurt me; I was suddenly sure of that. "I'm thirsty, sir. Do you have something to drink?" I asked.

The old man scratched his head awkwardly and then pointed with an outstretched hand at a leather pouch on the wagon. "Of course, girl, take the water bag there by the cart; it's full of fresh water from the oasis."

His eyes met mine and he nodded understandingly. Ashamed, he averted his face. "I wanted to wash you; you were covered in blood and dirt. I cleaned your clothes in the oasis there."

He seemed to sense my discomfort because he glanced briefly at me, then immediately away again and nodded a couple of times as if to apologise to himself. "I'm sorry, girl. Your camouflage was very clever, with your shaved hair and all ..."

I swallowed my pride bravely, got up, let cool water trickle into my mouth from the water bag, gurgled, rinsed and spat out the first sip. Only then did I take three large sips that moistened my parched throat and brought me to life.

"What are you going to do with me now, Master?"

I turned back to him suspiciously. The water was still dripping profusely from the corner of my mouth, and I wiped it away with my sleeve. I watched with interest as he slowly rolled onto his knees and then stretched one leg after the other as if his bones were hurting. He groaned, confirming my suspicion.

"I am Isaac ad Din Abu l'Abbas, a scholar from Persia and a student of Abu Ubaid Abd al-Wahid ibn Muhammad al-Juzdschani, a student of the even more famous Abū Alī al-Husain ibn Abd Allāh ibn Sīnā, also known as Avicenna in the Orient."

"I don't know either one or the other," I interrupted, unimpressed. Angry, his gaze wandered to me. His eyes still had a somewhat unnatural glow as if he had just awakened from a deep dream.

"Shut your cheeky mouth, girl!" he snapped at me. I realised that in his eyes I was a disrespectful child. Hot anger welled up in me, but I suppressed my desire to give him my opinion; after all, he had saved me.

With a stern look, but a little friendlier, he continued.

"Since I was not admitted to his hospital, I became a travelling Medicus. My way led me via Esfahan to Rey and from there to Baghdad. Yesterday at the market square, I saw something that shouldn't be." His weasel eyes now looked at me sharply. "Your hand should be off, but it's not. How so?"

His voice was implacable and harsh. He wanted to hear the truth, but I couldn't give it to him. I just shrugged

215

my shoulders and made him understand that I had no explanation, either.

He took two quick steps towards me and grabbed my good wrist. It was an unusually firm grip. His gaze fixed on me and he hissed through his teeth, "Why?"

I looked thoughtfully at my hand with the bandage. I nervously chewed my lower lip. Was it possible that such a deep wound could heal so quickly? Or was he just a good Medicus? Confused, I took another deep breath and looked straight into his clever eyes, which seemed to look deeply inside me.

"Damn it, I don't know why!" I burst out. "The executioner may not have struck hard enough?" But even to me, that seemed unlikely.

"Ha!" the old man said dryly, and again, "Ha!"

He turned around abruptly, took a few steps, and came back. In between, he looked searchingly into my face. Why was he so mad at me? Again, he turned and paced up and down.

"Say, Master ..."

He stopped abruptly with his back to me and lifted his head to hear me.

"Say, Master Isaac, why did you take me with you if you think something went wrong?"

As if to protect myself from his answer, I crossed my arms over my chest.

First, he turned his head and then his whole body in my direction. With two steps, he stood right in front of me and leaned forward, his head almost in front of my nose.

"I don't know. Maybe I took you with me because otherwise you would have been brought before the executioner again. Hopefully you realise that, right?"

I backed away, startled. "Did you have the right to do so?"

He raised his eyebrows in surprise, looked me up and down, and grinned. He looked malicious and gleeful.

"You, girl, have no rights; you are an escaped slave, and if no one else claims their rights on you, I will. You…" he spat and pressed his index finger to my chest, "… from now on, you will be my helper and replace my hands and eyes—until I know who or what you are!"

Disappointed, I closed my eyes. My freedom had been fleeting; the cross on my forehead had betrayed me. It was my wound mark, and it would remain so forever. My jaw clenched so tightly in my despair that my teeth ached.

He insisted on being called Master Isaac, claiming it was his rightful title. To me, he could have called himself anything—even imp—and it would have suited him just as well. As so often, I resigned myself to my fate and did my best to assist him wherever I could.

After all, he showed himself to be a strict but just gentleman despite his bizarre nature. In addition to harnessing and disconnecting his draft horse, and keeping the wagon and all utensils clean, my activities also included accompanying him to the sick—apart from preparing food and of course, getting food.

Medicus Isaac estimated me to be about twelve years old. To make this point, he only gave me a quick look before turning back to his work. With his usual meticulousness, he rolled the little balls, which looked like granular powder, until they shimmered in every imaginable colour. I carefully filled the small but effective medicine into sachets. We were in the wagon that turned out to be more spacious on the inside than it appeared on the outside. It was pleasantly dim there, which was a relief for my eyes. I spent most of the day inside, always listening attentively to what my master said.

While I was sorting some of these bags into the drawer provided, we agreed that I should continue to look like a boy. After all, a girl was not allowed to visit male sick people, and the fact that my body was not yet showing any feminine features made my disguise perfect. When he asked, I soon gave him my real name, Enja, which I hadn't heard for so long. But he shook his head and said, "This is not an Arabic, Turkish, or Hebrew name. With the best will in the world, your foreign origins cannot be covered up, even if you speak Farsi and Arabic without an accent."

For a while, he brooded and stopped in his work, then he made up his mind and continued to roll his fingers over the little pearls on his work table.

"I will call you Eran from now on," he finally announced suddenly. "That is a Hebrew name, very common among the Jews. It means to waken; that suits you."

And he grinned his mischievous grin again. "Also, most Medicus are of Jewish descent. They have always been allowed to dissect people. In many other religions, this was forbidden for a long time..." he explained to me. He scratched the base of his crimped beard.

"But you are a Muslim," I replied, "so can't I have a Muslim name?"

"No," he answered firmly, and his hand wiped the subject off the table with a jerky movement. "A Muslim is never a Muslim's slave. We'll stay with Eran, and you'll work for me."

That ended the discussion for him, and he turned back to his pills and pastes with his usual passion. In time, I was glad to have met such a learned person as Master Isaac. I learned a lot about the art of healing and the connection between personal hygiene and healthy eating, which seemed to prevent most illnesses from reaching us in the first place. Despite dealing with the sick, and sometimes with disgusting body fluids, we were both rarely sick, and when we were, my master had a cure for it.

I watched with interest as he created concentrates from nature's sources. In response to my relentless questions, he told me that he made them with the help of steam distillation, a process that concentrated oily essences and made them durable. In addition, I learned to recognise plants and animals as remedies, to collect them and to preserve them. That included keeping his small collection of extraordinary creatures alive. Frogs, scorpions, and snakes had to be cherished and cared for. He soon entrusted me with his extensive collection, which he looked after with such devotion that I often wondered how he could still find time for his patients.

And their number rose by leaps and bounds as soon as we approached a larger city. His reputation often preceded us. Usually, the messengers of the rich families intercepted us at the gates of the city to escort him directly to a sick person.

He used his knowledge of nature and the animal world to treat any disease. He was particularly fond of snake venom. He spent a lot of time with the elegant, silently meandering creatures and soon showed me how I had to grab the animals behind their head in order to milk the fangs over a small clay pot. It took me a while to lose my fear of these deadly animals, but at some point, I realised their importance and uses.

Mushrooms, plants, animals, everything that was poisonous seemed to fascinate Isaac, and he showed me his notes and findings with increasing confidence. Everything that was poisonous, he kept claiming, could also have a healing effect in small amounts. It just depended on the dosage. I became increasingly interested in his experiments and even supported him with my own conclusions. After a while, I was finally allowed to mix his medicines and pastes and distil herbal oils. Only his little pearls, as he lovingly called the coloured balls, did he still turn himself with the mischievous grin on his wrinkled face.

His wagon was a travelling conglomeration of curiosities: dried monkey penises; sharks' teeth; eyeballs of varying sizes and colours, frogs, larvae, and shrunken heads. Master Isaac had good connections in Asia, who secured his supply of unusual extracts, but often it was the patients who traded these unusual things in exchange for his medical help.

I learned a great deal in my time with him, except for the make-up of the small pearls, which he refused to share. Of course, it was these that especially attracted my interest …

I could convince myself of their effect personally, as we arrived in a larger city with our wagon. The city's name was Tehran and was well known for its cultivation of pomegranates. It was a very effective plant, according to Isaac, who was sitting on the seat of the wagon with me, delivering a short lecture about the intake of a concentration of this fruit's juice for heart problems, as well as the common cold. He himself took this tonic for his ailments and needed a supply of the best pomegranate juice. With a twinkle in his eye, he explained that there was a popular tavern directly adjacent to the market where this juice was for sale, and that we could meet there later.

The thought that it would be an expensive shopping trip went through my mind, and I rolled my eyes knowingly. For me, this meant that at some point in the night, I would have to pull him out of a tavern somewhere and drag him back to the wagon so that he could sober up. Unfortunately, the dear master often forgot that he was unable to tolerate alcohol, and together with his opium habit, he lost his ability to reason all too often.

As I expected, and as so often before, I dragged him back to his wagon after a night spent carousing. Gasping for breath, I propped him up against the front wheel since I couldn't go any further with his heavy body in tow. I covered him with a blanket and let him sleep it off. He, however, made so much noise that one would have thought he wished to wake the dead who lay in the adjacent cemetery.

In the meantime, I began to pack his bag for a visit to a sick person who had sent for him. The awe for a Medicus that prevailed in the Orient filled me with pride, since I was his helper. It always filled me with great satisfaction when a patient recovered due to Isaac's extensive knowledge, which I absorbed like a sponge in water.

"When you look at a person who is ill, consider not only the pain, but also notice the eyes, the skin, and the urine. Allow all your senses to function. Often, an odour can say a great deal about an illness. Ask the patient about changes in lifestyle, eating habits, or sleep. Each one of these is a part of a patchwork that, like a carpet, is woven into whole cloth which provides insight into an illness. Most important are the eyes. One glance into the coloured circle around the black pupil, and I can already tell you which organ is affected," Isaac often said when he was trying to explain his methods.

Ask about illnesses in the family—father, grandfather … an illness often skips a generation. And I recognise every drinker by the nose! Be aware that the nose often changes colour to red or blue and swells up. A decontamination usually brings the body back into balance again. The help is temporary, however; these people don't often live very long. Either the liver collapses, or they fall off a wall while drunk.

And he said this with a mischievous laugh that sounded somewhat like a rusty mill. Again and again, I found his observations of the world and its inhabitants amusing.

Medicus Isaac woke up that morning with a throbbing skull. He simply couldn't manage to complete the simplest of activities successfully, and even wrapping his own head scarf turned out to be an impossible task. Without reproach, I began to fix it to his hairless head with a few practised grips, while he sat listlessly in front of the small fire like a heap of misery. The water jug for his first mocha of the day was already hanging there.

From his dull eyes, I knew that the mocha should be a little stronger today, and I dropped a second spoonful of coffee powder into the small cup made of the finest Chinese porcelain. Then I filled it up with the hot water from the jug. His trembling hands could barely hold the delicate handle to bring the steaming cup to his mouth.

"Are you ready to inspect the patient, Master Isaac, or should I send a messenger to postpone the appointment until tomorrow?"

I asked politely so as not to point out his bad condition directly. Defiantly, he took a swig of the bitter brown broth, shook his head gruffly, winced in pain, and grimaced as he rubbed his temples with a knotty hand.

"No," he croaked, licking his dry lips, "I've never cancelled a visit for such an unimportant reason. This woman has been waiting for me for a long time, and I will visit her today because her condition is getting worse every year."

With brave gulps, he drank the mocha completely, his red eyes cleared a little, and finally, he thoroughly coughed out the mucus from his lungs that had collected during his sleep. After what felt like an eternity, he got up cautiously and, leaning on my arm, wobbled a little unsteadily towards the wagon. He looked down silently at the city of Tehran, which was slowly awakening from its night slumber. Mainly it was traders who moved past us towards the market square at this early hour. The sun couldn't really be seen yet, but the warmth of the coming day was already creeping into the clothes and leaving behind the warm, damp odour of unwashed skin. We didn't have much time to reach the shady streets of the medina of Tehran before the onset of the midday heat.

"Sit down on the driver's seat. I'll tidy up here and put out the fire," I called to him while I hurried off to fetch the horse that was tied to the cemetery wall.

A short time later, we were on our way to the rich family who lived in a large palace in the medina. As usual, we were first shown to a guest area that was reserved for men only. Refreshments, mocha, and the datiln I cherished awaited us there, to be consumed until the sick woman was prepared in her room. Master Isaac was a special guest of this family, and the friendliness with which we were received amazed even me, accustomed as I was to oriental hospitality.

The palace rooms were pleasantly cool and clean, pure respite in the hot and dusty air of Tehran. Despite my washed feet and the clean clothes that the meticulous master insisted on, I felt unusually strange and almost dirty as we were shown through the hallways and rooms. The wealth of this family was reflected in every room and corner. The sick woman's husband, who had received us in the guest rooms and brought us to her bedchamber, withdrew a little but did not leave the room.

Fatima al-Fihri was an elderly lady, but she still had great charisma. She was sitting on the edge of her bed with her face towards us. Big black eyes under the headscarf looked first at my master and then at me, and a gentle smile appeared on her delicate face.

"Master Isaac!" She greeted us with warmth and a soft, melodious voice that did not indicate her age. "How nice to see you again!"

With an elegant gesture, she held out her hand to him. Her fingertips were dyed red with henna and the back of her hand was decorated with beautiful flowers and lines. Doctor Isaac bowed deeply, took her hand in great reverence, and pressed it against his wrinkled forehead.

"May Allah praise your beauty, Sahiba Fatima—my dear friend!"

"I am pleased with your words, Isaac, precisely because I suffer greatly from my dwindling eyesight. I can barely recognise you."

Isaac had straightened up again and looked worriedly into her face. Of course, I was ignored as a servant so I set about unobtrusively getting the Medicus's bag ready. I hurriedly looked for a chair to sit on, and the host pointed out a stool in the corner. I was about to carry it to my master when the next instruction followed.

"Eran," he ordered me, "open the windows, I need more light. And get the lens out of my pocket."

Immediately, I left the stool next to him and did as I was told. The windows were covered with delicate silks, and when I pushed them aside, I remembered our clothes in the Fahrudin Palace. The fabric felt similar, cool but soft, and it had that sheen that I liked. I suddenly saw Jasemin before me, and I had to swallow at the intense memory. Where was she now? Was she okay? I felt like I could even smell her scent.

"Eran!" The doctor interrupted my thoughts harshly. "Where are you?"

Torn out of my daydream, I hurried to his bag and handed him the lens that he had cut and polished himself from a piece of glass. It enlarged everything he was looking at.

He sat down on the stool in front of the lady and looked intensely with the magnifying glass, first into one eye, then into the other. He sighed and grumbled as if speaking to himself, questions and answers in one breath. Finally, he put the magnifying glass aside and let the woman count the fingers he held up in front of her eyes. Unfortunately, she didn't recognise a single one.

With an almost imperceptible wave of his hand, he called me over. He gave me the lens, which, following his example, I turned to the old lady's eyes. Based on the clouding of the eyes, he now explained to me how far the blindness had progressed. I could clearly see how both eyes had a milky discolouration behind the once black pupil that made them blind.

Fatima noticed that I was standing right next to her and looked for my hand with her slender fingers.

"Who is the tender boy here, Isaac? Your helper?"

She squeezed my hand gently. Her skin was warm and silky like a rose petal, while mine was rough and cold.

She was corpulent; the silk robe flowed over strong shoulders. The dressing gown that covered her completely barely hid the fullness of her feminine curves. Her hair was not visible under the veil, but it was sure to be streaked with grey. Despite her advanced age, her skin was still as soft and delicate as a child's. The busty body was surrounded by a scent that was sweet and beguiling at the same time. She must have been a beauty once and accordingly adored. What a cruel fate that the world around her now became as dark as the eternal night. But she did not seem despondent; perhaps her family loved her so much that the loss of sight did not sadden her?

I gently squeezed her hand back and she smiled warmly. Master Isaac cleared his throat.

"Eran is my student. He has been with me for a long time and has become an indispensable part of my work. At some point, he will follow in my footsteps when I can no longer work, and I am sure he will be a good healer."

I stared at him in surprise. So, he saw me as his successor, equal and worthy of his knowledge, which he gradually passed on to me. He didn't seem to mind that I was a girl. As old and moody as he was, he had a big heart, and even more, a good mind. My eyes got wet, and I withdrew my hand from Fatima to wipe the tear away. I quickly turned to put Isaac's lens back in the bag.

"Then can you or Eran help me regain my sight? I would love to see my grandson, who was born three months ago. I ask you, Isaac, help me!"

He looked at me, the small dark eyes moved restlessly in their sockets, and he smiled knowingly.

"What do you suggest, Eran?" he asked, testing me.

I straightened up to my full height. "We have to remove the two lenses. With this, she will not regain her complete eyesight, but she can at least recognise outlines and distinguish between light and dark."

Isaac nodded approvingly. His serious face twisted into a mild smile, and he turned to Fatima.

"Eran has correctly recognised that the lenses in your eyes are clouded with age. We have to remove them so that you can see something again."

"I would be so grateful to you, Isaac! So grateful!"

And instead of my hand, she took his hand. He was clearly uncomfortable, and he got up hastily to withdraw from her loving gesture with the necessary respect. At that moment, I wondered if Isaac had ever been married in his life, but I couldn't imagine it.

"Do you agree, Sahib al-Fihri? Shall I prepare everything for the procedure, or do you need a moment to make a decision?" the old Medicus asked the husband, who was lying on one of the soft leather pillows where he had settled down. Now he got up and went to his wife, took her hand in his, kissed her, and looked lovingly into her cloudy eyes.

"My wife's wishes are the way to her heart. I will do everything I can to make her happy, Master Isaac. You will be lavishly rewarded by me for your efforts."

With that, he turned to us and looked at us expectantly.

"No matter how long you need for the treatment, you will, of course, be my guests until my dear wife has completely recovered."

Isaac nodded resignedly and set about preparing the medicines and instruments he would need with me. And on this occasion, I saw it ... his hand, which was now conjuring the small silver star stitch needle out of the leather case, trembled like a leaf.

Startled, I looked him in the eye. At that moment, he knew I had noticed, and his lips tightened grimly.

"Can I do something for you, Master?" I asked, piercing the sudden silence in the room as I nervously dipped the instruments in hot water. With such shaky hands, he would miss an elephant's eyes!

Isaac turned to Fatima and gave her one of his pearls, which she swallowed with some water.

"Today you will perform the procedure, Eran, just like last time," he explained without looking at me. With mock calm, he tried to pretend in front of Fatima that I had done it before. That was, of course, not true.

"You remember the drunken priest in Baghdad?"

Irritated, I rummaged through my memory. In fact, there had been a drunken priest, but he had operated on him himself. So, he wanted me to play in his little theatre.

"Yes," I replied a little frantically, "I remember."

My stomach contracted with excitement. Isaac just nodded in agreement. The woman, it seemed, was no longer listening to us at all. Her head fell slightly on its side as if she had fallen asleep. Isaac now moved her gently to lean against his chest and held her head firmly with both hands. I sat down in front of her and held her eyelid open with my free hand. After a moment's hesitation and controlling my breath, I lifted the rigid needle and put its sharp point in the right place. With that, I pressed the clouded lens, which took away her eyesight, to the bottom of the eyeball. Fatima would then recognise outlines again, and perhaps her grandson as well.

When the operation was over, we put a clean bandage soaked in a healing solution on the woman's eyes.

"This bandage has to be worn for seven days to allow the wound to heal, after which it is all over. Fatima will be able to see again," the Medicus explained to the husband, not without pride.

"Eran did a good job; he has steady hands and a good eye." He put his hand on my shoulder, heavy and shaky.

I swallowed, my stomach tumbling, this time with joy. Could it be that after such a long time of wandering aimlessly, I had finally found my purpose? Should I become a healer?

We stayed as guests for a fortnight in one of the richest houses in Tehran. There was an unbelievable wealth of the finest dishes. For the first time in my life, I tasted fermented date juice, the low alcohol content of which catapulted me into the realm of dreams after just two cups. I discovered that I just wasn't made for this type of drink, and I secretly admired Isaac for how he managed to pour some of it into himself without losing his mind.

Fatima al-Fihri woke up from her sleep at some point and could hardly wait another day to take the bandage off. When the moment finally came, Fatima wept tears of joy at the sight of her little grandson.

Isaac and I finally said goodbye to the overjoyed family with many words and gestures, and even more provisions for the rest of the way. Most of it was in liquid form, which our good master happily imbibed, contrary to his own words of warning, so he went to bed drunk almost every evening.

I wasn't sure if his hands were getting shaky from the alcohol or if he would let me do his job because it would give him more time to get drunk. In any case, word of our success got around very quickly in Tehran, and we—or rather I— had a lot of work to do. With every further procedure, every further illness I cured, my self-confidence and experience grew. Isaac limited himself to spreading his good name, assisting me, and correcting me if necessary.

For many, we looked like father and son, our cooperation was so well-coordinated. We'd both long since forgotten that

I was actually a slave, and a girl at that. The black cross on my forehead was well hidden under my turban, and I began to become more and more aware of my freedom, albeit in a defined environment.

The day on which my life changed decisively again was actually a wonderful day. I had already packed most things in the wagon and made mocha as always before I woke Master Isaac for breakfast. The sun was high in the sky and illuminated the stony path that should lead us to Rey, the birthplace of Isaac. A cousin lived there, and he visited him from time to time. Perhaps I would learn about my master's family, a subject that made him monosyllabic.

How old was he? Well over a hundred, I guessed. But no one could get that old! I was pouring the hot brew from the silver jug into his narrow cup, while Isaac, awakened by the intense smell of mocha, lolled with relish.

At that moment, a group of four men suddenly stood in front of me. I blinked in disbelief because I hadn't noticed them approaching. There was no trace of their horses. The cup in my hand suddenly felt infinitely heavy, and I put it back when my hand began to shake.

The men stood in front of me like statues, looking at my master and me. They had their hands casually in their belts, in which the usual khanjar was stuck next to a long, pointed dagger. It was part of every male costume in this area, a curved dagger in an elaborate shaft. The men were dressed in a strikingly light colour. Even the turbans were white, and their beards were cut short, which, to my reassurance, showed me that they weren't Shiite.

Quickly overcoming my surprise, I straightened my back and welcomed the men. I pointed to the place by the fire next to Isaac and offered them mocha and datiln, as befits good Muslims. This eased the tension a little. They accepted gratefully, bowed to the Medicus and sat cross-legged with us. My master's expression was tense; apparently, he knew who he was looking at.

They were young men, no more than twenty-five years old. One spoke in a refined Farsi with an accent that I could assign to the Turkish Seljuks. He explained to us the reason for their coming: his name was Nabil Al-Hakam. He was said to be a prince of the Nizarite King Hassan I-Shabbah and had been sent by him to find a Medicus named Isaac who was currently in Tehran.

"When we heard that you had already left, we decided to hurry after you because the matter was urgent. Our illustrious Grandmaster Hassan I-Shabbah, the ruler of Alamut, suffers from an illness that causes him great pain and his Medicus could not help him. Therefore, we ask you to come with us to heal him."

During his speech, Nabil moved his head in a north-westerly direction, where Alamut was probably located. Isaac remained strangely mute, turning the mocha cup from side to side in his fingers.

"Wherefrom had the Medicus of the wise sheikh determined that the pain was coming?" he asked the prince carefully.

"He said that the pain comes from the middle of the body and goes straight into his bowels, poisoning the blood there and pushing it out again with its water," replied his counterpart politely, but with an unmoved expression.

"What did he do about it?" Isaac leaned towards him, interested.

"He gave him an enema. He said it was the stomach and put him on bread and water." After a pause, Nabil said hesitantly: "But the pain remained."

"What happened then?"

"Hassan's Medicus made him sweat in hot wraps. He said it could also be a fever of the stomach. For three days he made our wise sheikh sweat and suffer. But the pain didn't go away."

"And then?" Isaac put the cup down and looked at him expectantly. I bit my lip. The poor Grandmaster must have suffered terribly from this treatment.

Prince Nabil shook his head slightly and replied coldly, "Then we cut off the physician's head!"

Calmly, he crossed his arms in front of his chest.

Isaac's face went white. My left hand went unconsciously to the frayed collar of my tunic, which suddenly became very tight around the neck. I looked from him to Nabil and then back again. Would Isaac be next now?

He took a short breath and replied, politely but firmly, "I can't help your Grandmaster now. I have an important patient in Rey whom I can't keep waiting. Maybe on the way back I can…" He got no further.

Prince Nabil had jumped up and assumed the posture of a predator. With one hand on the hilt of his dagger, he gave Isaac a cold look from his dark eyes. He hissed menacingly: "How dare you let our Grandmaster, the wise Sheikh and leader of all Nizarites, suffer! I'll take you with me, and I advise you to pack your things quickly. Because the more pain our Sheikh suffers, the more impatiently he awaits his healing, and the worse his mood is …"

"I'll harness the horse, Master," I called out a little too loudly, then turned around and ran as if driven by furies to our loyal grey horse.

Isaac got up slowly, and without a word, washed the dishes in a bucket, then poured the water into the fire to put it out. The thoughts milled in the rusty channels of his old brain. I could literally hear it creak and groan. Only on the way to the driver's seat did he announce loudly, "Well, I'll have a look at your sheikh, Prince Nabil, and if I manage to cure him, you will let me go—me and my faithful companion, Eran."

He pointed at me with his bony hand. A little nervously, I stood next to the horse and waited for him to hoist himself onto the driver's seat. Then I quickly climbed up to him and shakily took the reins in my hands.

Prince Nabil nodded and relaxed his posture again.

"I am sure that my illustrious Grandmaster will show himself appreciative, Master Isaac. However, if he dies, you will follow him."

With that, he and his men turned in a north-westerly direction and led us to the horses they had left at a fork in the road. They escorted us all the way to Alamut.

"Why did I have to be around?" Isaac growled softly. "To what whim of Allah do I owe this fate?"

"I'm sure you can heal him, Master. Who else besides you?" I replied encouragingly and was glad that the dark prince had turned his back on us.

"Pah!" he grunted unwillingly. "What if Allah takes him from us before I can do anything? Then we'll both die. Inshallah!"

He clicked his tongue loudly, and the faithful grey horse pulled the wagon, which was groaning under its load.

"Who is this Hassan I-Shabbah? It seems to me that you have heard of him, Master?"

My curiosity had overcome my fear. The noise of the iron cartwheels that crunched on the stony ground on the long way to Alamut drowned our secret conversation. Isaac screwed up his weasel eyes and chewed his lower lip. At some point, he nodded as if it hadn't been some time, just a few heartbeats, and then began to explain.

"You know that in Islam there has always been a dispute over the legitimate succession of Muhammad."

Isaac looked straight ahead, as if he wasn't expecting an answer.

"It began with the death of Muhammad in the year 632. The Sunnis saw the Prophet's father-in-law, Abu Bakr, as the rightful heir to the Imam's throne, while the Shiites were in favour of the son-in-law, Ali. The heads of the Muslims should grow from the loins of this rightful heir."

As if thinking, he licked his dry lips with his tongue.

"With the sixth Imam, Schaafar, there was a dispute about the succession. Schaafar died 173 years after Mohammed, leaving behind a family quarrel that continues to this day. Some believers considered Ismail's son to be the rightful heir, and this resulted in the Ismailis, who followed the Shiite belief. With the death of the eighteenth Imam-Caliph, the Nizarites or Sunnis split off, and they established themselves militarily in Persia under the Grandmaster and leader, Hassan I-Shabbah. He is now in his bed and squirms in pain. The wise Sheikh Hassan, as he calls himself, grouped his followers around him and trained them to be perfect murderers who spread fear and terror among his enemies in his name. Hassan was the only one in this troubled country to make friends and foes equally fearful. Even the Templars left him alone, because the fear was too great that one would not live to see the next day when one of his assassins had found his bedroom that night. A cut and ...”

Without saying it, he put his hand to his neck with a movement that had only one clear meaning. I swallowed.

As always, when he finished speaking, he folded his hands over his chest, closed his eyes, and dozed off. I let my gaze wander and admired the rough but impressive rock formation of the Elburz Mountains. The vegetation had long since disappeared, and apart from a few tough grasses and herbs, the surroundings were desolate, almost hostile to life. Despite everything, a well-developed path led us to the fortress.

After four endless hours through the barren mountain landscape, the bright sandstone walls of Alamut, "The Eagle's Nest" as the fortress was called, rose a good four hundred and sixty feet along a ridge surrounded by mountains, several as high as thirteen thousand feet. As Isaac told me, after Hassan had escaped his captors, he used political tricks to steal this citadel. He skilfully gathered like-minded people around him and turned Alamut into a fortified castle. His fearsome reputation was based on his specialty in killing adversaries and enemies in a tricky and cunning way. He trained his assassins himself to strike effectively and purposefully— sometimes for his own purposes, often for those of others who paid high blood tolls. His wealth, power, and reputation brought him dubious fame.

Isaac would have been glad not to have to follow in the unfortunate footsteps of the previous Medicus. Who knew what the Grandmaster was suffering from and whether we could even be successful? Diseases often took strange paths. His followers like Prince Nabil seemed very devoted to him, and that made them very dangerous. Isaac's tension was literally palpable, and now, when the huge main gate finally opened, this tension also gripped me with an icy fist.

Inside Alamut, there was surprisingly lively activity— almost like the market in Baghdad, I observed. The scar over my right wrist itched. The cart creaked to a halt in front of one of the stone houses that leaned against the castle wall like a tired peasant. Now some boys in simple frocks and linen trousers hurried out to harness and feed our grey horse.

We were taken straight to the Grandmaster's apartment. Presumably, the pain made him forego any hospitality. The part of the castle that was reserved for the king actually consisted of only two chambers. The rest of the building was made up of the great hall and further chambers for the servants and supplies. Although the fortress was astonishingly large, it had to accommodate many warriors, slaves, and helpers.

The small group of assassins with whom we had come here were greeted by like-minded people who, with their elegant clothes, like Nabil before, reminded me more of nobles than of cunning murderers. The colours white and gold dominated their magnificent coats and turbans, and I felt as if I had been transported back to the time in Fahrudin's palace. However, there was a dangerous aura surrounding these men, which only heightened the smouldering fear that rumbled in my bowels.

In the middle of the bedroom into which we were now led was a large bed with a canopy made of heavy silk, shiny gold brocade curtains, and gold cords. The walls and floors were covered with ornate carpets showing oriental patterns and scenes from mighty battles. The groan of the hunched over person on the bed gave me goosebumps.

So that was he, the dreaded Grandmaster, Lord of the Assassins, the hostage of the Ismailis and the Crusaders, who was as feared as he was hated. A tortured face looked at us, grey with pain. Black hair, sticky with sweat, lay in a mess on his head, and his lips were dry and split open. Shaded eyes were in dark sockets. An alarming sight. Isaac next to me emitted a faint hiss. Strangely enough, his cough was better up here in the thin air. I knew exactly what he was thinking. Hopefully, it wasn't too late ...

We bowed low and introduced ourselves. Dark eyes looked at us with disgust.

"Another new quack, Nabil?" growled the sick man. A shadow of a beard had settled on his skin like a dark premonition. Nabil hurried to allay his concerns.

"The best Medicus in Tehran, my lord! He's our only hope now," he announced with a bow, his gaze brushing our faces. We noticed the unspoken warning in it.

Isaac had sweat on his forehead and my hands were damp. Nervously, I slid his bag, which I had carried protectively in front of me, onto a nearby chair and looked for the examination instruments in it. Ear tube, lens, urine cup.

The servants carefully sat the tormented man upright and supported his back with pillows. His upper body was bare and glistening with sweat; the black hair on his chest clung wet to his skin.

Isaac cleared his throat, sat down on the bed next to the suspicious-looking Sheikh, and felt the heartbeat on his hand. My mentor looked into Hassan's eyes with the care and thoroughness that was so unique to him, felt his stomach and back, talked to him about his pain, the nature, the frequency and the location. How, when, where—according to Isaac, the three most important questions a healer should ask.

Finally, he asked him for the urine, which Isaac examined intently. As was his way, he barely said a word about what he was thinking but let me be part of it all. The Grandmaster's companions became restless. The tension in the air seized me again when Isaac suddenly asked me, "What do you think, Eran? What can it be?"

I sensed that he only wanted to test me because he knew what was wrong with the wise sheikh.

"The gallbladder, Master. It has stones that go into the tubes and cause pain. They poison the stomach from the inside out because the digestive tract is clogged with the stones."

His look was full of pride as he nodded and asked in his rasping voice what to do next.

"We have to stop the poisoning, preferably with a tea made from nettle, sage, and ginger."

"What else?" he asked hoarsely.

"Maybe one of your miracle pearls against the pain?"

He smiled mischievously and nodded.

"Good! But how do we get the stones out of his stomach?"

I thought nervously as I searched his wrinkled face for inspiration. We recently encountered a similar case in one of the suburbs of Tehran. We gave the patient a liquid that loosened all the stones from the bladder. Unfortunately, he died a few days later. His body was already too poisoned by the gases in his stomach.

The thought made me swallow involuntarily, and I felt as if an ice-cold hand had placed itself on my chest and squeezed. I saw his approval in Isaac's attentive eyes, and he nodded to me almost imperceptibly. My breathing was suddenly hectic.

"Master, we should make him a brew. I will give him the brew during the night; tomorrow morning, he should then excrete all the stones."

Isaac looked at me, his dark weasel eyes shadowed by tiredness and worry, then he put his knotty hand comfortably on my shoulder.

"A good decision, Eran. So be it." He sighed resignedly and led me to understand that we were now dependent on God's help alone.

The pain subsided with Isaac's miracle pearls and first released him from his torment. While Isaac was boiling the brew in the wagon, I tried to pour the nettle tea into the Nizarite leader. I could see that his stomach was puffed up unnaturally—a result of the toxic fumes that had developed in his intestines. I tried hard to control my hands that wouldn't stop shaking. Hassan's breath slowly calmed down. I wiped off the sweat on his skin with the cloths his servants kept bringing me.

We were not left alone with the sick person for a second, and our actions were viewed with suspicion. My throat tightened at the thought of what would happen if he died under our hands. Isaac didn't seem to mind. Either he had better nerves, or he trusted his medicine completely—or maybe even more, his God? I wished I had a god at that moment, too. The only thing left for me to do was to trust in our knowledge, and in Isaac.

A little later, he came back to the bedroom with a knowing smile and the brew. While we were giving the patient the brew, he kept falling asleep, exhausted thanks to the painkillers. At night, I woke him up for the next portion of the brew.

While the Medicus was snoring in an armchair that had been provided, I didn't shut my eyes all night. This was due on the one hand to the brew that I had to give the patient over and over again, and on the other hand, to my fear that our treatment would not lead to the desired success. Just when I was about to give the last brew early in the morning, the sheikh suddenly was in a great hurry to get out of bed. He hurried to the chamber pot. Isaac and I glanced at each other, tense. Now it would be decided whether our drug had worked. After a short time, Isaac went to see whether the sheikh had passed the stones, and a little later, confirmed the success of our treatment. Those were, of course, the unpleasant sides as a Medicus, and I can assure everyone that a sheikh stinks just as much as a farmer when it comes to drainage. But I was never so happy to see the yellowish, spongy stones that, along with the digested matter, were ejected from his gallbladder. They were witnesses to our endeavours and ultimately the first road to recovery.

The tension in the room eased somewhat, and I even managed to smile encouragingly at the weary Hassan, who had retired to his bed again. He fell asleep immediately. It took another three days for his body to break down the poison. Countless teas and herbal brews later, the inflammation was diminished and the sheikh regained his strength.

Completely exhausted, I could hardly hold the bowl with the broth that the Assassin king was allowed to eat as the first food. Because of fear of failure, I had barely slept for the past three days and nights. Finally, Isaac took the bowl from me and sent me to bed with a stern face.

"Go to sleep, boy. You look like death. The wise sheikh will survive, that's for sure, and so will we. Go to bed now, and when you've had a good night's sleep, we'll leave."

His voice was gentle and understanding. He knew I had worked hard for both of us. Trusting in Allah alone would not have been enough for me. He smiled encouragingly at me, then sat down next to the bed and fed the rest of the broth to Hassan, who had a little colour in his face again.

I got up with my knees trembling. I bowed a little shakily to my Medicus and the sheikh and trotted with sagging shoulders into my little room, which was opposite. I fell on the bed fully dressed and fell asleep in the next heartbeat.

When I woke up, the sun was high in the sky and had warmed up my little room so much that I jumped out of bed wet with sweat, undressed, and used the bucket provided to wash myself. Meanwhile, thanks to Isaac, I had clean clothes. It consisted of the usual bloomers made of fine linen and a shirt that, instead of laces, even had silver hooks for opening and closing. The embroidered vest featured blue and red traditional patterns. The colours were repeated in the clasp of my turban, which I still wore over my forehead and neck. I now carefully tucked the end of the long cloth behind my ear and pushed the blue-red clasp over it.

With this, I felt strong enough to say goodbye to the Grandmaster. Full of expectation, I opened the small wooden door of my chamber and was amazed to find an armed young warrior with the assassin's light turban and a curved gold dagger in front of it. We were in the fortress of the assassins; maybe the young man was ordered to protect me?

On the way to the hall, to which he accompanied me because he was supposed to lead me to Isaac, I could already hear the stubborn voice of the Medicus ringing through the corridors.

"I'll go where I want! No one, grandmaster or not, has ever dared tell me what to do!"

I imagined his sullen face all too vividly; the small eyes could flash so angrily, and the hands could wave wildly in front of his wiry body, as if he were catching flies in the air. I couldn't help smiling at the thought. The narrow spiral staircase led directly to the hall from which the voices came, and I took two of the stone steps at once so as not to miss anything. My young guard stumbled hastily behind.

What I then saw left me speechless and swept the smile off my face in a flash. The recovered sheikh sat on an ornate wooden chair at the table in the great hall. He seemed to be arguing with Isaac. His gaunt face, still marked by the serious illness, exuded such hardness that I froze as I moved. His angry black eyes were fixed on Isaac like two daggers. His mouth twisted into a thin line, the muscles of his jaw working ceaselessly under the pale skin. There was a deep crease between his eyes. The wiry Isaac was standing in front of him.

"You will take his place, Medicus, whether you like it or not! In this castle, I decide," the assassin leader growled, letting his fist fall on the table. Startled, I winced and looked at the others at the table, who showed no emotion. His confidants sat or stood around him, including Nabil Al-Hakam, who leaned casually against one of the rough stone pillars and, bored, cleaned his fingernails with his curved dagger.

Isaac paced up and down in front of the table, his robe billowing, wrestling with arguments. The tassels on his knitted belt swayed from left to right, and his grey hair moved wildly in all directions. He urgently needed a shave again, I noticed absently. His face was red, and his eyes flashed angrily.

"I'm not going to be your Medicus! Not now and not later, never! No Shiite dog dares to thwart my intentions! Allah will crush you if you force me," he hissed, crossing his arms in front of his chest as if he were underlining his statement. His voice almost cracked. I had seldom seen him like this. He had to have a reason for his anger that he would surely explain to me later.

"One last time, I am not negotiating. I will pay you a princely wage—you and your assistant. I need you here and now until I'm tired of you. My word is law. There will never be a 'no' because that means your death. Do you understand me?"

Hassan's voice had taken on a tone I didn't like. He looked like a snake with a poisonous bite; cold, calculating, and deadly weight in every word. His voice grew lower and lower.

The hall had become as quiet as a mouse. All I could hear was Isaac's loud huffing.

As if lost, I stood in the middle of the great hall that had been built on the rough rock floor. It was amazingly cool. All the blood drained from my face when I realised what was going on, and I stared at the two adversaries in horror and with my heart pounding. At that moment, I held my breath and inwardly prayed that my master would make the right decision.

Isaac balled his fists, drew in a heavy breath, and clenched his teeth angrily. His gaze fell on me, and I saw in it his conflict, almost a guilty conscience. Suddenly, he turned around with a jerk, stomped to the front door, and only hissed a disparaging curse that made the heat shoot up in my face.

He couldn't get to the door. Two assassins, positioned to the left and right of the door, shot forward, drew their long daggers from their belt in one fluid act, and pierced the old man's chest. He probably didn't even feel the dull thud of his body on the rock floor. Isaac hadn't even raised his arms to fight back. So, his decision had been made: he would rather die than lose his freedom. Was this Allah's Will?

A terrible fear and despair seized me. Before I could scream, I felt a shadow slip past behind me. Nabil Al-Hakam's face appeared in front of me for a split second before a hard blow to the head sent me into a black void.

Chapter 11

Scotland in the summer of 1305

The dragon's head on the bow of the ship seemed to glide out into the open sea as if by magic. For the last time, I glimpsed the faces of my loved ones in the front row of the crowd, bathed in the early morning light. I tried to etch my father's face into my memory forever—his fair hair fluttering in the wind, his visage glowing with kind eyes.

"I will never forget you, Papa!" I cried out desperately. I kicked the blanket, which had nearly suffocated me in my dream, sending it flying to the stone floor in front of my bed. Wide awake now, my body trembling and drenched in sweat from the nightmare, I sat up, swung my feet over the edge of the bed, and tried to steady my breathing.

It wasn't the first time such a dream had pulled me from a deep sleep. Over and over, the images from that time haunted me. But now, for the first time, I sensed that something was wrong with my dream. The sadness of my mother on the ship, the final farewell. Had it always been a point of no return? Did my family know where the ship was heading?

Many of the images in my head were blurred by the filter of time. As the years passed, the certainty permeated my consciousness that all the girls before me had been sacrificed back then. My mother's words were still very clear in my memory ... When you see your parents once again in the hereafter, you will be like the gods. You alone have the power to do so with your destiny.

She had come to terms with sending me to my death as the chosen one. The volcano Hekla, as our grandfathers had often said, had already cost many people their lives, and so every village was to appoint a girl once a year to honour the gods. Only now did I begin to understand what purpose I should have served. If the ship hadn't sunk, I would probably no longer be alive.

Wide awake and agitated, I brushed my hair back from my face. It was so similar to my mother's: white-blonde, silky and smooth. It was true that she had worn her hair loose, sometimes braided, but never combed back as strictly as I did; it was the most beautiful adornment that she possessed, next to a silver brooch with the clan mark.

With renewed energy, I sat up and called for my maid, who was sleeping on a wooden mat in front of my door. It was less than three seconds before she knocked politely on the door.

Vika was an orphan who survived a fire in her village as a child. Her eyes and long, wavy hair were dark, but her skin had a milky complexion that almost made her rosy cheeks glow. She would have been considered a beauty had it not been for the overgrown scar on the right side of her face, which ran from nose to ear and covered the skin with thick adhesions. This resulted in slightly distorted facial muscles and affected her beautiful smile. Now she stood in the doorway, curtsied, and held out a bucket of steaming water to me.

Apparently without much effort, she ran barefoot with her heavy load to the simple wooden water basin next to my bed and poured the hot water into it. In the meantime, I took off my shirt, which was still damp from the sweat of the nightmare. With practised movements, she helped me wash myself and comb my hair, while I rinsed my teeth with sage and cleaned the gaps with silk thread.

With one look out of the window, which had been open all night, I could see that the sun hadn't risen yet. The castle was in a deep sleep except for the guard who checked the gangways of all castle walls at regular intervals. The hills and valleys that rose gently like waves in the water around the castle were still a misty grey. Birds and insects hesitantly started their daily concert of singing and chirping.

Vika got my black wrap pants, which could be tied at the waist, and my long-sleeved black shirt, which was laced at the front. Finally, I slipped my arms through the leather vest Vika was holding ready for me. It was closed at the front with silver hooks. All weapons, from swords to throwing knives, were ready to hang in the loops and pockets.

The scabbard on the back was exactly at the angle required to pull the weapon blindly overhead with the right hand. Left and right on my chest were the throwing knives and the castration sickle, a very useful weapon. The tailor-made vest was indispensable when faced with an enemy and fit like a second skin.

The scabbard with a Highlander dagger hung on the belt that I wore over the leather vest. This was a handy short sword with a sturdy, pointed knife blade. There were also various loops for axes and quivers of arrows on this belt, but I only hung them on when necessary; otherwise, they would have hindered my freedom of movement.

Finally, I slipped into the sturdy leather boots and pulled the top buckle to close. With a nod. I dismissed Vika, who shot out of the room like a whirlwind to prepare my mocha in the kitchen and to announce my imminent arrival to the stable boy.

I calmly gathered my straight hair with a leather band at the back of my head. Then I twirled my shock of hair and tied another leather cord around the knot. I took the silver scabbard with the little dagger that Jasemin had once given me and tucked it between the hairline and the knot. I often wondered if I should just cut my hair off, as I did when I was still disguised as a boy. But it was one of my few feminine traits.

Smiling at my touch of vanity, I went into the great hall to enjoy my mocha with two datiln. The scent, warm and sweet, reached my senses on the stairs. Vika had already put the small cup in my place in the great hall. I had quickly got used to the fixed daily routine.

At the table, I greeted my two warriors Kalay and Winnie, who were already busy with a bowl of porridge, as they, like me, began their combat exercises early on. The two were quite different in their appearance as well as in their nature, which ensured constant amusement with their mutual teasing— one blond, tall and slim, the other black-haired, short and strong. They would never have admitted it, but actually they were inseparable.

I ate a bowl of porridge, and a little while later, I got up to meet my horse. The little stable boy was already standing in front of the gate with my groomed and saddled stallion to spare me the trip to the stables. Taycan snorted. I looked around for a moment. Besides the servants and maids, I wasn't the only one up so early.

Hal was already sitting on his huge white horse, one leg across in front of him, as if he had made himself comfortable on one of Saladin's seat cushions. He was bored and chewed on a piece of jerky that he must have taken from the kitchen. He might look terrifying to anyone else, with two axes in his belt, but I had gotten used to the sight of him long ago.

Probably none of the kitchen maids dared to refuse his wishes, and at least three of them had ignoble thoughts. It was a mystery to me what induced the maids to admire his manhood. I still saw the boy in him that he had once been, albeit with a few more muscles. I blinked inconspicuously at Hal, who only now noticed me and shoved his foot back into the stirrup.

"Pretty late today, leannan!" he growled hoarsely. There was no movement in his face. He often called me "sweetheart" in Gaelic because he knew it would annoy me.

With a flowing movement, I swung myself into the saddle, and with the click of my tongue, gave Taycan the signal to leave. On the way to the big castle gate, I passed the strong white horse of my comrade-in-arms, who joined me. I measured him from the top to the stirrup, leaned over to him a little, and whispered ambiguously: "Sweetheart dreamed of you today, Hal! Believe me, I would have preferred to wake up earlier." I gave him a mocking look and rolled my eyes theatrically. "Every minute was torture ..."

Hal's face twisted into a grimace. He shook his head and pretended to actually laugh.

"If I've made it into your dreams, I am a gifted man. But I doubt I managed to make a special impression there. In any case, in my dreams, you are always unattainable."

I grinned. "Not only in your dreams, Hal, believe me!" I gave him a loving nudge with my fist.

Laughing and smirking, we finally rode out of the open gate onto the wooden platform that reached far into the lake and formed the ramp to the ferry boat that was tied up there. The two horses, without hesitation, found their way onto the boat with the flat hull, which was built like a small part of a bridge.

On a rope that ran over a pulley in opposite directions, a donkey at a wooden wheel pulled the ferry to the other bank, on which a similar platform made of masonry stones had been built.

Caerlaverock Castle was built in the middle of a lake. There was probably a monastery there earlier. Today, the three castle towers, which were surrounded by mighty walls, rose like threatening fingers from the water. The triangular layout of the castle was something completely new to me. It was considered impregnable, as the Maxwell clan credibly assured me.

In the last attack by the English king, however, it was so badly damaged that the Maxwells had quickly built a new clan seat a few miles away. Shortly before winter and without an army of workers, the chief had no other choice. The clan's new fortress was only a few miles distant and would be their headquarters for the next few years.

I was now the mistress of the castle Caerlaverock, and I had rebuilt her with the help of the Maxwell clan. We were still working on adding another keep for the valuable horses. The idea of replacing the bridge to the large gate with a ferry had not only saved us the effort of rebuilding, but another decisive advantage was that in the event of an attack, we would not be vulnerable if we destroyed the ferry beforehand.

In a few minutes, we had reached the shore of the lake. The horses trotted effortlessly out of the boat onto the mainland, and we made our way to Corbellay, the highest hill in the area.

The fog was still deep over the wet meadows. The horses' hooves made a sucking sound with every step. A few full-throated toads promised themselves the blue of the sky, which at this point in time was still more of an ash-like grey with a few light stripes. They already gave a foretaste of the light of the rising sun, which quickly spread its warmth over the land in the summer.

Most of the time, we made it to the summit in silence, but today, Cathal, as Hal's full name was called in Irish, seemed to have something on his mind. He rode his good-natured white horse next to me, shifted back and forth in the saddle a few times as if he couldn't find the right place, and kept his eyes straight ahead.

"Do you remember the Douglas clan from whom I picked you up after your ..." He stopped.

"Mmh ... accident?" he finally asked.

"Of course," I replied, surprised. "I enjoyed their hospitality long enough." The memories of this stay inevitably focused on a person I hadn't got out of my head for some time.

A few breaths later, he continued hesitantly, "The clan has been attacked by King Edward. The old chief, William Douglas, was arrested and brought to London, where a trial for treason awaits him."

I hoped Hal wasn't looking at my face because the news got under my skin. I couldn't help thinking of stubborn old Douglas, who was so proud of his resistance to King Edward, and of little Matthew ...

"What happened to his family?" I asked as casually as possible. James came back to my mind—the noble face, the man with the fine manners and the warm eyes.

"His wife was killed on the spot, as were many of his followers," Hal said matter-of-factly, but I felt the gruesome news like a blow in the pit of my stomach.

"His sons survived the attack, and they were probably thrown into the London Tower dungeon with their father. They will also be tried if their betrayal can be proven."

Hal's sources were always reliable. He would never divulge anything that wasn't true. The shock was deep; deeper than I wanted to admit to myself. William Douglas was certainly not an easy man, but something about him had won my heart—perhaps his unwavering belief in a united Scotland. James, on the other hand, was the only man besides Hal who had impressed me so much that he kept creeping into my thoughts.

Strangely, my heart was pounding restlessly. My words when we parted came to mind. I had promised him that I would help him should he ever get into trouble.

"Why are you telling me this, Hal?"

I stared straight ahead. My stallion seemed to sense my tension, for he had craned his neck and pricked up his ears as if he were expecting the worst.

"Well," he stretched his answer and ventured a sideways glance. "I thought that you cared somewhat for the Douglas clan, or more precisely, about James Douglas ..."

This cursed pig-faced knave! Since that time, he has kept on teasing me about the handsome son of the clan chief. He poked the wound again and again, even though I had only made one comment in his presence.

Taycan immediately stopped at my signal; so did Hal's horse, and we assessed one another over the horses' backs.

"Cathal Conchobhar Ó Searcaigh." I addressed him in a very formal manner, using his full Irish name so that he knew I was angry. His eyebrows, hidden by a thick layer of black ink, shot up. He hated his full Irish name.

"James is the only man I've ever spoken to you about," I continued sternly, "but that doesn't give you the right to see more in it right away."

I took a deep breath. My anger couldn't mask my grief. I wanted to end this tiresome discussion once and for all.

"I don't want to hear any more about it. Understand?"

Without waiting for an answer, I firmly pressed my heels into my horse's flanks, whereupon it obediently began to move. For a few excruciating minutes, my thoughts were with James and his family, and Eleonore, who had so changed her older husband for the better.

My God, little Matthew, what may have become of him? The face of Callie, the bright young maid, appeared in my mind's eye …

When Hal caught up, I burst out, "I have to do something, Hal. You know very well that I can't pretend I don't know anything. I'll ride to London; maybe I can help him."

I suspected he was grinning and didn't look back at him; otherwise, my fist would have landed in the middle of his face.

Later, I took out my anger and frustration on him. In our daily morning exercises on the flattened peak of Corbellay, Hal was left behind this time. He took my blows with stoic equanimity, and by the time he finally surrendered, I had vented my greatest anger, sweating and panting.

Exhausted and breathing heavily, I sank to my knees and felt the heated waves of my emotions give way to a clear mind. What remained were sore muscles and the determination to help James and his family.

Hal stepped up to me and offered his calloused hand to pull me up. My gaze fell on his mildly smiling, sweaty face, which looked so terrifying with its martial painting. But underneath was a man with a big heart. Strangely moved, I grasped his hand, which grabbed mine like a vice and pulled me up.

"The timing was well chosen," I blurted out, still catching my breath as I stood. He tilted his head, questioning. Thoughtfully, I released his hand and turned away, preparing to mount my horse again.

"Anger is a poor advisor. The combat practice has channelled my energy properly. My mind is now clear for what I must do."

Hal knew the moment he shared the news with Enja that she would set off for London. He had heard it from a merchant in Dumfries, with whom he had traded for many years. The word had spread like wildfire throughout the area, as the Douglas estate was one of the largest in the region, and the family had been a powerful ruling dynasty in southwest Scotland for decades. The English occupier, Lord Cardiff, was a thorn in the side of the Scots, for unlike his Scottish predecessor, he had no concern for the welfare of the people. On the contrary, he intended to bleed the land dry as punishment for the Scottish resistance.

The Scots' uprisings took on dramatic proportions due to the brutal occupation. It was only a matter of time before Caerlaverock and the Maxwell clan would be held accountable. The long overdue question about the transfer of ownership of the castle to its rightful owner—Princess Enja I-Shabbah ibn Hassan I-Shabbah—should be clarified at the London Court. At least this was the pretext that now urged Enja to leave for London. So far, neither the Scottish lairds nor the English king took their claims seriously. Actually, she was only tolerated on this land, which she had received from the Maxwell clan.

Of course, it was as clear to Hal as the water in the Highlands that Enja was concerned about the well-being of her life saver, James Douglas, and his family. With more force than intended, he lashed the girth of his white horse, which had to take a step to the side to compensate for the strong jolt on his saddle. No, he wasn't jealous of this upstart, he just didn't like the look in Enja's eyes when she talked about him. He had firmly believed that she was immune to the advances of men. Had this varnished monkey James Douglas managed to break through her defences? Had she been fooling him, Hal, all these years? He looked over at her inconspicuously as she gave the final instructions to her entourage. They hung on her beautiful lips like tadpoles on water plants, Hal thought angrily, and let the saddle flap fall back with a clap. Why should they be any different from him?

Everyone had come to say goodbye to their mistress and their clan chief. The warriors whom Enja had trained, as well as the healers, the teachers, and the infantry. A motley crowd of grateful women, men, and children whom Enja had devoted herself to in the last few years and for whom she would have fought to the last breath. The awe was written on the people's faces, but also the fear that it would be a journey of no return for their leader.

Not only were the roads to London dangerous anyway, in addition, there was the merciless attitude of the English king towards Scotland and the difficult legal position of women. Hal doubted Enja would ever be able to claim property as an unmarried woman, whether as a gift or not. In this country, men ruled.

An uneasy feeling had been with Hal all morning without him knowing why. They knew the country well enough, knew which way to take, and were well equipped for the dangerous journey, but convincing Enja of the dangers of her mission was just as fruitless as explaining to the Scots that uisge beatha was unhealthy. This stubborn woman did not want to hear about it. She insisted on entering the royal court to present her petition. And if this would not be stupid enough, she would speak for the Douglas family—what madness!

Tenderly, he scratched the neck of his white horse, who probably sensed that his master was tense and now nudged him with his dark nostrils, as if he could thereby dispel his brooding thoughts. Hal shook his head. The fire in Hell would sooner be extinguished than he could bring this madwoman to her senses! He had no choice but to accompany her on her way to the lion's den. Of course, if he had to, he would fight for her until the end. Hal had taken this woman into his heart, even if as a man she, in her own words, needed him "as much as a wart on her bum."

But that was exactly what attracted him to her. Why did he have to bind himself to this woman who would not hear him? After all, he was by her side, closer than any other man. This was enough for him as long as no one else took up this space.

It was our first trip to London, and the time of year was suitable for such a long excursion. In mid-August, the rain was repeatedly interrupted by pleasantly warm hours in which the sun dried soggy clothes, leather, skin, and hair.

Unlike Hal, I loved the Scottish weather. I didn't mind the rain or the wet; on the contrary, the sun drove me away rather than the rain. When Hal basked in the sun, shirtless, I would retreat to the shade and doze under my plaid—a long, woven scarf that the men threw over their shoulders or attached to the saddle. It protected me from rain and cold as well as from the sun. The women in our clan had designed an inconspicuous pattern for me that consisted only of grey and black colours. I carried it proudly over my shoulder, like all Scots in this country. It hadn't taken long before the grey and black striped checks of my plaid appeared on my people's clothes. Visible to everyone, they wore the mark that proved that they belonged to a very special clan; a clan that consisted of a wild mix of people from all over the world—my clan.

To have this confirmed and recognised by the reigning English King Edward, a king who hated all Scots, would be a difficult task. Scotland still did not have an official king. After the last ruler, Alexander III, died without an heir, Scotland was initially left without a monarch. Sixteen successors were vying for the Scottish throne at the time. Sir William Wallace, who had returned from exile in France, fought desperately against the annexation of Scotland by the hated Edward.

Wallace officially called himself Guardian of Scotland since he had no right to the throne because of his descent. In spite of this, or precisely because of that, the Scottish nobility did not stand united behind him. Torn by the wars against England and the feudal power structure that denied the nobility claims to the country in a war, it was still not possible to appoint a king. In addition, after the Battle of Dunbar in 1296, large numbers of the Scottish aristocracy were still incarcerated in English prisons. The deeply rooted hatred between the two countries was felt in every corner. Edward was desperate to nip any rebellion in the bud and wanted to make an example of William Wallace, the hero of the Scottish Resistance. The last message I had received from my clan friends was the successful capture of the charismatic fighter. It had been a slap in the face of the proud Scots. Would Scotland be humiliated and crushed once and for all after Williams Wallace's death—which I assumed?

So, what could I do but take the path of support for a clan laird in the middle of the border area? It was time to introduce myself to the English court. After all, I was a woman with a title who had received a lot of attention in the Orient but was hardly worth a penny in this country. Even so, I would demand my rightful claim on Caerlaverock and its lands. It had been given to me by Clan Maxwell, more precisely by Clan Leader Roderick Maxwell, as a thank you for saving his son.

Hal stretched his massive torso and then rolled over on his side with one elbow propped up. The black ink drawings covered his skin. I remembered his standing before me as a young man, awkward and helpless—a sight that could only soften one's heart.

Nobody would have bet an ounce that he would become such a strong warrior. He had considerable ambition and despised death like no other. His emerald green eyes met mine. He assessed me under the cover of the plaid and gave me a smile. If I didn't know better, I would say that I had a special place in his big heart.

"Should I catch a fish for us? The carp should be spawning," suggested Hal in his hoarse voice and straightened up. "A bath wouldn't be bad, either," he added. "I guess I should catch the fish first before I drive away everything living in the water with my stench!"

That made me laugh. I jumped up to enjoy the cool water and took off the leather doublet that held my weapons.

"Turn around!" I asked him, but he just crossed his arms on his chest and grinned.

"I won't think about it in my dreams," he replied with his deadly serious roguish demeanour, which really suited him.

"If I ever meet your mother, I am going to have a word with her about your manners ..."

I turned away from him with a smile. After the vest, I took off my shirt and pants and walked the few steps to the lake, which glistened invitingly in the sun. As soon as the water washed around my legs, a shiver of relief went through me. Sweat, tiredness and the constant eye pain that I felt when I was exposed to intense sunlight were suddenly gone, like magic. Behind me, I heard a big splash in the water, and Hal snorting and wheezing.

I dived quickly and glided through the dark waters of the moor lake. We were in the northern marshland and the waters here were murky and dark. Nevertheless, it awakened my spirits in this unbearable summer heat. My head broke the surface of the water to get a breath of air.

Hal had only waded into the water up to his waist and was splashing water over his massive torso. He didn't like to swim. Water was only good for him to drink. The muscles beneath his Celtic tattoos played, and drops of water pearled from his goosebump-covered torso. I eyed him openly. Shrivelled evidence of his manhood dangled lost between his thighs.

I was about to dive down again when I saw movement next to our horses out of the corner of my eye. My eyes stopped just above the surface of the water. Two men dressed in rags were trying to steal our two horses. They pulled and tugged on their halters.

The horses just shook their heads reluctantly and continued to graze calmly. When the men realised they weren't getting anywhere, they sneaked over to rummage through our belongings. They came across my discarded leather vest with the weapons.

Because Hal was still making loud noises in the water, they became bolder and pulled my sword out of its sheath. In a flash, I dived and swam past Hal to the bank, jumped naked onto the rocky edge, and in a few steps, was at the two thieves, who stared at me in horror. One held my vest, the other the sword, which he now put in front of him as if to defend himself. What an idiot!

The anger boiled hot inside me. What were they thinking? In a few seconds, I assessed and grasped the situation. Hal's pile of clothes was closer to the bank than mine, and the two axes were still beside his belt. But even these weapons were too far away. Without further ado, I took a handy stone, many of which lined the bank, and threw it into the perplexed face of the thief who was closest to me. His head was thrown back from the force of the impact, and he dropped his prey in shock. Another stone followed, and another. Again and again, the precisely thrown projectiles rained down on the bodies of the poor street thieves. They ran away, completely frightened, as if they had only just noticed with whom they had become engaged.

Behind me, Hal stormed out of the water. With fervour, he let out a battle cry that accompanied the two of them on their hasty retreat and made me turn angrily to him.

"Don't roar like that! I'm not deaf!" I yelled over my shoulder, causing him to stop in his tracks.

"Besides, they are already gone. You don't have to pretend you have the situation under control!" I continued caustically, with clenched fists. When I turned around and saw him standing in front of me with nothing on except his brightly painted skin, I suddenly had to laugh. He looked at me as if I had gone crazy. His eyes darkened noticeably.

"The two could have robbed us," he muttered. "We wouldn't have gotten far without weapons." His gaze slid down to me. "And especially not without clothes."

A dangerous flicker crossed his green eyes, the low sun made them shine like lush green moss. I had to admit that at times I had a lot of respect for him. He was an assassin like me, and a damn good one at that. He seemed to notice my scrutinising gaze and looked past me quickly, as if to hide his emotions.

"Come on," I urged him in frustration, "we have to move on; the worst heat is over."

With that, I grabbed my clothes and got dressed. Hal did the same, silently, and followed me back down the path which, although winding through a dangerous area, was the shortest route to London. How fortunate for us that this trip had so far gone without any major problems. Even the horses kept up the constant fast pace, and the breaks at the inns on this much-travelled route were good for us.

Only our appearance seemed to irritate some of the simple people along the way, as we were armed to the teeth and ready to fight. Hal didn't have to strain to nip unsolicited questions in the bud; one look from him was enough and we mostly had our table to ourselves. Except for this little incident in the English swamps, the gods were kind to us ...

London, August 23, 1305

The deep ruts on the road to London were a clear sign that the ground was usually muddy, but today the streets were dry. The two riders gave their horses loose reins, allowing them to cautiously navigate the crusty, uneven tracks without stumbling. As soon as they passed the city walls, they were met with a stench that could only come from a place teeming with people. It was a blend of manure piles and rotting compost, mixed with the scents of roasting meat and yeast. Hal always wondered how people could live here, but he supposed their sense of smell must have dulled over time.

Quite a few people stopped and watched them make their way through the dusty and dirty city. In many places, the paths were sprayed with water to bind the dust, and the rivulets that formed in the process often contained the faeces of the local residents.

The horses bravely trudged through the mixture of dust and rubbish until they came to the city gate, guarded by Edward's soldiers. The guard suspiciously stopped them and asked what they wanted. With their striking clothing and martial weapons, they differed from the pedestrians who otherwise moved through this gate. They looked at Hal, so he answered for Enja, who didn't even look at any of the soldiers.

"We are a delegation of the Maxwell clan, seated in Caerlaverock to petition the king," he said in his hoarse voice. The older of the two soldiers, who was probably also of a higher rank, made the two of them wait for another soldier to accompany them to the castle.

The young man with the goatee who escorted them through the city proudly explained the location. London was the island's capital, and its population was growing rapidly. Life in the city was dominated by Norman merchants and local artisans who found plenty of work here. Other, less fortunate residents ended up on the gallows or in the gutter, as the two of them saw as they passed through. Beggars, minstrels, charlatans—Enja looked fascinated at the multitude of people who were looking for happiness in the streets of London, or simply a change in their monotonous life. Rich and poor, farmers and knights mingled here in the hustle and bustle of the markets, and there was even a horse market on the edge of the town market. From there, loud roars and nervous screeching could be heard over and over again.

The Tower of London, fortress of King Edward, rose farther in the background like a threatening fist. It was built by William the Conqueror on a hill to the west of the city and had been expanded in recent years. Hal wondered if the stories surrounding the dreaded fortress were true; it was always imposing.

Not far behind the city gate, the street noise was drowned out by loud roaring and whistling. Another market? But the closer they got, the more it became clear to them that it was a gathering of people attending an execution. From the backs of the horses, they had a good view of what was going on at the podium, which attracted the attention of the audience. Spellbound, Enja and Hal stopped their horses in the midst of the howling crowd. A man sentenced to death was being tortured by an executioner on a block of wood in front of them.

The agonised screams of the victim were dreadful enough to course through the body and soul of every person with good hearing, all the way through the bone to the marrow, but those present did not seem to mind in the slightest; on the contrary, they cheered the executioner on. Hal looked at Enja, who followed the scene with interest, then watched the audience and stared back at the half-dead victim, who had now passed out. With a precision that could only have come about through years of practice, the executioner now severed the head and held it up by the hair. A frenetic cheer broke out among all the bystanders.

As the crowd gradually dispersed in all directions, Enja turned to the young man with the goatee who had politely stopped with the two of them.

"Who was the delinquent up there, and what was the crime that condemned him to such a cruel death?"

"A Scottish traitor, my lady," he replied politely. "His name was William Wallace; he had stood against King Edward and thus against the English crown." And with a glance at the market square, he added with fervour: "No one else deserves death more than he does!"

Enja looked again at the gruesome scene in the market square and unconsciously rubbed the scar on her wrist. Slowly, the scope of what was happening in London dawned on her. She had witnessed an example here. A monstrous display of Edward's power and sustained destruction of Scottish resistance.

"How is it that this condemned man was not executed with the sword? You'd think King Edward was afraid of this Wallace, that he'd send him to such a death?"

The curiosity in her voice cleverly masked her true feelings.

"Well," said the young soldier patiently, "it is not my place to form an opinion on the culprit there, but since King Edward, this manner of death is the only punishment pronounced for treason. Thieves or murderers die by hanging. Heretics, on the other hand, usually die by burning."

"Ah," Enja added with interest, "then heretics will also be burned here?"

"No, because of the stench and the fire, they are burned in the eastern market square, where the city wall is right next to the place of execution. It can better withstand flying sparks."

Bored, he indicated that they should go on, and Enja thoughtfully detached herself from the execution scene on the podium, in which now hardly anyone seemed to be interested. A few of the groups were engrossed in lively conversations that were certainly related to the death of the freedom fighter Wallace.

Enja silently turned her horse back in the direction of the road. She didn't show her discomfort. Cruelty and brutality were no stranger to her, but such a disgusting method of sending a convict to the afterlife required a stable stomach.

Had Hal been less religious, he would have worried about Enja. But he had wisely sent numerous prayers to his God that she should be put under his protection. Anything could be expected of a king who was so merciless with his enemies. And if God didn't care about Enja, then he was still there.

Soon afterwards, they were in fact received at the royal house. The news of a Scottish delegation visiting to clarify property ownership had piqued King Edward's interest. After all, the Maxwell lands were in the border region and could potentially be of interest. Following days of hearings by the king's chancellors, Enja and Hal were finally granted an audience with the king. In the meantime, they had found a room in a small inn not far from the English royal residence.

For the third time within a week, they rode through the mighty castle gate of the third ring of the fortress. Today, at last, they were to be admitted to the king; their patience had been put to the test in the last few days, so they made their way to the fortress with corresponding expectations. The day greeted them in the morning with a sad grey, and the clouds kept dropping raindrops, sometimes so suddenly that there was hardly any time to take shelter. The two noticed how many workers were working feverishly on the outer ring of the castle. The men huddled together like a wild anthill to cart stones, rubble, and sand to the construction site. They all seemed to have a common goal.

This time, the household guard actually allowed them inside the castle, which was protected by two additional fortress rings. Inside, a massive building of light sandstone with four outer towers rose, the size and extent of which reached a height and form that even towered over the cathedrals of that time.

Enja tipped her head back to look at the towers.

"This is also where the king's bedroom is located," Hal said, reminding her of the young soldier's proud remarks on arrival. With a mixture of curiosity and discomfort, they got off their horses, which were immediately led away by a stable boy. They were surrounded by the king's bodyguards, who brought them inside the castle. Again and again, they met servants, courtiers, and clergymen who stared at Enja, in particular, with undisguised curiosity.

Unfazed, she strode proudly through the ranks of soldiers towards her goal—King Edward. Today, she had even donned her golden belt, a symbol of her recognition as a warrior. She also wore her diadem of pure gold, with a sapphire set at its centre, large enough to completely cover her slave's cross. It symbolised her high rank as a princess and bestowed upon her an authority that commanded considerable respect from the court servants.

Many glances lingered first at the diadem, then at her face and her hair, which she had pinned up with the silver dagger as always. She did not correspond at all to the usual image of a woman. They had left the long swords at the palace entrance, as was customary at court.

Hal shrugged as the two wings of the ornate wooden door to the great room opened and a long line of dressed up courtiers stood before them, bowing to them. A marshal loudly announced the guests from Scotland and drew the attention of the king, who sat on his throne at the end of the room and spoke animatedly with his confidants.

The mention of Enja's title made some of those present sit up and take notice. The king's shrewd but not particularly kind eyes looked the newcomers up and down and hung on Enja's golden diadem. The large sapphire on her forehead could easily compete with the splendour of the English royal family.

Enja and Hal bowed to the king, who had laid his arm casually on a backrest and now asked them to speak with a wave of his hand. Enja took a step forward and carefully began to speak in French, the language customary at court.

"Your Majesty, it is an honour to stand here before you and to express my request. I have travelled all the way from Caerlaverock, previously owned by the Maxwell clan, to make my request for an instatement of this property. Since I was not born a Scot, I would like to show you my claims as my king and serve you as mistress of the lands and as a loyal subject."

Edward's cold eyes narrowed and his gaze bored into Enja, who was not unsettled by it. His Majesty's black-grey hair looked dull and stringy, as if it hadn't been washed in a long time. Overall, the king looked tired, as if he were ailing. His complexion was a little yellowish and his eyes were wrinkled. His mouth formed a pinched line.

"You are not a Scot. You are a woman, and not even a Maxwell. What in God's name makes you want to make any claims?"

Enja swallowed but was not deterred. "Caerlaverock Castle was given to me by Roderick Maxwell, head of the Maxwell clan, as a thank you for saving his son. I took refuge there for my people, and for years as a vassal of the Maxwells, turned the castle into a fertile and economic place. For my enfeoffment by Your Majesty, you would receive taxes directly from me and my loyalty as a vassal of the English crown."

With the last sentence, she bowed her head politely. An excited whisper among the courtiers present suggested to

Hal that they hadn't seen many women with such a confident request. He was proud of his leader, who had come from a life as a slave to such wealth and influence.

And to present her request to King Edward and thereby build a gate to Scotland for him was a clever move. Should that succeed, she had a good chance of standing up for James Douglas as well. Hal could see that the king was considering this possibility, too. He leaned back a little and crossed his arms.

"So, she's a stranger in this country? Where did she come from then?"

One of his advisors pointed out who was standing to the left of the king—a stout man with bags under the eyes and a grey beard Enja turned to him.

"I don't know in which country I was born, but I grew up in the Orient and was under the care of King Hassan I-Shabbah, who also gave me the title of princess because of my boldness."

"Then you are not a princess because of your blood?"

"No", Enja replied, irritated, "this title is an award for training to become the highest warrior and gives me the right to acquire property as a free woman and also to grant fiefs, similar to what a knight is allowed to do in this country."

A lean nobleman with a prominent nose snorted mockingly and said, "Knight, eh? That doesn't mean that we have to recognise your title as such in this country. Where would we be then!"

Approving murmurs and nods from bystanders accompanied his derogatory announcement, which worried Enja a little. What if he was right and they didn't even recognise her title? Nevertheless, she remained calm because only a cool head could move strategically on the chessboard of politics.

"Roderick Maxwell personally signed the property over to me, and as a free noblewoman, I accepted his gift. Recognition by the English crown would give you my absolute loyalty ... "

She got no further because the king got up hastily and took a step towards her.

"Enough!" he interrupted her. "What nonsense to claim land as a woman, especially with a title that anyone can come up with. If you want to continue living there, you just have to marry a Maxwell, and then there will still be a Maxwell laird there and not you, Princess Enja!"

His voice had grown louder. His advisors nodded their heads pleasantly. Enja swallowed. Her pride had suffered a severe blow. Still, she didn't flinch and stubbornly lifted her chin. Her voice took on that resolute tone Hal knew all too well: "I'll never get married just to keep this castle. It already belongs to me."

"Then you defy my will and the laws of my kingdom?" The king's demeanour suddenly looked threatening. His slender, sinewy body leaned forward like a cat before a leap.

Hal suspected what was going to happen and tried to pull Enja back, but she shook his hand from her arm.

"Here at your court, it's probably all about titles and men. If my loyalty is worthless to you, I must turn to the future

Scottish king to clarify my ownership claim. Maybe Robert de Bruce is ready to listen to me."

Hal closed his eyes in horror. Enja had never understood when it was time to withdraw. It was her damned temperament and the insistence on her rights that would eventually kill her. He had prophesied that to her many times before.

The English king blushed at the mention of his archenemy and then roared at the guards who were to arrest Enja for treason.

They had to get out of this room alive. Hal prevented the worst by grabbing Enja by the arm and whispering to her not to fight back now. He would get her legal counsel, and she would be free in a few days.

What occurred next happened incredibly quickly and was completely out of his control. The guards took off her weapon skirt and tied Enja's hands behind her back with a rope. Her furious gaze fell first on the king and then on Hal, who was forced to watch helplessly as she was taken away. He had persuaded her not to make any effort to defend herself. Now he had to stand idly by and watch as she was brutally dragged out of the hall by the king's henchmen to the loud cries of those present, who demanded her death for treason. And she had actually come to ally herself with the king.

The next three days were pure torment for Hal, and the nightmare had only just begun. He paced back and forth in the small chamber of the inn.

The trial had been set in three days while Enja was incarcerated in the infamous Tower of London, so he had three days to work out a solution and find a lawyer who could contact her, and he had to inform the clan.

Sending a messenger to Caerlaverock was not difficult. The attempt, however, to find a lawyer who was willing to represent Enja against the king, was almost futile. But finally, with a few extra gold pieces, the jury chairman agreed to hear him.

Sir Archibald Cowley did not care about the plight of the accused or the Crown—they were all the same to him. He always judged at his own discretion because nobody was interested in his opinion anyway. Hal's hair stood on the back of his neck as this conceited so-called scholar explained the hopelessness of the endeavour. But it was his only chance of at least getting Enja's personal belongings back. They had been kept by the jailer and given to Sir Cowley. He was refused a visit—even under supervision—because he was not a relative. He could only imagine what Enja was going through under custody. Mercy on anyone who touched even a hair on her head!

He would only see her again in the courtroom, in front of the assembled jury and on her own. Hal was her only supporter in this trial, the outcome of which was already determined. Hal clenched his fists. He would love to march into this tower, get his leader out, and get out of London as quickly as possible. Frustrated, he paced around his chamber yet again.

I wanted to scream with rage! But silence was better; silence made those damned Englishmen furious, as it was a way to show them my contempt. I wasn't afraid of the cold, the damp, or the hunger. They had given me a solitary cell, probably out of fear that I wouldn't survive the communal cells with the men until the trial.

Even so, I was constantly humiliated when the guards passed my cell. But the insults were mostly limited to jokes and obscene offers. I was able to avert an attack in time when, despite my hands being tied, I was able to kick an intrusive guard in the soft tissues. I got a blow to the head for that, but they kept their distance after that, which was a relief.

The trial was due to take place the next day. What a farce! It was already clear to the chief judge which sentence should be passed to please the king. The court of judges and the jury entrusted with the case certainly wished to avoid upsetting the king, not as a jury, and at least twice as much, not as judges. My hands clenched into fists.

A noise startled me from my dreary thoughts. A wooden bowl was pushed under the door once a day. I carefully picked up the shallow bowl with my fingertips and sniffed it. The little light that fell into my cell through the barred air vent in the wall high above my head made it impossible to tell what it contained. But I smelled oats and something sour, maybe bread dough. I felt for a piece of bread and was able to shovel a little porridge into my mouth. To my relief, it tasted like nothing.

Good, better than bad meat! I even swallowed a few bites before my door rattled. It sprung open, squeaking and creaking, and a little monk in a habit, carrying a candle, entered. He stood silently by the closed door and waited for me to finish my meal. I pushed the bowl back under the door and leaned against the wall with my arms crossed.

He was a Franciscan monk, as his dark brown habit indicated, and in his prime. The fringe of hair was already grey, and the areas around his eyes, which looked completely black in deep sockets, were already wrinkled. Nevertheless, they did not miss any of my movements; he was watching me very closely.

"I am Brother Theobald and have come to hear your confession, if you wish."

My lips pressed together tightly. I stared defiantly at him.

The monk patiently waited a minute and then just sighed. "Are you baptised at all?"

No reaction. Brother Theobald was now a little restless and looked nervously at the door, behind which the guard was probably standing. He quickly crossed himself, bravely took a step closer and whispered to me confidentially, "If you admit to being a heretic, I could get you to experience a quick death by burning instead of a much more painful one as a traitor!"

I flinched. In his eyes, I was already guilty.

"No judgement has yet been passed and you are already negotiating my death?" I responded angrily while he crossed himself nervously again. He'd probably seen the dangerous glow in my eyes.

"The presiding judge will ask you the same question as I do, and if tomorrow I convincingly show that you copulate with the devil, but believe in your heart, then I can see to it that at least your soul is saved!"

The voice of the monk sounded a little unsure now.

"How do you know that I'm in league with the devil?" I asked him with a warning undertone. He held his hands protectively in front of him.

"The sign," and a hand pointed accusingly at my forehead, "that on your forehead, the upside-down cross of Christ. Only a devil would carve the mark of humility on the faces of his henchmen! Did he paint it there himself with the black paint of damned souls?"

I stared at him. So that was it! Of course, who wore a black sign of the cross in the middle of their face? Just a heretic ...

I turned around furiously so that he couldn't read the expression on my face.

"Get out of here!" I snapped at him without turning back. "And tell your God that he can't help me!"

"God help us sinners, in heaven and on earth, amen," the monk said, then let the guard lead him out of my cell. I got a lump in my throat. So, if the king couldn't do it, the church would take me to the grave. What did Isaac always say?

"No god in the world can do anything against human stupidity. Inshallah ... "

For the trial, they shackled me and led me into the designated hall. I had not been outside a single time since my arrest. They had guided me through endless dark corridors and windowless rooms, underground, before bringing me into this space, where the daylight streaming in from above was blinding. I struggled to blink against it. I stood in the middle of a vast room. High above, I could make out a carved wooden ceiling that sloped into a row of windows. The floor of the hall was lined with rows of seats that rose towards the back. In the bright shafts of light filtering through the skylights, I could clearly see the glittering dust that, stirred up by the many people, was settling back onto the tables and benches.

A large part of the benches was taken up by members of the jury, who were to decide my fate. They cast curious and disapproving looks at me before I was led to a seat on a bench in front of a large table.

The presiding judge of the Assize Court, who was now sitting in front of me at the black table, was dressed in a splendid velvet coat and wore a strange headdress that looked very much like a scrivener's leather cap but was made of fine velvet. His eyes were half open, and his sleepy, bored gaze rested on a thick roll of paper, presumably the indictment, that lay spread out before him.

To the left and right of him sat clergy in their brown robes; Franciscan monks, in my opinion. A pale man who also wore a similar cap had made himself comfortable in front of my seat. Apparently it was a mark of jurisdiction. He introduced himself to me as Archibald Cowley, with a little bow, not looking me in the eye. He was the chairman of the jury, and my heart beat faster; after all, they had bothered to call some people to my defence.

Some people, unknown to me, had gathered behind me. Only Hal towered above most of them, and the bystanders kept a respectful distance from him. The sight of him had never felt more comforting than here in the middle of the lion's den.

I allowed myself a quick wink, which he returned with a serious nod. His brow furrowed slightly when he looked at me, but there was no other movement in his face. I could tell from his posture that he was very tense—his jaws grinding and green eyes glittering dangerously. No one in the hall could have even remotely suspected what a volcano was seething in their midst under the black tattooed skin.

English soldiers lined up to the left and right of the rows of chairs and behind me. In the event of a conviction, for which I was prepared, they would immediately put me back in the tower pending my execution. How long would that be? A week? A month?

The judge now stood up with a solemn expression and read the indictment: from consorting with the enemy to abstruse conspiracy theories, holding secret meetings and espionage, everything was listed. Every single point was in itself a reason to charge me with treason. Edward and his damned court really played it safe. The crowd whispered approvingly on every charge.

Now the monk who had visited me in my cell yesterday entered the courtroom. He was entitled to read out an indictment suggesting my heretical intentions. He demanded that I be burned.

My so-called defence attorney found me guilty on all counts and proposed death by the sword to save me unnecessary agony. The first boos rang through the hall. The blasé chairman who, because of the noise, must have been annoyed to be deprived of a well-deserved nap, asked me to plead guilty, either to treason or heresy.

Furious, I got up and shouted so loud that everyone could hear me through the babble of voices. "Since there seems to be no doubt about my guilt, at least condemn me as a traitor because, as such, I am considered the king's worst enemy, and that is what I will be from today on."

The chairman's hammer hit the table with a powerful sweep. The bang drowned out most of the voices, which were now all talking over one another.

"Quiet!" he shouted, demanding that those present stand up for the guilty verdict.

"Princess Enja I-Shabbah ibn Hassan I-Shabbah"—he managed, admirably, to pronounce my title and full name without stumbling—"you are found guilty of high treason. You will be hung by the rope, then emasculated, uh ... I mean ... "

Here he paused and briefly consulted the monk again. The laughter in the rows was audible. "Yes, just have fun at my expense, you dumb people!" He roared angrily, then he straightened up again, hit the table again vigorously with the hammer to finally calm things down, and announced solemnly: "... after you have been hung by the rope, you will be gutted directly, then quartered, and your head will be hung on the city wall as a deterrent. The judgement will be carried out tomorrow in the marketplace. May God help us!"

Tomorrow already! My heart stopped for a moment.

The audience had become restless. The speed of implementation seemed to surprise some. Someone threw rotten eggs, which I was able to avoid cleverly, and which instead hit Alexander Cowley. The man twisted his nose in disgust and began to wipe his stained skirt with a small handkerchief.

I looked over my shoulder at Hal. He had turned pale, and I felt deeply connected to him at that moment. The most intrepid man in the world feared for my life. Suddenly, he jumped up, threw up one arm and yelled to Archibald over the hustle and bustle in the hall.

"She could have a child under her heart, you idiot! You have to suspend the sentence until it is certain that she is not pregnant!"

I stared at Hal in surprise. Before Archibald could react, the chairman who had heard the objection struck the table with the hammer and the noise subsided a little. Then he announced loudly and clearly to the audience, "The convict will be given four weeks. Should she provide proof of pregnancy by then, the judgement will be suspended until the child is born. Otherwise, the judgement will be carried out as it was set today."

Four weeks. I closed my eyes in relief, hoping I would come up with something by then. I cast a grateful glance at Hal. But he didn't seem to notice me at all. He shook his head and quickly looked down; was he crying? It was the last time I saw him before the soldiers shackled me and dragged me out of the hall. The stench of rotten eggs followed me all the way to my cell.

Chapter 12

Alamut in 1297

Had it not been for my pounding headache, I could have sworn it was all just a bad dream. But every slightest movement brought a throbbing pain to my head like nothing I had ever experienced before. My eyelids felt as heavy as lead. Each attempt to open them was met with a shaft of light slicing through my eyes, the bright light cutting like a knife, causing me to groan. Instantly, a damp cloth was laid across my forehead, and a soft, soothing voice began to speak.

"Everything will be fine, Eran. The pain will be gone in a few days; just the bump won't diminish that quickly."

It was the voice of a boy I didn't know. He was sitting on my right. My vain attempts to speak were prevented by a big lump in my throat; nothing more than a hoarse croak came out of my mouth.

"Here, drink this. It will do you good."

A hand slipped behind my shoulders and gently pushed me up. The pain shot through my skull again and I doubled over. But the need for water was greater, and when a cool bowl was held to my lips, I drank greedily.

"Slowly, sir; otherwise, you'll swallow the wrong way!"

How did I get into this bed? What happened? Such pain raced through the convolutions of my brain, I could no longer think clearly.

Isaac ... My thoughts vanished again, bursting like delicate bubbles in my memory. Where was I?

The pleasantly cool hand pressed me gently back onto my bed. The soft voice enveloped me, and a wondrous weariness pervaded my body. Thankfully, I sank back into the deep sleep from which I had just awakened. I simply left the pain behind in the present and felt strangely relieved.

When I opened my eyes this time, I saw someone crouched beside my bed in the dim light of the room. A fly buzzed near my ear. I felt only a slight tug as I turned my head. The person immediately noticed my movement and removed the cold object from my forehead. Hesitantly, I lifted one hand and then the other, staring at my fingers. They danced hazily before my eyes. Gently, I felt my forehead and discovered a swollen lump.

I cleared my throat and tested my voice.

"How long have I been lying here, boy?"

Amazing, I could even speak again, although the voice sounded strangely far away and a little choked.

"Six days, sir. You took a good blow. We thought your skull was cracked at first, but then I felt your pulse and we brought you here, where it's cool and calm. I continuously cooled the bump on your forehead with a wet cloth until the swelling went down."

Six days of darkness. The blow must have been heavy. It was really a miracle that my head was still whole.

"Thanks be to Allah that you have recovered. Can you remember everything?" the boy asked me thoughtfully.

"Isaac!" I cried out.

"Master Isaac is dead, Master Eran. You are alone now; or, rather, you have me now."

"Isaac is dead," I repeated faintly as the memory trickled down to me. I wanted to swallow, but my dry throat would not allow it. "But who are you?"

"I am your new servant. My name is Ilyas, and I will help you with your work."

Help ...?

"Our King Hassan has appointed you to be his personal Medicus."

"What if I don't want that?" I croaked in that choked tone, as if my neck had swelled up to twice its size.

"Then he will kill me, sir ..." said Ilyas meekly.

By all the gods ...

I was now fourteen years old. I kept my hair short under my turban and tried to look manly. My spindly body was a good disguise for me.

My new helper, Ilyas, turned out to be a smart little guy with great charm, and I played the opposite of our two roles. This made me appear many times older and more mature than I actually was, and won the trust of King Hassan and his princes. According to the king's instructions, I was to take care of them as well as my limited knowledge allowed. Thanks to my knowledge of the human physique, I was also consulted in order to bring about the fastest and most silent killings possible—a frightening demand because I had been trained to heal.

On the other hand, it also gave me an insight into the work of the Assassins, who were supposed to sneak up as close as possible to their victims and kill them with a single stab. If it was aimed correctly, a stab at close range was instantly fatal and the murdered person never even felt the pain.

A great help in my further education was Master Kang Shi Fu, a Chinese Shaolin monk who had to flee from his homeland, and who had found a job with King Hassan as a highly regarded martial arts trainer. He never mentioned why he had dared to undertake the arduous journey from his homeland to the far-off Orient. But almost everyone who went into hiding in any way with the Assassins had their very own story to tell, which was not always intended for foreign ears.

From the taciturn Shi Fu, I learned a lot about Asian healing arts, acupuncture, and therapeutic massages. I, in turn, taught him the use of poisons and herbs. We saw it as a kind of symbiosis that brought each of us further skills.

Shi Fu was between twenty and a hundred years old, wise as a centenarian, and agile as a twenty-year old. In addition, his face was always a mask of friendliness; whether he was in a bad mood or happy, no one could tell. He treated everyone with respect and courtesy. He never said a word too much; on the contrary, he was a master at hiding words and feelings, and I decided to learn this skill from him. Well, at some point, I had to admit to myself that I wasn't very good at this.

A special friendship developed between us. We were united by a great interest in nature and the duel. It was therefore inevitable that we often met for combat practice that took place early in the morning before our actual working hours. These special circumstances and the fact that I did not want to deliver Ilyas to Hassan's mercy moved me to accept Hassan I-Shabbah's generous offer and work for him as a personal physician.

I was still haunted by the violent death of Isaac, which, according to Shi Fu's theory, was his own fault. Because no Sunni would be willing to work under a Shiite, Isaac was forced to refuse Hassan's dictate because of his creed.

Did Hassan know? Had he intended to get rid of Isaac anyway and left him no choice with his offer? Such a cunning crook as Hassan did nothing without calculation.

Another advantage of my employment was the medical care of the valuable horses that were part of Hassan's horse breeding interests. These animals, which were his pride and joy, were very slender and elegant, not too big, and proudly held their heads with the bridge of their noses curved upwards. I have never seen horses that were faster, more intelligent, and with more stamina than these thoroughbreds. Hassan himself rode and trained them with a passion that was contagious, and I really had a lot to learn from him in that area.

While Ilyas busily and zealously struggled with my little plants and animals, making ointments, pills, and vials to alleviate the discomfort of the castle population, I had enough time to learn to ride, understand horses, and even help the mares foal.

I was particularly taken with a black colt. We literally had to pull him out of his dam's womb on the day he was born to help him into the world. But after the first anxious hours, he recovered and became stronger. I was allowed to name him Taycan, which means something like "young horse" in Arabic, and he seemed to react to it from the start.

Hassan showed me in his strict and determined manner how I had to deal with the young stallion and how he was tailored to his future rider without putting too much weight on his young back. Soon the docile animal followed me closely and listened to my commands.

The unfortunate day that Taycan broke his foreleg, therefore, hit me all the harder. The Nizarite king had the idea to adorn his fort atop the ridge of the Elburs Mountain range with catapults in order to repel his enemies. Hundreds of workers laboured night and day to erect these heavy, wood constructions in the prescribed area. An enormous amount of wood was transported to the ridge from the valley below. This was accomplished with the use of oxen hitched to wooden carts. Oxen were the only animals that were strong enough to be able to climb the steep hill with the heavy load on their backs.

Just as the two-year-old horses were being brought back to the Eagle-Nest from the meadows in the valley below, the shaft of one of the wood carts tore loose. The heavy conveyance rumbled backwards, tipped over on its side, and under the hysterical cries of the workers, a number of the felled tree trunks rolled noisily down the steep incline. The horses panicked and ran uncontrolled in all directions. Taycan found himself in the middle of them. A rolling tree trunk hit him in the middle of a wild gallop and drove the legs out from under him with its impact.

Even before I could reach him and assess the scope of the accident, I knew that he was suffering terrible pain. He was lying on his side and struggling for air. Again and again, he raised his head and let it fall, helplessly. Only the whites of his eyes were visible as they rolled to the back in panic. I dived toward him, held him tightly, and tried to calm him.

Feverishly, a variety of different healing methods crossed my mind, but I had never treated a broken leg on a horse.

Hassan hurried up with his caftan fluttering, his dark eyes full of worry and pain—an unusual sight for this imperturbable man. Three other animals had also been hit. They were so badly injured that Hassan's men released them from their pain. When they and Hassan finally came up to me and Taycan, my throat tightened. Panicked, I held the disturbed animal's head against my shoulder. I sat down to keep it on the ground. I threw myself protectively over the stallion's neck.

"Wait!" I shrieked as Hassan, with a rigid expression on his face, set the knife himself to kill his precious stallion. Distraught, his gaze wandered into my face, the dark eyes sad, and his mouth pinched by suppressed grief.

"If I can cure him," I asked him, my voice trembling with fear, "when he gets well again, may I keep him?"

He looked at me in silence. The corners of his mouth twitched. At some point, he realised I was serious, and his eyes suddenly softened. It was the most human thing I had ever seen him do. Indeed, a smile crossed his face. He looked over at the heavily breathing animal and looked back at me.

"I don't want him to suffer, Eran."

"He will not suffer, My King, I will take care of him myself," I urged him. "He will live. I swear I'll do everything to make sure that he does. Please, let him live!"

I put all my strength into my voice; he just had to believe me. I clearly saw doubt in his dark eyes. The fracture was on the right foreleg below the knee. The bone protruded, bloody and pointed, from the black fur, and the rest of the leg bent to the side at an unnatural angle.

The blood pounded in my veins. In desperation, I closed my eyes and prayed to all the gods I knew.

And I was heard. With a sigh, the dreaded head of the Assassin nodded and pardoned Taycan, placing his life in my hands. The cold man, followed by death and suffering like a shadow behind his billowing caftan, felt pity for a creature. And I was the key to it.

"So be it, Eran. If you can save him, he is yours! Inshallah ..."

My shoulders slumped forward; I was so relieved. Tears fell on Taycan's black fur as I trembled and held his snorting head. The lump in my throat was so thick, I couldn't make a sound to express my gratitude. I just knew that I would do everything I could to make my Taycan well again.

Everything ...

Never had I been as challenged—emotionally and professionally—as with this patient. The sheer size of him, the difficulty of keeping him stable yet calm, and my limited experience in treating horses—all of these factors were against me. Hassan's men seemed to hold me in high regard, and I didn't want to disappoint anyone, least of all myself. I will never forget how all the helpers willingly fell under my command.

After I had managed to numb him with the correct dose of diluted snake venom, I was able to calmly straighten his leg, sew the wound, and make a solid splint of wood and bandages soaked in lime. Finally, I tied his injured leg up in the front and attached it to the ceiling with ropes so that he couldn't accidentally put it on the floor.

Now I had to wait for the next few hours and hope that he would come to. That night, I found a place to sleep next to Taycan. When he woke up dazed, my knees went weak with relief. And when he carefully began to eat hay and drink water, I almost burst into tears.

The men patted me on the shoulder in appreciation, and even Hassan looked in disbelief that things were going well. I believe that that day, I climbed to another level of his respect. He assured me that he would keep his word.

Many weeks of intensive work went by with the constant fear of losing Taycan to a fever or unintentional weight on his broken leg. But he was young and still growing. The bone seemed to be as stable as before. After many weeks of waiting, I took the splint off him for the first time. Taycan was careful; he barely stepped on his right front hoof and hobbled. He seemed to enjoy my attention, and over time, had become used to me and gained confidence. We became friends first, and since he was mine from then on, we became something like partners.

No other event could have strengthened my influence at Hassan's court as much as the healing of Taycan. Not only did Hassan stick to our agreement and let me have one of his best stallions, but from then on, he seemed to me to be extremely well-balanced and shared his thoughts not only with his closest confidants, but also with me—a decision that made his followers very suspicious of me.

At best, I was tolerated in this group, and of course, completely ignorant of war strategies; consequently, I always held back with my opinion. Only here and there did I throw in what I felt was a clever thought that wouldn't affront anyone if I were questioned. Until one day, when I took the chance to show my courage—even if not entirely voluntarily.

The Shiite Nizarites, who grouped themselves around Hassan and won entire areas for Hassan's fight against the hated Sunni leaders, asserted themselves as a respectable force in their own country. Of course, Sultan Saladin could not tolerate such an independent empire in his country and declared war on Hassan I-Shabbah. Soon, the numerically superior troops of the Seljuk head of the empire were marching up the broad path to the fortress.

We had been preparing for a long siege inside the fortress for weeks. Our pigeons became important messengers, announcing the arrival of the Seljuks on the exact day. The pigeons had been trained and bred by a trained Assassin— an extremely effective way of getting messages across the country quickly. This enabled Hassan's numerous scattered sympathisers to warn him long before the coming attack. That gave him plenty of time to prepare for a siege, and he did.

Water and grain had therefore been stored in abundance for weeks, and cattle and weapons were increased in multiple quantities. With Ilyas's help, I doubled my wound preparations, pain reliever potions, and instruments. We had enough time to wrap clean bandages and pile rags. With Hassan's consent, I was allowed to set up a small hospital room that could accommodate up to three men at the same time. With noticeable tension, everyone was preparing for the coming onslaught.

And that came in the form of a huge army of Seljuks. Thousands of soldiers of the Sultan under their leader, Saladin's governor and General Nisam al-Mulk, streamed up the slopes of the mountain range on which the Eagle's-Nest sat, impregnable. On horseback and on foot, the loyal Saladins tormented themselves to try to reach the inhospitable heights and stand in front of the impenetrable sandstone fortress that surrounded Alamut like a protective shell.

The first wave of attacks by numerous archers subsided, almost without causing any damage. This was due on the one hand to the high walls of Alamut, and on the other hand, to the force of the projectiles mounted on the battlements, which caused far more losses to the enemy than anticipated. The second wave of attacks was almost as fruitless and left more dead on the Seljuk side than inside the fortress. The walls of Alamut were as good as impassable, as the war general Nisam al-Mulk discovered at some point. But if the enemy couldn't get in, then the Alamuts couldn't go out, either. Nisam ordered his soldiers to prepare for a long siege.

So, while the Seljuks waited for weeks at the gates of Alamut, the water level in the fortress sank, as did the mood of the inhabitants. We struggled with limited nutrition, bare nerves, and dwindling supplies. Every evening, Hassan called his confidants into his personal chamber and waited for inspiration.

After almost eight weeks of siege, we were plagued by camp fever. The number of sick people suddenly went up, mainly due to knocked out teeth and broken noses, which resulted from the multitude of fights with one another. The nerves of all the men were tense: they would rather fight than wait idly.

On the fifty-eighth day of the siege, Hassan I-Shabbah called his closest confidants to find a solution to the conflict. We met in his private room, as we always did when he wanted to be undisturbed. That day, there were only six confidants;

the rest were in the sick bay. The mood was irritable, and the men looked tense. The king himself paced nervously up and down in front of his bed, arms behind his back. It was the bed in which I had found him dying with Isaac that time. With its heavy canopy made of dark red brocade, it dominated the room, which was otherwise poorly furnished.

The chamber was darkened so as not to let the heat penetrate the walls. Only a few oil lamps lit the otherwise dark room and painted the men's faces in a mysterious colour. Almost like a conspiracy, we had cut ourselves off from the rest of the world. My position within this circle was special. Despite my age and gender—no one there suspected that I was female—I was able to influence a man whom all the Persians and the enemies of the Persians feared like the black plague. He was flesh and blood, of course, and yet there was an aura of a superhuman about him. I often felt as if he was manipulating people's minds. Mine, too, as I had to admit.

I looked around eagerly. Everyone was calm about the situation, but not all could hide their feelings like Master Shi Fu, whose face looked as mask-like in the light of the oil lamps as his Buddha statues. Above all, Nabil al-Hakam was showing his inner restlessness. He urged Hassan irritably to risk failure, regardless of loss.

"We could launch a surprise attack. None of the damned Seljuks expect us to dash out of the gates into the middle of the unsuspecting opponents," he exclaimed excitedly to the group, throwing his arms in the air to express his frustration.

He earned some nods of approval, but also sceptical looks. Among them was Hassan's, who crossed his arms over his chest.

"They would mow us down with their arrows immediately. We would have no protection, and the gates would be open," he replied to Nabil's daring suggestion, and nodded appreciatively, "but your courage impresses me, my friend."

He turned slowly to the other confidants and raised his strong voice. "Be patient, my friends. At some point, the Seljuks will also notice that we have more willpower than they do and leave things without having done anything. Trust me!"

"But I'm not going to sit idly here for months; it drives me crazy!" Nabil said hotly, and the other princes loudly agreed. Only Kang Shi Fu held back. He watched the action from a due distance.

I stayed inconspicuously near the window. From there, it was easier for me to sound out the situation and assess those involved. But now I took a deep breath, stepped forward a little to be noticed, and raised my hands. Indeed, some turned to me and studied my slender frame, including the king. He raised his eyebrows expectantly.

"I have an idea that doesn't need a horde of brave men, but just one." My voice sounded uncertain, even to my ears. Now the last in the group fell silent, too. Hassan encouraged me to continue.

"Hundreds of men are camping down there with all their servants and henchmen and tents. One more individual is not particularly noticeable. What if we just smuggle a man into the camp who deliberately kills the vizier Nisam al-Mulk?"

A murmur went through the small chamber.

"That would be exactly our way ...", I heard a voice from further back reply, which also encouraged me to continue.

"We would just have to smuggle someone out of the fortress unnoticed, who then sneaks into his tent. Best at night, when al-Mulk is sleeping," I explained with a little more self-confidence. "The only problem is, how does he get back?" I looked around questioningly because I hadn't thought that far yet.

"Not at all," said Nabil angrily. "He'll be killed on the spot, and if he's lucky, with his skin on his flesh."

"A suicide commando?" Shi Fu asked thoughtfully. It was the first time my teacher interfered. I tightened my body with this encouragement.

"Sure, if that person is caught. But if he manages to get out of the tent unnoticed, then he could go back the same way he got out of the fortress," I replied, looking around triumphantly.

Everyone looked at me as if I had just declared that I could fly. Nabil, that poisonous snake, finally pursed his lips unkindly.

"And how could a man manage to just walk in and out of there like that?" he scoffed cynically. "Let alone kill a man who is very well guarded in the midst of bloodthirsty Seljuks?" His voice hardened with every word.

"Well,"—I waited without losing my composure, then presented the second part of my idea—"when the granaries were built, hatches were provided through which the grain can be filled into the chambers from outside. Somebody could get outside through there, completely unnoticed, because the hatches are sunk into the ground—and come back in the same way."

Big laughter broke out now, and I felt the heat rush to my face. Especially Nabil, that arrogant peacock, neighed like an unyielding mare. What was the matter with him?

"And which of us should fit through the hatch, you blockhead? It is made for grain and not for a person!"

He snorted and everyone else laughed with him.

He was right, it was just a narrow opening, just big enough for a child …

Before I could think about it, I burst out: "A child or a thin boy would fit through!"

Again, it was Hassan who calmed things down by raising his hand imperiously. With a determined look, he stared at me with darkly shaded eyes and nodded appreciatively.

"Your idea is good, Eran; which boy were you thinking of?"

His words made me wince a little. I really hadn't taken the idea that far. Once again, the thought had just formed in my head and slipped out of my mouth carelessly. What boy would be capable of killing a man in cold blood in his sleep? And squeezing through a grain chute at night?

I closed my eyes thoughtfully. Was it possible? A wave of inexplicable confidence must have gripped me as I opened my eyes again and looked into the amused faces around me. Their amusement only made me more determined. With a deep breath, I defiantly pressed out, "I, My King, I will do it!"

My hands clenched into fists, which I pressed against my neck in my excitement to stop the throbbing there.

Nabil threw up his hands. "A boy who heals people wants to play an Assassin! Go back to your dreams, little one!"

Most of them laughed with him; nobody thought I could accomplish such a daring coup. Only Shi Fu gave me a thoughtful look from his narrow eyes, giving me enough confidence to go on.

"I know how to kill a person." I threw my chin proudly at Nabil's objection. "I lived among beggar children in Baghdad. If I can't squeeze through the shaft and move quietly in the dark, who else can?"

Convinced of my abilities, I folded my arms over my chest. Now that I had trumpeted it to the world, I was suddenly really convinced that I could do it.

Hassan brooded and hesitated. Doesn't he trust me to do that? Finally, he turned to Nabil and Shi Fu with a thoughtful expression but a determined voice.

"You two will show Eran how to move unnoticed among enemies. Show him how to silently kill his opponent. Give him a weapon he can handle."

And he ordered the rest of the men just as briefly: "And today you will clear the access to the eastern granary, right next to the entrance gate."

Tired, he put his hands on his hips and looked seriously at the group, who listened breathlessly. "It's a good chance, and if Eran succeeds, then they'll either leave without a leader or try to attack with anger in their guts, both of which would be fine with me. But there will finally be movement in this damn situation ... "

My heart was beating in my throat, my mouth was dry, and my legs wouldn't obey me. What had I gotten myself into?

Within a few days, Shi Fu and Nabil had shown me how an Assassin thought and acted; how he moved and silently killed a person.

Now I was standing up to my knees in the grain in this granary in the dark and saw the black opening of the shaft in front of me. It was as narrow as my throat; only a tiny bit of light fell in through the air vent above me and poorly illuminated the scene. My eyes had to get used to the darkness in there quickly because it was completely dark in the shaft as well.

Shi Fu instructed me to wear tight black clothes. My head was wrapped in a black cloth, with only narrow slits left free for my eyes. No part of my body was visible in the shadows; even my feet were in black stockings. The pointed dagger, which had to be stuck through the eye of the victim to the brain, was inserted in a sheathed shaft on my belt, custom-made by Nabil. Shi Fu and Nabil insisted on accompanying me to the entrance of the shaft, where they would wait for me until I was back.

"Good luck, Eran!" Shi Fu wished me, swallowing the R in my name, as always.

"Zhù nǐ hǎo yùn—good luck", he added and bowed politely to me.

"Xiè xiè!—thank you, my friend," I replied, and we shook hands.

I took a last deep breath and then resolutely pushed myself into the narrow, square shaft. It wasn't long, but I had to extend my hands first to open the hatch at the front of the entrance. My freedom of movement was extremely restricted, not to mention my fear of simply getting stuck in the middle. The small, unlocked door at the end of the shaft opened easily, however. Even though my body was so narrow, my hip bones got stuck in the frame of the narrow opening. Forcibly, I pulled myself through with my arms propped up on the outside, scraping off the skin on one of my hip bones.

The way to the tent was easy. Nobody expected the Nizarites to fall out of the protective walls of the fortress, especially not at night. Still, I was careful. My entire body was taut like a bowstring, and I watched every step. I heard the besiegers chatter and drink loudly as if it were a celebration and not a siege. The smell of roasted meat was seductive to my nose. This had become a rare dish for our people, and the portions were also rationed. My mouth went watery, and I swallowed angrily. Turn off your thoughts; focus on your goal! Shi Fu, with his instructions, was always in the back of my mind.

The descriptions of the tent and the vizier were part of my intensive preparation. It would be fatal if I accidentally killed the wrong person. There, between the two smaller tents, I paused for a moment and saw a darker tent with a red banner. How stupid to draw attention to yourself like that, I thought to myself. But he had to feel safe with so many of his soldiers. And a crazy boy who crept into the camp alone in the middle of the night ... who expected that? Again, fear overwhelmed me like a cold wave. Inhale, exhale—shakily, I counted the seconds until my racing pulse had calmed down again.

In fact, there were a lot of tents standing around. I counted at least fifty men here alone on the eastern side of the ridge. With all my strength, and Shi Fu's good advice, I stalked cautiously. The stones under my socks barely crunched as I slowly crept past the tents under the cover of darkness. The night was moonless and cold, ideal for my project. Blinded by the campfire, the besiegers did not see far into the shadows surrounding them.

In an arc-like pattern, I crept to the back of the tent. I could only hope that the vizier wasn't sleeping right behind the tent wall. A distant snore indicated that Nisam al-Mulk had chosen the strategically correct spot at the back of the tent.

With the razor-sharp dagger, I cut a line in the canvas level with my chest and down to my feet and quickly pushed myself through it. I stood breathless and let my eyes get used to the dim light inside. To my left, I could see the sleeping place with the furs, and on it the outline of a voluminous body, the chest rising and falling evenly. To his right was a candle, half burned down. I held still for a while until my breathing became even and calm again. Pay attention to your breathing, Nabil had taught me, and so far, my heartbeat and my breathing had been in amazing harmony. With the dagger in hand, I moved slowly towards the sleeping figure. Only a few more yards.

I faintly made out the details of the vizier. Curly grey hair, a fat paunch, and short stature—the description fit. Now I was standing next to him, my hand with the dagger on my right, the other hand resting over the half-open, snoring mouth. Then everything happened very quickly: I covered his mouth while I thrust the dagger into his head with my upraised right hand. The fat body reared up, then it went limp; death came quickly and without much fuss.

I found it eerie myself how easy it was for me to do everything, as if I had done it before. My breath whistled out of my mouth. The candle flickered. It occurred to me that I should extinguish it, or someone else would come into the tent.

With my eyes fixed on the tent entrance, I crept around the sleeping area and suddenly bumped my feet against something soft and warm. A groan came from below me, then I heard a soft voice.

"Sahib, what is ...?" It was the sleepy croak of a child.

Damn it! Suddenly, my heartbeat and breathing were no longer in harmony at all. I stood petrified with horror. At the same moment, the boy who had slept at the foot of the bed noticed that there was an intruder in the tent. I only heard him take a breath to scream and instinctively put my hand around his throat. His fingers clutched mine to pull it away, and the force of my movement made us both fall to the floor like a wet sack. The child's head crashed against the wooden pillar that held the tent upright. It wasn't a violent impact, but it was obviously enough to make him lose consciousness.

There was a faint shout outside the tent. I froze. Now my pulse was racing, and my heartbeat and breathing were back. I quickly got up and extinguished the candle. A head shot through the tent entrance.

"Are you okay, Sahib?" It was probably the guard in front of the tent.

"Psst", I whispered urgently from inside, "not so loud, the vizier is sleeping!" I hoped my voice didn't sound too strange.

"I had heard something!" he whispered back now as well.

"I dreamed! All right..." I soothed him again in a whisper to disguise my voice, and he actually turned back outside with a grunt. My goodness, that was close ...

With the greatest effort, I tried to get my uneven breathing under control again. It was pitch dark in the tent. But as my eyes quickly got used to the darkness, I found the slit in the tent wall. In order not to take any chances, I took the same path back, opened the hatch, and wedged myself back in with my feet first so I could close it with my hands behind me. The narrow opening had scraped off another piece of skin on my hip, but I no longer felt it in my excited state.

As soon as the hatch was closed, I noticed someone pulling my feet into the granary. It was Shi Fu, and in the pale light, I saw him grinning for the first time, ear to ear. Without saying a word, he hugged me tightly and slapped me on the shoulder. It was good that he supported me because my legs were soft as butter.

I had come back. I actually made it! For the first time in my life, I had killed—I could hardly believe it! One life for that of many. I enjoyed the approval of the other Assassins, who took turns patting me on the shoulder or shaking hands. It was exhilarating.

Indeed, the day after the violent death of Nisam al-Mulk and his unfortunate servant became known, the tents of the Seljuks were dismantled and the troops withdrew without having achieved anything. Unfortunately, I never found out whether it was because Hassan paid the Seljuks off, or because an Assassin had managed to break into the camp and kill the vizier among his own people.

Courage must have left the Seljuks as quickly as the vizier's soul left his body. In retrospect, I did not find my own role in this drama to be quite so brave; after all, the vizier had been asleep, and his servant was still a child. I was fortunate that he had passed out or I would have had to kill him, too. My guilty conscience had caught up with me. I struggled with killing someone in cold blood. My sleep was tormented by sweats and repetitive images.

The men around Hassan saw it quite differently, however. Killing the vizier in his sleep was a real masterpiece. They encouraged their king to grant me the honour of Assassin training as a reward for my services. This incredible recognition had, at first, relieved me of my guilty feelings. It was Allah's will, they said.

In fact, this was only the beginning of a deep self-criticism, because I soon began to quarrel with Hassan. I did not see any of the princes who often invoked Allah to justify their actions, ever praying. It seemed that their king was closer to them than Allah.

In the morning after the first prayer, the Nizarite king had me called to his private room, which he always used for his secret meetings. Only Nabil stood next to him, a strange smile on his face. It almost seemed to me that I had made a big mistake and was preparing myself internally for a punishment. But the king only asked that I describe my nocturnal adventure to him again. He stood directly in front of me and looked at me with those eyes that rather frightened me. It was the way he looked at me.

I bowed my head as I spoke because his pupils were as black as the rest of his eyes, and I felt as if I were looking into a deep chasm where there was no light.

Again and again, he encouraged me to taste the wine he had provided. Since I didn't want to cloud my senses, I declined with thanks, but accepted the datiln and the mocha, which he generously handed me. At the end of the story, I admitted that I mourned the vizier's soul, and he raised his black eyebrows in question.

"Why do you mourn the vizier, but not the many soldiers who fell before him?" he finally asked me.

"He was lying there defenceless and doing nothing to me," I replied meekly. Now I raised my head and looked into his black eyes again.

"And if he would have stood in front of you with his sword?" he asked again.

"Then I would probably no longer be alive," I replied resolutely and cocked my chin.

He was right. I would have been easily killed by a man.

"They would have grabbed you, peeled off your skin, and thrown your head over my walls," he continued. Irritated, I swallowed and looked down at the floor again.

"Look at me, Eran!" I had to look up into those black eyes that were so hard and yet so smart. Now they eyed me with an intensity that made my hair stand on end. What did he see in me?

"You are a brave and skilled boy, Eran. What you did that night may have saved the lives of many people here. It only happened to one grand vizier."

He put his right hand on my shoulder.

"The Seljuks have given up the siege. We won this time, but they will be back. And maybe then we'll have to kill another man so that others can survive. Or another vizier."

How did he make me feel like a mouse in front of a snake? I couldn't take my eyes off him, and just nodded resignedly. My head began to whir, and circles appeared before my eyes. I heard myself breathing, loud and unnaturally fast. The pressure on my shoulder became tighter, hot, and heavy.

"Will you kill again next time to help us, Eran?"

My head just nodded mechanically, and I let out a hoarse "yes". Why did I say that? Where was my mind?

"Then I will train you to be an Assassin, a warrior like Nabil Al-Hakam, and one day you will be free," I heard him say. "You will be a free man and serve me as a prince. Do you understand me, Eran?"

With that, he placed his second hand on my other shoulder. His eyes were still staring into me, and I felt strangely hollow.

"Yes, Master ...", I managed to say, before my legs went weak. I slumped to the floor and stammered, "Thank you, Master ..."

My body and mind were as weak as if I had a severe fever. My knees and palms supported me on the soft silk carpet, and my breathing was jerky. I was beginning to realise that I had just made a promise to become an Assassin.

The spell of his gaze was released, and I could breathe and move freely again, yet it seemed to me as if a stranger had just forced his will on me, someone. Someone more powerful than my own soul. A stranger who took possession of my thoughts. How was that possible?

Nabil helped me to my shaky legs and grinned as if I had actually drunk too much wine. Angry and still a little dazed, I pushed him away from me.

"What happened to me?"

Now he was laughing. "You just sold your soul. And I'll show you what you have to do for it."

His laughter sounded like mockery to my ears.

Chapter 13

London in September 1305

They had put me back in the same filthy cell. The bucket of stagnant water was still in the same place. They could at least have cleaned it in the meantime, I thought bitterly. Don't be ridiculous, Enja; they had no intention of doing that.

I had four weeks to think. Four weeks to find a way out of here. How could it all have happened? I had offered Edward my support. Was it simply because I was a woman, or shouldn't I have threatened him with the future Scottish king?

My anger was only matched by my despair and the worry about dying here in London and leaving my clan alone. I had failed. If I couldn't even save my own life, how could I save an entire clan?

I walked back and forth in the tiny cell, taking small steps. I had to do something; move, scream, or put my fist through the wall. But it didn't help. I couldn't undo it and called myself an idiot.

Hal's reaction to the judgement was heartbreaking. He almost jumped over the wooden barrier and dragged me out of the room by force of arms. I gave a slight shake of my head, signalling to him that we had to find another solution.

But the more time passed, the more desperate my thoughts became. I hit the rough rock with my fist furiously. The stabbing pain was good and cleared my crazy thoughts. The knuckles were already bloody and scabbed. My only hope was Hal. He would help me; I was sure of that. He just had to think of something.

But the Tower was impregnable. There were always two guards on constant patrol, with two more stationed in the guardroom at the front. The patrols were unpredictable, the cell searches unannounced, and meals were never delivered at the same time. Someone was doing their duty with meticulous precision, and it was slowly becoming clear to me why the Tower of London had such a fearsome reputation: No one got out of here unless they were allowed to.

The days and nights blurred down here; the sun never rose or set here. Therefore, I spent the waking hours in a kind of meditation that helped me survive the oppressive time. Or I tried to keep myself physically fit with limited exercise, which was hardly possible in this small room. But at least my strength-building distracted me from the monotony for a while.

After about two weeks, I was awakened by noise in front of my cell. It sounded like the rumbling voice of a man who cursed the soldiers, then the king, and finally God himself, in a language that was pretty familiar to me: Gaelic!

Startled, I ran to the door and stared through the barred peephole. If he was who I thought he was, he shouldn't be here, not in the Tower of London!

"Sir William Douglas!" I shouted loudly, clutching the bars. "What are you doing here in this hole? Is there no more uisge beatha in the Highlands?"

He turned to me and simply dragged the two soldiers who accompanied him with him. The sturdy man took a few more steps towards me, but the English henchmen forcibly held him back.

Old laird William Douglas, father of James, stood before me in person. He was slimmer than I remembered, but still a powerful and tall man. He knitted his bushy eyebrows and squinted at me. His reddened eyes stared thoughtfully at me. Only after a few moments did he recognise me and shouted in his loud and already rather hoarse voice, "Lady Enja, what are you doing here?"

He shook his head with the tousled grey mane that fell to his shoulder. I heard his regret to find me here within these walls.

"I had no choice but to hand over my life to these filthy English bloodhounds. But this is no place for you, here!"

"The English have arrested me and want to execute me as a traitor. I didn't even get a chance to explain myself properly," I burst out angrily. "Should you be brought before the court, it would be better not to hire a lawyer; it will only make things worse ..."

The soldiers tried to drag William further down the corridor, but he could not be moved an inch. Serious and disappointed, he looked at me and nodded down the hallway.

"I am already sentenced. I am already considered a traitor for my opinion and my attitude towards the English crown. The English piss their pants for fear that the Scots might set up their own king!"

He spat contemptuously, right in front of the feet of one of the two soldiers, who slowly seemed to be losing patience and screamed for reinforcements.

"They're taking me to be tortured. They're going to kill me one way or the other." William's mighty voice drowned out the soldiers' shouts. "I'm going to die in here, and I'm going to follow my beloved Eleonore with pride. These English pigs have her on their conscience. They simply killed her and Matthew, my little boy…"

He hissed the last words, bitterness diminished his voice, and the two soldiers tugged at his arms again. One even hit him with a club. He cursed and damned the English crown as the two soldiers dragged him down the passageway.

"Where are James and Hugh?" I called after him as he stumbled forward, cursing, my hands desperately clutching the bars. With a wild glance, he looked back and called to me, "I don't know. They were taken away, but I have no idea where. Maybe they are still alive ..."

And with that, he was gone from my field of vision. His words echoed cavernously in my ears. Maybe they are still alive! If James and Hugh were still alive, where were they? Wouldn't they have returned long ago to help their father? Or maybe they had been moved to another prison? Young men were often misused as workers for the numerous war structures of the crown. Since the father had to pay for his debt in death, his sons could not be executed for the same crime. But even if they were sent to a labour camp, their death would eventually be the inevitable result.

My cramped hands were cold. Thoughtfully, I put my forehead on my fists, still clutching the bars. I had to get out of here. I had to find out where the two men were and help them. If I believed in any goddamn god, I would have said a prayer then for the soul of William, for those of his children, and for me…

On the morning of the scheduled execution of the Governor of the tower, a healer confirmed that I was not with child, so he commanded that the royal sentence could be carried out. The news spread like wildfire through the city and made people hurry to the market square in eager anticipation. In keeping with the occasion, the English sky was overcast. The unusually warm summer days in London had ended with a violent thunderstorm. Autumn wetness had covered London with a grey veil that let people breathe deeply after the heat.

"What pissing weather for this damned execution," grumbled Hal, who was standing under a small canopy at the end of the market square. He pulled his foot back from a puddle in which the dirt from the streets was collecting. Numerous onlookers had already gathered here on the market square to experience the highlight of the week with their own eyes. A few birds were looking for worms, snails, and rubbish in the puddles. Even in the rain, they didn't let themselves be deterred from scavenging.

For the first time in London, a woman was to die the death of a traitor. A woman, a traitor to the English crown, who was to die a most gruesome and slow death, agitated even the laziest lay-about in town.

Next to Hal stood Kalay, a tall, slender woman with red-blonde hair that fell in a thick braid down her back. Again and again, her grey eyes strafed the men and women who had gathered here. She wore the simple robe of the traders, a tunic that was held at the waist by a belt, and a skirt that clearly showed signs of wear, with a few pulled threads at the hem. Even so, her clothes were clean and showed off her slim figure. A basket covered with a cloth dangled from her right arm.

"She'll probably come in a cart; Winnie has already found that out. We have to wait until she gets out of the wagon," she said quietly. Standing next to Hal, she could have been a seller offering him her wares. None of those present paid her any attention. Hal had pulled the hood of his tunic over his head to hide his eye-catching face. With his arms crossed, he was now standing in the shadow under the canopy.

"We changed the guards at the north gate through our people. Everything went smoothly," Kalay whispered, then put on a practised smile.

Hal just nodded casually under the hood, and his satisfied gaze slid back to the audience, which was now joined by an instrumental group that had previously made music in a different place. Their colourful costumes stood out against the uniform grey of the backdrop of the marketplace. The musicians were still quite young, girls and boys in a good mood, who mingled with people while carrying their instruments. Obviously, they didn't want to miss the exciting performance, either.

Hal was glad that he had managed to notify his clan in time and bring some of his warriors to London. He had used a brilliant trick that Enja had shown him once. Enja's stallion was trained to run home. They had also practised that with his white horse, and the animals actually seemed to take the cue: no matter where they released the two, they always ran straight to Caerlaverock, right into the stable. He had done that with Taycan this time, with a small note in a leather

325

pouch on his mane, which was enough. Freed from saddle and bridle, he was back in Caerlaverock in no time.

The news of Enja's imprisonment had caused great concern. Kalay had used the time to gather the best warriors and set out for London, determined to save their leader. They had brought Taycan with them to use it for Enja's return.

Thank God the group from Caerlaverock had arrived a few days ago, and a stone was taken from Hal's heart because without the warriors around Kalay, his plan would not work—a plan that even Enja would have welcomed, he was sure of it.

But she wasn't free yet, and his nerves were strained to the breaking point despite the casualness on display. Kalay smiled nervously at him again, bit her lip, and anxiously checked the contents of the basket.

Enja's best friend craned his neck and stepped out of the shadows when the crowd suddenly moved as a wagon was being pulled from the eastern path into the market square. It was a simple, one-axle wagon with a donkey in front of it, and on it stood Enja von Caerlaverock like a statue, her hands tied with a rope in front of her.

A murmur went through the crowd. Hal and Kalay glanced at each other hastily. Whistles and shouts resounded while Enja looked straight ahead, completely immobile. They had loosened her hair, which now waved around her like a veil. She was in a penitent shirt that the delinquents had to wear on their last journey. On her temple, visible from afar, there was a laceration with coagulated blood that had run down her ear and neck and stuck strands of her hair together.

An unprecedented rage crept up to his throat and constricted it. It was all his fault. If he hadn't asked Enja not to fight back, she might not be standing there on that disgraceful cart.

How could he have done that to her? Who knows what else she had to endure in the tower? His fist clenched around the handle of the axe tucked in his belt. With all his might, he had to calm down. He couldn't screw it up now; otherwise, all would be lost. But the horrific sight had kindled his anger.

Nobody should dare to touch a hair on this woman's head! She had once saved his life and soul. If it hadn't been for her, he wouldn't be standing here in the marketplace today and opposing the English. She had given him the strength he now possessed. He would sooner die than leave Enja to the English.

Again, his gaze fell on the crowd. English soldiers appeared on the sides, including the young man with the red beard who had escorted them to the castle two weeks earlier. That person was going to die today, Hal decided grimly, and not just Redbeard but some of his comrades as well. The prospect of that made him focus on his goal again.

Suddenly, he became very calm. His advantage was the ambush. None of those present would be suspicious; the action was not allowed to start earlier than planned. Reluctantly, he let go of the axe, relaxed again, and sought eye contact with Enja to draw her attention to him.

Enja gave neither him nor the priest nor the hangman a glance as she was pulled down from the cart and pushed up the stairs to the dais. The shirt only covered her legs up to her knees, and the drooling crowd gazed unabashedly at her bare skin. The bulge of her breasts could be seen through the coarse fabric.

The henchmen dragged her to the rope that dangled from a gallows. The priest in a brown robe, armed only with a rosary and a Bible, spoke to her. But she just shook her head impatiently, whereupon the clergyman stepped back, visibly annoyed. A bailiff in a dark tunic and a crooked cap climbed the few steps to the dais and stood in front of the crowd. He had a whip in his left hand. With his right hand, he laboriously opened the parchment roll and read the judgement in his nasal voice:

"We, Edward, King of England, Lord of Ireland, and Duke of Aquitaine, convict the defendant Enja I-Shabbah ibn Hassan I-Shabbah, also known as Enja of Caerlaverock, for treason against the English crown. She got …"

At that moment, the instruments of the musicians who had gathered in the square sounded with a noise that spread over the entire market square like a carpet of sound and swallowed the speaker's words. They played a wild dance, which was accompanied by rattles, whistles, and a bagpipe. However, no melody could be recognised. It sounded like the one on the left didn't know what the one on the right was playing. If someone had thought about it, they should have been surprised why the group had played so harmoniously in the streets of the city before.

The bailiff gave up his speech, red-faced and exasperated, and waited impatiently for the group to stop playing. The amused people applauded politely, and the musicians bowed. A smile crept into the mask-like face of Enja, who was waiting next to the gallows.

When the crowded market square was finally quiet again, the bailiff started again and read in a loud voice, "And, therefore, she was sentenced to death by hanging, disembowelment, and quartering, and her head will later be on ..."

At that moment, the musicians began to play again, even louder than before, as if they had just really enjoyed their performance. They pounded the strings and whistled with such fervour that there was something funny about it. Even Hal and Kalay were grinning now, and most of the people in the square laughed openly.

On the wooden pedestal, the humiliated bailiff now looked completely angry. That had never happened to him before! And the crowd pretended that this was a fun interlude. He had a job, after all, and the proclamation of a royal judgement should earn the respect of his compatriots!

Sullenly, he ordered the soldiers to calm things down. But when they got closer to the musicians, there was suddenly a commotion in the crowd. As if on an invisible command, a few of the onlookers rushed up to the soldiers, tore them from their horses and killed them. Two or three of them jumped onto the dais, cut the delinquent's handcuffs, and pressed a strange-looking sword with a hilt of carved ivory into her hands.

With his mouth open in horror, the bailiff watched as the accused cut off the hangman's head in one flowing movement and the hands of the astonished priest, his hands still holding the Bible. His terrified scream boomed in his ears and mingled with the roar of the horrified and frightened crowd.

In a feline movement, the woman in the penitential tunic jumped straight at the bailiff. Startled, he took a step back and held his hands with the parchment in front of him. He was trembling like a leaf and began to whimper, begging for his life. But instead of chopping off a part of his body as well, she grabbed his robe and shouted at him, "The king has made me his enemy. If he wants me, he'll have to fight me. And if he fights with me, then he has to fight all of Scotland. Tell him that, you useless oaf!"

She let him go, and the bailiff, who had soiled himself in fear, collapsed onto his trembling knees. Helplessly, he watched as a horde of horses was driven into the now completely chaotic crowd that filled the marketplace. The women and men who had killed the soldiers with eerie precision now held the bystanders at bay with their swords, forcing them to retreat and form a passageway. Slowly, as if he had all the time in the world, an imposing man on a white horse approached, his face hidden beneath a hood, leading a black stallion by the reins. He halted before the wooden platform.

With a swift leap, the woman in the penitent's gown mounted the stallion, who tossed his head fiercely. Both horses then bolted into a full gallop, tearing through the crowd towards the northern gate.

A cry from the people followed them. Together, they rode unhindered through the deserted city gate. How could this be? There wasn't a single soldier in sight to stop them. Had they hidden? Were they all dead?

It had to be the work of the devil. Yes, that was the only explanation!

The bailiff let the verdict slip from his hand, clutched his head in despair, and collapsed to the ground. The terrified shrieks of the wounded priest reached his ears as if from a great distance. He was certain that the devil himself had come to free the heretic woman. Gratefully, the bailiff slipped into merciful unconsciousness, escaping the horrors of this world.

Chapter 14

Alamut in the year 1299

The abyss stretched infinitely. My body fell for what seemed like an eternity, far too long, before finally hitting the surface of a mountain stream with a resounding crash. The stream roared as it swelled into a raging river, and I swam fiercely against the relentless current, trying to get closer to the shore. Time and again, I collided with rocks and boulders that scraped against my skin like pumice. Again and again, I was swept away from the bank, pulled deeper into the swirling waters.

At last, my flailing arms struck a rock, and I managed to cling to it. My senses were already fading, and I had little hope of reaching the shore alive. With the last of my strength, I hauled myself up onto the rock and lay there, utterly exhausted, gasping for breath.

When I looked down at myself in confusion, I found that I was naked. The current had torn all the clothes off my body. I lay trembling and bleeding on the cold stone. I wouldn't have minded if I'd died at that moment. I had never felt such a longing for death before.

I saw my mother in front of me, her head getting smaller and smaller in the water. She yelled something at me. I saw her mouth open and close again. But I couldn't understand it. The language was alien to me. What language did my mother speak? Where did she come from? I couldn't remember anymore. My father had said something to me when he said goodbye to us. What were his words? I had forgotten. His face? Just a vague outline. I had promised him that I would never forget him …

Panic welled up in me. I pushed myself up on the smooth rock, swayed, and tried desperately to get my feet on the slippery stone. As if in mockery, I suddenly heard laughter over the rushing water. It came from the bank and my burning eyes searched for people among the trees.

Indeed, there came Nabil, Shi Fu, and my servant Ilyas. I waved and screamed with all my might. It was a long time before the three of them finally noticed me. They ran to the opposite bank, pointed excitedly at me, and shouted something in turn that I couldn't understand. My head was not able to form a clear thought. The water rushed and the noise made communication impossible. Only when they put their hands in front of their mouths like a funnel and kept shouting a word did I understand: "Woman!" they shouted with all their might. "You are a woman!"

I got dizzy. Stars danced before my eyes, and the world suddenly turned around me until I felt the water that caught me in its icy arms and carried it away. Mama ...

I woke up drenched in sweat. With a panicked look, I yanked back the covers, looked at my undamaged body, and took a deep breath. I had only had a bad dream. I sat up in bed, dazed, and rubbed the tiredness out of my eyes. When I tried to get up, I noticed the fresh blood that had collected between my legs and seeped into the sheet. Did I hurt myself?

I got up hastily and felt myself for any injuries, but nothing hurt me. There wasn't much blood, but I continued to bleed, and I felt grotesque panic about what to do now; and, most importantly, how to explain it to Hassan. The flush of shame rose in my face.

I had talked to Isaac once about the reason for menstrual bleeding and the cycle of female sexual maturity, but never about how I had to deal with it. I couldn't even get dressed without getting everything bloody. It was good that, as an Assassin, I now had my own chamber, which was simple but functional. Next to my horsehair mattress was a small wooden table with a bowl and a water jug on it. I started to wash off the blood with a sponge. I bit my lip nervously. How should I keep this fluid at bay while I wield my sword and fight?

My eyes fell on my bag with all my medicines and vials; it was lying next to my bed on the wooden bench. A bold idea arose in my head when I thought of the arrangement of the genital organs. If I could stop the bleeding already in the body, no more blood would flow out ...

I found a suitable size from the different sized linen bandages in my pocket, and applying firm pressure, rolled them into a tight roll that was about the size of my little finger. Then I tied the roll with the silk threads I had knotted myself, and just let the rest of the thread hang. I introduced them carefully, straightened up, and walked around my room. Due to the curvature of the uterus, it did not slide out any further, and the blood was stopped for the time being. I quickly turned a few more rolls and tucked them into my cloak, which I always carried with me. I was proud and at the same time relieved that I had found a solution to this feminine disadvantage. Nobody would find out yet that I was a woman.

I quickly tied back my breasts, which were small but had grown noticeably in the last few months. When I was fifteen, I had adjusted to this physical change. It would soon be more difficult to explain my high voice. I had to come up with something. My beard growth also left a lot to be desired. My whole body had changed, too. I had grown taller and become more muscular thanks to the combat exercises. The jokes about my sparse beard growth were, therefore, only sporadic.

My blonde hair was back to shoulder length, and I bound it with a leather strap at the back of my neck like most men here. Long hair was a sign of freedom and prosperity. A beard had to be short and should only partially adorn the face. My clothes had also changed since I became an Assassin. Wide, fine cloth trousers with a tunic that was gathered at the hips with a gold-trimmed belt, the obligatory khanjar, and the curved Arab dagger naturally tucked into them. The fabrics were sand-coloured, not dyed; only my cloak was embroidered with many coloured patterns and interwoven with gold thread. I was very proud of it because I had received it as a gift from Hassan in honour of my third consecration. I now slowly put it over my shoulders, pinned the ends of the gold and richly decorated brooch over my chest, and slipped into my soft leather shoes, which had been cut to my feet by Hassan's shoemaker. With them, I could move as silently as if I were walking barefoot.

Dressed up like that, I went down to the great hall where the new recruits were received. I should prepare them for their tasks together with Nabil. As always, I was curious to find out which interesting people had come, because not all of them were suitable for the tough training to become an Assassin. Again and again, men came from all corners of the country who volunteered to serve Hassan and wanted to be trained by him. As a military leader, he sent out numerous scouts who kept their eyes open for him and recruited people. The sultan's constant persecution and reprisals against the Shiites encouraged enough desperate men, tired of his tyranny, to run into Hassan's net.

The steadily growing following of the leader of the Nizarites was thus spread over the whole country, and according to my estimates, amounted to several thousand men—and one woman. Hassan's Assassins were true and loyal to him. He appointed the best princes as his personal staff, and these in turn were allowed to determine who would succeed them. As a Medicus and Assassin, I had a special position, although I had not yet received the highest ordination. I was brought in on official occasions. It was unthinkable to be indisposed because of a menstrual period on that day of all times!

The three newcomers standing in the hall today were the fruit of Hassan's efforts to raise an army that worked, murdered, and struck in secret, destined to serve as Saladin's greatest enemy. There was no sign of this euphoria in the three boys between the ages of twelve and sixteen. They stood next to each other with their arms hanging down. Their clothes were stiff with dirt and their faces were as emaciated as our cook's soup chicken. Not even the begging children in Baghdad were in such a sorry state.

One of the three caught my eye, in particular: he was tall and shockingly thin. His hands and feet looked way too big for his emaciated body. His hair, sticking out in all directions, was the dirty brown of street muck, and his nose looked unnaturally large on his flat face. Everything about this boy seemed ugly; only his eyes were a fascinating bright green. He was of Western descent, and the inverted cross on his forehead was a witness to his fate

I didn't know what had brought him here, but my heart instantly opened to this poor soul, whose wretched state touched me deeply. The moment our eyes met, I realised I had encountered my kindred spirit. He may have been unkempt, but his green eyes told a different story, and I was curious to learn more.

Hal was aware that he had no choice but to become an instrument of the dreaded Hassan I-Shabbah. After his adventurous escape from Saladin's palace, he wandered barefoot, begging and wearing only rags for nights on end— always looking for a way to get out of this cursed country that he had learned to hate so much. After all the humiliating shame he had endured, it seemed like a beneficial omen when the splendidly equipped troop of his new master came to a stop before him. They stood there proudly with their billowing gold-coloured cloaks and their impressive horses with elaborate bridles, as if they had come straight from the fairy tales that the women in Saladin's apartments told each other.

The men in gold-embroidered cloaks told him of their great leader, Hassan I-Shabbah, and his heroic deeds, of his indomitable fortress, and Saladin's great fear of the Assassins. In the end, the temptation to leave this country as a free man and with considerable wealth was greater than the homesickness that overcame him again and again, and so he had followed the men into an uncertain future.

Now here he was with the two other homeless children who had joined them, meeting the notorious Alamut Assassin leader and the rest of his gang. Hassan eyed him with his deep, penetrating eyes, and at his gesture, two princes received the three to prepare them for the first consecration. The men escorted them to the washroom, where they could change, shower, and get dressed.

Hal felt it was like a liberation to finally get out of his stinking rags and, now freshly washed, put on clean trousers and waistcoats. The pants were a little too short, but he didn't mind. He was, as he proudly stated, the tallest of all the men present, whom he towered over by far more than a whole head.

The young man with the blond hair who had brought him here with the others only came up to his shoulders. But otherwise, he was an impressive figure: strong arms and legs on an athletic body. The man was certainly a good and persistent fighter. His face was even, with high cheekbones, a straight nose, and skin as white as milk. If he'd been a girl, he'd be pretty. He looked rather menacing with his black eyebrows and blue eyes.

But what fascinated Hal most about this man, whom they called Eran, was the fact that he had the same tattooed cross on his forehead as he did. That connection gave him, a son of Irish farmers, the courage to get through all of this.

He looked at the fair-skinned Assassin and wondered if he would look like that one day, too. The pride with which he wore his cloak impressed Hal. Yes, he wanted to be like that one day—an Assassin, but a free man.

The first consecration of the three newcomers reminded me of my own the year before, which had been so formative. Nabil and I led the three boys into the holy halls—that's what we Assassins called the underground vaults that were under the actual fortress. A narrow staircase, laboriously carved into the rock and lit by the flickering light from a multitude of fire baskets, led into the dark heart of Alamut.

Fearfully, the three boys groped their way forward in the narrow corridor until it led into a large hall in which the other princes had already gathered. This hall served us for combat exercises because hardly a sound penetrated upstairs. Accordingly, the walls were peppered with all sorts of weapons: swords of all sizes and lengths, axes, lances, knives, crossbows and arrows. Next to them were shields and other strange devices that I had never seen myself. Hassan appeared to collect such weapons and also tested them on several occasions. Overall, there was something martial about this room; it literally smelled of death and violence.

The princes in their precious cloaks now stood in a circle in front of a granite block that always reminded me of an altar. Nabil manoeuvred the three intimidated boys into the centre of the circle and made them kneel down. Grandmaster Hassan stood in front of the granite block and crossed his arms in front of him. On his head he wore a black turban with a huge sapphire clip over his forehead. He looked awe-inspiring with his long black robe and precious silk robe. His neck was adorned with a chain of gold and lapis that hung heavily to his chest.

Even at my own consecration, I was deeply impressed by the complexity of this ceremony, and again the magic of this moment captured me. The three boys watched with wide eyes as Hassan turned and ignited a liquid on the granite block until the flames licked the entire surface of the stone. The children gasped. The light from the flames was reflected in their wide-open eyes.

The leader's sapphire sparkled bluish in the warm glow of the firelight, and the warmth of the flame was all too palpable. It even reached my skin, although I was standing a little apart from the group, for I had not yet achieved the title of prince. Hassan now raised his arms, looked into the fire, and began a chant in a language I had never heard before that ritual. Nabil suspected that it could be Old Arabic, an ancient language from a time long past. Nobody could understand the exact content here.

Hassan spoke faster and more urgently. The princes also began singing, which gave me goosebumps. It was only a hum, but it caught all the senses and formed the language of Hassan into a strange soundscape. The fire on the granite block seemed to burn by itself. Suddenly, Hassan's outstretched hands caught fire, and he stopped chanting. The princes stopped humming and there was a strange silence.

The leader turned and beckoned the three children to come over to him. One after the other shyly stepped forward, kneeled, and swore to serve the wise Grandmaster Hassan, and to give his life for him and Allah. Then Hassan put his fiery hand on the recruit's head and scorched his hair. Startled, he touched his head, but all the hair had burned off where the hand had lain.

I vividly remembered my own consecration. The smell of burnt hair lingered in my nose for a few days after this ceremony. I was just as shocked at the sudden loss of my hair as these boys. From then on, the hair would grow into a new life, which should symbolise a baptism.

The fire on his hands went out, and underneath, his skin was completely intact. The heat, which we ourselves felt as a hot wind, didn't seem to bother him in the least. Frozen with awe, the boys looked at the man in the black robe, who stared at them with his bewitching eyes.

"From today on, you are my children, and you are under the protection of our community and Allah," I heard Hassan say in his mother tongue, Farsi. "You will learn to kill enemies in my name and to love me so that you would die for me. Are you ready for that?"

"We are ready!" the three of them responded, and they were allowed to kiss their new leader's hand gratefully. Hassan was a charismatic man, and he knew how to cast a spell over people, and even let them die for him. At some point, I would ask him about the trick with his hands that was always impressive to all of us.

Personally, I had great admiration for this man who appeared so heartless and brutal on the outside, but who led his people smartly and wisely. His mind was unique, and his actions were determined by skilful political moves. No one else, whether monarch or Knight Templar, was so feared and at the same time so respected as Hassan I-Shabbah.

His principle was simple: purposefully and with only a few Assassins, he eliminated his opponents—sometimes for a fee, sometimes without—and thus kept his enemies in constant fear. He deliberately left his enemies in the dark as to who might be next and boasted of his misdeeds. It was not uncommon for clients to pay additional money to Hassan in order not to become victims of his Assassins themselves. Bribery was literally one of his best weapons.

From the perspective of an outsider, everyone would claim that Hassan was a ruthless murderer. But I would prefer to call him an opportunist, for he skilfully exploited the enmity of people, especially the religious conflicts, to his advantage. He knew how to never get caught between the fronts, neither between the Crusaders and Saladin nor between the Arab and Persian sultans. On the contrary, he preferred to hunt down one, then the other, for a fee, collecting his payment and letting the enemies loose upon each other again.

The leader of the Assassins was as hated as he was needed. His network spanned all of Arabia and large parts of Persia; he was an undisputed powerful figure, only he never made the first move himself. I couldn't help but smile at the thought of how Hassan played with powerful rulers like a cat with mice, and yet no one could eliminate the cat. Today, three new boys had been inducted into the circle of Assassins, and the number continued to grow. The newly initiated children of Hassan were now being invited to his table in the great hall to celebrate their induction with a feast, and they smiled with relief. As I accompanied them back up the stone staircase after the ceremony, the smell of burned hair still lingered in my nostrils.

Master Kang Shi Fu looked at me as if I had just grown a second head. I had forced him down on the exercise room floor several times. Here the cold rock floor was covered with carpets and pillows to dampen the fall. Shi Fu was the master of hand-to-hand combat and was able to perform all the exercises with me that were only intended to be practised after the sixth consecration. This was due to my ambition and persistence in performing each new exercise with the utmost precision until I mastered it perfectly.

Even today, he kept me fending off his attacks with merciless meticulousness, which he carried out sometimes with a knife, sometimes with his fist; and each time, I saw his movements as if in slow motion, saw his blow before it hit me, and could effectively hold him off and defend myself quickly.

Frustrated, the Chinese puffed through his nose and shook his head in disbelief.

"You fight, Eran, like you know exactly what I'm up to," he growled in his signature accent.

"If I hit this way," he said, waving his fist against my neck, "then you turn my fist and punch me in the face. If I hit here," he added, his fist pointed towards the abdomen, "then you step back and kick my balls. How you do that? Can you see into my mind?"

He was visibly upset, and I would almost have laughed if he hadn't meant it so seriously. I scratched my ear, embarrassed, and pulled my earlobe. How should I explain that without appearing arrogant again, as Master Abdallah had already chalked up against me? I tried a vague explanation.

"I don't know how I do this, Shi Fu. I just see what you're going to do and react before you move your fist. And it doesn't matter if you attack me with a knife or if someone shoots an arrow at me—I see it in advance."

My earlobe snapped back.

I hadn't really realised it myself until then. Now that I had said it, I began to think about it. For some reason, I guess I had something like a sixth sense that warned me when I was in danger.

"Isn't that the case with you, Shi Fu?"

I couldn't imagine that a trained fighter such as he wouldn't have the same instincts as I. It had never occurred to me that I was alone in this.

The wiry man looked at me thoughtfully and ran his left hand over his goatee, which hung thin and frayed from his chin. Finally, he nodded as if he understood, bowed briefly to me, and then said solemnly, "If you have the gift to see the immediate future, then you have long since deserved your seventh consecration. Shi Fu can't teach you anything anymore. Your strength and courage are those of a lion. I bow to you."

I was strangely moved that a man who had so much experience and knowledge himself would praise my skills so much. I couldn't really see into the future at all. But secretly, I had to agree with him, because one experience had occupied me for a long time: when an arrow flew in my direction during an attack by the Seljuks, I was able to see it before it hit me. It was as if time stood still for a moment. I could look at the arrow in peace and quiet, and only had to bend to the left to avoid it. Catching it wouldn't have been a problem, either. Apparently, the faster the threat approached me, the slower the images became. Was that it? Was that the perfection Shi Fu spoke of so often? The perfection of a warrior who has received the seventh consecration.

Shi Fu had turned to the wall with the strange weapons that I didn't recognise. Dutifully, I followed him without his asking me to. Finally, he took a slightly curved sword from a wooden stand and pulled it out of its scabbard. He held it reverently in front of him, then placed it on both palms of his hands to hand it to me with a little bow.

It was wonderful! The handle was carefully carved ivory, and the blade gleamed in the torchlight like a crystal in the sun. I accepted it with a reverent nod. It felt heavy and cool in my hands.

"This is the katana of a great warrior from a faraway land," Shi Fu explained. "He died a long time ago. No one can wield this sword unless he is perfectly balanced in arts and war. You are a great warrior. It should be yours now."

I caught my breath for a moment. The admiration for my skills that he gave me by handing me this weapon pressed on my chest and made my heart beat faster. The sword, an Asian katana, was extremely rare because the warriors were usually buried with their swords. I didn't know why Shi Fu had one in his collection, but apparently he was happy to pass it on to me. So I thanked him, and while I pretended to look at the unusual weapon, I tried to swallow that big lump of unbridled pride that was stuck in my throat. Was I even up to this unique sword? Would the great warrior who once owned it approve of my possession?

I weighed it in my hand with deep awe, and I quickly felt as if the weapon was made for me. The hairs on the back of my neck stood up as I looked lovingly at the sword. The edge was so sharp that I cut my finger as I passed it.

"By all the gods," I said, withdrawing my bleeding finger, "how can it be that a sword is so sharp!"

Shi Fu nodded knowingly and crossed his arms on the front of his chest as if he had known what was going to happen. "The blade is folded and hardened a thousand times. Much harder than iron or steel. Few people know how to do this. A katana is very valuable; it means a lot of power for its right owner."

Shi Fu smiled his mysterious smile again, and his goatee trembled. "But you have to know how to do it. Shi Fu will show you."

That day, he started training me with the Asian sword, which would become a deadly weapon in my hands. It seemed to me as if it were an extension of my movements, flowing and deadly at the same time. Nabil once told me that a weapon looks for its right owner and not the other way around. Maybe the weapon had found me now. It was actually what I was missing to be a perfect warrior. This sword and the art of wielding it gave me the power to wipe out life in the blink of an eye.

In the life of a warrior, setbacks were inevitable. Even the greatest fighter had a vulnerable spot. After three initiations, I had achieved all that I had set out to accomplish. However, there was one thing missing that the other men would always have over me despite my rigorous training: sheer physical strength. I was swift and knew where to strike or stab to take down an opponent. But if a man were to surprise and overpower me, he would have the advantage in sheer muscle power.

This was my carefully kept secret that only Shi Fu knew. Sometimes I felt that Shi Fu knew all of my secrets, including that I was a woman. With such close physical contact, which inevitably developed in hand-to-hand combat, he had to feel that I was missing an essential piece of my alleged manhood. As was his style, his facial expressions didn't reveal anything, for which I was very grateful. But he trained with me much harder and more intensely than with the other Assassins, because he seemed to sense that I had to fight harder than the others.

"You have the body of a woman," he once revealed to me at the very beginning of our friendship, "but the spirit of a man with balls. You can work with your body; your mind is very strong!"

Did he know? With a weapon like this unique sword, I was sure I could keep men at bay. Because the katana was far too dangerous as a practice sword, we used large bamboo sticks with wrapped handles.

I had never had more bruises and aching limbs than at that time. I quickly learned to dodge his blows. Soon the others who were practising with me in the hall noticed us and looked on with interest. As always, I lost myself in this kind of defence play with Shi Fu: dripping with sweat and groaning.

In the heat of the practice fight, I noticed at last that a special pair of eyes was watching me eagerly. They were bright green eyes, and they registered my every move with due respect.

Chapter 15

Leicester Castle in the year 1305

With a mighty swing of his iron hammer, the rock block shattered into pieces. Ignoring the flying splinters, the workers swiftly gathered the fragments with nimble hands and stacked them into the designated carts. A groan escaped James Douglas's throat, and the effort was etched into his face. Tired, he leaned the hammer against the rock face, took a short break, and wiped the sweat from his brow with the sleeve of his dirty shirt.

It was a cold December day, and the men froze if they didn't move. Hardly anyone had the iron will and strength like James to pull off the hard work. The steam from his body created little clouds in the cold, and his thin shirt was soaked with sweat. Dark, wet strands curled around his face, which showed the hardships and privations of the last few months. His once pale skin was now dark from the sun, and the winter cold drew tiny red veins down his cheeks. The vertical crease on his forehead was already a deep furrow in his face. Reluctantly, he picked up the hammer again and struck another blow. Immediately, the brittle stone gave way and burst into pieces the size of a child's head. The muscles on his arms and shoulders were clearly visible under his thin shirt. The hard work was a much tougher exercise than sword fighting had been in his youth.

The harshness of the labour camp took its toll. Many of his followers died miserably from illness or accidents despite having enough food. His younger brother, Hugh, had broken his arm in a rock fall. There were no healers in this hole, and James had tried to splint the arm with a fragment of wood and scraps of his shirt, but the break just wouldn't heal. A fire raged in the bone, and it seemed as if Hugh were getting weaker every day. He was holding on to the cart because another fit of weakness forced him to take a break when one of the English guards brutally hit his back with a stick.

"Work, you lazy piece of shit!" he yelled at Hugh, and he winced from the blow. Dazed, he stumbled towards the stones lying around and picked them up with his uninjured hand. Since he pressed the broken arm to his chest, he could only pick up one stone at a time and put it in his shoulder bag, which he unloaded into the cart provided.

James held his hammer so tight that the knuckles of his fist were white. His jawbones ground. Another moment and he would have landed the hammer on the soldier's head. He had imagined it so often in his dreams when he looked up at the stars in the open air at night.

Hugh swayed with every step he took but held on bravely. James felt heartbroken when he saw him suffer like this. As prisoners of the Crown, his men and brother had been brought with him to the labour camp not far from Leicester.

Under the strictest guard, they had to break the stones for the expansion of Leicester Castle. It was to be a grim castle with which King Edward wanted to demonstrate his power. Stone-beating was a job that required an incredible amount of strength and was carried out by James with stoic calm. As long as they didn't cause trouble, he and his brother were treated well. The English had made this clear to him before they sent him to the quarries. In doing so, they bought his cooperation and the loyalty of his followers.

But his brother's poor health worried him. He urgently needed a healer who could straighten his arm and fight the burn in the bone. Frustrated, he hacked the rock with the hammer again, which gave way under his anger and burst.

"We're about to have lunch, Hugh, then you can rest," he uttered breathlessly between two blows of the hammer.

"I'll talk to the officer on watch whether you can take a break today, and I'll go on with Lachlan alone."

In fact, his foreman and loyal friend Lachlan MacKay had stayed by his side here in the quarry. Lachlan, who had been there when they killed his father's young wife and brother, Matthew, harboured a deep grudge against the English who had confiscated Clan Douglas property. He had also been there before when James's father and his wife, Eleonore, convinced the Earl of Carrick, Sir Robert de Bruce, to fight for the Scots.

Like James's father, Lachlan was an ardent admirer of the Scottish heir to the throne. In fact, Sir Robert had come on the orders of the English King Edward to storm the castle of the rebellious Douglas family, but there—to Edward's great annoyance—had professed his Scottish homeland. Now, with the help of his compatriots, Robert was on his way to becoming king of Scotland. And James's father, William Douglas, was dead, allegedly killed in the Tower of London by the severe abuse of the English henchmen.

Angry, McKay threw the stones at the cart, which was already bending under its heavy load.

"Damn it, Scotland is finally about to win land against Edward and we're going to the dogs here!"

He spat without interrupting his work.

"If the boy doesn't get help soon, then he won't live to see the Scottish victory ..." With a movement of his chin, he pointed to Hugh, whose sweaty face was already pale. One of the English guards looked over at them suspiciously.

"My request for a pardon has been signed by Bishop de Lamberton and he will present it directly to King Edward. He has to let us go; this is an instalment execution ..." James whispered quietly to his foreman. "I pray every day that Hugh will hold out for so long."

McKay barely shook his head. James rolled his eyes. Oh, how he hated being stuck here while the Scots rebelled everywhere. One day, he would get back what King Edward had taken from him and his family. As long as he lived, he would fight to make amends for what this English bloodhound had done to his family—alongside a Scottish king. With suppressed anger, the hammer landed with a crash on the rock, and the stones flew in a high arc through the air and pelted the wet earth.

"The guards change every three hours. The work begins at sunrise and ends when the bell rings for evening prayer. One hour break at noon."

This is how Enja summed it up in her usual sober way. Her otherwise strong voice was just a low murmur. Hal lay flat on the ground next to her on a rise, peering down into the labour camp, which spanned an area three times the size of all of Leicester Castle.

Hale was glad that Enja had been freed from Edward's angry henchmen and had not been dragged back into the tower, but he had believed at first that they would hurry back to Scotland as quickly as possible. Everything would have gone well if they hadn't met these craftsmen in the shabby tavern. While Hal and Enja slept in the stables or in the woods, well masked because of their striking appearance, Kalay and her friends spent the evenings in the taverns drinking with the travellers to obtain information about the situation from them. It was only by chance that they discovered the trail leading to the Douglas brothers.

Hal remembered the name of the dive—Maiden's Inn—a name it didn't really deserve. That evening, after returning to her hiding place, an exhausted Kalay had told them with a heavy tongue of craftsmen leaving Leicester Castle and heading back to London to look for work. It had been skilled workers who drowned their frustration in ale in the inn where they had stopped. Before they forgot the reason for their trip, they revealed to Kalay after a few mugs of the strong brew that Sir Simon de Montfort, the Earl of Leicester, was now using Scottish slave labourers to build his castle instead of the expensive craftsmen. Among these, the two talkative men revealed in great secrecy, were probably also many of the broken Douglas clan, who were looked after by the wives of the craftsmen. Word of the stay of the unwelcome Scots quickly got around, but at the same time sparked the anger of the craftsmen. Kalay had thanked him, paid the bill, and let the two unlucky fellows ponder on behind their mugs.

The day after this meeting, on Enja's orders, they had changed their route towards Leicester to get a closer look at this labour camp. Hal thought that he had heard de Montfort's name in connection with Edward's generals. Certainly, the earl had good contacts to get slave labourers who should be sidelined on Edward's behalf. There was no question that the Douglas clan mentioned must be the remains of the once influential Scottish family.

Hal had noticed the look on Enja's face when Kalay had talked about the encounter and had kept his concerns to himself. There was no question that he would help her free James. And he hadn't flinched when she had her black stallion travel a little further west. Ever since she had met this James Douglas, she had been behaving strangely. Almost as if she owed him something. He had only found her and taken her with him. In Hal's view, he hadn't done anything to explain her sudden empathy for James.

He grumbled quietly to himself. His gaze fell on Enja, who was lying on her stomach next to him on the grass and was staring intently down into the labour camp. Her beautiful face looked almost stern in profile with the straight nose, and the tied-back hair accentuating the high cheekbones. It tempted him to brush the strand that had come loose back behind her ear. But he kept his hands on the ground as best he could.

Hal had nearly died of worry when her stallion Taycan appeared in front of the lake that surrounded Caerlaverock. Wet with sweat and trembling with exertion, he had hardly been calmed down when they wanted to take him to the courtyard on the ferry. The saddle, her bow—everything had seemed untouched, only no trace of Enja and her famous sword. Without thinking, Hal had saddled his white horse to look for her. His search eventually led him to the Douglas clan, who had rescued Enja after her encounter with the English soldiers.

It seemed to Hal as if Enja had a cloud of constant threat around her that fell upon her like a swarm of wasps. Enja was a mystery to him, but an enchanting one. Like a little child conquering the world with curious eyes, she ran from one adventure to the next. Hal worshipped her as one could only worship someone who, like a deity, was so completely out of his reach. Hal was her right hand and her conscience. And he couldn't be more for her—that had always been clear to both of them. But he disliked her apparent interest in this James Douglas more than he wanted to admit. The thought of him darkened his mood.

His gaze returned to the front, down to the camp where Douglas and his fallen clan worked. At some point, Enja would get tired of this puppy, too; he was sure of that. He couldn't hold a candle to her.

When she turned her head and smiled encouragingly at Hal, all concerns were blown away; for that smile alone, he would have carried her in her hands as far as Jerusalem.

Like ants, the workers down there in the grey stone hole kept moving in the same rhythm. There were the strong who beat the rocks, the nimble who gathered all the stones and piled them in the carts, and the weak and old who pulled the donkeys with the carts to the fortress.

The division of labour was effective, and the building grew correspondingly quickly, except that the people down there didn't do it willingly. James's sturdy build was easy to see as he hit the rocks with a hammer to crush them. His clothes were dirty and torn, his hair was shaggy, and the dark beard on his face hadn't seen a shave in months. Next to it, a smaller, similarly bearded figure picked up the stones and threw them into the cart. From his looks and size, I immediately suspected it was Lachlan McKay, James's longtime friend.

Another man worried me more: his slim, beardless figure moved unsteadily between carts and boulders; his arm bent at his chest. Even from a distance, I could see Hugh in pain. Thoughtfully, I pulled my lower lip between my teeth and assessed the situation.

"Hugh's condition calls for faster action, Hal. Yesterday, the rest of the warriors from Caerlaverock arrived with the ponies we were waiting for. We'll change the plan and switch three of the girls at once. We cannot delay his deliverance any longer. We should also send a healer; she can look at Hugh's arm."

Hal turned his head to me with a terrifyingly sombre look, raised one of his eyebrows, and looked at me questioningly. "And how are you going to explain that all of a sudden three new girls are coming to the kitchen, and that one of them happens to be a healer?" He grumbled angrily.

"A fever," I said spontaneously, glad of my brainstorm. "The three girls were replaced because they got sick. Maybe they got it from the prisoners, and now new ones are coming with a healer who is supposed to check the prisoners, too."

I looked at him challengingly from the ground, my head close to his. He had averted his eyes again and was staring stubbornly down at the camp. If I hadn't known better, I would have said that a flaming volcano was simmering again beneath his superficial calm. I was curious to see when it would break out.

"Hal, we have to get down there tomorrow, and we need the weapons that the cooks smuggled into the camp," I warned him urgently. "Hugh is getting worse every day since we've been watching him."

"Mmh," was all that Hal said.

I mentally listed the names of those I wanted to send down there to cook for the prisoners. Up until now, it had been done by the women from the village who had been assigned by the English, mostly women of the craftsmen who had been employed to build the castle. Our plan had been to gradually replace them with our female warriors, but that was taking too long. The boy urgently needed help.

"Kalay goes with Winnie first," I thought out loud, "and then Moira comes as a healer."

"Moira is not going anywhere," Hal snapped hoarsely.

"Moira is our best healer," I replied, irritated.

"Moira stays where she is!" The anger in his voice made me curious. I looked at him sideways again.

"Moira ..."

"... stays here!"

Hal hissed angrily and suddenly pushed his face very close to mine. His green eyes shone menacingly under furrowed eyebrows. What was the matter with him all of a sudden? Under my guidance, Moira had become one of the best healers I had ever trained. She was my right hand and organised the sick area completely independently. Her cleverness rivalled her beauty, and Hal must have fallen for her. If he was so set against Moira going, he should make a suggestion.

"Who else should I send?" I asked him.

He didn't respond.

"Hal, I'm sending two warriors along; nothing will happen to Moira!"

"What if we attack and she gets caught between the fronts?" he suddenly responded, his forehead furrowed.

"I'll let them rappel down to join the prisoners in the pitfall," I suggested, surprised again by his concern for Moira. Hal took a sharp breath. And knowing what was to come, I quickly added, "There are decent men there, not savages, and they will protect them, believe me. They will immediately see what is going on and their fighting instinct will guide them to protect the women. No Englishman will voluntarily get lost in the pitfall."

I was certain that this daring plan would work, and we could save valuable time, time we so badly needed. I crawled back carefully and got up. Hal followed me, and while I was still brushing the dirt off my clothes, I pushed the topic further before he could change his mind; "Come on, let's go back to the camp and talk to the girls."

With that, I turned on my heel and went down to the horses. But I could still hear Hal's sullen hum at my back.

James Douglas had been observing the behaviour of the women working here for some time. They were polite but distant, and there was no direct eye contact—clearly, they had been intimidated beforehand. The food was surprisingly good for a labour camp, contrary to his fear that they would starve him and his men. The distribution of food was handled by three women from the village. They arrived early in the morning, served breakfast, prepared lunch and later dinner for the prisoners, then cleaned up before returning to their homes. The English were carefully ensuring that the women spoke to the prisoners in English, so they couldn't exchange secret information in Gaelic.

Hugh had to work that afternoon despite his fever; James's intercession had not been able to soften the commandant of the camp. The young Englishman was new to the job and unsure how to deal with the prisoners. His dismissive face showed no understanding for the poor health of the young Douglas.

Drained and tired, Hugh still lacked an appetite, and he barely made it through half his dinner. He fell asleep feverishly after dinner, only covered with a blanket to protect against the bitter cold.

To sleep, they climbed down into a kind of pitfall using a ladder that was pulled up as soon as the last of them was down. It was a little over ten feet deep and overhanging at the edges. The walls were smooth and slippery. No man had ever managed to climb out of this pit. There were straw and blankets laid out for the prisoners. Crowded together, all twenty-four men had ample space. So, they survived the cold nights to some extent.

Better than a cell somewhere in a dark basement dungeon, James thought, turning to Hugh, who had fallen asleep with his back to him. Carefully, he touched the sixteen-year-old's lean body, which felt hot despite the cold. Christ, don't let him die, James thought, sending a quick prayer to heaven. He is all that I have left of my family.

Sadly, he put his hard work-calloused hand protectively on Hugh's shoulder and fell asleep, exhausted. The stars glittered graciously above them on the clear December night, as if they too had an eye on his sick brother.

The next morning, it was suddenly three unknown women who were distributing the bread and porridge—a circumstance that amazed James because the English were very suspicious of strangers, and for good reason. Where had the other women from the village gone? Had they had enough of the daily sight of the ragged figures?

But when one of the three women who introduced herself as Moira immediately took care of his brother, new hope sprouted in James. She seemed to know a lot about sick people, and maybe that was the reason for the change of cooks. Moira exuded a maternal warmth that seemed to defy even the chill of the quarry, and a gentle but determined nature. She made not only Hugh smile, but every Scotsman, and even the English. She was a very pretty girl with a petite, feminine figure. The simple linen dress flattered her every move, and a leather belt accentuated her slim waist.

The men turned their heads when she floated past them with a fluttering skirt and put on her warmest smile. The Scots paused in their work, and for a moment, the English forgot to guard their prisoners.

With practised movements, she straightened Hugh's arm, wrapped a cooling herb wrap around him, and gave him a makeshift splint. In addition, he was given a special tea that he should drink as often as possible. It was also Moira who made sure that he could take a break from work. A smile from her, and the captain on watch let Hugh rest in the trap with his tea and a warm blanket.

After breakfast, the English guards let the entire troop line up in a row. The young officer informed the prisoners that the women from the village had contracted a fever the day before, and that it may also be rampant among the prisoners, adding that a healer would examine the men for typhus.

James let Moira—under close supervision—also examine his face, overgrown by the shaggy beard, and his upper body for reddish spots. She looked him in the eye and plucked a louse from his beard with her pointed fingers. Now he was able to admire her face up close and understood straight away what so enchanted the men. Fine fair skin, an even face, the lips were full and sensual, and the eyes were the colour of mature uisge beatha. To men in his situation, she had to appear like an angel. He muttered thanks in English for her treatment of his brother.

"He'll be better soon," replied Moira in a lowered voice—in Gaelic! James hid his surprise behind his cupped hand with a cough and checked with a quick glance to see if one of the officers on duty had noticed the exchange. Moira turned his head in the other direction with one hand and looked at his face. Then she felt his forehead with soft, warm hands, looked directly at him, and blinked one eye. His heart stopped for a few seconds. What did she mean by that? Finally, she turned and shook her head in the direction of the commander to signal that this Scot had no fever. Determined, she turned to the next prisoner in line.

He couldn't get the woman out of his head. Something told him that she didn't belong here, not even in the village with the other women. She didn't really suit them at all. He couldn't wait to queue for lunch to look at the other two women. One was tall, slender, with a long, red-blonde braid that came down to her waist under her hood. She made a robust and tough impression. She could have been from the Highlands, with grey eyes and lots of freckles on her face. She wore a simple linen dress, as was customary with the maidservants and peasant women from the village. Still, it seemed somehow out of place with her. She exuded a peculiar nonchalance in every movement she made.

She held the handle of the soup ladle like a weapon, and despite working quickly, did not spill any precious food when pouring it into the wooden bowls. The tall girl didn't look at anyone, but only concentrated fully on her work.

The second, on the other hand, was a cheeky thing. Completely wrapped in a dress that was a little too big, her body looked noticeably small. But she made up for her lack of height with her appearance. She grinned boldly at him from below and held out a piece of bread. When he was about to take it, she dropped it, and he hurried to catch it. He almost spilled the soup. Was she crazy?

With a theatrical gesture, she bowed apologetically to him. Some of the row could barely suppress a grin. Even the English laughed along as if she were here to entertain them.

The little one allowed herself to have fun a few more times and conjured up a small smile on the mournful expressions of his fellow sufferers. With her short black hair bobbing around her face, blue eyes, and little snub nose, she definitely looked different from the average. Her lively facial expressions underlined the impression that she was a real bundle of energy until one of the officers on duty finally reached the end of his rope and urged her to stop.

Then she turned around and countered with a squeaky voice, "Your lieutenant said we are not allowed to speak to them, but he has not forbidden us to joke with them. And if you don't want to find a rat's tail in your plate, you better shut up now!"

The soldier's eyes widened in shock, then he blushed, turned angrily away with clenched fists, and took up another position a little further away. The little one grinned into the ranks of the prisoners, who couldn't believe how confidently she had won the round. Moira, who was cleaning the dishes, laughed openly at James, and he winked at her.

James was sure now that none of the women were from the village. But who was she then? He simply could not fathom how the three had arrived at this desolate place. They must have been sent, but by whom?

The presence of the pretty and intrepid women, who brought a little colour to the dreary grey of the quarry, had made the workday easier for many prisoners. Even the English understood that a little variety didn't hurt and joked with the girls who were allowed to retreat to the soldiers' warm tent during their break.

Before dinner, a group of mounted men suddenly moved into the quarry, in the midst of which was Simon de Montfort, the Earl of Leicester. He might have been a handsome man when he was young. In his expensive outfit with the lavishly decorated breastplate, he drew the eyes of all the workers from afar, and the girls also looked up curiously from the dining area. His face was deeply furrowed. He looked as if he'd forgotten how to laugh at an early age. Accordingly, the good mood had vanished quickly, and a strange tension settled like lead on those present. Sluggishly, the earl rose from the saddle of his warhorse, who shook its head and tried to clink the bridle against his foot. Even the horse seemed tired of its disgruntled rider.

The commandant on duty had the prisoners line up and reported his troops, the daily success, and the condition of the camp. But that didn't improve the earl's bad mood. Nervous and freezing, the prisoners stepped from one leg to the other, foreseeing a disaster. It was so cold that their breath formed small clouds of mist over their mouths. Many rubbed their hands together to create a little warmth. At the earl's orders, the girls had to stop preparations for dinner and shyly approached the prisoners, who were lined up in two rows. Against the cold they now wore plaids over their shoulders to keep warm.

"Count through!" ordered Simon de Montfort in a harsh, commanding tone that did not tolerate contradiction. Each prisoner kept counting in his row until the last one announced the number twenty-three aloud. Dead silence.

"Last week, it was twenty-four and no deaths have been reported, so where's the missing one?" the earl snapped at the captain. He pointed eagerly at the pitfall.

"There in the pit, my lord. He is reported sick at the behest of the healer. He's feverish, my lord."

The earl's lips narrowed. He snapped at the commandant. "Bring that fellow and that cursed healer to me at once. Who in the devil's name are they supposed to be?"

Then everything went very fast. In no time at all, the drowsy and confused Hugh was pulled out of the pitfall, and Moira soon found herself next to her patient, whom she held carefully by the arm so that he would not fall. He was still suffering from the effects of the sleeping potion that she had given him.

With his arms folded behind his back, the earl walked up to them and stared at them with furrowed eyebrows.

"Young Douglas. I thought so ..." he said more to himself than Hugh. "Why can't you work, you lazy good for nothing?" he snarled. "Even with a broken left arm, you can still pick up the stones with your right!"

Moira took him courageously under her protection.

"His arm is not healing properly, and he has caught the fever. He cannot work for you; he would be useless in the quarry, and today I let him sleep with some medicine."

"While everyone else is working, that Scottish bastard is resting?" the earl spat at her. "And who are you, dirty whore, that you disregard my orders?"

"My lord, I am a healer, and if the young man does not recover, he will die and can no longer be of use to you," said Moira in a firm voice.

James involuntarily leaned forward. He was not far from the two of them and prepared to intervene at any time if the earl should harm this woman.

"So, healer," he mused suddenly, dangerously quiet. "What is your name?"

Moira swallowed visibly.

"My name is Moira, Moira Colhoun," she said hesitantly.

"I don't know any Moira Colhoun," replied the earl in a low voice that was much more threatening than his loud barking.

"I have only recently been in the village, my lord. My husband died, so I had to go back to my family in the village a few months ago."

Moira's voice trembled; the lie written on her face.

"I don't know any family by the name of Colhoun either, woman!"

Dead silence. The earl turned slowly to the captain, who was now also nervous. "Has she been checked?"

"Eh, to be honest, well, there should be a fever in the camp ..." stammered the young officer before de Montfort lifted him out of his shoes with a strong right hook.

"Take your things and get out of here, you beginner! I'll take matters into my own hands," he yelled after him with a blazing red face. The young man got up, distraught, and backed away from him.

"Fever, pah!" uttered the raging earl. "It seems to me that everyone can walk in and out of here as they please!"

His voice had the barking sound again.

"Guard! Whip this lazy piece of Scottish guts here that simulates at the expense of others. Eleven lashes, one for each of the missed hours today!"

Moira let out a cry of horror and rushed towards the earl. "You must not do that, my lord! He will die from it! He's so weak."

She even dropped to her knees in front of him, her headscarf slipping off as she begged him bitterly. "I ask for forgiveness; it was my fault. I ... "

She didn't get any further. His huge hand rushed down into the face of the horrified Moira, who fell back like a sack. The sound was like crunching bones, and James jumped forward, blind with anger. Roaring, he lunged at the earl, who was completely surprised by this maddened attack. Not only him, but all the men—especially Lachlan McKay—

suddenly seemed to be playing crazy and rushed with roars at the hated Simon de Montfort and his people.

He hurried back into the circle of his soldiers, who stood in the way of the attackers. An unorganised uprising against armed soldiers was brave, but extremely painful for the attackers. James received a blow in the stomach with a stick that made him crumple with a groan. A kick in the face finally knocked him down in a daze. His fellow prisoners were no different and were quickly incapacitated or surrendered.

James only vaguely noticed that he was being thrown into the pitfall by the soldiers. The soft straw caught him, but his bowels ached on the impact. The rest of the squad were allowed to use the ladder. Hardly anyone didn't have a black eye, a bleeding nose, or a chipped tooth here and there. Only Hugh was missing because he had to stay upstairs with the three girls.

James's head throbbed from the kick, and he gently felt his face with his fingers. He felt a bruised spot on the side of his chin where the boot had hit him and let out a curse that expressed so much of the pain, agony, and suffering he was feeling. "Hugh! My God! Hugh, what have I done …"

And when he heard the crack of whips from above, the terrified screams of Moira, and the agonised roars of his ailing brother, he closed his eyes and began to pray.

He didn't open his eyes again until he heard his brother's battered body pop up next to him. They had just thrown him down like an animal, and he landed heavily on his back in the straw, his broken arm twisted at an odd angle. He was unconscious, his torn shirt hanging in tatters from his bleeding back. James took him in his arms, tears in his eyes. He held the motionless boy tightly to his chest. The anger and horror almost took his breath away, and he stammered Hugh's name over and over again.

Shortly afterwards, one of the girls fell into the pit, neatly rolled over, and jumped up again nimbly. It was the little one with the short hair. Then followed the redhead, who came down with both legs, cushioned herself, and stood. Both tried to catch the third one, who jumped off the edge. The other men who saw this action helped them to keep Moira from getting hurt.

James saw the grinning English look over the edge. They smirked and spat on her. Apparently, the girls preferred to jump into the pit than to become fair game for the English. The wrinkled face of the Earl now rose above all of them, who uttered the guilty verdict on the girls audibly for everyone.

"They would rather stay with you cellar lobsters than spend the evening with us, so they should stay down there, too. Simon de Montfort can't be fooled, you understand. Tonight, you can think about which side you choose, my doves!"

The ugly laughter of his henchmen accompanied his cold words.

"If there is anything left of them tomorrow," he heard him say to his men, laughing as he trudged back to the tent to have his dinner.

The three girls clutched each other. Moira still seemed to be in shock. She looked around anxiously. The other two stared around motionless. They had stuck their chins out defiantly. There was no sign of fear on their faces. The men stood in a circle around the women but held back and waited for their leader's orders. Even in captivity, the hierarchy was perfectly clear—James Douglas remained their laird.

Suddenly, Moira's gaze fell on Hugh, and she rushed towards him with a horrified gasp.

"Let me look at it! My God, how terrible. How could you do that to the boy?" she exclaimed as she carefully laid him on his stomach with James's help. "And there is nothing I can do for him. My bag is upstairs. Maybe I can ask the English...?"

At that moment, her gaze fell on James and she fell silent. His angry look told her that apart from a few insults, she wouldn't get anything from up there. She put her hand to her mouth and turned away. Tears ran quietly down her cheeks.

James turned to the other two girls, who stood by and waited. "Who are you actually, and what are you doing here?" he said, demanding an explanation.

The bigger one spoke for the first time. Quietly and with impressive nonchalance, she pointed up with one finger and spoke in broad Gaelic: "We thought we would be safer here than up there." She grinned boldly. "My name is Kalay, and the short fellow with the loose tongue is Winnie."

Winnie bowed and grinned cheekily. "Forgive me, my lord, for us to burst in here unannounced, but I didn't know where to knock ..."

Kalay slapped Winnie in the back of the head with the palm of her hand and apologised to James.

"This dwarf simply has no manners, and certainly no decency."

"And your brain is closer to the sun and completely burned by the heat; that's why you're just speaking nonsense," Winnie snapped back.

James got up with a groan, stood up in front of the two as they continued to argue, and repeated in a surprisingly calm voice that did not reveal any of the turmoil in his heart, "Please, just tell me what's going on here. Who in God's name sent you?"

"Well," said Winnie, "something must have gone wrong."

She cocked her head as if the situation was uncomfortable.

"We shouldn't be here; at least Kalay and I shouldn't."

"Where else should you be?" James asked patiently, although his collar was slowly bursting.

"Well, up in the quarry, distributing the weapons and killing the soldiers," added Kalay, as if that were completely normal.

"You both? You alone?" he croaked, his head pounding again.

Winnie laughed. "No, you fool! With everyone else, of course!"

Kalay gave her a light push. "This is Sir James. You're addressing him in third person, and with my lord—can't you remember that?" she hissed at her.

"Oh yes, my lord, excuse me. Sir Fool?" Winnie corrected herself and curtsied.

James's shoulders sagged noticeably. It couldn't get worse. Three women trying to rescue twenty-four men from a hole in the ground, one of them half dead, and two of the women who didn't even seem to be in their right mind. He wiped his eyes with a hand. Suddenly, a leaden tiredness overcame him.

"Who sent you? Where are you from?" James tried again to get some clarity into what was happening. But the two dissimilar women were silent. No one wanted to say more about the messy situation than necessary, and they all had their arms crossed over their chests. Helpless and tired, he shrugged his shoulders, and wiped his hand over his eyes.

"We'll solve this tomorrow," he mumbled, then turned back to his unconscious brother.

His men, who had watched the goings-on in disbelief, became restless. They knew their leader had a strong personality and were now worried. Lachlan stepped forward and made a suggestion to bail out his laird.

"Shall we try to lift the women up at night so they can run away? If they keep drinking and eating up there, they might not even notice the three of them passing."

"You wouldn't be able to get past de Montfort's tent. There are guards stationed there, and that's the only way out of the quarry," James replied flatly and shook his head.

"No, you stay here for the time being; we'll wait until night falls. We have to come up with something to distract them."

James Douglas was frantically pulling his hair out. He had no idea how to get them out of this hole safely. They were trapped here, as were his men.

Sullenly, they parted the blankets and carefully wrapped the unconscious Hugh in one of them. Moira couldn't do anything about the broken arm but managed to get the shoulder dislocated during the fall back into place. Hugh was very badly off. The new wounds on his back and the loss of blood had only made his condition worse.

James lay down to sleep and hugged his brother. He was miserably exhausted and emaciated. They hadn't had dinner, and the hunger was also gnawing on his nerves. The women lay warmly together and waited for the night to fall. For a long time, the noise of the soldiers drinking in the tent could be heard as they were feeding Simon de Montfort with wine and a warm meal. How inhuman and obscene, thought James, when twenty-seven people shivered from cold and hunger in a nearby pit.

Eventually, silence spread through the quarry. A tranquility that was eerie after the noise of the previous hours. James awoke to it. He checked Hugh's breathing, which was thankfully steady. Then he listened again to the outside. Only the moon and the starry sky provided some light in the dark pit, and he could make out the bodies lined up under the plaids and blankets.

After a while, he realised what bothered him about the silence. Not a single animal made a sound, and that was a sign that someone was out there somewhere; someone even animals feared. No owl cry, no rustling rabbit, no howling wolf. He listened hard. It was like the silence before a storm.

And the storm broke out shortly afterwards. Some intruders in arms invaded the English camp. Screams of fear and death became loud; the roar of battle arose in which the soldiers' screams mixed with the noise of metal hitting metal. It was the relentless scales of death, a tune so familiar to James and his people.

Without thinking, James had his now wide-awake followers and the three women who peeled themselves from the blankets in alarm stand against the wall of the pit to protect them from flying parts. He himself held Hugh tightly against his body with both arms, limp limbs dangling lifelessly. In fact, a short time later, torches and weapons fell into the pit; whether on purpose or not, he couldn't tell. The men picked them up immediately before the straw could ignite. McKay had grabbed a sword, and the nimble Winnie had grabbed a knife that looked way too big for her. Everyone listened intently and breathlessly pressed against the wall while the battle raged above.

A particularly fierce battle seemed to be developing between two men whose grunts and snorts were getting closer and closer to the edge of the pit. Thuds and crashing bones were evidence of a relentless argument. Suddenly, James saw a body being thrown with force over the edge of the pit and it hit the straw in front of him. He tensed his body. In the light of the torches, he recognised Simon de Montfort, who was now trying to sit up in a daze. If James hadn't been holding his brother in his arms, he would have jumped and killed the earl with his bare hands.

But someone else got ahead of him: a second man jumped into the pit and landed with both feet. Even in the half-light, James could tell immediately who this fierce warrior was. It was the giant who had collected Enja from his parents' castle. Now he stood in front of him in the flesh, with an expression on his terrifyingly painted face, which, in the silvery moonlight, he could only describe as a lust for murder. The torches only vaguely lit the haunted scene, but the flames were reflected in his eyes. Without paying attention to the bystanders, he drew one of his axes from his belt and struck the head of the lord of Leicester Castle, who was getting up on all fours, with one powerful blow. The bone gave way with a crack. The warrior pulled out his axe again and left the motionless body lying there. Tense, with a slightly bent upper body, he looked around for a familiar face until his eyes finally landed on Moira.

"Moira!" he exclaimed, half relieved, half worried when he saw her swollen eye in the torchlight.

"We're fine, Hal. Winnie and Kalay are here; nothing happened to us," Moira soothed in Gaelic. She briefly explained the situation to him and introduced him to James Douglas.

James nodded his thanks and relief.

"I hope you can help us get out of here. My brother urgently needs help from a healer."

Hal could see that the young man in James's arms was closer to death than life, and he nodded.

"I'm Cathal Ó Searcaigh," he said, finally introducing himself and holding out his paw to him. "Call me Hal."

There was something unreal about the situation when James handed his unconscious brother Hugh to Lachlan and squeezed Hal's offered hand with all his might. It was more than gratitude that he wanted to express with this gesture. "Thanks, Hal," he said, choking and putting his left hand on top of it. "Thank you …"

Suddenly, a whistle rang out from above. Hal stepped back and whistled, too. He motioned for some of the people who were still standing against the wall to move to the side and grabbed the ladder, which was now being lowered. At the edge of the pit, there were now many faces grinning down. Happy shouts accompanied the three women as they climbed the ladder, especially Moira, who couldn't wait to get out of this terrible trap.

Hal climbed second to last. He took the unconscious boy over his shoulder and climbed the wooden ladder, which bent dangerously under his weight. At last, James Douglas climbed up and found himself facing a large number of unknown women and men who looked at him expectantly. The quarry was hardly recognisable, lit by countless torches; it offered a scene of horror. The English tent had been torn down and bodies were strewn everywhere. Apparently, none of the soldiers survived.

James swallowed hard when he saw his clansmen who had just received some bread and water to satisfy the worst hunger. The realisation that he was free, and that these unknown men and women had fought for him and his people, made him shiver. Someone also handed him bread and water, which he gratefully accepted. It was Kalay who patted him on the shoulder encouragingly. Moira was already taking care of Hugh.

Hal and a few helpers gathered up the weapons and tools that were still usable: a good yield for today. McKay walked up to James and they both hugged in relief. Then his gaze fell on the figure who came down from the hill and greeted each of the men with a handshake.

She was wearing black trousers, sturdy high leather boots, a tunic with a leather vest and a long dark plaid over it, which was held together at the shoulder with a clasp. The pale hilt of her sword, which was strapped diagonally across her back, peeked out from behind.

She was even more beautiful than James remembered her. Her long hair was pinned to the top of her head, with a strand or two hanging down the side of her ear. She was just coming up to him.

She moved like a cat, light and springy. Her fair skin looked even lighter in the torchlight. The eyes were almost black and shiny in the weak light, their features hidden in the penumbra. But he could see that she was smiling, and a strange pressure settled on his chest, his heart suddenly beating unusually fast.

She stopped in front of him and held out her right hand. "Lord James Douglas, I assume?" she asked formally, showing her most charming smile. She had named him by his title, a title that had once belonged to his father and now passed on to him—all that was left to him.

He took her cool, firm hand, cleared his throat, and replied just as formally, "Enja von Caerlaverock, what an honour to see you again."

And for the first time in a long time, a smile crossed his lips. "I suppose my men and I owe you the greatest of gratitude. But say, why did you free us from the English?"

"Thank you very much, my lord," she replied gravely. "But I have only paid my debt to you. You saved my life then, I now saved yours."

And with a slight bow, she underlined how important it had been to her to settle this debt. "Besides," she continued, "Robert de Bruce still needs fighters for his army. I suppose you still want revenge on the English king?"

James nodded grimly. That was to say the least.

"Then you will be happy to hear that a ship is waiting for you, and that I will bring you and all your men to him. Are you ready for a little trip?"

Enja looked at him briskly.

"I'd ride through hell myself if I could find Edward there. But how do we get away from here? We won't get very far on foot …"

His eyes were back on his men, who were wrapping themselves in warm blankets.

Enja followed his gaze. "Let that be my concern. Before dawn, no one will have noticed what happened tonight, and by then we will be over the mountains. Except for Hugh, the men are all in physical condition to ride a couple of hours to the coast. We don't take a break."

"What is going to happen to Hugh? I won't leave him alone. I'd rather stay behind…" James burst out. But Enja wiped his concerns away with a wave of the hand.

"He will be brought to Caerlaverock by my people and nursed back to health; do not worry. He is in good hands."

At that moment, James heard the sound of horses' hooves and a whole herd of Scottish ponies trotted into the quarry, flanked by two riders who were Enja's warriors. It was their highland horses that could run for many hours, sure-footed and undemanding. She was clearly ahead of the game with these scruffy animals.

"Let your men mount the ponies and then go!" Enja shouted to the leader of the Douglas clan in a loud voice, then put her fingers in her mouth for a long-lasting whistle.

"Hal, throw the bodies in the hole and stack stones on top of it. See you in Caerlaverock!"

She called to the tattooed giant and ran towards a black horse, who bolted like lightning out from behind the hill and came to a stop in front of her with slipping hooves. With her left hand on the pommel of the saddle, Enja jumped onto the back of the magnificent animal. A leather strap tied under his chin served as a rein, and Enja didn't even need that. Horse and rider merged into one, it seemed.

Amazed by the impressive couple, James let his men mount the horses and took one for himself. These tough Highland horses were ideal for the demands of this area, and also found their way in the dark. Enja's people had folded blankets on their backs that were strapped with a large leather belt, the simple version of a saddle.

The ponies did not move. James's hands clenched his thick mane. The four-legged friends seemed to be waiting for some signal from Enja, who now rode past them like a commander with five of her torch-bearing warriors. James saw Winnie sitting on the smallest pony he had ever seen. She winked at him.

Only then, as if on a secret signal, did the wiry horses start moving. At the end of the long line, five more of Enja's female warriors followed on their own horses.

They had exhausting hours ahead of them, but they were nothing against the fate that would certainly have overtaken them all here. His gaze went back once more and caught some of the men and women removing the bodies of the fallen by torchlight. Hal was dragging two bodies at a time by their feet and throwing them into the pit. In the distance he thought he could make out Moira at Hugh's side.

Saying goodbye to his brother had been difficult for him. Who knew if he would ever see him again? But Enja was right—Hugh would be much better off in Caerlaverock.

Relieved, he turned his face forward. In the flickering light of the torches, James glimpsed the fair hair of the woman who had saved him and Hugh. Her striking weapon swayed with each step of her horse. He closed his eyes in relief and sent a prayer skyward. Perhaps she was indeed an angel, sent by Almighty God?

Chapter 16

Alamut in the year 1299

The boy with the green eyes wouldn't leave my thoughts. I tried to earn his trust to learn more about him, but that proved easier said than done. For a long time, I had no idea if he even understood the local language, as not a single word passed his lips.

His fighting skills had a peculiar quality, somewhere between a broomstick and a dancing bear—a situation that clearly troubled him. His two left hands and awkward legs seemed to have a mind of their own, which even I found surprising. His accuracy was impressive, but getting into position seemed to be his biggest challenge.

I felt all the more his awe of my own skills. One evening, when I sat down on the steps in front of the great hall after supper and caught the last rays of the evening sun, he spoke to me for the first time on his own initiative. It was the only time of day I could be outside. My eyes and skin suffered from the hot rays, so I completely avoided the sun during the day. The night became my best friend. The best conditions for an Assassin!

The air was still pleasantly warm, and the updrafts of the mountain range came from the valley, blowing the dust over the courtyard in small eddies. I held my little flute, which I had carved out of bamboo, to my lips and blew a melody that I had rehearsed with Jasemin in Baghdad. It was a happy melody that we could even play in two voices at the time. When I closed my eyes, I could see her sitting in front of me, her little fingers barely covering the holes in the flute, her eyelids half-lowered in concentration.

When I opened my eyes now, Hal was standing in front of me with a shy smile. I stopped playing in amazement and looked at him questioningly. He didn't know what to do with his hands, so he crossed his arms, looked at the floor in embarrassment, and rocked back and forth on his feet. As always, his muddy-brown head of hair extended in all directions.

I nodded gently to him and motioned for him to sit down next to me. Hesitantly, I raised my flute to my lips again and started the chorus. Hal's face turned sad, and I wondered if the music reminded him of someone. When I finished playing, he confirmed it. "This song reminds me of my homeland, Ireland. My family was very musical. I had a drum."

He looked melancholy and I hardly dared to breathe; they were the first sentences I had ever heard from him. He spoke Farsi with the harsh accent of people who hadn't learned the language as children. His voice was low and hoarse, as if his voice was breaking. I stared at him expectantly, hoping he would reveal more, but he said nothing else.

"Do you miss your home very much?" I asked carefully and put down my pipe.

He took an audible breath and looked at the peaks that rose steeply to the right and left of Alamut; nothing but rock and stone.

"Yes, I miss Ireland very much—above all, my family, the green meadows and forests, and the smell of heather and moor."

Dreamily, he lowered his eyelids. I would have loved to be able to read his mind, and even if I had never been to this Ireland—if it was as green as his eyes, then I would like to get to know it.

"How did you get here, Cathal?"

I just had to know. He was in the mood to talk; maybe the music had moved him to it.

"My parents were poor with eight children, and there was barely enough food for each of us. The fewer mouths the better for my little siblings. When I was ten, they sent me as a boat boy on a merchant ship so that I could go to sea and support the family."

Again, his melancholy gaze turned to the surrounding mountains.

"The route took us from Ireland to Gibraltar. It must have been shortly before the Portuguese coast when pirates attacked us at night. They took everything they could carry and enslaved the crew. I came to Saladin's palace through a slave trader." Here he swallowed. "Whom I escaped from a few months ago. Now I am here to earn the crossing back to Ireland—as a free man."

He spoke the last words in a firm voice. So …we had a common goal. He was staring in silence again now. At some point, he put his elbows on his thighs and propped his chin up with his hands as if he were sinking into his own thoughts. Impressed by his words, I wanted to cheer him up with another song I had made up myself.

Later, when the sun had just dipped behind the rocky heights of the Elburs Mountains and only an orange-red glimmer was bathing the limestone walls of the Eagle's Nest in a warm light, I wanted to get up and go into my room. But at that moment, Hal turned his face back to me and looked at me with his eerie, green eyes.

"May I ask you something, Eran?"

His gaze flicked from left to right, as if to make sure no one was listening.

"You are a healer and a great fighter. I'd like to be like you, but I'm afraid I can't do it without help."

His tongue licked his lips as if they had become too dry for him.

"I mean, I mean … I need help!"

His hands kneaded his knee nervously.

"You don't have to tell me," I offered, to distract him from his embarrassment. I already suspected what was coming, and yet it was like a punch in the stomach when Hal said, "I have no balls. I mean, Eran, they made me a eunuch."

Now he was looking directly at me, intently, for my reaction as if it all depended on it.

Thanks to my experience as a Medicus, I did not show how I was shaken by his confession. I remembered my training and leaned forward with interest.

"How was it done? There are different methods of castration."

Hal raised his eyebrows in surprise. He probably didn't expect such professional interest. His gaze remained fixed on me as he described in detail the day of his emasculation. Isaac and I had seen some young men die in the process. Hal seemed to have suffered terribly in his young life, maybe that's why he was so shy and insecure.

I put my hand on his shoulder, understanding.

"That is the reason why the training is so difficult for you; am I right, Cathal?"

In a flash, I had extrapolated and compared his current condition with that of his peers. He literally lacked the balls to become a real man. His explanation provided me with the context of how things were going with his body. I had realised it but couldn't interpret it.

"Hal," he replied seriously, "please call me Hal."

"Hal," I repeated and nodded.

"I want to be a real man, Eran, just like you! I want to be able to fight and be strong. Can you help me?"

His gaze was so intense and hopeful that it made my throat tight. Tired and angry at the same time, I swallowed my anger, my eyes searched for the wounded soul in the young person. I took a few more deep breaths in and out, but the pressure in my chest just wouldn't go away. My God, if he only knew what secret I was hiding!

"Hal," I croaked, cleared my throat and started again.

"Hal, I'll help you. There are ways and means," I tried to encourage him, "but I have to look at my notes again. In the meantime, I'll start training with you differently. Meet me tomorrow at sunrise in front of the great gate. I will help you, Hal, and you will become the most impressive man Hassan has ever seen in his life."

Hal gave me a brilliant smile that revealed two rows of large teeth. Moved, I jumped up and helped him to his feet.

"Cathal, the terrible! What do you think of that?"

I tried to cheer him up and chuckled, because the way he stood in front of me, he was far from "terrible."

Hal laughed a little shakily.

"Hal, the terrible," he said. "That's enough. I don't particularly like my name."

Without thinking about it, I kept his hand in mine. He looked relaxed and relieved, as if a heavy load had fallen from his shoulders. I had this big awkward boy in my heart, whether I wanted to or not. He had just offered his soul to me, and I would cherish it. Forever.

That same evening, I disappeared into my sick room with an oil lamp. I patiently rummaged through the papyrus rolls and notes Isaac had left me and made my own notes. My job was clear, but just how should I do it? To turn a eunuch into a man again?

I actually found a specific reference to this subject in the notes of the old Medicus. In a separate chapter, he mentioned the clinical nature of boys who were castrated before entering puberty and who suffered from weak muscles and bones throughout their lives. He described the physical consequences of this mutilation, much of which applied to Hal as well. He mentioned a series of experiments in which he reduced male urine to crystalline extracts by distillation. The daily administration of a small amount of this powder led to a clearly more masculine appearance in the castrati. A wave of relief seized me, and I sent a prayer of thanks to my old companion.

Then Isaac had probably managed to develop an extract that gives the castrated man back what was naturally produced in the removed testicles. Unfortunately, he had never spoken to me about it, so I could only try it with the help of his notes and the remains of this powder. I wondered why Isaac hadn't made such an important achievement in his medicine public, but as so often happened, I couldn't understand the thoughts of this strange old man.

In my honour as a Medicus, I now felt obliged to Hal and would do everything in my power to help him. Ilyas, who had grown into a fat and talkative boy, helped me prepare the powder using resin that we had scraped from the pines in the valley. I had found the small, inconspicuous leather sack with the significant inscription in Isaac's carefully guarded camp, inside his wagon. Relieved, we began to knead the powder with Ying Yang hao, ginger, and dried powdered camel penis—an insider tip of our master Shi Fu—with a little tree resin and rolled it into small balls. Perhaps the little pearls weren't as round as my old master's, but the effect should be the same.

Isaac had also left a few recipes to help build the stunted muscles. Meat and fat were the two pillars on which Hal's diet had to be based. Isaac had sworn by raw eggs. Then poor Hal would have to swallow that, and in that I could …

An idea matured in me, but for that, I needed Shi Fu. He was still in his practice hall, but afterwards, I had an intensive conversation with him.

It wasn't until late that I found rest on my mattress made of stuffed horsehair. Tired but satisfied with the results of my research, I fell into a deep sleep.

The sun hadn't really risen yet. In the bluish, diffuse light that fell over the ridge, Hal stood in front of the gate. He looked a little nervous and shifted from one foot to the other.

His face was pinched; maybe he was just wondering what I was going to do with him. His legs were covered by the usual wide trousers, which were wrapped and tied at the hips, over which he wore a tunic with a simple hemp belt in the middle. This was our usual exercise garment, which guaranteed a lot of freedom of movement.

I was dressed similarly, but had a scarf wrapped around my head that would later protect me from the sun. I gave him a friendly smile.

"How do you say 'good morning' in your language?"

"Maidin mhaith," came the hesitant answer, and the corners of his mouth rose a little.

"Meiiden meiiid?" I tried.

"Something like that," he praised me and smiled shyly.

"Then we'll greet each other like this every morning from now on," I said, tilting my head and making a decision.

"If you are successful in teaching me your language, Hal, then I will accompany you back to your home."

His jaw dropped in surprise. He started to say something, but then just stammered something that sounded like "It's far away" and absently looked at the mug I handed him.

He eyed the yellowish liquid that I had fetched from the kitchen early that morning and looked at me inquiringly. His eyes, which were shimmering blue-green at this time, looked suspiciously between the mug and me.

"Two raw eggs, beaten," I told him succinctly, and pressed the mug into his hand.

He sniffed it carefully and drank them down. He licked his lips and handed the mug back to me.

"Salty," was all he remarked.

"It's now prescribed every day before breakfast," I told him, and his face lit up as always when it came to eating. "The kitchen will prepare the mug for you every day. You just have to pick it up there."

We walked down the wide path that led from the valley to the main gate. The path took a fork that led along a rugged rock wall. Hardly anyone knew this path, which ended in a plateau that offered a breathtaking view of the massif and the valleys in between. This was where my personal practice area was, which I had equipped for my morning workouts.

Round stones of various sizes, sticks, and even loops of rope were on the wall, which I used for abdominal and back exercises. The rock wall was suitable for climbing. With that, we would have to wait with Hal until his hand-foot coordination had developed.

"Here, I train at the same time every morning until the sun drives me away. But the combat and weapon exercises still take place in the Eagle's-Nest."

The awkward boy swallowed and kneaded the back of his hand.

"Does Hassan know about this place?" His gaze wandered uncertainly over the rock formations in front of us.

"What doesn't Hassan know?" I asked him the counter-question, and he smiled his shy smile again, which, as always, found its way straight into my heart.

"Let's warm up, then get started."

We started with chiselling stones. I had every muscle in his body in view. In between, I let him translate words into Gaelic that came to mind while doing the exercises, and we both sweated profusely.

Hal actually showed up on time the following morning and every day from then on. He toiled, lifting stones, lifting heavier and heavier weights, and I encouraged him to give a little more every day.

Already six months later, a man stood before me who, despite still struggling with his motor skills, showed impressive progress. Hal had gained nearly forty pounds thanks to his hearty appetite, and his arms and legs had become more muscular. The regular training sessions with him had also benefited me, as lightning-fast fighting, climbing, and jumping soon became my trademarks.

Little by little, I told him my story without him ever asking about it. It was a sign of our growing confidence, and all I kept to myself was the fact that I was a young woman. When we compared our résumés, we found that we had to be roughly the same age.

One day, I asked his full name. He shrugged his shoulders in disgust. "I don't like how my family called me," he admitted.

"My name is Cathal Conchobhar Ó Searcaigh," he croaked, dropping his shoulders again.

I looked at him blankly. I persistently made him repeat his name three more times before I could repeat it.

"That's enough," he finally demanded. "The name is not so beautiful that you have to repeat it so often!"

That was the end of the subject for him. He threw himself on the floor and pressed himself into a push-up.

When I completed my seventh ordination—Shi Fu had insisted on prioritising it—my training was complete, and I was made prince in an elaborate ceremony.

"Prince Eran I-Shabbah ibn Hassan I-Shabbah" was my title from now on, which made me a descendant of Hassan and a free man. The sheikh himself crowned me with a gold coronet, which he proudly placed on my head. A large sapphire was set on the front of the coronet; large enough to cover my slave mark. With the title, I finally regained my freedom. It was an intoxicating feeling. The sapphire covered my past and opened the way to power and wealth. Hassan's gift—this beautiful gem—meant a lot to me.

All the princes and recruits were gathered in the great hall to celebrate my coronation in style. Nabil, Shi Fu, and Hal also accompanied me through this solemn act. And despite my excitement, I did not fail to notice that there was a strange tension between Nabil and Hal.

Just as I was walking up the stairs from the subterranean hall in the embroidered cloak and my gold coronet to invite the guests to the banquet, I caught a gesture by Nabil that was quite clear: he drew his palm horizontally over his neck. But he didn't look at me; his cold black eyes bored into Hal's, and Hal returned his deadly gaze.

Undeterred, I continued up the stairs without showing that I was deeply affected. Did the two of them have a problem with each other?

It had been clear to me from the beginning that the two had no sympathy for one another, but that was the case with many of the men here. Every Assassin was endowed with a good deal of suspicion. Seldom did we develop friendships like Hal and me. I had to find out what was going on because if the two attacked each other, one would die.

Feeling that neither of them would tell me what had happened, I began to investigate. I suspected it was about a woman.

Hal knew exactly who Nabil's obscene gesture was aimed at: his tutor and best friend, Eran. If Hal had his way, Nabil would already have no head on his shoulders.

Nabil had discovered Hal's weakest point: his friendship with the man who had changed his life. Friendships were almost never found among Assassins, and there was a valid reason for this. He had made it all too clear that this snake, Nabil, was threatening to kill Eran if he divulged something. Hal's fists opened and closed in anger. He didn't care if Nabil fucked Hassan's mistress, but Nabil felt under pressure. This knowledge made him, Hal, his enemy.

Hal had retired to the stables to sort out his feelings. Here in the company of animals, he was not alone, but neither did he have to talk to anyone. With his hands behind his back, he marched up and down the long corridor, trying to find a way out of the dangerous situation.

Of course, he could understand that the Assassin was in a tight spot, but the fact that he was dragging Eran, his only friend, into the story was just too much. The thoughts that kept revolving around Eran, who had grown so dear to Hal, raced in his head.

"Ifreann!" he shouted with all his might, hitting the wooden wall with his fist. In his anger, he used his mother tongue, an expression that meant 'hell'.

The wall trembled under the force of the blow, and the horses snorted nervously. Dust trickled from every crack and glittered like fairy dust in the light that penetrated the windows and cracks.

"Cursed, insidious murderer ..." he started, but he couldn't think of enough swear words in the Persian language.

"I don't know what louse ran down your liver, but these words are not exactly the result of your good upbringing."

Eran's calm and clear voice made Hal flinch and jerk around.

"What are you doing here, Eran?" he replied, surprised, and was immediately annoyed that he had caught him here. His anger had made him careless. But Eran had the quality of moving like a cat.

Eran looked at him strangely with his piercing blue eyes, and his black brow furrowed suspiciously. He held the gold circlet loosely in his fingers, his arms crossed. His lips were pressed together as if he were angry. The hand with the gold band tapped his upper arm. Strange, not a hair sprouting on his chin, Hal suddenly thought, as he had to shave himself daily to keep his beard under control.

"What happened between you and Nabil?" Eran asked directly. A sombre look hit Hal square in the eyes.

Apparently, nothing escaped him. Accursed Nabil ... Hal thought feverishly. How was he supposed to explain everything if that was exactly what was putting him in danger? He crossed his arms and said nothing.

"Trust me, Hal, I'll find out anyway." Now it was Eran's turn to get angry. "I don't know who would be worth covering by you!"

Eran turned and stomped away angrily. From a distance, Hal could still hear how he complained to his horse, Taycan, about the stupidity of some people, and finally left the stable.

Hal leaned against the wall of the stable. He never dreamed of divulging any of his knowledge. It was a matter between Nabil and him. His anger had subsided, and slowly, he saw more clearly again.

It had all started quite harmlessly with his habit of taking a walk before bed. Well, actually he just wanted to be alone with himself for a little while because that way, he could confess his love for Jesus unobserved. Despite his many years here in this distant land, he had never stopped praying to Jesus Christ, as was the practice in the religion with which he had grown up. The evening prayers had helped him get over the difficult time of his slavery. His bad memories still haunted him. The nightmares of his emasculation had plagued him for years, causing him to wake in a sweat and shaking, struggling to regain his self-composure. Only the prayers brought him back to mental equilibrium and let him find sleep.

That evening, he had also taken a walk inside the fortress to pray his rosary in silence. He wanted to prove to God that he had not forgotten him in this strange land, even if there was no church to be seen far and wide.

His path usually led him behind the living quarters of the palace, which were reserved for Hassan and his harem. Sometimes, the laughter of individual girls' voices wafted over to him. Just as he was about to pass the wall of the keep, he heard the whisper of a woman and the dark voice of a man.

Hal paused, withdrew behind the corner, and listened. The man's voice was dark against the bright woman's voice. Tender words followed, and the woman laughed softly. Then it was quiet; only the sounds of passionate kisses, occasional low moans and grunts could be heard. Finally, they both slipped secretly through the door up to the keep that led to the women's quarters.

Hal had completely forgotten where he left off with the rosary and started all over again. With that, he continued his evening round. Somebody had approached one of the sheikh's wives, a nasty crime that was punishable by death. But Hal wouldn't be Hal if he judged someone for it. It wasn't his problem.

However, it did involve him when he unexpectedly met this couple again. It was the evening before Eran's seventh consecration. He had imbibed a lot of wine, and Eran had laughed at his tales from Saladin's harem. When they said goodbye, it was late.

The loving couple had chosen Eran's hospital room that evening. On returning from his prayer tour, Hal saw a movement in the flickering light of an oil lamp that fell from the window of the stone chamber. Sensing something bad, he pulled his dagger from his belt and cautiously crept to the door. Eran had a lot of valuable equipment and medicines stowed here, so the door was always locked.

Hal pushed the door carefully. It was open, and with one step he stood in the interior, which had room for two hospital beds and contained lots of shelves, boxes, and cages with strange animals. In the weak light, Hal immediately recognised who he was looking at: it was Nabil.

The dark-haired Arab stood with his pants down in front of a woman who was lying on her back on a hospital bed. The woman uttered a choked scream, which Nabil immediately tried to muffle with his hand.

"Shh ... quiet, damn it!" he whispered to the woman. "Do you want to wake everyone up?"

"Take your cock and get out of here, Nabil, before I whistle to Hassan. And you're dragging the woman into perdition. She could die for it, you idiot!"

Hal's voice revealed all the contempt he harboured for this man and his inglorious deeds.

Nabil pulled up his trousers and no longer paid any attention to the woman who was bashfully straightening her clothes.

"Listen, you damned ox, you don't scare me! I'd rather slit your fat belly open before you can say a word to Hassan."

Hal took a step forward, stood up in front of the smaller and thinner Nabil, and held the curved dagger threateningly in front of his nose.

"I would now like to detach your stupid face from your head and cover my drum with it, then I could smack your face with pleasure at any time ..." he uttered in his hoarse voice.

His cold eyes were fixed firmly on Nabil's black eyes, and Nabil must have felt the seriousness in his gaze because he was silent.

The woman approached the two opponents carefully and even pleadingly tugged at his sleeve.

"Sahib, please let us go. Nobody should see us here, I ask you."

Hal turned to her and looked into her frightened face. There was a beautiful, if serious, expression on it. Her hair was dishevelled, but individual curls had fallen gently on her shoulders; they were as dark as her eyes. He withdrew his hand and put his dagger in the sheath on his belt.

"Get out of here," he growled at the two of them, "before I change my mind."

He had shaken his head unwillingly and went straight to his room. To this day, he had paid no heed to this incident.

The day after my ordination, and after the unfortunate encounter with Hal in the horse stable, I decided, as the new prince, to return the grandmaster's favour and to practise the finer points of the rhetorical arts. I announced myself to the sheikh through his servant and promptly got access to his private rooms.

When I entered, Hassan examined me with a look that didn't bode well, and motioned for me to do something else because he was talking to Nabil. Shi Fu was also present next to him, wearing a mask of courtesy, as always.

Nabil was visibly nervous; he kept kneading his hands behind his back and throwing angry glances at me. Had the wise sheikh perhaps also seen the obscene gesture at the consecration yesterday? Then he would stir up Nabil with a severe reprimand. That would explain the sizzling tension that had hung in the air since I arrived.

Once I was forced to wait, I sat at the ornate table on which a Shatrandsch—a Persian chess game—was set up, the figures of which were all carved from precious ivory. One set was of a light hue, the other coloured purple.

While I waited, I considered my first move. Shi Fu sat across from me and waited for my opening. I pushed the bright king's pawn forward. Shi Fu waited a moment and pulled his purple-coloured knight in front of the figure I had just placed.

"Nabil is not good," he whispered through his thin lips. "Nabil tells lies."

"What does that have to do with me?" I asked, just as subdued.

Shi Fu looked at me strangely. "You don't know anything?"

I shook my head in confusion. "What?"

"Hassan caught a woman last night. She came from, from ..." He stuck his finger into the rounded thumb and forefinger of his other hand.

Without taking my eyes off Nabil, I nodded and pulled the pawn on the marble plank. My mind raced. Did Hal have ...?

"Did Nabil see who it was?" I hissed across the table, and almost knocked the purple king over with my shoulder.

"Worse! Nabil found something," came the answer unobtrusively, and the Chinese coughed into his hand. With his left hand, he also pulled his king forward. Hell.

"What?" I swallowed. Good heavens, what was Nabil's game?

Shi Fu shrugged. I stared at the table. Mechanically, I lifted a figure and put it somewhere. On the eve of my consecration, Hal had made his evening rounds when I had ducked into my room. What happened?

Hassan's voice hit me like lightning.

"Eran!" he called. "I have to speak to you! Please come to me."

Sensing something bad, I got up slowly and went over to the grandmaster, who was standing with his other princes in his black caftan and barely grey-streaked hair. They politely took a few steps back to allow me in front. Nabil grinned at me, somehow triumphantly.

"Prince Eran", Hassan addressed me seriously, "one of my women was caught when she came back from outside the harem chambers on the day of your consecration. She admitted to meeting a man but wouldn't reveal who she was with. An examination showed that she still carried the man's semen in her, and ..."—here his facade of the cool distance crumbled a little—" ... we found out that she has been pregnant by him for three months."

Hassan's gaze became dark and directed into the distance; his jaw muscles were working.

Why was he so sure that the child wasn't his? The thought stayed with me as I watched him closely. He folded his arms behind his back and breathed in and out a few times. As I watched his chest rise and fall, I barely dared to breathe. Finally, he went on with surprising calm.

"She hasn't been with me for more than three months, constantly apologising with discomfort." His voice was controlled; he behaved well, keeping himself in check, and gave me the answer to my unspoken question.

"She didn't reveal who it was," he continued, "but she did reveal where it happened."

Only now did he look me straight in the eye again. Why did he tell me all this?

"It was in your hospital room, on one of the beds."

So that was it. His eyes were scrutinising mine. I stood up to him directly and without a guilty conscience.

"Is that why you suspect me?" I asked as calmly as possible. A small wave of panic suddenly gripped me.

"Well, it is certain that the door to this chamber is mostly locked and that you have the key, Eran. In addition, Nabil found something in this chamber that belongs to you."

My face had turned red from anger. What did this unsuspecting ...

"Everything in this chamber is mine, Grandmaster!" I said through clenched teeth. So that was it, I should play the scapegoat. I looked at Nabil angrily. He had the nerve to look me in the face. Only then did I realise what he was triumphantly holding in his hand: my gold circlet.

My hands twitched and clenched helplessly into fists. I wanted to tear the damn crown out of his hand. He must have stolen it from my room.

"We all saw that you had it on before you said goodbye for the night."

Hassan looked at me coldly and pointed to the crown in Nabil's hands, which he was now holding up for everyone to see. "Was it you, Eran? If you turn yourself in, you will save this woman from cruel torture."

"I don't know this woman, wise sheikh," I replied calmly to keep my composure. "And I have nothing to do with her. I can only guess how the crown got into Nabil's hands. But I did not put it in my hospital room."

The air in the room was getting too thick to breathe; it literally crackled. And into this silence burst Hal's gigantic figure. It sounded as if both the door and my friend flew into the king's private apartment. The servant hurried after him excitedly; apparently, Hal hadn't let him stop. Now he was standing in the middle of the room and fixed his eyes first on the grandmaster, then on Nabil and me.

"What's going on here?" he said in his deep, hoarse voice.

"Hal, I didn't call you to appear," Hassan remarked sharply.

"Why is the woman out there being dragged to the dungeon?" Hal hurled at him. "What did she do?"

My gaze shot to Nabil, who put one hand to his neck as if he were gasping for air. Hal's gaze fixed on him.

"And what are you doing about it now?"

"He helped to find the man who made her pregnant," Hassan intervened angrily. "What do you have to do with it?"

"And who was this man supposed to be?"

Hal was still staring Nabil into the ground.

"We found Eran's crown in the sick bay," added Hassan, disconcerted. "Do you know more about it, Hal?"

"I know it wasn't Eran, dear Sheikh. But as much as I'd like, I can't tell you who it actually was."

Now a little defiance surfaced. Nabil watched him like a hawk, his hand conspicuously reaching for his dagger in his belt, and it was not a nervous gesture. Something was wrong between the two of them. Was Hal protecting Nabil?

Hassan threw his arms in the air indignantly.

"You pledged your allegiance to me, and now I don't even get an answer to my question?" he roared. "My best Assassins tear themselves apart because of an unfaithful woman! Where is your respect for me?"

"Why don't we just call the woman in?" I suggested to reassure those present." If she is here, and one of us is her lover, we will know, I'm sure."

Hassan took a few more audible breaths, finally shrugged his shoulders, and called his servant. "Let the woman be brought in, then we will hear what she has to say."

I sat down again at the table with the Schatrandsch game and toppled Shi Fu's pawn with my knight. In the exciting performance taking place here, he had completely forgotten to move him out of the danger zone. While I appeared calm and deliberate on the outside, I was seething inside. What if this woman actually accused me to protect her lover?

The already badly damaged door creaked in its iron brackets as it was pushed open, and a frightened woman stumbled through. She had probably been pushed because she fell, got up and straightened her clothes, which were soiled by the dirt in the dungeon. Her hair was in a mess on her head, her lip was split open on one side, and there was a bluish swelling under her right eye. Beside me, I heard Nabil inhale sharply.

The servant who had brought her grabbed the poor woman by the mop of hair, dragged her in front of the grandmaster, and forced her to her knees. She was breathing frantically. I could see that even in this condition, she was beautiful with her dark eyes and black curls ...

I stared at her. By all the gods! That just could not be!

"Jasemin!" I shouted without thinking. "Jasemin, it's you!"

Her frightened eyes widened when she recognised me. Tears ran down her cheeks, and with a sob, she called out, "Enja!"

Chapter 17

Dumfries in Autumn 1306

James Douglas cursed and spat. It had rained all morning, and even the bread they had enjoyed for a small midday meal was soggy from the moisture. The fields and meadows were misted from the cold downpour that had sharply lowered the temperature. It seemed the brief summer had already ended; the few sunny days had been exhausted. The nights had turned sharply cold.

Lachlan McKay, riding not far behind James, muttered curses under his breath. His clothes clung to him like a second skin, and the waxed plaid could barely keep out the pervasive dampness.

Slowly, dusk fell on the two riders who rode through the Scottish hinterland on their tough Highland horses. They deliberately avoided the main roads, and with them, the English troops. In addition to their two horses, they had two pack animals with them that carried a stretcher strapped to bars between them. An almost lifeless person lay on it, covered with blankets and furs. He too was exposed to the forces of nature and soaked.

"I hope we'll be there soon," muttered McKay. "Otherwise, I'll get webbed feet and gills ..."

"It can't be far. Lochar Water is already five miles behind us. But in this fog, you can't even see a castle, even if you're standing in front of it ..." James admitted worriedly. His gaze wandered sullenly to the two ponies, who bravely carried their load through the harsh Scottish weather. Concern for the health of the sick man on the stretcher was clearly written on his face.

After Enja and Hal had freed him from the labour camp, a ship belonging to the McLeods of Skye, who supported Robert de Bruce, brought him to his army. James Douglas quickly became one of Robert's closest confidants. His courage and his tactical fighting style earned him the great respect of his compatriots. And now he had been entrusted with this very important mission, which weighed like a heavy stone on his shoulders.

Suddenly, his horse stopped as if it had hit a wall. James looked around carefully. Something made the animal nervous, and the other horses snorted in alarm. He and McKay pulled their broadswords out of their sheaths almost at the same time to be prepared for an attack.

Before he could see anything, his four-legged friend winced under him. James's heart jumped and he narrowed his eyes to stare at what the animal must have spotted before him. Directly in front of them was a black horse with a rider completely wrapped in black, as if planted there by magic.

James's neck prickled, as it always did when he sensed danger. His pulse was pounding loudly in his throat.

The strange rider stared at them from under the hood of his cloak, completely motionless, as if he had frozen into a pillar of salt. Only the dark mane of the black horse moved a little in the refreshing breeze, which now also drove away the annoying clouds of vapour that had stolen his and McKay's view for several hours.

James swallowed. He had neither heard nor seen the rider coming. Had it been a trap, they would certainly have been lost. Damn Scottish weather! He cleared his throat and spoke to the dark rider: "Greetings from God, noble lord! Can you help us find the way to Caerlaverock?"

The rider seemed to be laughing at him, or at least his shoulders shrugged. Then he grabbed the hem of his hood and slowly pulled it back. White hair came out from underneath. Her blue eyes shone bright and clear even in this weather.

"You have already found Caerlaverock, Lord James Douglas." He heard her laugh in that full voice that he remembered so well.

Enja! He should have known. No one else sat as proud on this magnificent stallion as this woman! Despite the debilitating tiredness that had taken hold of him, he managed to send a faint smile in her direction. Relieved to see her beautiful face again, he said: "It is a pleasure to see you again, Lady Enja von Caerlaverock. Here and now more than ever. Rest assured, we come with good intentions because we are looking for your help with a very important matter."

He could see Enja's gaze falling on the seemingly lifeless man on the stretcher.

"He is a nobleman and high officer in our Scottish Army and urgently needs your medical attention," Douglas said straightforwardly before she could ask him. "We have been on the road for days and ask for your hospitality."

The woman to whom he owed his freedom had already jumped from her horse and stepped alongside the stretcher. Only a dark head of hair could be seen in the bundle of furs and blankets, and Enja looked into the face of the pale, unconscious man, felt his pulse on the carotid artery, and raised the lids of his sunken eyes. Her expression gave no indication of what she was thinking, but she nodded briefly and motioned for the two men to follow her.

In one smooth movement, she swung onto the stallion's back and directed him past Douglas into the thick fog they had just come out of.

"Be my guests," she invited the men. As if he had another choice, James thought, grateful for her help. He was not in the least ashamed to come to her as a supplicant. He would take anything for his king, and it seemed as if it were a matter of course that she would help him.

Not far from where they met, she stopped her horse at the edge of a lake. Thick swaths moved over the surface of the water and enveloped the air in a wet grey. Night had fallen in the meantime, and with it came new moist air. The fog was particularly thick here by the water. James Douglas looked for a bridge or a boat but couldn't see anything. Only a winch could be seen on the bank; the ropes themselves led towards the water and disappeared into nowhere. Even the horses and their riders were nothing more than black shadows.

Lachlan McKay looked at him questioningly when they were surprised by a long whistle that Enja let out with two fingers in her mouth. They were amazed to see how the winch started moving, and finally a flat ferry boat with a boy emerged from the fog. Illuminated only by the torch the helper held out to them, Enja led her stallion onto the boat and supported the two men to free the ponies from their load and also to bring them onto the ferry. Finally, they carried the sick man onto the wing of the ferry, which was large enough to easily accommodate twice the number of people and horses.

The long whistle came from her mouth again, and the ship moved in the other direction. Except for the nervous snorting of the animals, who did not feel comfortable in this unfamiliar situation, there was hardly a sound to be heard from the veil of mist that wrapped itself around them like a heavy cloak. The only thing that could be heard was Lachlan's voice, which was intended to calm the animals. Now and then, light waves slapped against the bow.

In the silence, Enja said to James, "Is the sick nobleman the only reason you took the long way here? As far as I know, the Scottish Army is much further southeast ... "

James looked in the flickering light of the torch into her face, which was again in the shadow of her protective hood.

"Caerlaverock has a reputation for having the best healers far and wide. This man's health is very important, he ... he is very dear to the king," he said hesitantly.

"Besides," he pushed on and searched for her eyes under the hood, but could only guess where they lay, "you know exactly what brought me here."

She said nothing, but he thought he saw her smile. He was here to visit his brother. It had been a year since the news of his recovery; a difficult year in which he and his men had fought for the interests of their King Robert de Bruce.

The fact that he was here with Lachlan in person and with the utmost secrecy had to make it clear to her how important his mission was. She hadn't asked him about it yet, and he didn't want to tell Enja anything about the identity of the person he was so desperately trying to help. He hoped it wouldn't be necessary, either.

James still carried Enja's message in his leather pouch around his neck. With her clean, clear handwriting, she had written him personally in a few words that Hugh was doing better. His arm would take time to heal completely, but he could move all fingers, and his appetite had returned. Involuntarily, his hand went to the small leather pouch around his neck. That was what he had been clinging to all this time—the hope to see Hugh again and this woman who accompanied him in his dreams. He eyed her furtively, as she stood upright at the bow and looked into the grey haze for something he couldn't see.

Finally, pebbles crunched under the bow and announced the shore. At the same moment, Lord Douglas could see the torches in the hands of some people. In her commanding voice, Enja announced James and McKay, whereupon they were greeted warmly by numerous women, men and children. Now James realised that the winch was powered by a donkey, surrounded by children who disconnected, petted, and fed him.

Helpful hands lifted the sick man from the ferry and brought the ponies through a large stone gate. Only then did James realise that they were inside the castle. Little was visible in the vaguely torch-lit haze. It had to be a big castle, because in the courtyard many people came running to greet Enja and her visitors, including numerous women in dresses and trousers, three of whom he recognised immediately, even in the dimly lit area: Kalay, the girl with the red braid, and little Winnie and Moira, who immediately bent over the sick man.

Lachlan was a few years older than he and had a charm of his own that was always well received by women. And with so much friendly attention, his good mood returned despite the tiredness. He even managed a smile for Kalay and was joking with the slender warrior.

"Take the man on the stretcher to the sick bay!" Enja ordered two of the men, pointing with her hand in the general direction. "And set up the guest chambers for our guests," she added to two women with bonnets and aprons.

"No!" replied Douglas, standing in the way of the men. "I will stay with the sick person. He is my responsibility."

Enja's strange look hit him with full force.

"You will not be able to help him, Lord Douglas. Your presence in the hospital is not welcome."

There was something urgent in her tone, and yet James did not want to leave his companion alone.

"I swore I would do everything I can to save him. Now I'm here and I won't leave him," he said firmly, pressing his lips together, his hands on his hips.

He winced when Enja's hand touched his shoulder. He hadn't noticed how close she'd come to him.

"Hand him over, James," she said in a low, soothing voice. "You cannot help him with your mere presence. My healers will do everything in their power. Better pray for him; he will be able to use it."

He was tired and exhausted. His shoulders sagged. The task was a heavy burden, but he would now hand it over to people who knew better about disease than he did.

With a heavy heart, he gave in to Enja and avoided the two helpers, who carefully picked up the limp body and disappeared into one of the entrances, accompanied by Moira. He wiped his hand over his face as if that would drive his exhaustion away. Enja's hand was still on his shoulder. Why did he suddenly feel this power emanating from her? He looked wearily into her familiar face, a bright spot in this dark time. Eyes as clear as crystals glittered in the torchlight.

She looked at him seriously and piercingly. Had her mouth always been sensual? Were his emaciated senses playing a bad trick on him?

"Take a rest, James. You are at the end of your rope. Take a hot bath and have a little warm beer. I'm sending for your brother. He's doing well."

He nodded as if in a distant dream. A young maid, with her hair cut short at the nape and covering the left side of her face, curtsied before him and led him to his chamber. The way there he scarcely perceived.

Thoughtfully, I kept turning the clay cup in my hands. The scent of the mocha bean awakened a deep melancholy in me that affected both the past and the present. James's arrival this afternoon had drawn me right into the heart of the troubled Scotland scene. This castle was a piece of home for me and all the people here, and that did not depend on the taking of sides. I didn't feel like an Englishwoman or a Scot. But I still knew that I would have to position myself and my confidants politically in the future.

The sight of James Douglas had shaken me deeply. I did not recognise the carefree young man I had met a few years ago at Douglas Castle when I was weak and hurt myself. Instead, a man stood before me who had been marked by the hardships and horrors of war. James's aristocratic pallor had given way to a dark, rough complexion that made the furrows on his face seem deeper. The worry line between his eyes was now a notch carved into tense features that spoke of the heavy burden that lay on his shoulders. The once so friendly brown eyes had lost their shine and lay in deep shadows. What could they have seen, those sad eyes? His lips were cracked and chapped, and barely allowed a smile. Even under the trimmed beard, I had seen his jaw muscles working.

How could a person change so much? His body had gained significantly in muscle and mass. The once so fine-minded man had become a tough fighter. His demeanour was almost martial, and tiredness didn't take away any of his dangerousness. It was frightening to see what the war made of a man who had lost everything and was now struggling simply to survive.

Robert de Bruce had gathered many such men to assert his claims on the Scottish land—frustrated and angry Scottish nobles who had lost their land, prestige, and often loved ones under King Edward's brutal hand. It was not for nothing that he was nicknamed "The Scots' Hammer," which he had earned during the years of the struggle for Scottish independence.

For me, however, the Scottish King Robert, Lord of Arnandale, was a hopeless case. After the murder of his rival, John Comyn, by his own hand on February 6, 1306, in Greyfriars Church in Dumfries, and his unauthorised coronation barely seven weeks later in Scone, not all Scots were sympathetic to him. Support for his cause was hesitant, and the August defeat by the English armies at Methven had been another major blow to the young but ambitious king of the Scots.

I was well informed about the progress of the war through the Maxwell clan, as they were in close contact with Robert's followers. Some of the clan's feudal men also fought at his side.

In the turmoil of the Scottish War of Independence, Caerlaverock had slipped out of the focus of the English king, who harboured a personal grudge against me. No wonder, since I had evaded my execution and had had a few of his followers fall victim to their own justice in the middle of London.

With the help of the Maxwell warriors, we were able to withstand the two English attacks on Caerlaverock, a castle that I had turned into a stronghold of enormous proportions with the help of the clan. It became my people's refuge. I never wanted to go to war with Edward, but his actions forced me to take a stand against him. So far, I had successfully defended my claims. Unfortunately, this did not help me in my endeavour to assert myself as the official owner of the castle.

If I had at least known where the Scottish king was at the time, I would have liked to confront him with my request.

However, de Bruce had a serious problem after losing the Battle of Methven. It was said that he fled to the north of the country from the English troops. Maybe he was already in Skye, a strategic retreat controlled by the McLeods clan?

In a few steps, carrying my steaming cup, I reached the room in which we were treating the sick man. James hadn't told me who he was. Certainly an important man from Robert's highest circle, probably a nobleman. I only hoped that the English had not yet found out about his stay with us; otherwise, we would have the army at the gates again in the next few days.

Annoyed by the course of events, I took a long swig of the bitter drink and pushed open the door to the chamber. Moira and her assistant had just washed and shaved the sick man when I entered. Apparently the expression on my face wasn't exactly friendly because they both paused in their work and looked at me in shock, so I cleared my throat, put on a laboured smile, and spoke in a neutral tone. "Any insights?"

Moira nodded and gave me a brief report on his condition. "The patient is about thirty years old; his pulse and breathing are regular. He must have passed out a few hours ago. The pupils are slightly dilated, the white has a yellowish tinge, and the skin is cool. Except for slight hardening in the lower abdomen, no external signs of inflammation."

Isaac would have been proud of my student. I put the empty cup on a table with some of my utensils and stepped next to the man, who was naked except for a sheet that covered the lower half of his body. He was muscular, with strong arms and shoulders. His hair was dark and continued, sometimes more, sometimes less, in small curls on his chest and arms. Large and small scars were drawn all over the upper body. Apparently, he was a nobleman who did not hold back when it came to a fight.

My hand slid over his right upper abdomen and felt the swelling level with the liver that Moira had already noticed. The colour of his skin was hard to tell in the light of the oil lamp, but it was probably a shade of yellow, too. The liver seemed to be working hard; I had known that when I briefly inspected his eyes on the stretcher.

We had to find out what damage the organ had suffered. James had informed me that the patient had been complaining of nausea, abdominal cramps, and pain for weeks. The few healers in the Scottish camp had not been able to help him so far, and he seemed to be getting sicker. After all, James had seen the only way out as to see me. Alcohol was ruled out as the cause because the patient allegedly only rarely drank wine or beer. Given the dire situation in which the Scottish Army found itself, my guess was that it was malnutrition. Maybe meat or fish poisoning? The word poisoning made me think.

"Did he drink water?" I asked Moira while scanning.

"We were able to give him almost half a litre; at least his swallowing reflex is still intact," she replied.

"Give him broth since he absorbs liquid so well. He needs salts and fats," I instructed her, and she immediately sent her maid out. "I'm going to examine his urine. Were you able to collect something?"

"No, unfortunately he didn't produce anything. It will take some time before he urinates again."

Thoughtfully, I looked into the patient's face. His lips were cracked like James's. He had probably not had anything liquid, let alone nutritious, provided to him for many hours.

"I need proof of poisoning."

"Poisoning?" Moira looked at me with an open mouth. "How do you know there's been a poisoning?"

"The liver is badly affected. Maybe a rotten fish, a poisonous fruit or ...", I thought for a moment, "or a poisonous mushroom accidentally slipped into a dish."

I looked at the patient's face and added thoughtfully, "Or on purpose."

Moira stepped to the other side of the bed. She looked very serious. "Why should someone poison this man in their own camp?"

I shrugged. "Maybe he had become too important for someone; who knows?"

There was something I didn't like about the situation, and an inexplicable fear constricted my chest. To avoid showing my concern too clearly, I hastily added, "Maybe it was just a jealous woman."

Moira smiled weakly. "Women are capable of anything, aren't they?"

She blinked at me with her amber eyes, and I nodded.

After Moira took some urine from his bladder using a special metal tube, I sent a prayer of thanks to Isaac. Because of his interest in the poisons of nature, I had a whole hodgepodge of possible comparative substances, which Moira now lined up in small bowls in front of me. The colour, composition, and smell of urine changed in people who had lost their physical balance through illness.

I was now used to recognising these differences. Moira poured the urine into a silver container to intensify the smell.

With actions that were routine, I took the small vessels and smelled the poison extracts that I had prepared. I stopped at one. It was the poison of a white death-cap mushroom and had a similar odour to the urine sample. So, my guess was correct: the man had mushroom poisoning. It was a miracle that he was still alive; presumably, he had received the poison in small doses. Someone had tried to kill him slowly and painfully.

I stared thoughtfully at the sick man's pale face. What made him so important that someone wanted to kill him? The English wouldn't go to such an effort to kill a Scotsman, even a noble Scotsman, in such an elaborate manner. A sword cut would be the first choice.

But maybe the man had enemies in his own camp? How should I reveal this to James? If this man survived—and that was still written in the stars—what would he do?

I unconsciously sought Moira's gaze; I saw helplessness in her face, too; her finely curved eyebrows curled with worry.

"Give him an extract from the fruit of the milk thistle. Best as tea with plenty of water," I instructed her. "Do we still have some of the concentrated coal pearls?"

She nodded hastily, knowing what that meant.

"Was he poisoned by his own people?" Clever girl.

"I can't say that, but everything points to a long ingestion of the poison. Probably a white cap mushroom, very aggressive."

The realisation almost took my breath away. The damage to the liver was my main concern. He had the stature of a battle-hardened knight, but a small white mushroom robbed him of vitality. Would he come through it?

James Douglas and his companion were seated at my table in the great hall. Here, the floor was covered with carpets and pillows that I had brought from the Orient. All the children were eager to sit on the soft pillows and listen to the music that was played in the evening. The social system at my castle was based on a flat hierarchy. The gates of Caerlaverock were open to everyone who sought protection and wanted refuge. This resulted in a colourful mix of people from different origins. Some came from my time in the Orient, others found shelter and a family here. Often, it was children and orphans who were washed up against my walls like driftwood from war. The number of men, women, and children reached over a hundred in these days, and I was very proud of how peaceful their coexistence was.

The children of my clan were my children, too, and they were allowed to be around me without restriction. They were taught and raised collectively by the educated women while the mothers and fathers did their work. There were many mothers in our community whose husbands had perished in war or illness. There were also many orphans among the little ones.

When I entered the great hall, many of the children ran up to me and greeted me enthusiastically. My heart jumped, so fine was the joy that was written on the children's faces. They were hanging on my arms and legs, and I lifted some of them in my arms to kiss them.

I was particularly taken with the silent Thorvil, who could only make himself understood with his hands. With him in my arms and the cluster of children in tow, I made my way to the large round table at the end of the hall. We had pulled up the ruined walls of the old castle and given the hall a wooden ceiling with a dark coat of paint. It muffled the noise, as did the numerous knotted tapestries that told lively stories from the world of the Orient. Some of them I had brought back from Hassan's treasure trove; others had been woven for me by the women of my clan over years of weaving, and each of these colourful works told a further story from the Orient and Occident. The children all knew them, and in spite of his grumpy moods, Hal, in particular, had excelled as a great storyteller, with the children hanging on his every word.

On the way to the high table, I greeted the fighters of the battle guards and the musicians who delighted the guests with light harp music. A few girls had gathered to sing together. Thanks to Hassan I-Shabbah's extensive library and his court architects, I had incorporated the principles of the Orient into the reconstruction of the hall. Even when played softly, all instruments and voices could be heard over the entire area of the hall, thanks to the sophisticated wooden construction of the ceiling.

With relentless strength, the children pushed me to my table, where the two guests had been seated, and past the large stove in the middle of the room, which provided such pleasant warmth. The men stood up and bowed to me, hands flat on their chests.

"I see that the kitchen has already provided you with food and drink. Please don't let me disturb you; my people are now entitled to a little of my attention," I said, explaining the rush of children. I let little Thorvil slide off my arm onto the chair next to mine and sat down at the table to the right of the freshly washed and shaved James Douglas. The other children sat down all around on the pillows and listened mesmerised to the music.

Amazing what sleep, a little food, and a good bath can do for a man. Tiredness and exhaustion had disappeared, and the expression on both their faces was a lot friendlier than on arrival.

"We thank you again for your generous hospitality. We really enjoy being welcomed so pleasantly and with such accommodation in your midst," Lord Douglas confirmed with his warm voice, and quickly added: "And I am also indebted to you forever for the medical help, my lady."

"Please sit down, Lord Douglas, and tell me what happened to you and the poor man. Your brother's arrival will probably be delayed a little longer. He was on the hunt with Hal, and as night fell, the return was probably delayed."

His brown eyes were serious and scrutinised my face. Finally, he nodded. His dark hair was still wet from the bath and fell in heavy strands on his shoulders. His long, calloused fingers clutched the wooden mug with the warm beer. The crease between his eyes drew deep into his forehead. He wiped his eyes and sighed heavily, as if he had the burden of a century on his shoulders.

"In the middle of June of this year, Perth fell to the English." James took a deep breath and began to speak. "Robert de Bruce, our king, was quite angry and wanted to retake the city with an army of four thousand men. Since we had arrived at the gates of Perth late, none of the damned English could be lured out of the town. We therefore set up camp nearby on the Methven River. Our majority had left the English unmoved, and they surprisingly attacked us in the middle of the night."

I drew in a sharp breath and interrupted him in an unfriendly manner: "How could it be that the Scots did not hear an approaching army? Were no guards posted?"

James scowled at me.

"Bruce was sure that they wouldn't dare to step out from behind the city walls while the Scots were camped in front of them," he admitted, contrite. "That was a fatal mistake."

He lifted his mug and took a long sip.

"It was the Earl of Pembroke, Aymer de Valence, who led the English troops out of town and killed us unprepared. Only a few hundred were able to escape. Lachlan and I kept the men of Valence at bay long enough for Robert de Bruce and a few of his knights to escape. Together, we made it with difficulty to the nearby Inchaffrey Abbey. During the night, the monks led us on adventurous paths northwest. Everything would have gone well, too, had it not been for the men of John Dougall MacDougall and the MacNab brothers ambushing us at Dilrigh. They had sworn retribution for Bruce's murdering their relative, John Comyn, in a church."

James's hand moved erratically through his hair.

"They were close enough to grind us into dust."

He pressed his index finger onto his thumb to emphasise the drama with the gesture.

"They almost pulled Bruce off his horse by his cloak before Lachlan could pull him out of the tussle at the last second. He literally overran one of the MacNab brothers with his horse, tore the brooch off his damned cloak, and galloped away with Robert."

"I almost lost a finger," McKay intervened. "They didn't want to let the king get away that easily." He held out his hand to me with a grin, and the right little finger actually hung a little crooked at the joint.

"I should take a closer look at it tomorrow."

My tone made it clear to him that I was serious, and his grin disappeared.

Even the corners of James's mouth finally moved upwards; he was obviously having a hard time getting into a cheerful mood again after the days of hardship.

The musicians had meanwhile switched to flutes and the little drums that they called the bodhran here in Scotland. The girls sang a folk song about an unhappy love between two young people. I was just about to send the restless children, who were frolicking in the pillows around the table, to dance, when the large gate on the south wing was thrown open. The flames in the great fireplace flickered nervously.

Hal, in his full height, was standing there and he didn't seem amused. His bare head glistened with moisture, and the fur coat dripped onto the stone steps. The maids immediately ran to him to take the cloak from him. Underneath, Hal wore his leather vest with the scales of impenetrable layers. His axes were still in his belt when he made his way to us at the table.

The children hooted to greet him. He grabbed two of the cheeky boys and tossed them through the air and onto the pillows next to our table, where they landed screeching with joy. He stopped next to our table. James and McKay had stood up and greeted him with a firm handshake.

Hugh, on the other hand, who had entered the hall after Hal, threw himself into James's arms with a cry of joy.

He laughed and sobbed against his brother's broad chest. James held the younger Douglas close. His war-scarred face twitched vehemently. Again and again, he wiped his hand over his eyes.

I turned away respectfully to give the two brothers a little time and thought for a moment about my brief stay at Douglas Castle. My thoughts lingered on James's family that he had lost: Eleonore, William, and Matthew.

My gaze fell on the silent Thorvil next to me, who was gnawing a rib with relish. It literally turned my stomach when the idea shot through my mind that someone was going to break his skull open. Exactly at this moment, two huge hands grabbed him, lifted him out of the much too big chair, and threw him into the soft cushions next to the other children, where he emerged grinning from the sea of pillows.

Hal dropped heavily onto the chair, which groaned under his weight. His leather vest creaked with his every move. He put out one of his paws, grabbed the nearest tankard, and in a few gulps, poured the beer down. With a bang, he put the beaker back on the table and wiped his mouth with the back of his hand. As he did so, he noisily released the excess air from his mouth.

"Why are you staring at me so angrily, Enja?" he hissed at me from the side. "Am I bothering you while you are flirting with your admirer?"

Oh, hence the bad mood!

"Hal, you're always disturbing," I hissed back.

His green eyes under the menacingly lowered eyelids looked deep into mine, and as always, he seemed to be able to read my mind. It was like communicating with me through his eyes, and I clearly sensed his warning—regarding James.

Unimpressed by our brief exchange of words earlier, McKay had hugged Hugh warmly and slapped him hard on the shoulder. Hugh towered almost a head over the stocky Lachlan. James's younger brother had gained not only height but also body weight since they last met, and the lanky, skinny boy had become a sturdy young man. With his short dark hair and kind brown eyes, he followed in the paternal Douglas line. He was almost a younger image of his brother, without his hard features and deep furrows. His grin exposed the left incisor, half of which was left after he and Hal had fought a brave fight with wooden sticks. He hadn't stood upright for thirty seconds, but still he won the hearts of the girls—much to Hal's annoyance.

Despite his difficult arm injury, he had become an agile, tactically clever fighter. Except for a few scars, nothing reminded of his severe wound. Only his loose mouth still distinguished him from his brother, whom he always emulated.

After his gruff greeting, Hal told me in a few words about the result of his hunt, which had ended successfully with the shooting of a stag. The children danced to an instrumental piece, and most of the men and women clapped along enthusiastically. The atmosphere was very lively, and the joy of the reunited brothers gripped our table. As the hostess, I made a toast to our guests, who raised their glasses.

"To the Douglas family—may the power of God shine through your deeds!"

I solemnly raised my voice and put my mug to my lips.

"To Robert de Bruce, the King of Scots!" Hugh shouted afterwards, causing me to choke. I cleared my throat audibly for everyone.

"Hugh," I reprimanded, a little brusquely, "as long as I have not sworn allegiance to either king and they do not recognise me as mistress of Caerlaverock, I will not drink to either of them."

Hugh winced; he must have forgotten what a sore point this was for me. But then he showed his mischievous smile and raised his glass again.

"Then just to Robert's health, and to Enja's nursing him back to health!"

All blood drained from my face.

Hal bumped up from his chair and banged his fist on the tabletop with a roar, making the plates and platters bounce.

James and McKay also stood and stared at Hugh, then Hal and me in alarm. People in the hall stopped laughing and stared at us.

The music stopped; the ridiculous rumble of one of the pipes was the last sound that came to my ears. Then there was dead silence.

Chapter 18

Alamut in the year 1299

A s a child, I always knew exactly where Mama kept the honey jar. Honey was a rare treat, so it was something special. Without thinking about the wrongness of my actions, I crawled through the flue of the wooden fireplace, which led into the large kitchen and connected to the pantry.

Naturally, one mouthful wasn't enough; I dipped my greedy fingers several times into the small pot of that rare, sweet temptation. Satisfied, I climbed back the same way. In my naïveté, I believed that no one would notice the disappearance of the precious honey.

The next morning, it became clear that draining almost half the pot had been a bad idea. My father summoned Jalla and me early in the morning to the kitchen with an ominous tone. He had placed the honey pot on the wooden table in front of us. Jalla nonchalantly sucked her thumb while I stared at the floor in embarrassment. My father looked first at Jalla and then at me and straightforwardly asked who had stolen the honey.

I didn't admit it was me, of course, and just looked accusingly at my sister, who was just as crazy about honey as I was. Although I also washed my sticky fingers so as not to arouse suspicion, my father directly accused me of theft and of lying to him. How did he know? Of all people, my sister Jalla, this traitor, hung me out to dry. Grinning, she took her thumb out of her mouth and ran it over my cheek. A streak of black ash darkened the thumb. All the while, the proof of my theft had been written upon my face, and I had felt so assured...

Exactly this feeling of shame crept into me again now—that the truth was visible on my face for everyone and that I had pretended to be someone else to the end. This roughly described the feeling that hit me in its full force in the presence of Hassan, Hal, Nabil, Shi Fu, and of course, Jasemin, like my father's accusation.

"Enja!" my old friend called again.

In Hal's shaken look, I recognised reproach and disappointment. Shi Fu just nodded silently, as if he had always known, and Hassan just laughed out loud in all the confusion that Jasemin's exclamation caused.

"A woman!" he shouted, holding his stomach and laughing. "A woman who made my mistress pregnant?"

He probably thought the idea was funny. That he limited the circle of suspects to Hal and Nabil did not seem to have occurred to him at that moment.

Nabil, on the other hand, did, because he opened his dark eyes and drew the scimitar with lightning speed. He was about to go for Hal when I threw myself against my friend's body with lightning speed to push him out of Nabil's reach. Nabil caught him anyway and cut his neck, ear and part of his cheek. Hal compensated for my impact with a step backwards and put his hand to his bleeding face. I, on the other hand, kicked the completely surprised Nabil on the temple with my heel. At the same time, I caught the arm he was holding the dagger with and used the momentum to ram the weapon into his stomach myself. Everything happened very quickly, and it took a few seconds for those standing by to understand what had happened.

Shi Fu just nodded as if I had done one of his best exercises to his satisfaction. Hassan had stopped laughing, and Hal shouted angrily a few curses in his mother tongue that no one understood. Only Jasemin gasped in horror and jumped to the side of her dying lover in a treacherous gesture.

"Nabil!" The choked cry escaped from her mouth, and with a desperate request, she turned to us. "By Allah, help him!"

Nabil writhed on his king's precious carpet and struggled with death. The curved dagger had cut a deadly path between the lower costal arch and his liver. Blood oozed from the deep cut, and it would only be a few minutes before Nabil would come to the end of his time. Jasemin held the dying man's head, sobbing. Nabil had closed his eyes; the shame was still written on his face even in agony. Hal looked at me from the side, confused, and when I turned to him to repair the cut in his left ear, he jerked away and disappeared from the chamber with heavy steps.

So, I had no choice but to take the desperate Jasemin in my arms and gently caress her dishevelled hair, which had lost much of its former lustre.

Shi Fu and Hassan weren't in any way surprised. As I had surmised, they had long since suspected—Hassan more than Shi Fu—that I was a woman. Nevertheless, they had decided to accept me as an Assassin.

"I saw it in your soul, Enja," the grandmaster later confirmed to me when Nabil's body had been carried away and the carpets had been cleaned.

"On the day that I accepted you into our community, I looked deep into your soul and saw the truth."

I shuddered to remember that strange moment of weakness. Hassan had penetrated my head then, into my thoughts.

"You are something special. You have a strange power that I cannot describe. I wanted you to myself; I have to apologise for that. But you have to admit, you've found your place here."

I smiled at him in agreement. He always turned everything to his advantage.

"Indeed, my Grandmaster, what better could have happened to me?"

He was right in a way—where would I be today without him? Still a slave with no rights or property. From then on, he called me Princess Enja according to my position at court.

Shi Fu had quickly noticed that I was a woman because of my body, and because he knew that Hassan was also in the picture, he had accepted it without comment. He had always made sure that, despite my femininity, I could assert myself against all odds. And I was connected to him for this for all time.

I was worried about Jasemin. As a slave and former mistress impregnated by a prince of Hassan, she had forfeited all rights to her life. That Nabil tried to shift the suspicion to other members and then carried out an assassination attempt would only have ensured her death sentence.

But as a result of my work, she got a chamber in the fortress, in which she could stay until the birth of her child, knowing that her death was only delayed by a few months. Hassan's disappointment in her wrongdoing outweighed my friendship with her in his eyes. I had to control myself not to openly show my displeasure, but here I couldn't speak for her any further. Strangely enough, since Jasemin was a very devout person, she seemed to come to terms with her death. Because if Allah had planned this for them, then may Allah stop it.

Over the next few days, Hal avoided me again and again with a skill I hadn't believed him capable of. Not that I resented him; after all, I had robbed him of his greatest illusion. Eran the Strong was just Enja, a woman.

I literally had to stop him like a thief on one of the evenings that we usually spent together in the stable to look after our horses. He was just coming out of the stable lane, bridle in hand, when I cut him off. He noticed his carelessness, stopped and took a deep breath.

"I need to talk to you, Hal," I remarked dryly and stood up slightly with my legs apart and my arms crossed in front of my chest.

Hal snorted. Then he hung the bridle on a hook and finally turned to me. It was the first time that I had seen him since that fateful day, and his cheek had healed well. Ilyas had looked after him competently in my place. The left ear was severed at about the middle of the lower half and was still slightly swollen. A thick scab had settled on the wound.

Like two opponents in a duel, we stood across from each other in the passage and stared at each other. Green eyes against blue. Anger versus frustration. At one point, I shrugged my shoulders.

"If you want to say something to me, now you have the opportunity", I offered him as an opening.

He grunted meaninglessly.

"How about Why didn't you tell me you were a girl?"

I helped him to come to the point.

"Why didn't you tell me that you were a girl?" he repeated promptly.

I let the air out of my lungs with relief.

"I was afraid you wouldn't trust me."

Again, there was no answer.

"My goodness, Hal, I was in a strange land with a slave cross on my forehead and my teacher was stabbed to death in front of my eyes. Should I give up the only chance of freedom for the fact that I'm a girl? Would I still be a hero to you if you had known that I was a girl?"

"If I had known, I would never have told you that I am only half a man," he responded defiantly. That seemed to have bothered him very much.

"And yet you were always a whole man to me, Hal. And my friendship with you was real, whether man or woman. I have always helped you and I will continue to do so in the future. Can't you just overlook the fact that I'm a woman and see me again as I was before? A good friend?"

"A good friend ..." he repeated, already a little more quietly.

"My offer is still open," I started again, and he looked at me again with those intense eyes. I saw the disappointment in them. Desperately, I drew my last trump card: "I will accompany you on your way home if you still want to take me with you."

Satisfied, I saw his Adam's apple hop treacherously. The shell had already broken open and the seed could sprout. I slowly turned towards the exit and casually tossed over my shoulder: "If our friendship was worth something to you, then I'll be happy to wait for you. You know where to find me."

I smiled to myself, self-satisfied. I had reached his heart, that was all I needed to know.

The next day, we continued our common combat exercise. Friendship was a precious treasure; it would endure forever, regardless of whether man or woman.

From a certain moment on, Hal's teaching turned out to be extremely one-sided. With his body mass, he could neither achieve the speed nor the agility of a slim assassin, which presented Shi Fu and me with a new task. Hal was pleased, his sheer strength doing more damage than my well-placed kicks could ever do. Still, he had to find a weapon that wouldn't burst under his force. In my mind, the big hammer he used to shod horses' hooves was the right instrument. But Shi Fu shook his head.

"Hal must have a weapon with a punch, but it must be sharp like a knife." He crossed his arms over his chest, as he always did when he did not want to argue.

"Are you thinking of a broadsword?" I asked him curiously. When Hal first wielded it in his practice sessions, the huge sword in his hands looked like one of Isaac's little pipes. He later forged one with a different centre of gravity and a wider blade. At least that made his movements look a little more balanced. The only problem was that he could hardly find a suitable opponent to carry out his exercises. Few had anything to counteract his blows with this sword. Even the exercises with the bamboo stick were always guaranteed to be painful with Hal.

It was a small observation that inspired the idea of Hal's personal weapon. Not so long ago, a cook from distant Nepal had set out from the earthquake-buried city of Pokhara to find a new place to stay. He and his little daughter embarked on a new future via the Silk Road and arrived in the Orient. What he had arrived with was the girl, her pots and her little metal tips with which he could prick ink under the skin. Not only was Sarvesh a good cook, but he was also an accomplished tattoo artist who taught his daughter, Indra, the art of body painting.

One evening, to the horror of all of us, Hal caused a breathtaking moment: during dinner, he appeared in the great room with a black bar on his forehead that stretched from the left side of his forehead to the right. It wasn't pretty, but it suited Hal and it served the purpose of hiding his slave mark. He didn't seem to be bothered in the least by the laughter that poured over him all evening. On the contrary, the next evening he came into the great hall with a shaved head. Now the black stripe reached completely from the back of the head to the forehead. The stripe sat like a black crown on the top of his head and gave him a really martial look. In a country where hair was an ornament, Hal decided to forego all masculine attributes. He just didn't need any.

From the love for Indra, the love for his tattoos had grown. One day, I saw him kill a chicken for Indra's father's soup. Hal pressed the nervously fluttering animal onto the wooden stake, and with a precision that I would not have believed him capable of, the axe whizzed down onto its thin neck. With one blow, he severed the head.

I had an idea that I wanted to discuss with Shi Fu—an idea of which weapon seemed made for Hal: powerful, destructive, and precise like the axe that had just cut the chicken's neck.

Shi Fu's goatee trembled a little, then he nodded. To train Hal at the axe—that would never have occurred to him himself. He would also teach him to throw that axe. With the Northmen, it is customary in combat to throw the heavy axe at a target. If set correctly, such a throw was fatal.

Hal was able to fight swords, sticks, and even the infamous Morning Star with his axes, against which hardly any herb had grown.

He proudly stuck two axes crosswise in his belt. In addition to the increasing number of Celtic symbols that stretched from his head over his shoulders down to his back, it was these two axes that made up his appearance. There was nothing left of the Hal that I had seen for the first time before his first consecration. Only his intense green eyes, which sometimes looked at me so vulnerably, allowed the old Hal to shine through like the rays of the sun through parchment.

He had remained a friend since we spoke but had distanced himself from me. The looseness with which we had dealt with each other before had given way to a nervous bias. It hurt my heart that our different genders forced us to a distance that sometimes made me miss the earlier times.

One day, I wanted Indra's father, Sarvesh, to paint my skin, too. So, I decided to go to the older man, who looked at me in shock. He just nodded and asked me into his tent, which was his living room and place of work. We agreed on a dragon motif, which he had already painted by the hundreds for the most famous warriors in his country, and which Sarvesh still mastered despite his fading eyesight.

I was lying on a table and Indra was sitting on a chair next to it, smoothing the skin with her fingers while her father tapped the first strokes into my white skin. In between, she kept mixing up new colours—copper oxide for the green colours, lapis lazuli for a strong blue, and for the red colour, she crushed purple lice in small porcelain bowls. Again and again, she wiped off the blood and excess paint that had run off Sarvesh's needle and cooled my skin with a wet rag.

The next moment, Hal entered the tent and stared at me in disbelief. Then he stomped back outside to vent his anger—as he always did when something went badly against his grain—with a series of rich Irish curses. Indra suddenly got up with a sob, apologised, and ran after Hal, distraught. It was then that I realised that I had entered territory that I had no idea about. Hal and Indra were a couple. Now I understood it, too ...

For a brief moment, I caught the look in Sarvesh's eyes. They were gripped by a vague fear, but only for a brief second, until he turned back to his work in silence and mixed the colour for my dragon's eyes himself.

It took another two weeks for Sarvesh and Indra to finish my dragon. He couldn't work more than two hours at a time, so I was forced to sit in his tent every day and drive away the two lovers. How happy I was when the finished dragon finally graced my back. Its mouth was wide open on my shoulder blade, one of its claws reached up to my neck, and the long tail curled up over my bottom to the back of my right leg. It was a true masterpiece in such unique colours as only an artist like Sarvesh could put on your skin.

Unlike Hal, I've never had another tattoo done again—neither by Sarvesh nor by his daughter.

Alamut in the year 1300

Hülegü Chan was a grandson of the powerful Genghis Khan and led a huge armed force that flooded the Orient with a wave of violence and oppression. At what the Persian and Turkish sultans could not do on their own, the Mongolian military leader soon succeeded.

The Sunni Abbasids had ruled Baghdad since 750 before Christ, but the rulers of the Orient had no chance against the overwhelming power of Hülegü Chan. The Mongol leader, Chan, now conquered the city with a severity that was unique in the eventful history of Baghdad. He killed over half of the population at the time and set most parts of the city on fire. What did not fall victim to the flames ended up in the waters of the Tigris, which, in those days, turned black and bloody.

The powerful Grandmaster Hassan I-Shabbah, leader of the feared Assassins, stood with his first commanders Enja and her constant companion Hal at the window of his chamber. The sky over distant Baghdad turned a glowing red. The flames of the devastating fires brought death and ruin to the once vibrant city.

As they entered the hall, they listened to the report of the messenger who had just arrived from the overrun city. Hassan's face had given way to a stone mask. It became clear to him that with Hülegü he had to face a completely new, much more brutal power that could hardly be influenced politically.

Baghdad's valuable library—centuries-old scientific works and academic records on endless papyrus scrolls—fell victim to the destructive flames or disappeared in the black waters of the Tigris. Hassan's stomach almost turned when he thought about the treasures alone in his library in Alamut. If these were lost ...

Perhaps he should draw up a plan to save at least parts of this collection, should it come to a takeover.

He shook his head. No, it just couldn't get that far. With his entire army, he would face these cursed Mongols. They would fight to the last breath. Chan's wife, Princess Doquez-Chatun, was a Christian, and it was said that he was joining forces with Byzantium because of her.

Damn Mongol! He had to hold this fortress at all costs; otherwise, the West would finally be overrun by Christianity.

"Have the outposts been reinforced that block the access road here?" he asked again.

"Yes, my Grandmaster!" Enja answered patiently. After the death of Nabil as hereditary princess, she was automatically the highest-ranking commander. It was so dictated by Hassan's law, and her authority, despite her seventeen years, was not challenged by any of the other princes.

"The outer ring was closed, the ranks of soldiers doubled, and the animals were brought from the central valley to the side valleys."

The taciturn man next to Enja nodded in agreement. The two had a friendship that Hassan found very strange, since

452

there were usually no friends among Assassins. Maybe it was because they shared a similar fate. Both had been sold into slavery and both ended up as warriors in Alamut.

"And Hal," added the tall woman to her report, moving her chin in his direction, "has checked all the weapons again and refilled the powder stores."

As quiet as the mighty warrior was, he really knew about weapons. Thanks to him, the throwing accuracy of the slings became much more effective, and the bombs were even more powerful in terms of their explosive effect. When he withdrew into the catacombs with Shi Fu, a new weapon or an improved effect of the existing one usually emerged. A very useful warrior who not only carried out orders but also used his wits, as long as he didn't have to talk!

Thoughtfully, the grandmaster turned back to the window and looked at the chaos in the distance. His dark eyes were transfigured, as if they were seeing something quite different there from the destructive work of the flames over the sinking city. In the meantime, he had grown a beard. This was much whiter than his main hair, which was still mostly streaked with dark strands. It made him appear far older than his forty-three years. On that day, he felt like he had aged another ten years.

"How can we get the valuable papyrus rolls—or at least parts of them—to safety?" asked Hassan, frowning, as if his mind were elsewhere.

"Papyrus?" Hal, who otherwise liked to hold back, exclaimed in disbelief.

"Papyrus," repeated Hassan sternly, and Hal looked passively at the floor again.

Enja had better control of herself and didn't show her surprise when she asked, "Why do you think the papyrus rolls are not safe here?"

The grandmaster looked at her pale face, searching for some clue that she wasn't taking him seriously, but her crystal blue eyes were absolutely serious.

"If we are overpowered here, the Mongols will destroy everything I have collected, including the library. In Baghdad, the barbarians have already destroyed too many of the valuable records. Data, facts, and scientific knowledge that can no longer be obtained."

His voice grew louder at the end of the sentence as emotions surged in him. He could clearly see how the two looked uncertainly at each other.

"We will not give up, dear Sheikh. We will fight to the end!"

He heard the resolve in her voice and was touched by his leader's courage to fight, but he persisted. "I want to keep some of my writings safe. Also, some artefacts, precious carpets, and part of my gold reserves."

With that, he reaped silent astonishment. He had never deposited anything outside of Alamut except his horses and farm animals.

"Enja, I want you to choose fifty of the best people and bring the most valuable part of my collection to my fortress in distant Masyaf in Syria. There, the library is safely stored under the orders of my commander Raschid ad-din Sinan. If something happens here, at least the other half of my treasure will be safe. Nothing is as valuable as the written word!"

The young woman with the silky white hair gave him a strange look. Her size was about the same as his own, and her eyes were now level. Those eyes searched his face for an answer that she hadn't even asked yet. But he would also be able to give her such an answer.

"No, we won't see each other again," said Hassan gently. "Leave here with everything that has grown dear to you and form a new unit of my influence. When you have handed over the records and the gold, head north and secure a new fortress, castle, or island to expand my power. Don't come back here."

Hassan clearly saw how surprised she was at his command; she had to swallow. Apparently, she made her decision unexpectedly.

"Of course, dear sheikh." With a bow, the tall commander turned around and was about to go through the door when Hassan called her back again.

"If something happens on the way," and he made a clear gesture in the direction of the window and the Baghdad burning behind it, "or the Masyaf fortress no longer exists, then take everything with you to safety. No matter where, bring my message and my name out into the world, Enja. Send a messenger as soon as you are safe."

This time, Enja seemed to hesitate before she wanted to turn away again. Something was still important to her.

"I will do what you wish, my wise sheikh. I only have one more request … "

She was standing on the step that led from his work area to the rest of the living area with the Sharantsch table. She had put one foot on the step and one arm rested on her thigh. The long, embroidered coat fell just below her knee, proof of her stately size. For most warriors, this cloak covered the entire length of the body, except for Hal, of course.

Hassan gestured to her that she should make her request. She looked first at Hal, who was already standing in the doorway and waiting for her, then back at the grandmaster. "It's about Jasemin, Your Highness. She will give birth to her child in the next few days. I promised her I would bring it into the world. Can we wait that long with our journey?"

Hassan cocked his head as if he were considering the matter. It was an unpleasant story about one of his many mistresses. Jasemin had betrayed him with one of his princes, and after the birth of her child, she was destined to die at his hand. Had so much time passed already?

It was time to finally end this matter. As an answer to Enja's question, he simply nodded, and as if the thought had just come to him, he asked Enja by the by what should happen to the child.

Surprised, she shrugged her shoulders as if the thought had never occurred to her.

"Don't you wish to adopt it?" Enja asked.

Hassan raised his eyebrows and placed his hands behind his back.

"No," he said decisively, "its mother will receive her rightful punishment, but the child of a traitor and a whore has no standing in my house. After the birth, I will personally take her life for her shameful betrayal. How could I receive this child of an illicit love affair when its mother's blood still stained my hands?"

Hassan could see how Enja winced at his harsh words. But even his patience with this unfaithful woman had to come to an end. With concern for her feelings, his tone became somewhat softer.

"Take the child with you on your journey; perhaps it will remind you of your friend." And, after a pause, he added: "Alahu Akbar—God is great!"

Enja's mouth fell open for a moment. She hadn't even considered this possibility. But she regained control of herself immediately, bowed, and rustled out of the room with her fluttering cloak. Hal, equally confused, ducked under the arched door and followed his leader.

"How could he do this to me, Hal?" Enja hissed angrily through her teeth. "What am I to do with a child on such a dangerous journey?"

Hal's face, as always, was an expressionless mask under the black drawings which Indra constantly enhanced. I noticed absently that now half of his ear was decorated with small stripes that played across his ear-muscle like a spider's web. Looking more closely, I even recognised a spider in its nest cowering under the curve of the outer shell-like cup. Irritated, I stuck my finger in Hal's ear, forgetting my anger for a second, and I earned a grumpy grunt in return. He wiped my hand away with one swipe. It wasn't a real spider, I realised to my relief. Indra really did have an astonishingly good hand for details, I had to admit. In the past, her motifs on Hal's skin were more of a flat nature.

Returning to the subject, Hal grunted again before he added in his hoarse voice, "We'll have enough servers, maids, and animals with us. A goat for milk and a wet-nurse for the baby, more or less …"

He shrugged his shoulders as he spoke as if my imagination would serve to finish the rest of the sentence. As a matter of fact, we would have a number of camels, horses, and beasts of burden with us to be able to transport the great number of writings and artefacts.

I had a transport list of all of the items prepared and gathered the animals that we needed for the ride through the Elburs Mountains. No wagon was able to pass through the out-of-the-way paths that were occasionally used for tracking. We were busy for weeks with the logistics alone, and the Eagle's-Nest vibrated under the tension of its inhabitants.

In the middle of the hustle and bustle, I received the message that Jasemin was going into labour. Ilyas had already put together my things for me days ago, which I needed to give Jasemin medical assistance. He only brought hot water and clean towels, which he carefully piled next to the expectant mother's bed.

I sat down next to Jasemin on the modest bed and held her hand tightly in mine, just as we used to do as children when we shared a bed. Her chamber had been her prison for the past few months, even if it was never locked. With the equanimity of a Muslim woman who had surrendered to her fate, she waited for the day of the delivery and thus also for her redemption at the hand of Hassan, whom she had so shamefully betrayed with Nabil.

I wasn't sure whether to admire or regret so much equanimity and trust in Allah. For Jasemin, it was nothing more than an intermediate step on the way to paradise. If the belief was so strong that death was received with head held high, why did I doubt it so much? Could I ever give myself into the hands of Allah and stop fighting for my life every day? And just accept my fate?

Jasemin didn't need to answer this question anymore; she would give life to a child and then leave the worldly plane; it was so easy for her.

Her dark locks were now soaked with sweat, and the effort to breathe in the steady rhythm of recurring pain could be seen on her flushed face. I kept wiping her face with a damp cloth to cool it down. The labour pains that had plagued her for hours now came at closer intervals, a sure sign of imminent birth. Again and again, I checked the width of the cervix and was able to estimate how long we would have to wait for the last phase.

During the gift of those few free hours, we spent intimate moments together telling each other our different stories for the first time. After all, I wanted to tell the child something about its mother, whom it would lose so early. And in the few respites between the pains of childbirth, I found out what happened after I secretly left the litter that day in Baghdad.

Jasemin had actually arrived with the caravan at the court of Prince Chalil, who had so generously stocked up on new ladies via Fahrudin. My disappearance was noticed, but only noted with regret. It was probably deducted from Fahrudin's pay, which elicited a hearty laugh from both of us, Jasemin and me, as we imagined his face when he was confronted with the fact.

Prince Chalil, however, turned out to be a loudmouth—Jasemin had used a different expression here, but it came to the same thing—who was less concerned with the satisfaction of his desires than with the size of his harem as a sign of his class and his wealth so that he could compete with his father. Jasemin protested that she had hardly seen him since her defloration. On the other hand, she confirmed to me the longstanding tradition of cruelly mutilating large numbers of boys so that they could do their work in the harem. The description made my hair stand on end, and Hal moved a little closer to my heart.

The prince suddenly died one day of an inexplicable illness and the harem was dissolved. The main Arab women were incorporated into his father's harem, while the other girls were sold by the Grand Vizier to men who did not mind that they were no longer virgins. Jasemin did not have to describe the humiliation of such a transfer of ownership to me in detail.

It was Hassan's castle-manager who had bought them in Baghdad and brought them to Alamut. Hassan did not leave the fortress once in all these years but sent his chief to take care of his master's affairs. So Jasemin reached Alamut, which would be her final resting place. The affair with Nabil was the first and only love she had experienced in her life. She confessed to me that she didn't regret it, even if it was just a very one-sided love.

Nabil gave her something she had never known: a purpose to exist. If only it was for this child she would give life to. Allah wanted it that way.

On the evening of July 3, 1300, calculated according to the Christian calendar, I was able to usher in the birth of a healthy Sunday's child with the help of Ilyas. It wasn't exactly an easy birth because the girl's head didn't want to go through the narrow birth canal, and I had to help out a little. With a painless little perineal incision for Jasemin, I finally ensured a quick and gentle entry into the human world. As I held the little creature in my arms and its eyes still looked uncertainly into the unknown world, I let my tears of joy run free.

With every birth, I thanked the Creator of this world for a new life and was delighted with the attention to detail that went into every creature. With my own hand, I counted the fingers and toes of the tiny limbs and marvelled at the perfection of this creation.

"God is great—Alahu Akbar", as Hassan always used to say. Where could his greatness be found but at such a moment!

Jasemin lay exhausted in her bed; a tired smile flickered over her lips as I put the newborn on her breast.

"What would you like to call her, Enja?" she asked me in a low voice, her big eyes shining deep black in the glow of the oil lamps.

"Shouldn't you give her a name? Something that will live on with us as memories?" I managed hoarsely, my voice still troubled by my thoughts.

Jasemin closed her eyes for a moment, maybe because she was tired, or because she wanted to think. The ensuing silence was only interrupted by the satisfied smacking of the baby's little mouth on her breast. At some point, she opened her heavy eyelids again and, without hesitation, popped out a name: "Rachel. I want her name to be Rachel!"

I was very astonished at that. "Isn't Rachel a Hebrew name?"

Jasemin nodded. "According to the Bible, Rachel secretly took the idols of her husband Jacob with her on the trip to Beersheba. How appropriate, you are now taking little Rachel with you on your journey. You are no more a Muslim than I am a Christian, Enja. But if she becomes your daughter, if she is now free and not a slave, then she shouldn't have a Muslim name. I hope that she becomes like you: a little rebel who secretly takes his gods with him."

I was touched that she didn't want a good Muslim as a daughter, but one who wouldn't conform, and she made sure that she bore a name that wouldn't stand in the way of these goals. How did Jasemin know the Bible so well? Hadn't she just read the Koran?

I would not have been surprised if she had read the papyrus scrolls in Hassan's library, which also contained a partial copy of the Bible. I knew from Hassan that he had studied it. She was always well-read and curious. Was she serious about making a Christian out of her daughter?

Just as I was about to ask her about it, the guard who was still standing in front of Jasemin's door made himself known. Considerate and courteous, the young man announced a visit, and a few seconds later, Hal's tall stature filled the tiny room. He knelt down in awe by the bed and took the bundle of humanity from Jasemin's hand. In his arms, the newcomer looked as fragile as a soap bubble on my hand. Hal looked tenderly into the pale, shimmering face. Small black curls still clung to the head, and the dark eyes, which could hardly be perceived as outlines, looked into the wild face of Hal, whose green eyes took on a damp shimmer.

It suddenly crossed my mind that he would be a good father, and I had to force myself not to think that this moment would never happen for him. But maybe there was a kind of fatherly love for a child who did not come from his loins. The way I saw him here, he might as well be Rachel's father ...

Hal kissed the girl tenderly on the forehead and, as carefully as his huge hands could do, gave Jasemin the bundle of humanity back to her breast. "If she becomes as beautiful as her mother, she will be the most adorable creature I have ever seen!" he said, full of admiration, and gave her his blessing. Jasemin looked at him with such adoration that I had to turn away so as not to be overwhelmed by my feelings again.

As if Allah had heard the prayers of his daughter Jasemin, he saved her from a violent death and let her sleep peacefully in the child's bed the next day. The newborn's head had likely torn open one of the large veins in her uterus as it passed through. I could have tried to save her life of course, but for what? A few days later, she would have died brutally by

Hassan's knife anyway. This saved her further pain, and I was able to say goodbye to her in peace and quiet while she was bleeding to death in front of my eyes.

Losing someone always hurt my heart terribly. But to see how Jasemin fell asleep—satisfied with little Rachel on her breast and embedded in our prayers—took her last breath with a smile on her lips filled me with a deep calm.

After a busy three weeks, the final preparations were made. Almost a hundred camels, horses, goats, and sheep stood ready for our trek over the mountains. Escaping over the mountain ranges was our only chance. There was no possibility of taking the route directly into the valley; we might have run into the hands of the Mongols there. In the weeks before, scouts had discovered the best route, and it led us deep into mountains, spat us out again in a dry riverbed, and from there we should go quickly towards Masyaf.

Grandmaster Hassan I-Shabbah showed his human side briefly when he allowed Jasemin to be buried as a Muslim in the garden of his private rooms, with her head turned towards Mecca. Allah had brought his disobedient daughter to him before anyone could judge her. My reasoning seemed to make sense to him and moved him to this fine act of infinite goodness.

When the entourage set off with a good half of the valuable writings, carpets, gold, and silver coins, the moving moment of parting had come. I personally selected Hassan's fifty best warriors, our cook Sarvesh and, due to Hal's endeavours, of course, his daughter Indra. Along with at least two hundred other warriors, Ilyas had to stay with Hassan to ensure medical care. But he helped me divide up my supplies of medicines and get some of my venomous snakes and spiders ready for travel. The rare medicinal plants I cultivated also came potted in my luggage. Hal had put together a small flock of sheep and goats that were guarded by two shepherds. I had a few sachets of his 'man's elixir' mixed for him, so as not to get into an emergency situation. It wasn't that easy to make the valuable extract that Hal had to swallow every day. He could sooner omit the goat seed and raw eggs than Isaac's precious acquisition.

In order for us to continue Hassan's horse breeding, he also granted us precious rarities from his stable: two more stallions besides my Taycan, eight of his best broodmares, a racing camel for Hal, who was just too huge for the delicately built pedigree horses, and of course, little Rachel, who came with her personal wet nurse who found space on one of the carrier animals.

What a responsibility! When I was barely eighteen, I was in command of one of the most valuable caravans that were on the move, comparable to the alleged treasures of the Knights Templar. I stood proudly in my riding gear with a turban next to Hassan, who had turned grey in the last few weeks, and looked towards the departure of the huge caravan. Animal by animal lined up in the long line that broke out into the unknown. We wanted to leave early in the morning to reach the first resting place—a high valley—in the evening hours.

Both Shi Fu and Hassan shook hands with me in a solemn gesture, knowing that it was the last time we would face each other.

"May Allah protect you on your journey, Enja. If he had a daughter, she would have been resurrected in your person, and who knows," Hassan suddenly whispered mysteriously and winked at me with his dark eyes, "if you don't even have a divine destiny."

I couldn't speak of so much presumption, but then Hassan wasn't someone who feared God's wrath. I bowed politely at Shi Fu's offered hand, took it with both hands, and thanked him politely for so much trust. I did the same with Hassan, whose hands I kissed again to express my attachment.

When I straightened up, deeply moved, and looked into Hassan's face, which was lit up slightly orange by the early sunlight, his eyes suddenly shone unusually bright. In the otherwise black pupils, a blue shimmer could be seen, as blue as the sapphire in the crown that he wore at our consecration rituals. It reminded me vividly of a last encounter with a person who wished me dead in the market square in Baghdad. It was the nobleman who took Laith and me prisoner with his Akasires. Since then, I had never encountered this phenomenon since, which I attributed to my imagination. But now I had seen it again, all too clearly.

I instinctively withdrew my hand from him. There was something dangerous, something deadly about this glimmer. What did that mean? Could others see it too, or was it just me?

I turned away from him, irritated, the telltale twinkle fading as quickly as it had come. Did he consciously send me to my death? Was it a trip of no return? Half-baked thoughts burrowed like snakes through the coils of my brain. I would not be the first of his assassins whom he sent on a suicide mission. But why should he then send me away with his treasures? An uneasy feeling crept into me that wouldn't leave me during the trip.

Now we were both standing next to each other and my gaze wandered to Hal. He was sitting on his new racing camel, which he gave the appropriate name ifreann, which probably meant "hell" in his Irish language. At least he always shouted that word with all his might when struggling with the cattle. It was a dignified paraphrase of his character and his disturbed relationship with his rider. The stoic look with which Hal followed the goings-on from the back of his infernal animal was in any case the same as his animal paid to the whole thing. I found more similarities between the camel and Hal, but I preferred to keep my mouth shut so as not to end the day in the morning.

Without a word, I got onto my Taycan, who was already prancing uneasily on the spot, and turned to Hal, who was waiting on his camel. Only when the last animal was on the way into the mountains did I look back again and raise my hand in farewell to those who stayed behind. It was going to be a great adventure that brought me closer to my destiny, I was sure of that. As long as paradise was in front of me and hell was under Hal, it should be fine with me!

Chapter 19

Caerlaverock in Autumn 1306

The clumsy Hugh had, of course, recognised the ailing King immediately in the sickroom. Robert de Bruce had already visited his family's castle when he was still a young boy. His father, William Douglas, had been a great admirer and supporter of de Bruce, a circumstance that had ultimately cost him his life. The distinctive face with the broad nose and prominent brow had been instantly identified as that of his king, even though it was now smooth in sleep and marked by hunger and privation.

He hadn't dreamed that he would trigger such a surge of indignation. His brother, James, was furious, having brought the king here himself. McKay just swore foully and rummaged through his deepest Gaelic vocabulary. Hal even tried to pull one of his axes out of his belt before Enja grabbed him from behind and stopped him.

A wondrous silence had fallen over the rest of the hall because the eyes were fixed on the hustle and bustle at the high table. While the Scottish guests wanted to tear each other apart, Enja insisted on sending Hal, foaming with anger, out of the hall, which he reluctantly did. His axe flew into the frame of a massive door with such force that the metal head got stuck completely in the carved border. With this token of his displeasure, Hal left the room.

"Quiet!" Enja shouted with uncompromising authority in her voice at her guests at the high table. "Do you want to be quiet?" she repeated again and hit the wooden plate with her fist. Little by little, the angry screaming died down and James reluctantly let go of his brother's collar.

"Follow me into my office! All three, immediately!"

Her tone brooked no argument. The Caerlaverock clan, who fell silent together, sensed that something unforeseen had happened that enraged even their level-headed and experienced mistress Enja.

By all the gods, how tired I felt! I wiped my eyes several times on the way to the office. When I left the hall, I didn't look back, nor did I pay attention to the embarrassed faces of my people. How could this have happened to me? Ironically, the warlike King Robert de Bruce was in my sick-room and drew either the anger of the English against me and my clan or the anger of the Scots, if he died. Either way, I held bad cards.

And all because of this damned James Douglas, abandoned by all good spirits, who had tricked me into this situation. Angry and tense, I kneaded my hands while pacing up and down in front of the somewhat sad-looking guests. Without arguing, they followed me into my office, which adjoined the great hall through a narrow door. Not particularly large, but functionally equipped, it offered space for the endless flood of papyrus rolls that I had once rescued from Alamut. On the other hand, there was a large table made of Scottish oak, which was enthroned on the noble Persian carpets that also came from Hassan I-Shabbah's possession. The mix of different cultures was not only reflected in the furnishings, but also in the people. Approaching the subject delicately, James tried to smooth out the messy situation. His face had again taken on the worried expression with which he had arrived here. He cleared his throat.

"Please let me explain the situation, Lady Enja, before you come to wrong conclusions. Far be it from me to put you and your clan in danger, but I had to keep the transfer of the Scottish king a secret under all circumstances; otherwise, we would not have got here. Forgive me if it came to your ears in this way. I wanted to tell you about this myself ... "

"And when did you want to do that, say?" I interrupted sharply. "When Edward and his army stood before Caerlaverock?" My voice dripped with sarcasm, but James took the swipe bravely.

"I would have told you tonight, after supper. We would have left again if you hadn't accepted us as guests. We were just so exhausted, and the king would not have survived another journey. Please forgive ... "

His face and whole demeanour were that of a loser, as if his mind and will had been broken. Seldom have I seen someone so desperate and depressed as this man who had lost so much and clung to the last hope that I could save his king.

Should I judge him? Should I turn him down? James took me in, badly injured, many years ago without knowing who I was. Is this how I should pay my debt to him? In order not to endanger my clan, I should have sent them all away as soon as possible, but I couldn't bring myself to do it. James had put me in a tricky position that forced me to make a decision that I would have liked to postpone. My thoughts circled; an uneasy feeling had crept into me and took hold of me like a fever. With a deep sigh, I turned to the dejected men who now awaited my decision side by side.

"Tell me about your way here. Tell me what happened to Bruce," I asked James. "Maybe it will help me to understand the whole situation better before I make a wrong decision."

Their relief was palpable. The shoulders tightened a little again, and the rising glimmer of hope made James's face brighten. In a calm voice, he summed up the amazing history of the Scottish fighters, while McKay occasionally added something. It was an incredible story indeed.

"Robert and his followers were on the run from the MacDougalls after the devastating defeat. Only a hundred men survived the Methven slaughter and the English ambush. On the run, we were driven further north towards the Scottish Hebrides. It was only in Skye that we had a chance to think about what was going to happen now, and it was there that Robert got so sick. We couldn't go back—they would have killed us on the spot—but with such a sick king, we couldn't flee any further."

His voice cracked at this point, and he wiped his hand over his face again, as he always did when trying to cover up his feelings. He crossed his arms and looked at the floor.

"I decided to bring him through enemy lines with McKay, who knows the country like the back of his hand. Our other fighters, meanwhile, led the English by the nose to distract them from us. You were my only chance, Lady Enja!"

At that moment, he looked at me intensely with his brown eyes. Despite his harshness, he was so vulnerable. His king meant so much to him that he had put his life and that of his comrade at risk. What a daring coup to get the king out of danger in the protection of the Scottish backwoods exactly in the other direction!

There was a pleading undertone in his voice now. I clenched my teeth hard not to reveal my feelings—I had to follow my reason.

"No healer from the Campbells of Skye has been able to recognise and treat his illness. But they told me of your abilities, and we saw our chance. If anyone could do it, it would be you, Lady Enja."

I was embarrassed by his belief in my abilities. I cleared my throat, took a deep breath, and surprised him with another question: "What if I can't do it? If he dies here—under my hands?"

"Then it's God's will," he replied meekly.

"And the wrath of all Robert's supporters would come after me and my clan," I exclaimed uncontrollably, my clenched fist rushing into the palm of the other hand with a loud clap.

"I would never let anyone blame you, my lady!" James was suddenly right in front of me, grabbing my shoulders. "You have to believe me, Enja!"

What a beautiful deep brown his eyes were, with little yellow flecks—eyes that glared at me like two amber stones in the light of the setting sun.

"I was driven by this only hope of finding you. And I was right—you found a way to help him."

"And with that, I turn the anger of the English King Edward on me and my clan ..." I said, finally looking away from his shimmering eyes.

Again, he grabbed my shoulder. "I will not let anything happen to you. Please believe me, Lady Enja."

They held me captive, those hands; that look from his warm brown eyes, and I felt my inner calm return. How did he have such an impact on my state of being?

My tone became more conciliatory, my mind set in again, and with it the healer in me came to the fore.

"Now that I can hardly send Bruce away again, he'll stay here until he's healthy. If the remedy works, he will soon wake up. If not, you will disappear with the corpse, as

476

inconspicuously as you came. Either way, you have to get out of here as soon as possible. I cannot allow my clan to be endangered by your presence. Please understand me … "

"Thank you for your generosity. I will never forget that."

James 's voice moved something inside me, and when he bowed to me, took my hand, and kissed the palm of my hand, I held my breath for a moment. I was impressed by his presumptuousness. Finally, I invited him and McKay to be my guests until the king was recovered.

Later, I met Hal in front of the fountain in the middle of the courtyard; he was chopping a stump of wood. A sizable pile of wood was already chopped by the well, and two stable boys piled the finished logs against the wall that supported the well roof.

I stood next to him with my hands on my hips and waited for him to put his axe in front of him. Sweat ran down the bare skin of his head, and his tunic clung to his massive torso. The veins on his arms protruded from the exertion. He leaned on the handle of the huge axe and put the other hand on his hip as well. He glared at me belligerently in the torchlight.

At that moment, I decided not to explain anything to him, and just told him that we would have guests for the next few days. With that, I turned around again and started to go towards the hospital. I had expected another outburst of anger, but the force of Hal's words hit me harder than I thought.

"Why do you allow a fanatical supporter of this Scottish king to endanger all of our lives?" he hissed in his hoarse voice. "Has he already turned your head so that you can no longer think clearly? What if we all get killed here? I don't give a damn about this accursed king; he's going to drive us all to ruin!"

Deeply upset, I stopped and turned back to him. I replied in a firm voice: "First of all, this man is my patient right now and not the king of Scotland. Second, he'll owe me a favour. And third, it is my decision, Cathal Conchobhar Ó Searcaigh, whether this man is my guest or not, and no bloody Irish hothead will stop me!"

Furious, I trudged on to the hospital rooms. I would take care of Hal later, especially his jealousy that I had to get under control before he did anything stupid. Despite my inner turmoil, I felt it was my duty to at least stop by my patient before retiring. His condition was still unchanged, but I wasn't expecting anything else. Tired, I went back to my room.

That same night, I received news that Robert de Bruce had opened his eyes, albeit for a short time. A good sign: it meant the milk thistle was working.

At least I had already won the fight for his life. However, it would be some time before his liver was working normally again. And with that, my guests' stay would probably take a while.

Hal insisted on making James uncomfortable at every opportunity. One morning at breakfast, he demonstratively sat down at the guest table and served himself from James's and McKay's plates. An affront to all good manners! While Hugh acknowledged the unusual behaviour with a big grin, James had just risen from his bench to show Hal his understanding of hospitality. He wasn't going to be shown up.

At that moment, Enja rushed through the large gate into the hall, and with her, a cool morning breeze. The men stopped moving, and all eyes were on the lady of the castle. With one look, she immediately grasped the situation, and her eyes glared at the men angrily. Arriving at the high table, she addressed Hal with undisguised mockery in her voice: "You missed your morning exercises, Hal!"

He crossed his arms over his chest, leaned back a little, and grinned hypocritically.

"I'm very sorry, Mo Leannan. Yesterday, my grey horse lost an iron while hunting and I wanted to repair it as soon as possible."

Mo Leannan? My love? Enja frowned and opened her mouth to say something, then closed it again. She deliberately turned from Hal to the guests and put on a friendly expression.

"I hope you slept well, gentlemen," she said, gesturing for James to sit down again. Without even looking at Hal, she took a seat next to Lachlan. She grabbed one of the bowls carried by the table maids.

Lachlan took on the charming answer to her question: "We slept like in a mother's lap, my lady. The mattresses are wonderfully soft. What are they made of, if I may ask?"

"Horsehair."

Enja took a spoonful of the porridge that is widely used in Scotland, briefly blew on the hot mouthful, and explained: "We collect them in the stables. They are softer than straw and store the body's own heat."

"I am amazed by your wisdom and your sense of practical application. Where do your good ideas come from?"

James intervened. Hal just rolled his eyes.

Enja took another spoonful of the cereal porridge and explained, while looking at the empty spoon: "From my brain."

Hal leaned back and chuckled. James stared into her eyes and at first didn't understand the meaning of her sentence. Then Lachlan started laughing, and finally James joined in, too.

A white-capped maid came out of the kitchen balancing three small, red clay mugs on a silver tray, each filled with a steaming black drink. The scent was intense, almost penetrating; James had never seen anything like it before.

The maid handed over a plate with reddish-brown dried fruits which looked like plums. Lachlan and James secretly watched as Enja put the mug to her mouth, took a sip, and then put one of the fruits in her mouth. She pushed the food around in her mouth a little, removed the stone, and spat it back onto the plate. James and Lachlan did the same. While Lachlan grimaced in disgust, James let the strange taste melt on his tongue. The bitter taste of the hot drink combined with the sweetness of the dried fruit created a whole new pleasure. James closed his eyes.

"Mmh," he said and took another sip. "What's this? It tastes great!"

Enja smiled. "It is the brew of roasted and ground coffee beans that is boiled over hot steam. This fruit here …"—she pointed to the datil on the plate—"... is a dried datil from the Orient. It grows where I grew up."

And just as she was about to take the last piece of this exotic fruit, a small hand reached for the sweet bite. The boy ran out of the hall with his prey before anyone could stop him. Enja looked after Thorvil and began to laugh out loud.

James paid no heed to the boy, watching Enja's face, spellbound. Her open and beautiful laugh gave him a pleasant shiver that literally left him speechless. It was so completely without falsehood; unlike those he had unfortunately seen so often. He didn't notice Hal looking at him with bloodlust in his eyes.

Enja leaned back and noticed James's look resting on her face. She cocked her head slightly. Her worried expression came back, and something else he hadn't seen before—an uncertainty that wasn't there before, whenever she had looked at him.

James let out his bated breath in a long sigh, and Enja frowned at him. The strange moment was interrupted when a girl, barely older than Thorvil, with shiny black curls and dark eyes, came into the hall. She had grabbed the cheeky little thief by his tunic and pulled him firmly to the table at the end of the hall.

The girl pushed the contrite Thorvil towards Enja and began to speak in a foreign language that James had never heard before. Enja listened to everything in peace.

Enja answered the boy in Gaelic: "What were you thinking, Thorvil?"

There was a little break in their conversation as if she would expect an answer from the boy. But he just lowered his gaze.

"But pretty clever of you, I have to admit ..."

Enja had to smile, impressed by his skill. Then she turned to the girl, who put on a stern expression, and said affectionately: "Thank you, Rachel. You were careful. But if someone is so skilled and manages to steal from me, then I have to acknowledge that. So, you get half of the datil for catching the thief ..."—she took half from her little hand—"... and our little thief here gets the other half of the booty."

Thorvil blinked at Enja in surprise and quickly wiped the snot from his nose.

"But as a punishment, you have to clear the tables today, Thorvil. There is no stealing in this house!"

The boy nodded in relief, put half the datil in his mouth, and immediately began to clear the empty cups from the tables. Enja lifted Rachel onto her lap and stroked her hair. James sensed the intimate relationship between the two.

"Who is this pretty girl, and in what language did you just speak?" he asked politely.

Enja's smile died away and the tender look gave way to that uncertain expression. She hesitated imperceptibly, but then replied, "This is my daughter Rachel; she is now six years old and loves her little brother Thorvil very much."

A daughter? A son? How many children did Enja have? James had to swallow. Hal, on the other hand, grinned and started poking his teeth with his knife.

As if she hadn't noticed his inner turmoil, Enja continued, "She speaks Farsi, the language of my native Persia. She also speaks Gaelic, English, and is learning French."

She looked at the girl with maternal pride and kissed her forehead.

James tried to cover up his astonishment.

"You come from the Orient? But you don't look like you were born there. What brought you here to Scotland?"

His gaze touched the still grinning Hal, who pretended not to care about their conversation. Lachlan, on the other hand, looked spellbound at the girl on Enja's lap, who looked so completely different from the children here in the north, and listened with interest.

Enja told them briefly about her journey from the East to the West and how she had finally found a home on Caerlaverock.

"I am still striving to be recognised as the mistress and to be granted the lordship of this castle. I've been working on this castle for four years now. I have a growing number of clan people who help me to cultivate the land that belongs to it, and yet I still lack recognition."

Frustrated, she looked at James, who was impressed with what she had achieved in so few years. He nodded understandingly to her and exchanged a look with Lachlan.

"Perhaps you should ask the Scottish king for enfeoffment; after all, Caerlaverock is on Scottish soil," he suggested, and thus had Enja's full attention.

"If he survives, he will certainly be very grateful to you and show himself generous. You just have to prove to him that you are able to manage this castle and hold it against the English."

Enja straightened up a little. She drew hope from his words; he could see that clearly.

"Then let me prove it! I have successfully managed this property and can pay my taxes. The English have tried twice to take the castle, and we have successfully stood up to them."

She released the little girl from her lap and stood up. Hopefully, she added, "Come, Lord Douglas, I'll show you what a woman can achieve."

James followed, and Lachlan rose, too. Hugh, on the other hand, said goodbye and left the two guests alone with Enja.

"When Bruce gets well again—which I assume—and you are on your way home, put in a good word for me," she asked, then left the hall with the men and took little Rachel by the hand.

During her tour of the castle, Enja explained the structure and tasks of the individual groups with such fervour that James wondered whether he had promised her too much. She did her job as mistress of the castle perfectly, there was no doubt about that, but would that be enough to convince Bruce? James had serious doubts whether a woman—and especially a woman who was not Scottish—would ever be able to claim and successfully defend a castle in this country. Not even every nobleman succeeded.

Enja led him into the individual castle areas. One was the study chambers, where teachers taught the children to write and read, mostly learned women and nuns. Depending on interest, languages, medicine, or even arithmetic were taught. James, who had been allowed to study in France because of his father's position, marvelled at the knowledge of Enja's students.

Eventually, they went into another house, where several experienced and inexperienced women studied new remedies

485

and practices together. In this way, an enormous amount of knowledge could be accumulated, which had led to many successful pregnancies. Enja's midwives and healers were among the best in the area, and not infrequently they were also called on by the other clans.

But what was most astonishing for James was that not only the men but also many women practised martial arts. Now he also realised why they were all walking around in men's clothes: they were trained warriors. Enja proudly declared that the best archers in the area came from Caerlaverock. While she was trying to talk about it, Hal hit the blade of a glowing sword with senseless force over and over again with his hammer. The sword blade was supposed to be folded a thousand times. At some point, Enja gave up trying to be heard, gave Hal a murderous look, and sent James and Lachlan to the chapel, which was in a side wing of the castle. The men sat down on one of the benches, enjoyed the peace and quiet, and took time to pray.

While Enja was dealing with Hal, James was happy for the silence of the chapel. He didn't want Enja's foreman to be an enemy. Unfortunately, Hal seemed to be standing between him and the woman who he couldn't stop thinking about. He jealously watched over Enja, who was so completely different from all the women he knew. James felt a deep respect for her and for what she had achieved. The physical attraction he felt around her almost drowned him. Never before had a woman taken hold of his thoughts like this, even though she made no move to seduce him.

James looked around the chapel, which was mainly used by the nuns who taught here. A wooden cross hung over the simple altar adorned with fresh flowers. A marble slab was set in a wall with several names carved into it. Above it in slightly thicker letters were the words Memento mori, the warning reminder of one's own mortality. Beside him, McKay was lost in silent prayer.

The telltale images that had been captivating him for days returned to James's head: Enja in his bed, her long legs around his hips, the silky white hair falling loose and untamed over her back, her beautiful eyes looking at him confidently and full of passion ...

"Lord Douglas!" His head turned to Enja, who was now standing next to him. "When you're ready, we can still go to the stables."

James swallowed, startled, and just nodded; his face flushed slightly. He hoped she wasn't seeing what was really going on inside him. Hesitantly, he got up with McKay to examine the breeding of horses that seemed to be Enja's pride and joy. Should he one day have title and land again, he would take a horse from their breeding. The animals, which came from the Orient, had a casual elegance. They carried their heads with natural pride, which made for a beauty all their own. Very similar to Enja ...

487

I had told Hal at the smithy that I found his attempts to frighten my guests away from me childish. Thereupon, he pouted alone in the kitchen to allow himself a second breakfast.

I would have liked to ask him for advice. At twenty-four, I had never had any experience of the opposite sex, not even physical contact. When I looked at James, my stomach fluttered, my pulse quickened, and my thoughts became more difficult to sort through. I had never been so physically attracted to a man. I liked the way he spoke, the way he moved his hands, and when his mouth did smile, I felt an unexpected powerful energy pass over me.

Did Hal see what was going on between James and me? Was that why he was acting so strange? Hal wanted to protect me, but he was interfering with something I wanted to take into my own hands. It was clear to me that I would never get married, that no man would ever determine my fate. But still I was gripped by an incredible curiosity when it came to James, which aroused me strangely and carried me on a dangerous wave.

For the next few days, Hal and James had apparently agreed on a truce so that the tension that was palpable among my clan people would not be fuelled by the strange visitors. In this way, they tried to make themselves useful, as it should be with good guests. The squat McKay made himself available to practise hand-to-hand combat with the women.

He was really a charming and funny man who could establish an easy relationship with women. I estimated him to be over thirty summers. In the exercises, he showed himself to be an experienced and able fighter and not one to avoid the pleasures and demands in matters of love. I noticed the interested looks the girls gave him.

That afternoon, Robert de Bruce woke up from his long sleep. When I got the news, I hurried off and was glad to see him sitting up in bed, weak but upright. His eyes were still slightly yellow and were sensitive to daylight. Fortunately, he had a healthy appetite again and drank without hesitation the broth I had cooked for him every day. After my routine examination, I explained to him what had happened and how he had come to Caerlaverock. For now, I ignored the fact that he was a king hounded by all of England. He approached me with a kindness and a dignity that made a great impression on me.

King Robert wasn't a despot or a vain fool. Even sick and weakened, he gave everyone the feeling that he was taking them seriously and paying attention. His intelligence and fluent language were evidence of a good upbringing, and he made a lasting impression on me with his polite demeanour. He thanked Moira and me for the good treatment that had saved his life. However, he could not explain the poisoning, especially since he did not like to eat mushrooms. For me, this confirmed my suspicion that someone had deliberately mixed small amounts of the poisonous mushroom into his food. But I would discuss that with James, who knew the king's environment better.

James, whom we went to fetch soon after, was warmly welcomed by him; everyone in the room could feel how young Douglas had found in Robert not only a fighter for his cause, but also a kind of father figure. I soon said goodbye, not without warning Robert to go to bed, and left the two of them alone.

That evening, I wanted at least to share the good news of the king's recovery with my clan and arranged a small feast in his honour. The maids and servants ran around excitedly to decorate the hall and prepare the food. They decided to prepare one of our house pigs for the festival as the stag was not yet ready to eat. The kitchen was boiling over with the preparations for the meal.

Everywhere, candles lit the great hall, tables were put together, and additional chairs were brought in. The large fireplace in the centre of the room spat fire and warmth, hissing and crackling. The faces of the children who sat down in front of it glowed with anticipation.

As the host of a party in his honour, I had invited Robert de Bruce to our table, even if he could not stay long. But he felt honoured and saw it as a welcome change from his sick bed to be back among healthy people, at least for a short time. Hugh escorted him by the arm across the hall to our table, and I politely gave him my chair. James, Lachlan, and even Hal stood in awe and bowed.

It was time to inform my clan about the identity of our sick guest, so I got up. When Hal gave a sharp whistle through the hall, the conversation stopped immediately, and I thanked them for their attention.

"Dear women, men, children of Caerlaverock," I began, leaning towards the children at the stove, "today we are celebrating the recovery of our Scottish King Robert de Bruce, who was brought to us by Lord Douglas a few days ago. I am happy to have him as a guest in our midst on the way to recovery."

A murmur of amazement went through the room.

"The people of Caerlaverock, along with me as clan leader, wish you a healthy life and great strength to finally settle the political turmoil for a united Scotland."

My speech was a tightrope act that I had carefully considered beforehand. I couldn't profess a king yet; I just hadn't come that far. The people in the hall were now applauding, excited by the unexpectedly high rank of the guest in attendance, and Bruce bowed his head in front of me.

"Long may he live to Robert de Bruce, the King of Scots!" shouted an enthusiastic Hugh, and he almost fell from his chair as he raised his mug and shouted at the top of his lungs, "Slàinte mhath! Good Health!"

The others repeated the Scottish toast, habitually expressed as glasses were raised repeatedly and with relish, loudly and with rare unity. You needed that toast to accompany such a drink fest.

Bruce insisted on offering a few words of thanks to me and the people here but apologised for wanting to forgo the good

Scottish uisge beatha at table today because his Medicus had forbidden it. He winked at me.

Our guests were amazed when the tasty roast pork with vegetables were served, with fresh bread and cheese. There was also a lot of beer and French wine, which Roderick Maxwell had brought from France and which James especially liked. McKay preferred to enjoy the uisge beatha from Hal's own distillery and thereby became a friend of Hal, who was a lover of strong alcohol.

Hal behaved like a real host that evening, proving that his vocabulary was greater than three words. Perhaps the in-depth conversation with him in the forge that afternoon bore fruit after all, or it was the presence of the king. Only with James did he still not exchange a word. But as long as he didn't use him as a target for his throwing axe, it was fine with me.

I left the choice of music for the evening to Muriel. As one of the oldest residents of the castle, she used her extensive knowledge to teach the children how to use the various instruments. The Scottish dance songs, in particular, were very popular with children and young people. They just pushed the tables aside and started dancing. They were simple but catchy tunes, played by Scottish bodhrun drums and harps and accompanied by singing. Only rarely did the flutes completely replace the vocals. The lyrics were Gaelic and were sung along by many.

McKay proved to be a gifted dancer and was allowed to do his rounds with pretty much every girl that evening. He often asked Kalay to dance, her red-blonde braid swinging with every turn.

I saw my chance coming when I asked James to dance. Obviously amazed at my direct manner, he hesitantly took my hand and let me lead him to the crowd of dancers. Unfortunately for this piece, of all things, the musicians had started a form dance that was not danced in pairs, but in formation. Here, everyone danced with everyone in turn. In addition, the beat got faster and faster until everyone was either completely out of breath at the end of the song or gave up beforehand and preferred to return to the audience.

What bad luck! At this rate, I quickly lost sight of James as I had to concentrate very much on the dance moves. But at least until the end, I kept up with the ever faster turns and steps. James, Hugh, Lachlan, Kalay, Winnie, Hal, and Moira all gasped like fish out of water. Many of the other dancers had to give up and now applauded as spectators.

Spontaneous as I was, I had hoped to get another chance, at least after the dance, to get closer to James. As if she were deliberately trying to prevent me from doing it, Muriel and her ensemble now played a piece that she had composed based on my stories from the Orient. Together with Rachel, the old woman forced me to sing about the Persian King Cyrus. Rachel had inherited her mother Jasemin's talent, and her clear, melodic voice was wonderful.

Only after three more pieces was I allowed to return to my seat—of course, to the applause not only from my clan, but also from the guests, who in the meantime had already properly approved of the alcohol being served.

Hugh had brought the exhausted king back to his chamber. Relieved by the successful evening, I sat down and looked around with satisfaction. All seemed to be having a good time. James, too, had become friends with the uisge beatha and toasted McKay, Hal, and Hugh regularly.

Well, I noticed a little piqued, the alcohol actually seemed to effortlessly overcome irreconcilable differences ....

Unfortunately, I couldn't take much of it: a few sips of this heavy drink were enough to get me drunk immediately. One day, I simply decided to do without this hellish drink, which confused the senses and could turn mortal enemies into drinking brothers in one evening.

As the only sober person among all those who drink, at some point, I no longer understood the jokes and got up to go to my room. Next to me, James, red-cheeked and shiny, was talking to McKay, who seemed to be laughing himself to death at something. Hal danced exuberantly with Kalay, who hadn't left the dance floor all evening anyway. I paused and looked at James's serene face. Something was preventing me from ending the evening like this. Maybe I had to give him a clearer sign.

So, I stood right next to James, who paused for a moment in a confused conversation with McKay and appraised me from top to bottom. When his eyes reached my face, he seemed a little disoriented, but I indicated a small bow and gathered all my courage.

"I am now withdrawing, gentlemen. Lord Douglas, if it is not too late for you, and you find your way to bed before midnight, come to my chamber."

Seeing the amazement on his face, I turned and went up the stairs to the private chambers. Only at the landing did I turn around again and caught his startled look with amusement. McKay next to him just grinned stupidly. But that's the way I was. I pursued my goal and didn't care about conventions. Now I was curious whether he would actually find my chamber ...

At first glance, James Douglas thought he had misheard through the fog of drunkenness. The aloof, beautiful Enja, mistress of Caerlaverock, had invited him into her chamber? He looked in amazement at McKay, who was just as amazed as he was. He smiled wryly and then slurred a little uncertainly, "It seems, she's been a fool for you."

"But that's not possible," replied James, shaking his head. "I can't marry her. I have nothing anymore ... I mean, no country and no title ... "

Unsure, he took the last sip of his uisge beatha and set the mug down on the wooden table with a bang. What could he offer her?

McKay laughed out loud. "You and your moral standards. She doesn't want to get married."

He was also having difficulties expressing a fluent sentence. "Go to her and give her what she wants." He burped and took another sip.

James became thoughtful, his cheeks turning deep red.

"But I don't know anything about women. I've only kissed a girl a couple of times. I have no idea!"

McKay stared at him as if he'd grown two heads, his usually lazy eyes wide. "You," he began, "are you still a virgin?"

"Shhh!" James snapped at him. "Nobody here has to know that."

He looked around uncertainly at the dancing people, but the two of them were now sitting alone at the high table.

"Ha!" McKay said and poured James another generous beaker full. "Then let's have a drink to your evening, boy. My first time was a hell of a long time ago."

Together they drank another long gulp of the high-proof liquid. James swallowed, starting to get nervous. Lachlan wasn't exactly helpful.

Christ, Enja was unmarried, the mother of numerous children, and had probably already had many men, from the Orient to Scotland. She could have anyone; why did she choose him now? He wanted her—that was what puzzled him the most. He thought of her day and night, but her direct manner frightened him now. She would toss him aside like all the other men before him, he was sure of that. As a precaution, he took another long swig.

Lachlan slumped slightly with his eyes closed as if he were sleeping. Now he straightened up again for a moment and looked at him with eyes half-shut.

"You're still here, boy. Go on, go already!"

He laughed to himself, lifted his mug, and clinked glasses with James.

"So ... all right!" James's tongue was heavy. "I am going to her!"

With that, he got up and leaned on the table. The hall circled around him. He paused for a few breaths, trying to sort the images before his eyes. His gaze found the stone stairs up. Slowly, step by step, he approached this shaky thing. The sweat stood on his forehead. Damn it, why did he have to drink so much!

What was the matter with me? I would rather have fought an army of Vikings than to stand here in my room and wait for James to come or not. I ran anxiously from one side to the other. The fire crackled in the fireplace, filling the room with a pleasant scent of smoke and resin. The logs cracked and crackled loudly. How should I receive him? How did other women do that?

Annoyed, I rolled my eyes and looked at my large bed, my restless hands clasped behind my back. My maids had covered it with light-coloured linen. I decided to act just as I would any other night and took off my things then carefully folded them up. It shouldn't look as if I've ripped my clothes off.

I slipped naked under the fur on my bed and sat up straight. Again, an endless period of time passed in which I became more and more annoyed about my behaviour. In my overzealous manner, I might have angered James, and he was certainly not going to come now. My hand went to the stone around my neck, my mother's stone. I had to change the leather cord a couple of times already, but the plain black onyx had not lost any of the magic it held for me. The memory of my mother, who died for me, was preserved in it.

The thought of it made me feel sad. She had had a husband and a family. She was so different from me. Gentle, soft, loving. The onyx on my neck felt pleasantly warm; it had absorbed the heat of my body.

Suddenly, I heard a rumble at the door, as if someone had fallen against it. I jumped out of bed smoothly to see what had happened when the heavy wooden door flew open and the drunken James stumbled in. His eyelids were at half-mast, cheeks and nose glowing red. He stood swaying in front of me and grinned crookedly. I stood frozen between the bed and the door. My heart leapt.

"You are completely drunk," I stated unnecessarily.

"And you ... you are naked," he declared back at me.

I crossed my arms, hurt.

"Did you have to drink some more courage, James?"

His eyebrows rose and his gaze became unsteady.

"I've never ... I mean, never had a woman like you."

He staggered a step forward until his face was right in front of mine and I could smell the pungent smell of strong alcohol. He lowered his mouth, and his arms tried in vain to grab me because at the same time, I stepped back a little. It nearly threw him off balance, and he took an uncertain step forward.

I quickly reached out and held him away from me with my hand on his chest. How could he get so drunk?

His upper body leaned heavily against my outstretched arm. His gaze fell on my bare breasts, and almost at the same time, he began to gag. With presence of mind, I tore my basin off the block of wood and held it under his nose.

Suddenly, his knees gave way, and I had trouble getting the big, heavy man and the bowl down to the floor. It smelled awful. James didn't seem to notice much of anything. I sincerely hoped for him that the grace of oblivion would overtake him tomorrow. It was only with great effort that I got him to my bed, where he began to snore with his arms and legs outstretched.

Thoughtfully, I sat down on the bed next to him and looked at James, whose features were so peaceful in his sleep.

He'd rather get drunk than share my bed with me. A deep disappointment seized me and pulled me with an iron fist into an unprecedented sadness. I was too unattractive for such a man.

My size, my self-confidence, my way of getting what I wanted, they put men off. And then my appearance ... who would want a female warrior in men's clothing, and one who taught most people fear?

Deeply disappointed, I took another breath and ran my hand over his soft, dark brown hair. The smell of chimney smoke and uisge beatha filled the room and took away some of the harshness that the contents of the basin gave off.

From now on, I would concentrate on leading my clan again. Only once had I given in to my urge to be perceived as a woman. And now I had received the bill for it.

I slowly got up, picked up my folded clothes, and got dressed. Tonight, I would sleep in the straw at Taycan's, so I would not be alone, and my loyal four-legged friend was not bothered by my presence.

Of course, the next day, everyone knew that James had spent the night in my bed. Under the curious glances of the stable boys, I had set off alone for my morning combat exercise, since Hal's sour face was the last thing I could stand to see now. This encounter was only postponed because at some point, I inevitably had to walk into the great hall. There they all sat now and waited for me. I took my time, puttered around in the stable a little, but I couldn't avoid this meeting, so I straightened my shoulders, went up a few steps to the door of the great room, and pushed it open resolutely.

Of course, the murmur and laughter stopped as soon as I moved through the rows of tables. Everyone stared questioningly at me, and I wondered if they saw what I had done or not done as a sin in their eyes. There was no trace of James at the high table, and I didn't miss him, either.

McKay preferred not to look me in the eye; he just turned his spoon in his hand, embarrassed. He looked like he hadn't slept well. His dark hair stood out in all directions, he hadn't shaved, and his eyelids were puffy. Hal, the nasty rat, had leaned back in his chair and crossed his arms. His expression didn't let on whether he was angry or amused. The green eyes just looked at me keenly. He was probably waiting for what I would say about the rumours that the maids must have carried to every corner.

"Good morning!" I said happily.

No, I wouldn't show any weakness. I forced a smile and clapped a hand on Lachlan's shoulder in a friendly manner. He winced and held his temple, his mouth twisting into a wry smile.

"You should become a torturer with your instinct for causing pain to others, my lady."

"Oh, believe me, your friend will tell me the same thing today," I replied grimly.

"Is he still sleeping?" Lachlan asked uncertainly.

"I assume so. Since he didn't show up for breakfast, he's sure to be sleeping off his hangover."

The mockery in my voice wasn't intended to be overheard. With a quick movement, I grabbed a bowl of the warm porridge that a maid was serving on a tray, sat down next to Hal, and added a spoonful of honey from the honey pot. I enjoyed the sweet porridge with relish.

When I looked up again and my eyes fell on Hal, the porridge almost stuck in my throat. His eyes glared at me dangerously. The fist that was clutching his spoon was white.

"Did you sleep with him, Enja?"

I choked and coughed until the tears came. Only when I had my voice under control did I hold my spoon in front of me like a weapon and hissed out between my teeth, "That's really none of your business, Hal. I can do what I want in my bed!"

"I don't see it that way, and neither do the people here. What kind of role model are you when you act like a harlot?"

Bitterly disappointed, I put the spoon down and leaned back.

"A harlot? Is that how you see me? When a man gets involved with a woman, he is the hero. But woe, the woman who does that with a man; she is a whore."

"Enja!" He addressed me urgently and a little more quietly. He leaned over to me. "You cannot ignore the feelings of the people here and their convictions. What I think personally doesn't matter."

Now he had actually appealed to my duties as mistress of the castle. But, reluctantly, I had to admit that I had made a similar decision, and so I was able to credibly convey my good intentions to him.

"I just had a weak moment. Nobody here should ever see me in such a situation again. My duty as head of the clan is very important to me, Hal. I have my feelings under control; you can believe me."

Hal stood up, and still a little stiff, as if it were difficult for him, he bowed to me.

"I'll remind you of your words, Enja," he muttered, and his voice sounded unusually cool. "It is feelings that we have the least control over."

I got up with a lurch, too. I had to get out of here. If I hadn't had a bad feeling before, now it was there. It was Hal's very words that revealed my emotional facade.

I ran the few feet to the door, tore it open, hurried down the stairs, and disappeared into the small chapel. I braced my back firmly against the door and tried to catch my breath. I damned the men and especially James and Hal and anyone else I could think of. There weren't many.

The silence in the chapel was a relief. A candle burned at the front of the altar and bathed the small room in a warm light. Slowly, my blurry vision cleared. I was happy to be here, not to pray, but to find myself. But where was I actually?

The door behind me was suddenly pushed open with such force that I stumbled forward. Hal pushed his way in and let the door slam shut behind him. He snorted through his nose.

To get out of here, I had to get past him.

"Ifreann!"

"You can call it that!" he snorted angrily.

Did I say it out loud?

"You can't get out of here until you tell me what happened."

I damn well knew Hal was serious.

"There's nothing to tell." I desperately tried to sound normal.

"So?" His eyebrows rose. In the candlelight, the shadows on his face with its black lines danced a threatening dance.

As if to fend off his questions, I crossed my arms in front of my upper body.

"Nothing happened; James was way too drunk."

"Did he hurt you, the goddamn son of a bitch?"

Hal came up to me. My eyes desperately searched for a way out, but I couldn't get past him.

"Hal, please!"

I raised my hands in a soothing gesture. A lump formed in my throat. Why must this fellow always press so directly?

"What did he do?" Hal's voice was just a hiss.

My chest rose and fell frantically. Overrun by his rage, I looked everywhere except at his angry face.

"He … he", I stuttered like a little girl, "oh, hell! He got drunk because he finds me so repulsive."

Now it was Hal's turn to gasp.

"He got drunk because he ... what?"

I completed the sentence for him. "Because he couldn't share my bed with me sober." Hal seemed to be struggling to keep his composure. Anyway, I was glad I said it—now it was out.

Even before my breath had calmed, something happened that I have never understood to this day. Hal's large hands cupped my face. As tenderly as I would never have thought possible from such a large fellow, he pressed a kiss to my lips. It was a warm, affectionate kiss. When he looked at me again, his eyes were full of emotion—clear and deep as the Irish lakes.

"You are the most beautiful thing that my eyes have ever seen, Enja. Everything you do is honest, unconventional, and crazy. And I love each of your strengths and weaknesses. You know that I love you as if you were my wife. I also know that I can never have you. But I'll kill anyone who hurts you and doesn't appreciate you."

He meant every word seriously, I could tell, and it touched my wounded soul. A tear crept down my cheek; he ran his thumb over it. His face was a declaration of love, and I closed my eyes to take it in.

No, no man would die because of my offended pride! A jolt went through my body, and with renewed energy, I opened my eyes and put my palm on his chest.

"Weeping doesn't make me weak, Hal. Please excuse this emotional moment."

It was not easy for me to regain my inner balance. It was not for nothing that Shi Fu had repeatedly warned me not to show feelings.

"Feelings are not good, make you weak", he had always warned in his lessons.

Hal turned around wordlessly, went to the door, which hung a little crookedly on its hinges, straightened the top hinge, and ran out. It fell into the lock behind him. Restless and aimless, I stomped out of the chapel.

Chapter 20

Caerlaverock in Autumn 1306

Only well past midday did a dishevelled and hungover Lord Douglas stumble down the stairs. His hair resembled a bird's nest, and a dark stubble shadowed his weary face. Red-rimmed eyes scanned the large hall, still adorned with the remnants of the previous night's feast. Only the benches and tables had been tidied and the traces of the revelry removed.

His temples throbbed with every step. He desperately needed a drink and was relieved to spot Hugh with some of his men at one of the tables. He looked at him with bloodshot eyes, and his younger brother quickly pushed a jug of water and a cup towards him.

"By the saints, James, ye look as if a herd of cattle has trampled ye!" Hugh exclaimed in genuine sympathy, his brows raised and a crooked grin upon his face.

"I feel that way, too," James croaked, his neck thick and tongue heavy. He rubbed the stubble of his beard, scratching.

"Where's Lady Enja?" he asked as casually as possible. Something had happened yesterday, but with the best will in the world, he couldn't remember it. Maybe she could tell him what had happened.

Hugh's expression suddenly turned serious, almost embarrassed. "The last time I saw her was on the way to the sick bay. That was at least an hour ago."

James's gaze fixed on the door before moving awkwardly.

"I'm going to look for her." But before he reached the door, he stopped and turned around again.

"Um, Hugh?" His little brother cocked his head and looked at him questioningly.

"Did something ... anything happen last night?" He scratched the back of his head, embarrassed.

"Not that I know of," Hugh replied innocently, "you sat with McKay for a while longer and drank uisge beatha. When I withdrew and assigned the guards, I ran into the wet nurse, um ... she had problems with one of the babies." His cheeks were reddish in colour.

James paused. "So, the wet nurse," he muttered absently as he turned back to the door. Outside, glaring sunlight greeted him and made him blink because his eyes hurt. It was a cold but sunny October day. With one hand over his eyes, he searched the courtyard. It wasn't long before his gaze fell on the opposite castle wall. Some of the men and women on watch stood there excitedly and pointed to an area outside the castle.

Less than a minute later, the gate opened, and a horseman came chasing through like lightning. Before the steps to the great hall, Winnie yanked her pony back and jumped off, her short hair stuck to her forehead in the wind.

"Where's Enja?" she called, out of breath, and her short legs darted up the steps. Sweat stood on her face from the wild ride, mixed with dirt and dust.

"She's not in the hall," James intercepted.

"I'm here!" shouted Enja. She had come out of the hospital room when she heard the tramping of quick hooves.

Winnie turned to her and gasped excitedly, "An army is on its way here! They carry King Edward's banners, at least six hundred strong! Maybe a few hours away."

Enja paused in the middle of the movement.

"Edward? Here?"

The people in the courtyard were filled with horror, and chaos suddenly broke out. James shouted for Hugh to take the men outside and arm them. Hugh rushed over and ordered his men to get their weapons. And McKay yelled at Hugh to come with him to the west tower, to defend the other side in case there was an ambush. Finally, Enja roared so loud that she made herself heard in the commotion that she was in charge here. The panic slowly subsided.

Meanwhile, Hal, who had been on patrol with Winnie and had discovered the advancing army, was already fetching the horses from the pastures and handing them over to the numerous stable boys, who hastily brought them to safety inside the castle. A horn rang high above the castle battlements to bring the rest of the residents of Caerlaverock into the castle.

The residents worked feverishly through the routines they had learned in countless hours of practice. They took the bows and arrows from the armoury, the swords and shields, knives and axes. Tar was heated and water was collected in buckets. Everyone had a job; under Enja's command, nobody lost their nerve. Again and again, occasional shepherds and hunters returned to the castle via the ferry, then this was also pulled in and the ferry cable was cut.

James tried repeatedly to catch Enja's eye in all this madness. She paid no attention to him, but rather checked all the positions and made sure that everyone took their tasks seriously. At the same time as the stoic Hal told her that the old people as well as the children and babies had been safely brought into the underground vaults, James came up to them on the castle wall above the main gate from the opposite side. There was a strange, restrained silence between the three of them. James searched the closed expression on Enja's face and ignored the ill-tempered Hal, who was playing with the handle of his axe nearby.

"I would like to speak to you, Lady Enja, if you will."

It was enough for him that she had put him in his place when he was giving the orders, so now he tried a more cautious approach.

"Speak!" the response came curtly. Enja did not look at him but let her gaze wander over the battlements to the surrounding hills, looking for any signs of an advancing army. She had supported herself with her hands on the castle battlement, which was part of the masonry. Hal crossed his arms and diminished James in his blatant manner.

"If so, please, in private ..." James started again politely, without being able to make eye contact with her. He only saw her angry face in profile, along with her straight nose and her white hair carefully tucked away with the silver dagger. She didn't even look at him.

"Speak up, Hal is privy to it."

She was terribly dismissive. What was she thinking? James huffed angrily, and then, in a sharper tone than intended, began to explain, "I don't know what happened last night, but if I got too close to you in any way, I do ..."

He didn't get any further.

Without warning, Enja's fist flew into his face with lightning speed, and with a force that made him see stars. His legs failed, and he dropped to his knees and held his bleeding nose. Totally surprised by her reaction, he hadn't even seen her hand move, so that he could at least have protected himself.

"Apology accepted."

The cold-blooded warrior's gaze wandered over the hills again and was suddenly stopped by movement in its path. Enja pointed tensely to a point in front of her.

"They are coming. Everyone at their posts!" she shouted in a commanding tone.

James didn't even look at her, and Hal smiled maliciously. He seemed to be very amused by Enja's reaction.

Slowly and unsteadily, James hauled himself up the wall. So, something did happen that unfortunate night. Something that Enja hadn't forgiven him for. He couldn't get rid of the feeling that he deserved that blow to the nose. At some point, he would ask her about it. Despite his headache and bleeding nose, he knew what to do.

"I'll get the king out of here and to safety," he muttered, holding his swollen nose.

"The king stays here!" Enja snapped at him. "He's safe here."

Now she at least looked at him for the first time, albeit with cold, sparkling eyes, her lips pressed together angrily.

"King Edward is here because of me. If I get him out of here, maybe Edward will spare the castle," James replied, showing the utmost of his remaining dignity. His head continued to pound unbearably.

"Edward is here because of me," she replied grimly, pushing her chin forward aggressively. "How would he know that the Scottish king is here? This army has been on the move for days. How should they have heard of Robert's stay here? Nobody leaves the castle—that's my order!" she hissed in a tone that brooked no argument.

James swallowed hard. He was just getting to know a side of this woman that he had never seen before, and it both terrified and fascinated him. The orders she issued were as hard as her fist.

Did he always see her as an attractive woman? Was that why she was so mad at him? Did he say the wrong thing last night? Maybe also how beautiful she was? He groaned inwardly. What he would give to relive the last evening soberly.

But he pushed these thoughts aside for now because he had to concentrate on the problems in front of the castle wall. An army of six hundred men against a castle of maybe two hundred men, women, and children.

Damn it! Enja must have nerves of steel.

His gaze fell on a person who was struggling to drag himself up the stairs. Completely clad in his blue and white tunic, with the coat of arms of the Scottish throne on his strong chest, Robert de Bruce climbed the steps, exerting all his strength. He was breathing heavily, his sallow face was covered with a film of sweat, and his arms were trembling.

"King Robert!" James exclaimed, startled. "You should stay in your room!"

"Edward is at the gates and I should hide? What kind of king would I be?" roared the strong man's deep bass.

It was then that James saw a change in Enja's face for the first time. Slowly, it seemed to dawn on her what a dire situation she found herself in. The Scottish king was in their castle and the English king was at the gates.

James' eyes were caught in the pale contours of this brave woman. A first crack appeared in its otherwise cool facade as Bruce dragged himself up the stairs to the wall passage.

What would she do now? James wondered. Suddenly, he no longer felt the hellish pain in his nose; something else was throbbing in his head. She stood there proudly, straightened up, and with every inch of her body, she radiated a determination that filled him with admiration.

An uncertainty burrowed in her that she did not allow to the surface. She was the mistress of this castle and had to lead the people into a fight that they might not be able to win. Would she fight or hand over the Scottish king to Edward to avoid a slaughter?

The fate of his king, his people, and his own hung by a thread. An icy silence fell. Only Robert de Bruce breathed heavily, as though he had already fought his greatest battle. Even the constant clucking of the hens and the sounds of people in the courtyard below seemed to fade into the background. Everything went quiet. The fickle sky stopped raining on the heads of the people, and no annoying wind tugged at their hair above the mighty wooden gate. Enja's gaze moved across his face, then over each of the fighters present, and finally settled on the ailing face of the man James so admired, who was summoning all his strength just to stay on his feet.

Suddenly, James knew what Enja's decision would be. Her soul was so similar to his: hunted, hardened, and driven by a great heart. The proud heroine closed her eyes and took a deep breath. A moment for eternity.

END

For You Who Crave More:

Three Exclusive Options
Before Episode II Arrives

Again: My dearest reader! In everything you've read now in this first episode of The Highlanderess, you feel how strongly I believe in the extraordinary power of women, freedom and leadership inspired by higher values.

You saw how Enja was pioneering her own fate and the fate of others, and when you hear about leadership today, you may wish that there was some heroines like her just now…

For the best benefit of all.

Well, perhaps there are heroines like her out there. If so, I bet they exist in the everyday lives of ordinary people—unrecognised by the public, yet creating wonders by overcoming ordinary challenges, surviving in a world that, in many ways, isn't much different from the 14th century. Truly, isn't this a strange time we're living in? I wonder if the Middle Ages were really more grotesque than the years 2020 to 2024. The world needs natural-born heroes and heroines like Enja, and I believe they exist. Now, ask yourself a very important question: Why not you?

Sometimes you just need to find somebody who believes in yourself and who empowers you long enough so you then can believe in yourself, too, as much as the other person does.

I want to believe in you and I would love to prove this statement.

Of course, I can't (and I don't want) to help everybody in the world, but if you're cut from the same cloth as I (and Enja), then there is a possibility I wish to open. When you are like me, you intend to know more, learn more, have more and give more and if you are like me, what you want right now is much more than just the next Episode, The Quest!

Do you?

If this is the case, here are the good news. Now you have the choice between three magnificent options.

As someone who resonates with the values and themes of The Highlanderess, I'm excited to offer you a chance to take part in something truly special.

What if there would be a clan which is destined to bring these values to your life and this clan's only mission would be to make you stronger!

Following this, you will find three distinct opportunities to engage with me and our community of inspiring women.

Option 1:
Your associated membership in "The Clan"

Join a carefully curated community where value creation by and for powerful women is the cornerstone. However, we also warmly welcome every brave and strong man who enriches the group! As an associated member, you'll gain access to exclusive resources, events, and opportunities alongside other driven individuals committed to making a difference. This isn't just about networking—it's about being part of a tribe that values growth, emancipation, and empowerment. To become a member, you'll need to complete a short survey. If our admins determine you're a perfect fit, you'll be welcomed into the clan.

Option 2:
The Clan's Mastermind

For those who are serious about mastering their leadership and achieving their deepest desires, this mastermind offers a powerful platform. Work alongside other selected members in a dynamic environment that fosters growth, accountability, and shared wisdom. The synergy of the group will help you elevate your vision and leadership to new heights.

Admission to the Mastermind is by application only, ensuring that each participant is fully committed and aligned with our mission.

Option 3:
The Clan's Inner Circle!

This opportunity is for those seeking a more personal and transformative experience. As part of the Inner Circle, you'll work directly with me to uncover your unique strengths as a leader and pioneer of a thriving future. This isn't just an amazing mentorship journey—it's a deep dive into your full potential, with tailored guidance and support.

Given the intimate nature of this experience, selection is based on an application process. If you're ready to discover your superpowers and embrace your role as a trailblazer, this path is for you.

How to Apply? I am highly selective about who I work with, as my time is valuable and I am committed to making a meaningful impact with those truly ready for this journey.

While Option 1 requires completing a survey and receiving admin approval, Options 2 and 3 involve a personal application process.

To begin your personal application, please email my team at application@highlanderess.com with exactly five (not four, not six) brief truths about yourself.

This is your chance to share your vision, passion, and why you believe you're a great fit for our community. I look forward to learning more about you and potentially welcoming you into our powerful, purpose-driven clan.

For Option 1, please visit www.highlanderess.com/clan and follow the process outlined there.

See you on the inside!

Epilogue

Isn't it extraordinary what an opulent setting Scottish history provides at the beginning of the 14th century? Of course, my two main characters, Enja and Cathal, come from my imagination, but in this book, we find many real characters from the history of Scotland who have had such a lasting impact on this country: Robert de Bruce, King Edward, James Douglas, and last but not least, William Wallace, the one who is so revered today, but who hardly appeared dynastically in what was then Scotland.

During my research, I came across some material on the descendants of the Scottish royal dynasty and their wives, but little on the private life of James Douglas. It seems as if nobody bothered to document his love life—a treasure trove for me and my imagination. Did James Douglas ever fall in love? Was the unknown mother of his second son, who was obviously a mistress, not worthy of his class?

I found only the following information about him: James Douglas was born in 1286, about three years after Enja's fictional birth, in Douglas Castle, Lanarkshire. His parents were William "The Hardy" Douglas and Elisabeth Stewart, who presumably died at his birth. His sister, Barbara, had previously been born in 1280. William Douglas later married the younger Eleonore de Lovaine and had a son with her, Hugh Douglas, James's half-brother. It is said that after the death of his first wife, the elder Douglas first kidnapped his future wife Eleonore and then married her out of love. This would be another explosive story, but it would have taken place long before the time of my two main protagonists.

James had two illegitimate children, William and Archibald. Uncertain sources speak of a wife, Elisabeth, and a mistress. I assume that he was not averse to the female gender because of his lifestyle. How obvious to bring this hero of his time together with Enja!

The historical data on the course of the battle of the Scottish king are mostly available. Even the strange illness that befell the king on his flight and which left him sick for almost three months is documented. Of course, my interpretation of this is not necessarily proven, but poisoning would have been possible at that time.

I drew the place Alamut from another historical source. In fact, it was the headquarters of the Assassins. Hassan I-Shabbah was a colourful figure in those days of religious wars, and the most successful leader of the assassins, but he died as early as 1124 AD and missed Enja by almost a hundred and seventy years. Sultan Saladin also raged far before Enja in recorded history. But my artistic licence allowed me to resurrect him as a main character. Alamut was destroyed by the Mongols as early as 1256; here, too, I juggled with time a little and set the occurrence a bit later. I just had to weave the inglorious death of Nisam al-Mulk into my story when I read that an assassin boy had killed the poor man in his sleep.

Likewise, some of the surgical instruments that appear in my story were already familiar to the Egyptians and, as is well known, they had already dared to perform brain operations. My story here is based on such known facts. The Romans also performed the eye surgery described in the book. However, the success of this operation was rather doubtful.

Regarding the language used, I would like to say that I have not mastered Old Arabic, Old English, Farsi, and Middle High German, nor the earlier Gaelic, and have given myself the freedom to use our modern language, which is more pleasant to read in many ways. I only included a few original words that I put in italics.

The trade, which Enja operated intensively, was certainly possible in this form, but the mocha, which she enjoys drinking so much, did not come into fashion until a hundred years later.

The German biochemist Adolf Butenandt succeeded in artificially generating the androsterone obtained by Isaak in 1931. Somehow, Isaak seems to have managed to crack the code for the steroid that gave Hal back his masculinity in my story.

The exciting Scottish conquest lasted several centuries, and the Highlanders were unrelenting in their fight for freedom, which continued for many years.

Enja's fight will continue in a second volume, which will be released soon. In Germany, this book series became well known and led to five volumes. It is just now that the amazing warrior is published in the English market.

Eva Fellner

IMPRINT

THE HIGHLANDERESS

Eva Fellner

First edition: October 2024

ISBN: 978-3-949109-37-9 (Paperback)
ISBN: 978-3-949109-38-6 (Hardcover)

All rights reserved.

Copyright © 2024 Eva Fellner

LEAP PUBLISHING

Printed in Great Britain
by Amazon